COUNTRY OF
BROKEN STONE

COUNTRY OF BROKEN STONE

Nancy Bond

A Margaret K. McElderry Book

ATHENEUM 1980 NEW YORK

LIBRARY OF CONGRESS CATALOGING IN PUBLICATION DATA

Bond, Nancy.
Country of broken stone.

"A Margaret K. McElderry book."
SUMMARY: From the moment that she and her newly formed
family arrive at the isolated old stone
house in the north of England, 14-year-old Pennie
has a sense of foreboding that is borne out
by the events of the following summer.
[1. Remarriage—Fiction. 2. England—Fiction]
I. Title.
PZ7.B63684Co [Fic] 79-23271
ISBN 0-689-50163-3

"...and there is no gift like friendship."
—Rudyard Kipling
Puck of Pook's Hill

For Barbara and Brooks Bradbury with love

NOTE

There are four people I would like specially to thank for their help with this book: Anne Trembath, who read the manuscript and offered advice and suggestions, in particular on the dialect; Patricia Runcie and Katie Van Someren, who obligingly supplied all sorts of odd and invaluable information; and my father, who gave Sulpitium its name and thereby solved a knotty problem.

Although many of the places in this book are real, and the information about the Romans as accurate as I could make it, the characters and situations are wholly imaginary. Among the forts on the Roman Wall there is no Sulpitium, but anyone who cares to do a little sleuthing should be able to find its counterpart.

COUNTRY OF
BROKEN STONE

CHAPTER I

"I AM GOING TO BE LATE! MY FIRST MORNING AND I'M GOING to be *late!*" cried Valerie, scowling at her watch. "I promised Kenneth, solemn oath, that I'd be on the site Tuesday, July eleventh at eight thirty A.M. It's now twenty past eight. I've had half a cup of nasty instant coffee and I haven't packed a lunch. Ted, why on *earth* didn't you set the alarm as we agreed last night?"

Penelope stood in the doorway watching her stepmother bang cupboard doors and rummage through drawers, searching the unfamiliar kitchen for necessary utensils. By the time they'd arrived at Wintergap the night before, it had been too late to do anything more than untangle luggage and make up enough beds for everyone to fall into.

"Civilized people do not get up at half-past six," Penelope's father, Edward Ibbetson, said flatly. "You Americans may, but *civilized* people do not open their eyes until half-past eight at the earliest. I didn't think you were serious." He gave an elaborate shudder. Normally he chose not to observe early morning. Penelope and her brother Martin were used to making their own breakfasts and getting themselves off to school. They seldom saw their father until they got home again in the afternoon. It was much the best arrangement.

Valerie gave an impolite snort. "It's important for me to be at work on time, not whenever I happen to wake up, Ted. This is a *job*, and I've missed two weeks of it already. *I'll* set the alarm after this."

Edward made no response. He sat hunched in his dressing gown at the huge round table, his face hidden in his hands. He was obviously not going to make himself useful.

"I can do scrambled egg," offered Penelope tentatively. "If I can find the eggs." She retrieved a vast iron skillet from the muddle Valerie was creating and unearthed a slightly squashed pound of butter.

"Bless you, Pennie. Lou, do you remember where the eggs

3

went?" she asked, turning to her small daughter Louisa. "I know I packed a dozen."

Lou shook her head. "I don't like them." She was placidly eating cornflakes at the table across from Edward in disregard of what sounded to Penelope's unpracticed ears like the beginning of an argument. Penelope watched her chase bits of cereal around a bowl full of milk, and wondered if, in time, she would achieve a similar detachment. The little she had heard about Lou's father, Brian, led her to believe that Lou, at eight, was already quite experienced with domestic upheaval. Valerie's first marriage had ended several years ago in divorce.

Edward straightened up and scrabbled a hand through his thick brown hair. "I don't see why you're in such a taking!" he grumbled. "The fort's been there for close to two thousand years—a few more minutes *now* isn't likely to make any difference to it."

"Ted," said Valerie with exaggerated patience, "many people in this world actually have to live by the clock. I would think you'd appreciate that yourself, if only because of the time you spend waiting for the pubs to open."

Martin, just entering the kitchen, gave a little whoop.

"You had better keep out of this, old son, if you know what's good for you," his father warned.

Penelope found the egg carton under a pile of bath towels and broke four eggs into a bowl. She looked doubtfully at them, then added two more. Six eggs seemed terribly extravagant. "Do the twins like scrambled egg?"

"Don't ask, just present it to them," advised Valerie.

"I don't," said Lou again.

"No one would dream of giving you any, sweetie. Look, I've made a kind of shopping list for you, Ted. I thought you could—"

"Better give it to Pennie, her eyes are open," said Martin. "I like my eggs runny." He held out a plate. "Any toast?"

Edward looked at him as if he were some kind of aberration. "How can you possibly consider eating at this hour? It's barbaric."

Martin joined him at the table. "This is how the other half

4

lives, Dad. Welcome to the real world."

"As far as I'm concerned the other half can take your *real* world and go bloody—"

"Ted," said Valerie warningly with a nod toward Lou.

He gave a windy sigh. "I keep forgetting I've acquired children. You must give me time to adjust my self-expression. Hadrian's Wall wasn't built in a day."

"Crippen, he's waking up!" Martin exclaimed. "I think that was a joke." He smeared butter on two pieces of cold toast.

"Where are the twins?" asked Valerie impatiently. "I know I heard them thumping around. Martin, go roust them out, will you?"

"And the dawn comes up like thunder," quoted Edward. "I suppose I'd better make some tea. Things can only improve."

Penelope was regarding her parent with a frown. "What about us then? Martin and me? What are we, if we aren't children?"

"You haven't been children for *years*," he replied. "I sometimes think you're older than I am."

"So do I," Valerie agreed with a little smile.

"Whose side are you on?" demanded Edward, spooning tea into a very good Wedgewood teapot. It was the only teapot anyone had been able to find so far.

"My own. And that means that I am, in less than five minutes, going to walk out the front door and away from the bunch of you, no matter what state I leave you in. Can I count on you to do the shopping today, Ted? I only packed enough food to get us through the first few meals, and the twins seem to have made great inroads on it already. There's the list—all you have to—"

"I guess I know how to shop," he said irritably. "I've been doing it on my own for years."

"Not exactly," Penelope said. "Not if you count Mrs. Brice and me."

"Right. Have you got a pocket on you, Pennie? Good, here you are then." Valerie handed her the list written out on the back of an airmail envelope addressed to Dr. Valerie Prine, Department of Archaeology, University of London.

5

She stuffed two hastily made sandwiches into a paper bag along with an orange and a handful of carrots. "Ted, you *will* manage with all of them?"

"Of course I will," he replied grumpily. "You haven't much confidence in me, have you?"

She blew the hair off her forehead, but before she could answer, Martin reappeared. "They're coming," he reported, slightly out of breath. "I say, Valerie, you're not going off without me, are you? You promised you'd see about a job for me on the site."

Valerie hesitated, debating visibly with herself.

"Well, if you'd rather not bother—" he said with an edge of frosty politeness in his voice.

"Oh nuts! Don't get all stiff with me, Martin Ibbetson," she said. "Come on, if you want. We haven't time to make you a lunch, you'll have to scavenge."

"Hey," said Mark, stuffing his T-shirt into his jeans, "what about us?" He and Luke had thudded down the stairs barely a minute behind Martin.

"Absolutely not. You are staying here today. I am not going to clutter myself up with a lot of appendages this morning. Once I know what's what you can come over—later this week maybe. And that goes for Lou as well," she tacked on, forestalling the question on Lou's face.

With a mighty effort, Penelope saw her father pull himself together. "Not to worry, Val, the five of us are going to Hexham to do some exploring. Mark, Luke, sit down and eat your eggs before they solidify," he said in a voice of authority. Once he assumed responsibility for something, he could be relied upon to make sure it was successful; it became a point of pride. The tricky bit, Penelope knew from experience, was getting him involved in the first place, and somehow Valerie had managed that.

"All right," said Mark, "we'll wait 'til tomorrow. After all, you're the codirector of this dig, you ought to be able to do what you want."

"Exactly," Valerie agreed. "And right now I want to go over there without offspring." She blew them an indiscriminate kiss from the doorway. "Goodbye, friends, and good luck, Ted."

Once Valerie and Martin were gone, the twins could direct their full attention to breakfast. The carton of food that had looked so enormous to Penelope when her stepmother filled it two days earlier in London was alarmingly empty. The twelve-year-old twins pitched into every meal as if they were coming to it from a twenty-four-hour fast. On the two-day trip from London to Northumberland, Penelope had observed them at close range, packing away enormous meals and keeping themselves alive in between with fruit, chocolate, biscuits, porkpies and gingerbeer. They were, as Edward was fond of remarking, omnivorous and voracious.

Martin had always had a healthy appetite himself, but Penelope was used to providing for him. She and Mrs. Brice, the Ibbetsons' three-days-a-week housekeeper, were familiar with his eating habits. But the first six weeks of life with the Prine twins had been a revelation from which Penelope had not yet recovered. She was unused to having to compete for things in her own house. It still shocked her to find that the packet of biscuits out of which she had taken only two had been eaten down to the wrapper by teatime the following day. Or that four pints of milk had evaporated to an inch in the bottom of one bottle overnight and there was only a jagged crust left of what had been more than half a loaf of bread at breakfast. It was disconcerting and upsetting not to know what she could count on finding in what she still thought of as her own kitchen.

The food business was symptomatic of all the changes that had taken place in her life since her father had married Valerie Prine. The pattern she was used to had been rudely shattered by the addition of four new people, and she only realized when it was far too late to prevent it that the damage was irreparable. But she was sensible enough to see, once the panic subsided, that she had a choice: either she could mourn uselessly over the rubble, or she could set to work to build something new for herself. This wasn't the first time she'd faced such a choice; it had happened seven years earlier when her mother died, and again, three years ago when Grannie Lawrence had gone into a nursing home and Edward had moved his family to the house in Warburton Square, Kensington. Each time she'd managed, and she would again, even though it was bound to be harder now. In the course of her fourteen years, Penelope had developed considerable personal resources.

Mark and Luke between them polished off the scrambled eggs, the remaining milk, large bowls of cereal, and half a loaf of bread smeared with strawberry jam and peanut butter. Then Mark sat back in his chair and looked around expectantly. Edward was concentrating moodily on a cup of tea, and Lou methodically ripped little bits out of the center of a slice of bread, eating it from the inside out because she wasn't fond of crusts.

"Well?" prodded Mark after a minute or two of silence.

"Mmmph," said Edward.

"What're we going to do?"

"I've told you. We're going to Hexham."

"Yes, but *when?*"

"When I'm good and ready." Edward's voice was ominously flat.

"There's lots to do first," interjected Penelope, hurrying to head off a collision. "The kitchen to clean up, and we haven't properly looked round Wintergap yet." Even as she spoke, she felt again the draft of apprehension that had chilled her the night before at her first glimpse of the house, so isolated and uncompromising on its dark hillside.

There had been no lights shining out of it to welcome them, to soften its severe outline; only the double row of opaque, secretive windows. She had put her uneasy feeling down to arriving at a strange place late at night, tired and hot from a long day's traveling. She was anxious now, in the daylight, to dispel that feeling as quickly as possible. The Ibbetsons were to spend the summer at Wintergap.

"Hey," said Mark, "that's right. Come on, Luke, let's see what we can find outside."

Before Penelope had time to realize what was happening, he and Luke had magically vanished, leaving the ruins of breakfast behind. "Just don't go anywhere without us," Mark called through the back door.

Penelope snapped her mouth shut and turned to find Lou regarding her with interest. "You let them get away," she observed. "Now you'll have to clean up by yourself."

8

Taking his cup and saucer, Edward wandered slowly out into the hall. Penelope knew it was useless to complain to him at this point. Lou slid out of her chair and followed him.

"You can just make your own bed!" Penelope called after her crossly. She saw no reason why she should have to clean up after seven people; it wasn't fair. But years spent living with Grannie Lawrence made it impossible for her to walk out of the kitchen and leave it strewn with the remains of a meal. She struggled with her conscience and finally settled for a compromise: she put away what little food there was, ran hot water in the skillet, and piled the dirty china beside the sink. As she did the latter, it occurred to her again how odd it was that the only dishes they had been able to find so far in the house were an elegant and very extensive Royal Worcester dinner service. There were none of the usual mismatched, chipped cups, saucers, mugs, and plates she was used to finding in a rented flat or cottage. At Wintergap there simply wasn't anything "second best" in any of the cupboards.

Her conscience appeased, Penelope left the kitchen in an orderly form of mess and began to explore the house a little on her own. In order to get her balance in any strange place, she had found it necessary to learn the territory with some care. She began with her immediate surroundings; then, as they became familiar, she moved outward a little at a time, gaining confidence as she went, until she was comfortable with quite a large area.

Her impressions of the house from the night before were shadowy and distorted. She remembered the surprise they had all felt when Valerie, armed with a key, had discovered the front door unlocked. "Someone's trusting," she remarked, pushing it wide. To which Edward had replied, "Why not? There isn't a soul within miles aside from your own crew."

The imposing front hall was sheathed in dark paneling; a staircase with a massive banister climbed up the right-hand side of it to the bedrooms on the floor above. At its foot, just inside the front door, was a wide archway framed with heavy wood columns through which lay a formal drawing room, the furniture shrouded in dust sheets: pale, vaguely sinister shapes in the gloom. Martin had found the light switch, but the high, thin light only seemed to accentuate the thick dusk. Penelope had noticed that the edges of the stairs and the angles of the paneling and columns were clouded with dust. But there wasn't time, and no one had energy, for further exploration just then. Perhaps Wintergap wouldn't seem quite so inhospitable to Penelope if she knew more about it.

Two heavy doors opened off the hall opposite the staircase. Behind the one nearest the kitchen lay the dining room: a high-ceilinged, gloomy cavern, stiff with dark, ornate furniture. Down its center ran a dust-filmed table guarded by a battalion of chairs frozen at attention. The walls were hung with mud-tinted prints and mirrors in elaborate frames. Penelope hastily withdrew and closed the door. She could no more imagine her newly expanded family eating their cheerful, chaotic meals in that intimidating room than she could imagine her father eating fish and chips out of greasy newspaper.

She found him in the next room, contemplating a vast expanse of bookshelves; the walls were lined with them. Wherever he went, Edward Ibbetson automatically gravitated toward books. They were, after all, his livelihood, and he found them endlessly fascinating. At a glance, Penelope decided this room was a study. It seemed slightly less overbearing, but perhaps that was the result of the books. They furnished it with a suggestion of warmth, even though someone had arranged them in strict regiments according to size and there were a great many sets of volumes in identical bindings. Edward had bypassed these for the moment in favor of an inconspicuous shelf behind the impressive desk. This was jammed with gaudy, inexpensive paperbacks. He was holding one open in his hands and there was a pleased little smile lifting the corners of his mouth. Penelope caught a glimpse of the cover and recognized it instantly: it was one of her father's earliest thrillers, reissued about three years ago and embellished with a photograph of a well-endowed model called Sondra, wearing a slinky black dress and pretending to be a corpse. She was draped artistically over a roulette wheel—the book was called *Blind Luck*. Martin, who'd then been fifteen, had been outraged at the cover picture because, having read the novel from beginning to end, he knew there was no such scene in it. Didn't it matter to his father that that constituted flagrant misrepresentation, if not downright fraud? Not really, Edward told him calmly, not so long as the book sold well enough to keep Martin in football boots and school uniforms. It had. Ibbetson thrillers always did.

And Sondra, whose last name Penelope had forgotten, had spent the next five months or so trying unsuccessfully to charm Martin and Penelope and get Edward to propose marriage. All three Ibbetsons had been relieved when she got discouraged and gave it up.

Edward gave a guilty little start when he noticed Penelope. "Oh, hullo. It's you." With casual indifference he closed the book and replaced it among its fellows. "Quite a collection," he said brightly. "Someone's evidently made a careful study of the Roman Wall."

Penelope went closer to examine some of the titles. "I had no idea there was so much written about it," she said after a minute. "We've done the Romans at school, of course, but—I don't see how people can find enough to say that's different. *Handbook to the Roman Wall, Research on Hadrian's Wall, The Building of Hadrian's Wall, The Northwest Frontier of Rome, The History of the Roman Wall.* Hmm." She took down *The History of the Roman Wall,* which was thinner than most of its companions and bound in leather. It was printed in large type with *s*'s that looked like *f*'s, and on the flyleaf someone had inscribed the name "Anthony S. Whitton" with controlled and elegant flourishes in brown ink.

"Did you come looking for me?" asked her father.

"Did I—not really, no. Just wondered what was in this room." She closed the book and put it back. "Dad, does it seem odd to you that there are so many personal things still in this house?"

"Personal? What d'you mean?"

"All these books, for instance. And the good china, and the prints on the walls, and all this furniture." Penelope paused, then said, "It's the kind of stuff that *belongs* to someone, not the kind of stuff you leave behind."

"I suppose that's true," said Edward, interested. "Family treasures. *I* wouldn't leave the books behind, I can tell you. We'll ask Valerie about it this evening, she's bound to know something about Wintergap. Maybe we can find information

11

here." He turned to scan the shelves again. Penelope knew in another minute he'd have submerged himself.

"I do think we ought to get the shopping done first," she said hastily. "I don't know where the twins have got to."

Edward stretched and yawned luxuriously. "You're not going to turn into a nag, are you, Pennie?"

"Dad, there isn't any food left. If you want lunch—"

"All right, all right, point taken. I'll go shave and dress."

In slightly under an hour the five of them piled into Edward's yellow Volvo for the expedition to Hexham. Penelope asserted her seniority by appropriating the front seat next to her father, and left Mark, Luke, and Lou to sort themselves out in back.

It was a day as hot and dry as the two before had been; the sun burned a flaming hole through the hard blue shell of sky. Beneath it, in all directions, the open country spread away from Wintergap, humped and rumpled like an unmade bed. It was unbroken by any reassuring sign of human life. The only trees were the ragged firs clustered around the square stone house and its neglected outbuildings. Wintergap was dwarfed by the wild emptiness on every side. Penelope was both fascinated and disturbed by the country; it stirred something unfamiliar within her that she wasn't at all sure she wanted to acknowledge.

With caution, Edward drove the Volvo along the narrow, bumpy dirt track that had seemed last night to wind so interminably over the heaving moorland. They left Wintergap behind in a billowing cloud of yellow dust.

"Look up there," exclaimed Luke after a few minutes. "You can see Sulpitium."

They peered through the dust-streaked windows on the left-hand side of the car, eager for a glimpse of the Roman fort Valerie had come to Northumberland to help excavate. Penelope saw a farmhouse and outbuildings, tents, a huddle of parked cars, and a grassy field crawling with little figures. From a distance the hillside looked like an anthill that had been disturbed by some giant foot.

Only Lou paid no attention. She leaned back on the seat with her eyes half-closed, humming a thin private song to herself, which emerged now and then from the noise of the engine.

"It really wasn't fair of her not to let us go," grumbled Mark. "We haven't even seen the Wall yet."

"We certainly have," contradicted Penelope. "We saw it at Heddon and Brunton and Chesters, and at Carrawbrough and Housesteads . . ." That was the reason they'd been so late arriving; with Valerie as guide they had made very erratic progress from the city of York, where they'd spent the previous night, to Wintergap. Along the way they had stopped to hunt out broken bits of Roman road, the excavated remains of major forts, milecastles, temples, bridge abutments, and chunks of Hadrian's Wall itself standing by the east-west road, or off in the middle of somebody's cow field, or twisting along the top of the sheer cliff known as the Whin Sill like a hoary grey snake. It had seemed to Penelope that they were forever piling into and out of the two cars—her father's Volvo and Valerie's second-hand Mini—getting hotter and grubbier and less enthusiastic each time. Only Valerie and Luke had seemed able to see something new and exciting in each successive piece of crumbling masonry.

"Yes," Mark said impatiently, "but not *our* part of it—that's all somebody else's. It doesn't count."

"You've got the whole summer ahead," Edward reminded him.

"Yeah, but—"

"There's a section of the Wall behind Wintergap," said Luke. "We didn't go up far enough this morning—"

"We found some other things, though," interrupted his twin, successfully distracted. "One of the huts back there has most of the roof left on it. We're claiming it for our private clubhouse."

"Bully for you," said Edward mildly. "You'll get no argument from me."

"And there's a brook at the bottom of the gully beside the house, but there's hardly any water in it," Mark continued.

Edward nodded. "Looks as if it's been very dry up here. Everything's brown rather than green and it's only early July." He swung the car left out onto the paved road at the foot of the farm track.

"—and we saw a dog, too," Luke was saying.

Lou instantly sat up. "A dog? Where? What kind of dog?"

"Black and white."

"Not what color, stupid, what *kind*," she said with an impatient frown.

"*I* don't know," Mark said. "How should I know? Just a dog. We called it, but it wouldn't come. It ran off up the hill."

"Maybe it's lost," said Lou, her face animated. "Maybe I can find it tomorrow and make friends."

"It was queer," Luke said slowly. "It felt as if there was someone out there, watching us, but we couldn't see anyone."

"You're crazy," his brother told him. "It was only that old dog."

Penelope said nothing, but Luke's words reminded her of her own uneasy feelings about Wintergap. According to Valerie the house had been empty since the summer before, and it certainly looked as if it had been empty. But it didn't *feel* as if it had. In some inexplicable way the house was full of a restless, secret life that Penelope suspected went on no matter whether there were people in it or not. That sounded ridiculous—it was like admitting a belief in ghosts, and she didn't think she could. But as they had unloaded the cars in the dark last night, she certainly had had the uncomfortable sensation of being watched.

There were strings of traffic on the road to Hexham; lots of cars and huge silver-sided tourist coaches whizzing in both directions. Fine weather had brought swarms of sightseers out. The narrow streets of Hexham itself were snarled with cars, bicycles, and pedestrians in far greater quantity than they had originally been designed to handle several hundred years ago. When not preoccupied with fear for her own safety, Penelope spared a little sympathy for anyone attempting to conduct ordinary business in the midst of such a confusion of tourists. They were everywhere: clogging the pavements, blocking shop doorways, pausing in the middle of busy streets to consult a map or take photographs.

His jaw set like granite, Edward gripped the steering wheel and muttered curses as he navigated the obstacle-strewn route into the center of the market town. Martin, Penelope decided, was a far less nerve-wracking driver, even though he had only just acquired his license. With Penelope and Luke as passengers, he had driven Valerie's Mini up from London, in convoy with the Volvo, and done very well except on the last thirty miles into York when he had let his self-confidence override his common sense and gone sailing past his father, much to Edward's undisguised fury. There would have been an unholy row, right there in the hotel lobby, if Valerie hadn't intervened and steered Edward away for a pint of beer and some soothing conversation. Martin had gone out and walked round the city walls for several hours to work off his own temper.

"Bloody idiot! Shouldn't be licensed!" roared Edward as he wove dizzyingly between parked cars and oncoming lorries. "Look at this ninny, will you, stopped dead in the middle of everything. This is a main road, not a flaming car park! Keep moving, you fool!"

Penelope shrank down in her seat, thinking it might help not to watch. But that was worse. At last her father swerved left, out of the line of traffic, onto a broad tree-shaded street, and with his customary luck, located a parking place immediately. He slid the Volvo neatly into it, cutting off a red-faced countryman in an old Ford. Penelope glanced quickly away from the man whose mouth was working inaudibly; she could supply words that fit all too well.

"And here we are," Edward announced cheerfully as he switched off the motor. The tension of the last twenty minutes vanished from his face. It was, as Martin often sardonically pointed out, a kind of Dr. Jekyll–Mr. Hyde transformation.

Mark erupted from the back seat; he felt he had been contained far too long. The others got out less violently. On the far side of the street was a block of very square buildings: offices and a hotel; beside the Volvo lay a sun-splattered park, its grass dotted with people seeking refuge under the trees from the shriveling sun. At the far end of the street Penelope glimpsed the canvas roofs of market stalls and the continuous movement of people.

"Hey!" said Mark eagerly. "What's going on?"

"Gawd," said Edward. "No wonder the town's heaving with people—Tuesday must be market day! What wretched luck."

"Neat! Let's go see—"

"Hold hard!" commanded his stepfather. "No one stirs until I say so."

"Can't we just go *look?*" wheedled Mark. "We'd come back—"

"Ah, but when? You stay put, both of you."

"I'm hungry," Lou declared. "I want lunch."

"It can't be time yet," objected Edward.

"We really ought to do the shopping," Penelope put in, not because she was anxious to do it, but rather because she was anxious not to get stuck doing it alone later, when everyone else had scattered. She had seen that happen before. And the shopping had got to be done.

Edward was looking faintly disgruntled. "Bother!" he said, an uncommonly mild oath for him.

"You'd better feed her," Luke advised. "If you don't she gets cranky."

"I do not!" Lou's eyes hardened dangerously.

"Do so," teased Mark.

"Put a sock in it," Edward warned him, "or I'll beat you to a pulp. Very well, we'll have lunch." He glanced up and down the street. "Not, I think, in an hotel. Of course what I would really like more than anything is a corner seat in some unpretentious pub, where I could sit peacefully with a pint and a sausage roll and listen to the locals gossip. Pennie, I don't suppose you'd be willing—"

"No," she said firmly. She was not about to take responsibility for Mark, Luke, and Lou so her father could go off and enjoy himself. They were *his* responsibility, not hers; he'd taken them on with his eyes open when he'd married their mother.

"Why don't we all go to one?" suggested Mark with enthusiasm. "I've never been in a pub—Mom would never take us."

"It's illegal, old son," his stepfather informed him sadly.

16

"You would be stopped at the door and I would be the object of universal censure for attempting to corrupt the morals of innocent children. We'll have to settle for the mediocrity of a milk bar."

"That's rotten!" declared Mark. "I don't even like beer, I just want to see what the inside's like."

Edward shrugged. "We're both thwarted."

"But," said Penelope, "that's not—" Her father waggled an eyebrow significantly at her and she stopped. She knew perfectly well that children were allowed into pubs at lunchtime —she had often been, but she also understood that he preferred to keep this to himself. She guessed he would much rather explore the Hexham pubs alone and inconspicuously, not trailed by a small mob of curious and questioning dependents. With a sigh she acceded. "Well, let's stop moaning and find something."

They walked toward the market, joining the flow of tourists and locals, pulled inevitably in the direction of activity. The square was a hot, dusty jumble of stalls. The sun stood in the sky almost directly overhead, flooding the scene with fierce white light, so that walking into the open was like entering an overexposed photograph. Mark and Luke examined the merchandise on display avidly. There was every conceivable portable item: fruit, LP records, synthetic knitwear and bolts of gaudy cloth, cheap kitchen pots, dazzling fountains of costume jewelry, flowers of every natural and artificial hue, dolls and stuffed animals, heaps of imitation leather shoes. It was an ordinary country town market; Penelope had seen them before, but to the twins everything was new and intriguing. If it hadn't been for the lure of food, she doubted they would have allowed themselves to be pried loose.

"Dad, what's that?" asked Penelope. "There isn't a cathedral in Hexham, is there?" She was looking at the tall, gold-brown church, a benevolent presence that stood against the market square on the east.

"Hexham Abbey. Perhaps we should have a look round it this afternoon—once we've finished the shopping, of course." He gave her a teasing, sideways look.

"The shopping is, after all, what we came for," she reminded him primly. "Unless you want to starve . . ."

CHAPTER II

THEY WERE SAVED FROM THE MEDIOCRE MILK BAR BY LOU, who discovered a windowful of delicious-looking sweet and savory pastries. They stood in a queue for ten minutes, surrounded by people on their lunch hour, and emerged from the little shop with cold chicken, thick slices of veal and ham pie, coleslaw, and half-a-dozen warm apple tarts. At stalls in the market they added bottles of lemonade, ginger beer, and a bag of ripe plums, then made their way back to the park and collapsed on the grass. It was a very satisfactory picnic.

Edward settled with his back against an obliging horse chestnut tree and his legs outstretched, and let the twins bicker about who got drumsticks. He looked surprisingly paternal, Penelope thought. His stepchildren were, of course, getting to know him under the best possible circumstances— during that calm, relatively even-tempered interval between the acceptance of one of his manuscripts and the appearance of the first proofs. The twins and Lou had not yet been fully exposed to Edward Ibbetson, successful novelist, at work.

This time the interval had been unusually long, owing to the marriage and subsequent adjustments. Edward had put work temporarily out of his mind. But Penelope recognized a creeping restlessness and knew the calm couldn't last much longer. Even before the first batch of proofs for his new book arrived, she knew he'd begin casting about for new material, taking mental notes, asking those deceptively innocent questions that Martin objected to so strenuously.

Instead of resignation, this time Penelope felt apprehension. She tried to tell herself that she merely wanted to postpone the inevitable moment when her father would begin to withdraw from them, when the balance would shift and the real world would become less important to him than the world he was creating in his head. But it was more than that; there

18

were all kinds of unfamiliar problems to cope with now. She and Martin had grown up learning how to adapt to their father's absorption in his work. They dealt with it in their own ways: Martin turned to his legion of friends, Penelope turned inward, to her own resources.

However, this summer there were Mark, Luke, and Lou to reckon with. Well before the wedding, Valerie had announced her plans to spend the holidays as codirector of an archaeological dig in Northumberland. Edward had agreed to look after the domestic side of things while she worked, to keep an eye on the children and the house. But if he were suddenly seized by a creative urge, all that would go by the boards. The one thing Penelope was resolved upon was that she was not, as the eldest girl, going to assume any part of her father's responsibilities: for the house or the young Prines.

"You'll get stuck looking after Louisa," her friend Alison Sheppard had prophesied darkly when Penelope told her of the impending marriage. "That's what older sisters are for." Alison knew from experience. She had a brother two years younger and a baby sister.

"I'm not her sister," Penelope protested. "Not really."

"You will be once they get married. You won't be able to get out of it, see if I'm wrong. What you must do right away," she went on to advise, "is make it clear that you expect to be paid. You ought to be able to manage that with a stepmother. If you have to baby-sit, you might as well get something for it. What about the twins?"

"Oh, no," said Penelope, horrified. "They're twelve—almost as old as *I* am. I can't possibly!"

Alison was not reassuring. "Just make sure you ask for money."

That conversation had struck chill into Penelope's heart. It was the first absolute indication that life for her after her father's marriage might be radically different.

Well, life certainly was different with four additional people in the Warburton Square house. Compromises had to be worked out over all kinds of formerly simple things: bath schedules and television programs; who did what chores when; how loud was *too* loud in relation to the radio. But so

19

far there had been no personal demands made upon either Penelope or Martin, beyond that of making an effort to get along with everyone. That they were both prepared for. They had, after all, encouraged their father to marry Valerie. She was far and away superior to any other woman he had brought home. And it wasn't that she was merely the best of a bad lot, in their opinion. They really liked Valerie Prine; she was attractive, humorous, and straightforward. She said what she meant and she didn't try to hide things.

But now, sitting here on the grass in Hexham, meditatively eating a slice of cold meat pie, Penelope had the sudden premonition that personal demands were about to be made upon her. That willy-nilly she was going to find herself *involved*. She swallowed her last mouthful and looked up to see Mark and Luke hovering greedily over the two remaining apple tarts. Everything else had been devoured; it was a good thing she hadn't wanted a piece of chicken. One could not afford to drift into one's thoughts at mealtime with the twins around. She was *not* going to surrender her tart. They watched with disappointment as she claimed it, then decided that left them free to split the last one. Luke broke it into two scrupulously even pieces.

Edward was in the midst of telling Lou a carefully edited and imaginatively embroidered version of his adventures as a young man in New Zealand. He had grown up on a sheep station outside of Christchurch on the Canterbury Plains, hating the provincial, physical life of a farmer. As soon as he could, he had escaped to England and a place at Oxford University and had never gone back.

Penelope was fascinated by her father's stories of that other life, but she could never quite believe that the man who was her father had really ever been that boy on that sheep station in a country half the world away. His reality for her began when she was old enough to be aware of him; everything before that was the stuff of good stories. How odd, she thought as she stretched out on the warm turf, comfortably full of lunch and drowsy, and what a curious distance there was between knowing something to be true and believing it.

She woke to find her father nudging her. "It's enough to make a man give up storytelling altogether when his own flesh and blood goes to sleep in the middle of one of his best tales," he complained.

"I've heard it before," she pointed out. "Besides, I wasn't asleep, not sound anyway."

"Oh yes you were," said Mark impudently, "you were snoring!"

She shut her teeth against an indignant denial, realizing just in time that he was only baiting her.

"I liked the story," said Lou. "Especially about the lambs. I wouldn't mind hearing it again."

"You will," Penelope assured her.

"Enough idle chatter," said Edward. "Pick up your litter, children, and let's get moving before anyone else drops off."

"Can we go back to the market?" asked Mark immediately.

"Don't see why not. We can arrange to meet—"

"Stop," said Penelope. She could see them all disappearing like smoke, leaving her holding the shopping list. "I am *not* going to do the errands by myself while you lot go exploring. I don't see why I should."

Mark screwed up his face in protest, but Edward said, "All right. Let's see how quickly we can get it done."

They selected one of the supermarkets on Hexham's main street; there they could buy everything at once instead of having to trail round to half-a-dozen little shops. It ought to have been a perfectly straightforward task—Valerie had provided a comprehensive list for them to follow. But the trouble was that no one except Penelope even attempted to follow it. Everyone else went shooting up and down the aisles at random, collecting anything that struck their fancies: tins of spaghetti, lemon spongecake and Swiss rolls, coconut biscuits, anchovies, bags of toffee, custard powder. Although she would have died rather than admit it out loud, by the time they piloted the laden shopping cart to the checkout counter, Penelope knew in her heart that it would have been much simpler to have let the other four go their separate ways after lunch and to have done the job herself. She was feeling a little sensitive.

Mark eyed the mound of groceries with respect and said it looked like a winner from an American game show called *Supermarket Sweep*. "But," replied Edward, opening his wallet, "I don't suppose the contestants have to pay for what they take, do they? Not to worry, when you're setting up housekeeping, it's necessary to buy a great many basics."

"I don't see how you can possibly call minced clams and pickled beetroot basics," observed Penelope tartly.

"The concept of 'basics' is relative," Edward informed her as he paid the enormous bill. The five of them staggered back to the Volvo carrying cartons. It seemed much further from the supermarket to the car than it had from the car to the supermarket.

"All right," said Edward once everything had been stowed. "I'll give you each fifty pence and you can go wherever the spirit moves you. But we'll meet back here no later than half-past four. There's a clock on the Abbey tower, or you can ask someone," he added, forestalling Mark's objection. "I don't care what you're doing, be here. Is that clear?"

The twins nodded, took their money, and sped off toward the marketplace, Mark in the lead. Edward, looking after them, said, "I feel as if I'd been sitting on an active volcano all morning and only just got down before the eruption. Well, Louisa, didn't you want to go with your brothers?"

"No," Lou answered simply. "What are *we* going to do?"

Edward glanced at Penelope and Penelope looked quickly away. "You said we might go into the Abbey," she reminded him. Before the afternoon was over she suspected her father would find an opportunity to drift quietly away, leaving her to cope with Lou, and she was determined to postpone that as long as possible. She'd actually hoped Lou would choose her brothers' company; then she could have had her father to herself for a little while. But evidently Louisa stood outside the invisible circle that bound the twins together. With an uneasy mix of feelings, Penelope saw Lou reach out and take Edward's hand; they smiled briefly at one another. This might serve to keep Edward with them a bit longer, but Penelope wasn't altogether happy about it. She protected herself by seeming not to notice.

The Abbey was dark and cool inside after the dazzle of sun. A comforting reservoir of peace filled the vaulted space,

22

muffling the hum of sightseers who wandered through it. Penelope had learned about the Border Abbeys in history at school: the great monastic churches that had been repeatedly sacked and destroyed over the centuries by Vikings, Irish, Scots, and rebuilt until Henry VIII had finally, and in most cases permanently, disbanded the monasteries and left their churches to decay. Once, on a trip to Scotland, Edward had taken Penelope and Martin to see the great ruins of Melrose and Dryburgh, silent impressive skeletons: broken columns and empty arches, roofless choirs, naves carpeted with grass.

But Hexham Abbey was miraculously whole; alive and functioning. Two ladies in blue nylon smocks arranged urns of hollyhocks and delphinium in front of the rood screen, tucking and tweaking, standing back, then tweaking again. A thin, grey man in a clerical collar talked earnestly to a little knot of tourists. The notice board over the book stall fluttered with announcements about church suppers, Mothers' Guild meetings, Bible classes, and child-care groups.

Edward paused to buy a guide book. "Might as well know what we ought to look for." Expertly he began to skim the contents, extracting the most interesting bits. "Where are we now? Mph—yes, South Transept. '. . . beautiful in its simplicity . . .' Mmm '. . . large aumbrey . . . slype . . . most picturesque feature of the whole interior . . . night-stair . . .' That'll be it, there." Beside them, as they stood in the shadowy transept, rose a broad, handsomely proportioned stone stairway, each step worn hollow in the middle.

"What's a nightstair?" asked Lou without prompting.

"It was used at night by the monks when this was part of a monastery. It led to the canons' dormitory, which has been destroyed. They would have come down the stair to service. People have gone up and down those steps since the twelfth century—how many years, Louisa?"

"Mmm," said Lou. "What happened to the dormitory?"

"Nearly eight hundred," supplied Penelope and earned a frown from her father for answering instead of Lou.

But he went on, "The dormitory burned or was torn down long ago during one of the Border raids, no doubt, and was never rebuilt. This was a bloody country up here, Louisa,

23

lawless and violent for a great many years." He glanced back at the guide. "A lot of the stone used to build the Abbey was apparently taken from the Roman Wall and the forts."

"You mean people just stole it? They *destroyed* the Roman things to build their own?" Penelope was shocked at the idea. "Why didn't someone stop them?"

"There wasn't anyone. The Roman ruins weren't considered worth protecting as a national treasure until relatively recently," said Edward. "People would have found it much easier simply to dismantle them than quarry new stone. Yesterday in the car, Valerie was telling us that people took the stone for all kinds of things: houses, cow byres, doorsteps, field walls. Apparently Wintergap itself is built entirely out of stones from the fort at Sulpitium."

Penelope digested that sobering information in silence, while her father read on. "'Four recesses underneath . . . Canons' Library . . . eastern processional doorway . . .'"

She lost track of the words as she glanced around at the Abbey. Light splashed through the high windows of the clerestory, turning the stone of the nave to the color of baked meringue. It felt settled and calm, not at all like Wintergap, and yet they had both been built at the expense of the Romans, raised out of the ruins of their labor. Of course they had been built for entirely different purposes: one as a private house, the other as a place of worship. That must account for it; the Abbey was consecrated, Wintergap was not.

"—it's got a horse on it. See?" Lou was saying.

"Hang on." Edward ran his finger down the lines of print, and Penelope turned to see what they were looking at. "'Large Roman memorial stone, dating from the end of the first century . . .' The inscription reads, 'To the Gods the Shades. Flavinus of the Cavalry Regiment of Petriana a Standard Bearer of the White Troop. Aged twenty-five and of seven years service is here buried.'"

At the foot of the nightstair, in a niche by itself, stood a flat stone slab, taller than her father. Above the inscribed panel someone had carved a bas-relief of a man on horseback —meant to be Flavinus, no doubt—holding his standard: a shaft with a circle at the end.

Lou, who had been studying the monument with a frown,

24

said, "But who's that?" She pointed to another figure cut into the face of the stone. Underneath the rearing horse, crouched as if to defend himself, was a second man. He held a long knife point-upward, aimed at the horse's belly. The longer Penelope looked at him, the more uncomfortable she felt.

"That," said Edward, "is the 'naked Briton,' one of the barbarians the Romans built their wall to protect themselves against. I must say he doesn't look particularly subdued. He looks about ready to stab the horse and murder poor old Flavinus. I wouldn't like to bet on the outcome of a fight between them."

Neither, agreed Penelope silently, would I. "Perhaps that was the man who actually killed Flavinus," she said. "I suppose you could say the barbarians won in the end—they outlasted the Romans, didn't they?"

"They had to, it was their country," Edward reminded her. "They hung on until the Romans ran out of money, patience, and time; then they took it back."

Penelope found it surprisingly difficult to drag her attention from the bent little figure on the stone. A wild fringe of hair stood out around its head, but where the face should have been, there was only one eye and a bit of nose; the rest had been chipped away. It disturbed her in some obscure, wordless way.

But Edward lost interest in the memorial stone and began to walk up the nave, drawing Lou along with him. Deliberately, Penelope shook herself loose and followed, but instead of catching up with them she wandered at her own pace, pausing to examine whatever took her fancy. Her father had his audience in Lou and didn't need her.

Finally Edward hunted out the verger, an elderly gentleman with a pink face and a thatch of white hair and faded blue eyes that were unexpectedly sharp. He was delighted to take them down into the Saxon crypt beneath the nave. It lay at the bottom of twelve deep, uneven steps. It was squat and barrel-vaulted and smelled of stale darkness and dank stone. Penelope was aware of the whole massive weight of the Abbey bearing down on them; she felt oppressed and suffocated and concentrated very hard on what the verger was saying.

"The stones were brought by St. Wilfrid from the Roman camp at Corstopitum about 674 A.D. That was an altar stone, you can see a word or two of inscription. And over there the marks of the Roman masons." Many of the stone blocks bore a distinctive crosshatch pattern he told them was called diamond broaching. With as much pride as if he'd helped to build it himself, he said, " 'Twas built to last, the crypt. These stones'll bide long after we're gone."

"Yes," said Edward looking around, "I suppose a sense of permanence and continuity is comforting."

Lou said, "It's very dark down here."

Penelope was relieved to mount the steps back to air and light.

"Seen much of the Roman Wall, have you?" inquired the verger once they were standing again in the nave.

"Not as much as we're likely to by the end of summer," said Edward. "We're spending the holidays up here."

The verger nodded approvingly. "Aye, that's good. Most folk think they've seen it all if they spend a day or two, then go tearing off to visit something else. They've no idea what they miss. Would you be staying in Hexham?"

"No, about fifteen miles west of here. My wife's an archaeologist, and this summer she's codirecting the University excavation at Sulpitium . . ."

Penelope, who'd been breathing deeply to rid her lungs of the fusty air and only half-listening to the conversation, happened to be watching the verger as her father spoke. It was an odd thing, but at the mention of Sulpitium, his open, pleasant face changed; it became shuttered, almost wary. She saw it happen in the blink of an eye. Puzzled, she glanced at her father to see if he'd noticed, but his expression betrayed nothing unusual. He went on conversationally, "Actually we're staying at the house called Wintergap—do you know it? It was given to the University several years ago, along with the Roman site, I believe. Seems an interesting spot."

Penelope realized he was rattling on precisely because he *had* sensed the change; under the cover of talk he was observing the verger closely.

"Aye, I know it," said the old man reluctantly. He hesi-

26

tated, frowning, then added, "It has an unchancy reputation in these parts, Wintergap. You know that, do you?"

"What do you mean?" demanded Lou, catching the somber tone of his voice. "Is there something wrong with our house?"

" 'Tis nowt but talk, most likely. Some places seem to attract bad luck; then there's always too much talk."

"What kind of bad luck?" asked Edward, really interested now.

Again the verger hesitated, as if he would rather not talk about it. "It was never a lucky farm for the Robsons when they leased it. Best they could do was scrape a living from it. George Robson was fortunate to be quit of Wintergap Farm when the landowner took it back and moved the Robsons to Dodd Moss, but he'd never see that." He shook his head, troubled. "And now George's dead and left the farm to his son, bad feeling and all."

"I'm afraid," said Edward carefully, "that I don't follow you."

Instinctively Penelope felt she'd rather not hear any more. From Louisa's face, she could tell the younger girl shared her feeling, but her father was running like a foxhound on a fresh scent.

" 'Tis nowt but talk," said the old man briskly. "Should have been finished with years back. Now, what else can I tell you about the Abbey? Have you seen Prior Leschman's Chantry?"

"Hmm? Oh, thank you, you've been most helpful, but we're running short of time this afternoon," Edward replied. "No doubt we'll be back."

"Aye, 'tis better when you needn't see everything at once. Good day to you." With a nod and a not-quite-spontaneous little smile the verger left them and walked off toward another group of visitors.

Edward stared after him for a moment, then said, "Well, there you are." Before Penelope, who was still puzzling over the conversation, could guess what was coming next, he went on, "That leaves you not quite an hour before we're due to meet at the car. I'll see you there, shall I?"

"Where are you going?" But he'd left them before Penelope had finished asking the question. She knew the answer anyway. He'd spent the best part of the day being a parent, a role he was unaccustomed to, and concluded that he'd earned an hour to himself. She had no doubt he was off in pursuit of more information concerning Wintergap. When that glint appeared in his eye, there was no holding him back. Ordinarily Penelope wouldn't have minded; she was used to exploring on her own. But today there was Lou, watching her inscrutably from under her dark fringe of hair. Helplessly, Penelope resigned herself to the situation; less than an hour wasn't *that* long. "What do you want to do?"

Lou gave her head a little shake.

"I suppose we could go and look for your brothers in the market." That should dispose of the time without too much effort.

"Okay." Lou was neutral.

CHAPTER III

THE SUN GLARED DOWN ON HEXHAM LIKE A FIERY EYE. AS SHE stepped through the Abbey door, the heat blasted Penelope; it beat on her head and burned through the thin soles of her sandals, bouncing up from the pavement under her feet. She was dazed by it, knocked breathless, but Lou hardly seemed to notice.

The marketplace was all but deserted. Only a handful of people browsed limply among the stalls. The vendors sat in tatters of shade looking bored and discouraged; the few remaining vegetables were wilted, the cut flowers drooped pathetically. Here and there in the rows of stalls were gaps like missing teeth, where some of the hawkers had already packed up and gone. Business was so slow it hardly moved, except at the ice cream van where Lou and Penelope stopped to spend some of Edward's money.

Lou had just decided on a Lemonade Fizz, when they became aware of a sudden commotion on the far side of the square. The sound of angry voices was particularly audible in the stillness of the afternoon. Heads turned automatically, and people began to drift toward the disturbance; it sounded harsh and unpleasant and, to Penelope licking the drips off her ice cream, like a very good thing to stay away from.

But Lou cocked her head like a spaniel and exclaimed, "Hey, that's Luke!" She darted off in the direction of the growing crowd and Penelope had no choice but to follow her.

" 'Ere!" cried the ice cream man. " 'Ang on—she 'asn't paid! I want me money!"

Penelope thrust ten pence of her own at him and went after Lou. The smaller girl had managed to eel through the gathering crowd and penetrate right to the source of the trouble. Penelope, with a dripping ice cream in one hand, had rather more difficulty and wasted valuable minutes apologizing to the owners of the feet she tripped over. With a sense of foreboding, she persevered.

The sight that met her when she finally reached Lou confirmed her worst fears: one of the twins—Mark—was rolling about on the pavement locked in what looked like a life-and-death struggle with another boy whom she'd never set eyes on before. They seemed pretty evenly matched, which could account for the fact that no one had yet pulled them apart. Luke, who had been hovering on the edges of the fight, yelling encouragement to his brother, dashed over to join the two girls. He was red in the face and out of breath.

"What's going on?" demanded Penelope. "Who is that? Why are they fighting? Oh, *blast!* I'm covered in ice cream!"

"He started it," said Luke quickly. "Honest he did, not Mark."

"But who's winning?" Lou wanted to know, eyeing the tangle of arms and legs.

"What does it matter who's winning?" exclaimed Penelope. "Luke, can't you get them to stop?"

Luke looked horrified at the suggestion. "Me? He'd kill me if I tried—it's a fair fight, Pennie."

"What do you mean 'fair'?" she asked furiously.

"What are we going to do?" asked Lou.

"I don't know."

As they stood there the crowd around them grew denser.

Penelope glanced at peoples' interested faces and wished fervently she could slip away and disappear, leaving the whole mess to sort itself out. Barring that, she wished one of these gawping, useless adults would step in and exercise his or her authority to break up the fight. Why didn't someone *do* something?

"Needs a bucket of water," suggested a spotty-faced youth behind them. "Works with dogs."

"It's the heat," someone else remarked sagely.

"It's disgusting, that's what! Such carryin' on in a public place!" exclaimed a woman with damp, frizzy hair. "Shouldn't be allowed. You stay back out of the way, our Joyce, do you hear?"

"But, Mam, I can't *see!*" wailed the little girl, clutching her mother's skirt.

"Get 'im! Get 'im! Thump 'im good!" a grubby little boy yelled indiscriminately at the combatants. "Grind 'is nose in!"

They were both doing their best to oblige as they tumbled over and over on the ground; first Mark on top, then the other boy, punching, scratching, elbowing, grabbing, kicking. People seemed genuinely to be enjoying the spectacle; it enlivened an otherwise slow, hot afternoon. With mounting frustration, Penelope could only stand on the fringe and observe; she had no heroic and foolish intentions of wading in to try and stop the fight herself. She didn't begin to know how, and she knew if she got within range of the flailing fists she was all too likely to get hurt. Oh, *why* had her father disappeared? She was suddenly consumed with an unreasoning fury—at him, at Mark and Luke, at all these stupid, cloddish people, even at Louisa, tense and excited beside her.

There was a stirring on the far side of the crowd. Someone large and deliberate thrust his way through the onlookers, not bothering to excuse himself to anyone, and they pulled back from him, clearly not expecting apologies.

"What's gannin' on here, whey?" he demanded in a voice like thunder. "Randall?" He was a heavyset man, with great powerful shoulders and a thick neck. He was in shirt-sleeves, his shiny brown trousers held up with braces. There was a sudden silence; even the little boy who'd been cheering the

30

fight shut up and withdrew. In the quiet, the panting and grunts of the two boys on the ground could be plainly heard, but both were so obsessed with bashing each other that they were oblivious to the change in atmosphere.

"Who's that?" Penelope asked Luke in a whisper. He only shrugged in reply, his eyes opaque with anxiety.

The man took one look at the fighters, let out a furious grunt, and reached out to catch the uppermost by the scruff of the neck, then shook him roughly loose. It was Mark who happened to have the advantage at that moment, and he gave a cry of rage at being interfered with. The cry choked abruptly in his throat, however, when he wiped the hair and sweat and blood out of his eyes and craned around to see who had pulled him so rudely away. The expression that flooded his face would have been laughable in another situation.

"What's gannin' on?" the man repeated in the same loud voice. He thrust out a heavily booted foot and gave the other boy a rough nudge. "On yer feet wi' ye," he ordered, obviously assuming no argument. He got none. Mark's opponent scrambled up and stood panting, his hands clenched at his sides. It was hard to tell what he looked like under the ragged mat of dark hair and the streaks of filth on his face. His eyes engaged Mark's in a hostile glare.

"An' what's this in aid of, whey?" The man still had Mark securely held by the back of his T-shirt and showed no sign of turning him loose. "Speak up, Randall! Aa've nae been crackin' to hear masel, ye ken."

"What's he going to do to Mark?" asked Lou loudly.

"Shhh! I don't know," Penelope said.

" 'Twas just a fight, Archie," said the strange boy sullenly.

"Aa could bluddy well see thon, couldn't Aa? An' se could half the county! Ye been makin' yersel a right spectacle, ye numb gowk. Aa've a mind to lace ye good an' sound masel, but Aa divvent do ma private business in public! Pack off back to the pickup. *Now!*" He cracked out the last word with such force Penelope saw the boy called Randall flinch fractionally. He went, head held stiffly up, with not a backward glance; he walked through the crowd and out of the market. The man, Archie, watched him go with a black

31

scowl, then remembered Mark and gave him a vigorous shake. Mark's head jerked back and forth alarmingly and Penelope took an involuntary step forward. "An' wha is it claims this tyke, whey?"

"We do." Penelope contrived to sound braver than she felt. "He's with us." Luke and Lou stood dumbly behind her.

The man shifted his scowl to her and she wished she were anywhere else. "Yer brother, is he? The lad needs a keeper, Aa'd say."

No, she wanted to say, no, he's not my brother at all. But she couldn't. Instead she said, "He didn't start it. It wasn't his fault." She hoped fervently that Luke had been telling the truth, and that no one would contradict her. Mark looked rather ill under the grime.

"Aw, let 'im be, Archie," called someone among the dwindling crowd. People had begun to scatter as soon as the other boy left. The excitement was over. " 'Twas a fair enough fight, an' they come off equal."

"To hell wi' ye, Arthur Malley! Haddaway an' mind yer own business!" growled Archie. He gave Mark a final shake and released him. Mark rubbed his shoulder with a grimace. "Ye let me catch the two a ye at it again an' Aa'll give ye summick to think on, lad!" he said, pointing a finger the size of a sausage at Mark. "Ye hear me?"

"Tell *him* that," said Mark, keeping carefully out of reach. "He started it."

The man lifted his hand threateningly, then turned and stumped off in the direction the boy had gone.

"Take my advice an' divvent cross them two again," said the man called Arthur Malley as he walked past. "That ain't just talk."

"What did you have to answer him back for?" demanded Penelope, covering her nervousness with irritability. "Suppose he'd called the police?"

"Police?" Mark felt his jaw tenderly. "Naw. He couldn't have done that without getting his own kid in trouble, could he?"

"I thought he was going to belt you," said Luke. His face was unusually pale. "We couldn't have stopped him."

"You've torn your jeans," observed Lou. "You look awful."

32

"*I* didn't tear them," he retorted. Then added with satisfaction, "That other kid looks just as bad."

"Worse," said Luke loyally.

"There must be somewhere you can clean up a little before Dad sees you," said Penelope. "Why were you fighting in the first place?"

But she had a long wait for an answer to that. Just then Edward materialized, looking annoyed. It was a quarter to five and he'd come hunting for them. One look at Mark and he declared he wished he hadn't found them.

It was a very silent carful that he drove back to Wintergap. They were late, because battle scars or no, they had to stop for milk and butter and eggs on the way. Mark refused to talk about the fight. He stated flatly there was no point in having to tell the story twice—better to wait until everyone could hear it the first time.

"Well, all I can say is, this is one hell of a way to wind up the day!" said Edward crossly.

Luke looked anxious but honored his twin's silence.

Valerie and Martin were already at the house when they arrived, sprawled comfortably in garden chairs on the overgrown terrace. Martin had a bottle of lager in one hand, and Valerie was making inroads on a large glass of cider. They looked tired and sunburned, but cheerful.

"Just my luck," muttered Edward, adding with regret, "There's nothing for it but to face this head on, I'm afraid. I had rather hoped we could wash a little of the gore off before your mother set eyes on you, Mark. I'll be lucky if she doesn't divorce me!"

Penelope saw Lou stiffen as he said that, but the younger girl's face was unreadable. They lugged the provisions up to the house; Mark tried to make himself inconspicuous behind a carton.

"There you are." Valerie greeted them with a lazy smile. "We were beginning to wonder. I was sure you'd beat us home. Any adventures?" She lifted her face for Edward to kiss.

"Optimist that she is, she thought you'd have supper started by now," said Martin, blowing into the top of his bottle. "I tried to warn her. What did you do—buy out Hexham?" He surveyed the cartons with mild interest. His eyes widened as he caught sight of Mark. "Crippen!"

Edward glared meaningfully at his son, but it was too late. Valerie had noticed Mark, too. She snapped upright in her chair, glanced swiftly at Luke and Lou, saw they were unscathed, then turned back to Edward. "What on *earth* have you been doing?"

"It's not serious, Val," he told her soothingly. "We had a minor misadventure, but—"

"Misadventure? That's a *disaster*, not a misadventure!"

"It looks worse than it is. We hadn't time to clean him up before we left Hexham—I thought we'd have a chance before you saw him."

"Mark, would you kindly explain what happened?" asked Valerie crisply.

"I had a fight, Mom, that's all. Don't get steamed."

She pursed her lips. "Whom do you know well enough to fight with up here? Honestly, Mark, if your father could see you, he'd tan your hide."

"Well, he can't," said Mark rebelliously. "Why do people always want to punish you for getting hurt, anyway?"

"You've missed the point," Valerie told him as she steered him into the house by one arm. "The rest of you can set the table and get supper started. I don't care what we have."

"Well," said Edward. "That could have been much worse."

"In my opinion, you got off much too lightly," remarked Martin.

"Mark's been in fights before," Lou told them. "He got a real black eye last summer from Jackie Wilkes on the Freedom Trail."

"I won't ask why," said Edward.

"I wouldn't," agreed Luke.

He had a black eye this summer, too, as it turned out. The left one went a violent shade of purple and swelled shut before morning—the result of a lucky punch, he maintained. The rest of him was spread with an interesting assortment of cuts, scrapes, and bruises—nothing that proved very serious once the dirt had been washed away. He and his mother came down to supper just as Edward was dishing up savory mince and mashed potatoes. Mark looked extremely clean and unrepentant. Valerie looked quite stern for her.

Mark was ravenous. Between mouthfuls of supper he finally explained the circumstances surrounding the fight, his story corroborated by earnest nods and "Mmhmm"'s from Luke.

The two of them had spent an hour exploring the Hexham market. When they'd wrung it dry, they ranged further into the town to see what of interest they could find. In the course of their wandering they discovered a craft and hobby shop tucked down a narrow street, which sold all kinds of intriguing items from fishing tackle to magic tricks, model fighter planes to cricket bats and butterfly nets. The proprietor also ran a back-room sideline in taxidermy: he stuffed fish as sportsmen's trophies.

Here Luke couldn't keep from interrupting. "He offered to show me how it's done, but there wasn't time. He said whenever I came back I could see."

"Good Lord," said Valerie. "Stick to model airplanes, will you? At least they don't smell!"

"Neither does a fish," said Luke seriously, "not if it's done—"

"You don't want to stuff a fish, you want to *eat* it, for pity's sake," Martin broke in. "What good's a fish skin full of sawdust?"

"He doesn't use sawdust," replied Luke. He was talking a little too loud and fast and kept darting glances at his twin. "It's something else. And he puts wire inside so he can bend the fish to look as if they're alive. Then he mounts them and paints pictures around them."

"Pictures?" echoed his mother.

"Of rivers and waterfalls—things like that. Really neat."

"Only way to stuff a fish is with garlic, breadcrumbs, and mushrooms," said Edward. "Then bake it in a wine sauce with tarragon—"

"Look," said Mark severely, "I'm supposed to be telling you about this fight—we're not supposed to be discussing fish."

Luke look crestfallen.

"Do you want to hear what happened or don't you?"

"Yes," said Penelope and Valerie in the same breath.

"Well, then don't interrupt! That goes for you, too," he told his twin.

"Then why did you bring the subject up?" asked Martin.

Mark gave an exasperated sigh and launched himself again. "*After* we left the shop we just had time to go back to the market for ice cream cones. On the way we met this kid who asked us what time it was—he was waiting for his brother who was in one of the stores. He seemed all right—knew his way around Hexham, and we thought he'd be a good person to know, to fool around with this summer."

"I didn't mean to make him mad," said Luke. Mark glared at him and he lapsed into an unhappy silence.

"Anyhow, we asked him what his name was—"

"No harm in that, surely," said Edward.

"And he said Randall Robson," Mark went doggedly on. "Said he lived at some farm out this way, I can't remember the name."

Valerie gave him a sharp look but said nothing.

"Dodd Moss," said Luke in a small voice.

Valerie frowned.

"Yeah, that was it. Then he wanted to know who we were. So Luke told him and said we were spending the summer at Wintergap. And he looked at us kind of funny, as if he knew something about this place we didn't, but he wasn't going to tell us."

'So?" said Valerie. "I still don't see why you came to blows, Mark."

"Well, it wasn't right away," he said impatiently. "He walked back to the market with us, and Luke began talking about the Romans and Sulpitium and the excavation and asking him questions—you know Luke."

"After all, he does *live* here," said Luke. "I thought he could tell us—at *least* be interested—"

"He got stranger and stranger," Mark went on. "He wouldn't answer any of Luke's questions—*I* think it's because he didn't know the answers—and then Luke began asking him about the way he talked."

"What do you mean?" asked Edward.

Mark shrugged and Luke said, "I just asked him about some

36

of the words he used, like 'divvent' and 'whey'—he said them all the time—and he said 'ken.' I think that means 'know' but I'm not sure. From the way he talked it sounded almost as if he was speaking in a foreign language, but I could tell he wasn't 'cause I could understand a lot of it when I listened hard. I said I thought everyone spoke English over here. I wasn't making fun of him, honest I wasn't, Mom. But I guess he thought I was."

"Good Northumberland words," Edward said with relish. "Regional dialect—I heard it myself this afternoon. Fascinating."

"Well, this Randall didn't think so," said Mark. "He got very quiet and you couldn't tell anything from his face, and then all of a sudden he went for Luke. Just like that, for no real reason at all." Mark sounded outraged. "So what could I do?"

Valerie fixed him with a steely look and he wriggled slightly on his chair. "Went for him, Mark?"

Mark avoided her eyes. "Well, he was just about to. You should have heard what he called Luke," he said indignantly.

"What?" asked Martin.

"I'm not really sure," said Luke. "But it did sound awful."

"Oh, Luke," said Valerie.

Embarrassed, Luke looked down at his hands. "It should have been my fight," he muttered.

"He'd have murdered you," said Mark frankly and Luke gave a glum nod. Their partnership was based on a mutual recognition of what each did best, and the ability to make the most of their combined strengths. They were disarmingly honest about their own and each other's weaknesses, but let anyone outside so much as hint at criticism of either one and they immediately closed ranks.

"And that was all it was?" said Valerie. "Just Luke asking his usual somewhat tactless questions about the boy's way of speaking and his vocabulary?"

Mark nodded. "Anyhow, there we were having a private fight, just the two of us, when his brother broke it up. And I was winning, too."

Penelope didn't mention that from where she was standing it had looked far more likely that Mark and Randall Robson would fight each other to a standstill before either of them actually won. Mark had, after all, been picked off the top and maybe he would have stayed there if it hadn't been for Randall's brother.

Valerie regarded her son thoughtfully. "It sounds to me as if Randall Robson of Dodd Moss Farm would be a person to avoid in the future."

"Not if I see him again," said Mark with conviction. "We're going to finish what he started."

"No," his mother contradicted him, "you're not. I want you to steer clear of him, Mark, and I mean it. I have enough to worry about this summer without that."

"Do you want him to think we're a bunch of cowards?" he retorted indignantly.

"Frankly, my pet, I don't care what he thinks, but I think I can guess what set him off if he's a Robson."

"Do you know the Robsons?" asked Edward with interest.

"Only by reputation."

Martin said, "Someone at Sulpitium mentioned an Archie Robson."

The name made a sudden connection in Penelope's head. "We heard about the Robsons, too—at the Abbey this afternoon."

From her father's expression, she could see that he had made the connection before she had. "I picked up a little information about the Robsons myself," he said. "Of course, Robson is a Border surname—there are probably quite a few Robson families up here."

Valerie sighed. "The only Robsons in this area that people talk about are the Robsons of Dodd Moss Farm."

"They're the ones who used to live at the Sulpitium farm, over at your site, aren't they? Tenant farmers, I believe," said Edward.

"Yes. The Robsons had rented Sulpitium for generations from the landowners," Valerie replied.

"Then who lived here, in this house?" asked Lou. "That man in the Abbey said this wasn't a good place, but he wouldn't say why."

"I wouldn't worry about it, sweetie," said her mother, but

she herself looked worried. "One of the landowners, Charles Whitton, built this house as a country residence at the turn of the century. It had nothing to do with the farm. He was going to live here at Wintergap and let the Robsons continue to rent Sulpitium."

"Was?" said Martin.

She nodded. "Poor Charles never got the chance. He designed the house and supervised its construction, and just before it was finished he caught a chill, which developed into pneumonia and killed him."

"Poor sod," Martin commented.

"Is the house really built of Roman stones from Sulpitium?" Penelope wanted to know.

"Every bit of it. The stones were cut by soldiers in the second century, A.D."

"But why didn't someone stop him from tearing down the fort?" Luke demanded with the same indignation Penelope herself had felt earlier.

"Who? Charles Whitton owned the land Sulpitium stood on, so he owned the fort as well, and at that time he could do anything he liked with it. The idea of protecting Roman ruins up here hadn't occurred to anyone but a few eccentrics. Out of a wall built by the Romans seventy-three miles long, eight feet thick and twenty-five feet high, there are only about ten miles still visible and none still the original height. It's enough to give an archaeologist nightmares."

"So what happened to the house, if this guy never lived here?" asked Mark.

"Wintergap and all the land passed to Charles's brother, John. I don't know all the details of the Whitton family history, but according to Kenneth, several of them tried to settle here during the next sixty years, but no one ever stayed very long. They used it for summer vacations in between; then they gave it up entirely and left it empty." Valerie glanced at Lou. "I don't think they were country people—they came from Birmingham."

"But someone must have looked after it for them," said Penelope. "It seems so well kept up, with all the furniture and things."

"The Robsons used to keep an eye on it."

"Ah," said Edward. "Our Robsons. Now we're getting to it."

"What?" demanded Mark.

With some reluctance, Valerie continued. "Wintergap was eventually inherited by Charles's great-nephew, Anthony—"

"The books in the library!" exclaimed Penelope, remembering the inscription in one of them. "They must have been his."

"Apparently Anthony considered himself quite a knowledgable amateur archaeologist, and the idea of owning his own Roman fort appealed to him tremendously. He moved up here nine or ten years ago and evicted the tenant farmer so he could have Sulpitium to himself."

"A thoroughly unpleasant business, so I've heard," said Edward. "The farmer was George Robson, and he put up quite a fight. Only left when Whitton threatened him with legal proceedings. There was a lot of bad feeling on both sides, and even though George Robson doesn't seem to have been a very well-liked chap, local sentiment was on his side. Whitton was a foreigner, a member of the so-called gentry, while Robson belonged here and was an oppressed tenant farmer."

"Who made you an expert?" inquired Valerie.

"Oh, one hears talk," he replied airily.

"In other words you've been prying," accused Martin, disgusted.

"Asking a few judicious questions. If you don't ask questions you'll never learn anything, old son."

"But *your* kind of questions—"

"If he came from Birmingham, Anthony Whitton couldn't have been a foreigner, could he?" interrupted Luke to Penelope's relief.

"Indeed he could. I daresay you have to have been born up here in order to belong," Edward answered.

"And two generations before you," added Valerie. "There are places like this in the States, too. Very closed and self-protective."

"What happened to Anthony Whitton?" asked Penelope with an apprehensive frown. "Why did he give Wintergap to the University?"

"He didn't, his family did," said Valerie and hesitated.

Edward elaborated. "Robson and Whitton carried on an active feud until finally about three years ago there was an accident—no one I asked would be very specific about what happened, but the upshot was that Robson was found down a mineshaft just north of here with his neck broken, and Whitton had a complete nervous breakdown and had to be taken away by—"

"Sounds to me as if you managed to extract plenty of details," said Valerie dryly.

"I do what I can," he said modestly and Martin give a rude snort. "There are three Robsons left at Dodd Moss Farm: George's widow and two sons. Mrs. Robson hasn't left the farm since her husband died. They sound like a peculiar and thoroughly anti-social crew."

"I *still* don't understand," Mark persisted. "What's this got to do with us? Do you want me to feel sorry for this Randall?"

Valerie wrinkled her forehead and gave him a troubled look. "There are a lot of people who seem to think the feud didn't end when George Robson died and Anthony Whitton left Wintergap. They believe the Robsons won't rest until they've sent everyone else packing and have Sulpitium back again. Now I don't know"—she paused, then went on more firmly—"I don't *know* that there's any truth in that at all. But since the University took over and began to excavate the fort there has been a series of accidents on the site, and we cannot afford to take any chances."

"Where's Dodd Moss Farm?" Luke wanted to know.

"I was afraid someone would ask that. It's just north of the Wall, on the other side of the hill named Dodd Pike. You can almost see it from Sulpitium, and the sheep grazing on the far side of the Wall belong to the Robsons." Valerie made a wry face.

"Sheep?" Lou, predictably, perked up. "Can I see them?"

"All too close if you're not careful. Apparently a flock of them got loose on the site one night last week and trampled most of the tents flat before they could be rounded up."

Mark had quickly assimilated the information most pertinent to him. "If the farm's that near," he said, a calculating

41

glint in his eye, "we're bound to see Randall Robson again before long."

"Unfortunately you may," agreed his mother. "Which is why I have just spent my breath talking about all this, Mark Prine. The excavation has had more than its share of bad luck in two years, most of it not attributable to human causes. The first year they had weeks of rain—the whole site was a great glutinous morass. And then an epidemic of chicken pox put paid to the rest of the summer. The next season the director had a heart attack and no one could be found to replace him, so that ended the dig."

"Here, in this house?" asked Lou, wide-eyed.

"No, sweetie, at Sulpitium, and he's quite all right now. Anyhow, Kenneth and I are determined that this year the dig will be a success. If it isn't, like as not the University will lose interest and decide not to fund it again. It costs a great deal to run even a small operation, you know."

"But what's that got to do with us?" demanded Mark.

"Just this. I do not want any of my family to cause any kind of disturbance while we are here. *Any kind*, Mark, is that clear? If you do anything that in any way jeopardizes the excavation, you had better look for a foster home. Stay away from the Robsons. I mean it."

Reluctantly Mark nodded. "All right, Mom. *We* won't start anything, but I can't promise about him."

"I'm not asking you to. Just think carefully before you plunge into anything, okay?"

When dinner had been cleared away, with the attendant noise and confusion, Penelope managed to slip out of the house unnoticed. She escaped to the terrace with a copy of Rudyard Kipling's *Puck of Pook's Hill*, which she'd seen in the library. She hadn't read it in years, but it seemed to her that there was a chapter or two in it about the Wall, which would account for its presence on the shelves. She found a corner where she could sit on the warm flagstones away from everyone and be private. She needed a little quiet space.

The twilight thickened imperceptibly until she realized suddenly that it was too dark to see the words on the page comfortably, so she closed the book and just sat, unwilling to rejoin the others. As the night crept in, she felt herself grow invisible. A breeze breathed gently in and out of the fir trees in the little valley below the house; insects sang thinly from the long grass. A hazy half moon swung into the sky above the Wall, and over the fells came the cry of a bird: a lonely, wavering ribbon of sound.

Nothing was out of place, it all seemed calm, and yet there built within her a feeling of tension, restlessness; it was like the air before a summer storm. She was very much afraid it meant she would spend another night as disturbed as the previous one, hot and twisted among her sheets, unable to relax and sleep peacefully. The night before she had excused as the result of a long sticky day spent traveling, an unfamiliar bed, and the unsettling silence that lay thick around Wintergap. She was used to London where the night was never still; underneath the darkness lay the rumble and hum of traffic, footsteps on the pavement outside her window. And between her curtains the smoky-rose canopy of the London sky, like a great tent, stretched over the city. She had grown so accustomed to them—the noise and the luminescence—that she no longer noticed either one. Until they weren't there.

She looked, unseeing, at the dark tide spreading across the fells. Her uneasiness tonight was probably no more than the emotional effects of the day: the talk of Border Wars, subjugated Britons, modern feuds. Her father was right, this had not been a peaceful country; its history was scarred with one conflict after another. Underneath the bracken and coarse grass was it possible that the scars were still there?

She was being childishly fanciful. She shook herself and picked up her book, about to go inside, when a small figure emerged from the shadows and came silently to sit beside her. After the first heart-stopping second, she recognized Lou. Crossing her legs like a jackknife, Lou sat for a long time without speaking. Penelope reacted to this unexpected presence with a mixture of curiosity and resentment at being sought out. Finally she said, "I thought you'd have gone to bed by now. Shouldn't you have?"

"No," said Lou. "I don't want to go upstairs by myself. What are you doing?"

"Nothing."

43

"Oh." She accepted Penelope's flat answer without question. "It's very big, isn't it?"

"What?"

She gestured with a nod of her head. "Out there. There's nothing but dark. It's like the ocean."

"There are other people in it," said Penelope thinking how small Lou's voice sounded. "All the students at your mother's site, and people living in houses like this one."

"No," said Lou seriously. "I don't think there are other houses like this one. Not exactly."

"What do you mean?"

But she didn't answer, either because she didn't want to, or because she didn't know how, and the silence that wasn't silence at all washed in over them both.

CHAPTER IV

BEHIND WINTERGAP THERE WAS A PATH THAT RAN EAST AND west, along the line of Hadrian's Wall: a single furrow worn by constant use to bare hard-packed dirt. The twins discovered it first when they were exploring what they referred to as "the back yard." No doubt Anthony Whitton had used the path when visiting his personal Roman fort, but it looked as if many other people, before and since his time, had used it also.

"It goes on and on," Luke reported at supper one evening. "We followed it a long way and didn't come to the end. Where do you suppose it goes?"

It was Martin who knew the answer. He explained that it was a section of the Pennine Way, a long-distance footpath that ran from the Peaks in Derbyshire, north through Yorkshire, across the Wall and into Scotland to finish in the Cheviot Hills, two hundred and fifty miles from where it began.

"You mean people actually walk all that way?" said Mark.

"Mmm." Martin nodded.

"There are certain misguided people who do," amended Edward, helping himself to salad, "though personally I couldn't tell you why. If God had intended us to walk, He never would have allowed us to invent the internal combustion engine."

His son made a rude noise.

"Neat!" exclaimed Mark. "How far is it from here to Scotland?"

"Too far," said Valerie, guessing what was in his mind.

"But, Mom, we could walk a *little* of it," he wheedled. "It's right outside the back door—what a waste if we don't use it!"

"We'll see," his mother said noncommittally.

By talking fast and arguing hard, she had managed to dissuade her family from visiting Sulpitium for several days. She succeeded mainly because there were other things at Wintergap to occupy Edward and the twins. Edward happily spent the time investigating Anthony Whitton's library. Every time Penelope passed the doorway she saw him either contemplating the bookshelves or pouring over maps and volumes spread open across the desk. Something had clearly struck his fancy, and he was off in pursuit.

The twins established a headquarters for themselves in one of the outbuildings and made rather a lot of trips between it and the house carrying mysterious objects, whispering together, and scuffling on the stairs. Penelope suffered a momentary crisis of conscience when she saw them maneuvering a large table down from the attic—after all it wasn't their house and it wasn't their furniture; oughtn't she to say something? No, she told herself firmly, she'd only annoy the twins and involve herself in something she had no wish to be involved in.

For her own part, she read and spent the days considering her somewhat limited options. Before their arrival at Wintergap she had given very little thought to the kind of place in which they would be spending the summer. She had simply assumed it would be next-of-kin to the cottages and flats her father had rented during previous holidays: antique but discreetly modernized; out-of-the-way but not isolated; rooted in an attractive, congenial town well provided with shops, several good restaurants, a distinctive cathedral, a stately home or two, and an ample number of comfortable pubs. This last was an absolute requisite where her father was concerned; he gathered a great deal of the local color for his books in pubs.

She was not prepared for Wintergap, isolated in this wild sweep of empty country.

She couldn't help envying Martin a little. As soon as it became definite that they were all going to Northumberland for the holidays while Valerie worked at Sulpitium, he decided the best way to pass the time was to join the dig. Not that he was particularly interested in archaeology, but he enjoyed physical activity and being with people. He was fit and healthy and off to university the next year himself, so he expected to fit in easily with the students on the site.

But Penelope was only fourteen and doubted that she'd be much use digging holes, even if she wanted to do it. Excavating sounded hot and physical and not particularly attractive. She was interested in the idea of Sulpitium, but couldn't see herself getting involved in the work there.

There were always books to read: the ones she'd brought with her and the ample supply in the Wintergap library; but she couldn't spend the entire summer reading. She had her drawing materials of course—she never went anywhere without them. They were stowed neatly upstairs in the little back bedroom she had claimed for herself the first night. But she hadn't yet come across a subject on which she wanted to work.

Whatever Lou found to do all day, she did it quietly and by herself, drifting in and out of the house at odd moments. Every now and then Penelope would come to with a start and the feeling that she was being watched. Sometimes she looked up and there was no one there; sometimes she would find Lou regarding her. It really was quite disconcerting. Without saying anything, Lou would go away again, as if she had merely been checking Penelope's whereabouts. That, Penelope determined, was not going to go on all summer. Lou was not one of her responsibilities.

By the end of the week, there was no holding the twins back any longer. They were determined to see Sulpitium: Luke because he was avidly curious about the fort and the excavation, Mark because he was convinced that he was missing the action. Valerie gave in to their badgering only on condition that they allow her a couple of hours head start so she could organize the day's work before they interrupted.

In the end of course everybody went: Edward, Penelope, and Lou, as well as the twins. They divided a huge picnic lunch between the twins' rucksacks and set off about eleven in a string along the footpath.

There were no trees once they left the shade of the firs around Wintergap; the sun was high and hot overhead, the path hard as cement. Patches of bracken on the exposed hillside were turning prematurely brown, and the grass was bleached silver.

"Everything looks so dry," commented Penelope. "Is it supposed to?"

Her father shook his head. "The farmers are beginning to worry. I heard a lot of uneasy talk about drought the other day in Hexham."

There wasn't much left of the Wall between Wintergap and Sulpitium: only the foundation and a course or two of squared facing stones with the rubble core between them, like jam in a sandwich. Hadrian's grey snake, which Penelope had seen at Housesteads, was only a skeleton here, picked over by scavengers greedy for stone. But even in the bare bones of the Wall she felt a kind of power, as though it were still a line of demarcation, in spite of the fact that the country on both sides of it was united. People spoke the same language, recognized the same Queen, paid taxes to the same government, went to school, town, and church together—north and south of Hadrian's Wall.

It was actually easier to see the Roman fort from a distance than up close. Most of the site still lay hidden beneath a shroud of grass: an intricate pattern of humps, mounds, depressions, and ditches, further complicated by the presence of the modern farm buildings. By looking closely where Luke pointed, they could make out the shape of the fort, defined by a series of blurred but regular ditches and ramparts. Like the milecastle they had visited at Cawfields, it had been built so that Hadrian's Wall formed its north side. But Sulpitium was much larger. Luke explained knowledgeably that while a milecastle was meant to house only thirty-two soldiers, a major Wall fort held anywhere from three thousand to fifteen thousand fighting men.

"One of the neat things," he went on, encouraged by their

attention, "is that all the Roman forts had the same basic layout. Once you've learned your way around one you can figure out all the others—where the barracks were, and the headquarters, and the supply houses."

"So that's how they know where to dig," said Penelope with interest. "It doesn't look as if there's any system to it from here."

"Oh but there is. They plan it out very carefully before they start. Mom says right now they're working on the west gate and the bathhouse. There, and over there."

Indeed there did seem to be two centers of activity on the site: one was a trench some four or five feet deep along the western wall of the fort; the other was an innocent-looking patch of grass well outside the ramparts, to the southeast, where a small group of people was busy with surveying equipment: stakes and flags, tape-measures, and a theodolite on a tripod.

"But why isn't the bathhouse inside the fort?" asked Edward.

"They never were," said Luke. "Or almost never. Brian always says that as soon as you say 'never' you find the exception. They were built outside because of the noise. The bathhouses were kind of like clubs."

"It would have been like living next to a pub, you mean," said Edward. "That would have certain advantages, of course—" He looked keenly at his stepson. "You've been mugging up, my boy."

"What d'you mean?" asked Luke apprehensively.

"He just means you know a lot about Roman excavations," Penelope translated.

Luke looked relieved. "I like to know how things work, that's all," he said modestly.

"We'll never get there at this rate," Mark broke in. "Let's go!"

Luke hesitated half a minute, then with an apologetic shrug cantered off in the wake of his twin. Edward called after them, "Hi, you two, remember you've got my lunch in those packs!"

Most of the archaeology students were at work in or around the trench, toiling with picks and shovels, carting away barrows full of dry, hard-baked dirt, sifting buckets of it through wood-framed screens. They were digging out a long section of buried stone wall, and hot, tiresome work it looked, too.

"Mad dogs, Englishmen, and Americans," remarked Edward, quietly enough, Penelope hoped, so that only she heard him.

Most of the men were shirtless, their bare backs ranging in color from white to pink to red to brown, glistening with sweat in the fierce sunlight. The girls wore halters or shirts tied up to expose their pale, vulnerable middles. It was impossible to tell one person from another aside from that; the heat and dirt and uniformly casual style of dress combined to obscure any distinguishing characteristics. Cutoff jeans, shorts, dirty sneakers or boots and thick socks; dusty, untidy hair, grubby crew hats. Penelope felt conspicuous in her old school skirt, white blouse, and sandals. She could not be mistaken for anything but a visitor. She knew her father didn't mind looking different, but then he had an identity he was sure of and could live with comfortably. She was only a fourteen-year-old schoolgirl, and there was no distinction in that: there were thousands very much like her.

"I hope they heard me about lunch," grumbled Edward. "That was damn good deviled ham I made."

"You ought to have carried it yourself," Penelope pointed out. "Then you'd always have known where it was."

"Why do you think I married a woman with strong healthy sons?" he retorted. "Speaking of Valerie, where do you suppose she is in this confusion?"

"She's over there," said Lou promptly, pointing toward the group of surveyors. "See?" Valerie was standing in the middle of them, her arms spread wide, holding a large map.

"Let's go see what she's up to, shall we?" Edward strolled off, taking Lou with him. Penelope started to follow, then changed her mind. She decided to look for Martin instead and see if she could make some sense out of what looked like a very haphazard operation. It seemed to her that when you were dealing with Roman remains you had to take a great deal on faith and exercise an exhausting amount of imagination in order to fill in the gaping holes between what had been and

49

what was left of it. There was such a long distance in time and understanding from this grassy slope to a living fort, a settlement thronged with Roman infantrymen in short tunics and capes going about the serious military business of the Empire's northernmost frontier. All the cluttery, messy details of everyday life. Perhaps if you were an archaeologist, you grew so familar with the past that you could conjure it up whenever you required it.

She picked her way carefully across the turf, keeping an eye out for hazards in the grass: invisible stakes, pick handles, lumps of stone. She was so absorbed in her struggle to put the incomplete fragments together that she walked right past Martin without seeing him. She nearly died of fright when a hand unexpectedly reached out and grabbed her by the ankle.

"What did you want to do that for?" she demanded. "I might have fallen in on top of you, you twit!"

"Just trying to attract your attention," he said with a grin. He stood chest-deep in the trench, holding a shovel.

"There *are* other ways of doing it, you know."

"I said hullo to you twice and you ignored me, so I took direct action."

Her pulse returned to normal and she looked closely at him. No wonder she hadn't been able to spot him among the others: his camouflage was perfect. In less than a week he had become part of the excavation; with his shirt off, his toffee-colored hair curling damply all over his head like an old rook's nest, and his face streaked with little gulleys of dirt, he looked like all the other students. He had even, she noticed, sacrificed a pair of jeans by hacking the legs off above the knee. "Your shoulders are very red—aren't they getting sore?"

"They'll tan." He hunched them experimentally and his eyes crinkled a little, but he seemed unconcerned. That was characteristic of Martin: when he chose to attack something he went at it headfirst and accepted the consequences later, whatever they might be. At least he never tried to shift the responsibility to anyone else.

She sat down on the crisp, dry grass at the edge of the trench and crossed her legs. "What are you supposed to be digging up?"

"The west gate of the fort. And it's bloody hard work, I

can tell you. The ground is like cement! You have to chip it. If it weren't for that we could finish this bit much faster because it's all been done before so we needn't sift every spadeful."

"You don't mean someone dug all this up, then filled it in again? What a waste of time!"

"Amen," he agreed cheerfully. "But when this was being used as a farmyard they didn't want dirty great pits all over the place. The Robsons weren't concerned about Roman ruins. Farmers all along the Wall did the same thing—don't look so horrified. Archaeologists came and poked around, then the farmers backfilled the holes and planted kitchen gardens or grazed sheep." He hoisted himself up to sit beside Penelope with his legs dangling over the side. "There has always been a running battle up here between the locals and the archaeologists."

"How do you know what you're supposed to be doing?" she asked after a bit.

"Easy! I follow orders. Someone handed me this shovel when I came and said, 'Dig over there,' so I am. I'm a quick learner." He stretched lazily.

"And this is what you intend to do all summer?"

"Not much choice, is there? What are you going to do?"
She shook her head. "I don't know."

"Yes, well," said Martin significantly. "Actually, it's not as bad as it looks. It's healthy, it's out-of-doors, and there's good company. We might even find something while we're at it, who knows."

"Ho, Ibbetson! Knocking off, I see. Who's this then?" They were joined by a round, perspiring young man with a red beard. He wore a bandana on his head, knotted at each corner to make a kind of cap. "I say, you'll need a hat in this sun."

"My sister Pennie," said Martin. "And this is Jonathan Shaftoe. He's a second-year student at the University, doing fieldwork."

"Work in a field, more like," Jonathan corrected him. He pulled a second bandana out of the back pocket of his baggy shorts and moped his brow. "Strewth, it's hot! Ruinous to a man of my delicate constitution."

51

"I thought it always rained in Northumberland," said Penelope.

"And so it generally does. I've lived in these parts all my life and this is the driest summer I've ever clapped eyes on. Six months ago they were losing cattle in snowdrifts, now they talk of losing them because of the drought. I suppose it's all those chaps mucking about with the ozone layer, don't you think, Ibbetson? Shove up a bit, there's a good chap."

"You've got the whole rest of the ditch to sit on," complained Martin.

"I know, but I want your bit." With a grunt, Jonathan lowered himself to their level and smiled engagingly at Penelope. "Seems a hard way to earn a university degree, doesn't it? My dad says I'm daft. I'd do better to run the newsagent's shop with him, and there're days I have to agree."

"Depends on what you want at the end," said Penelope seriously.

"Just what I tell him," agreed Jonathan with approval.

"Good Lord, what's that?" exclaimed Martin.

Jonathan and Penelope looked up to see a huge silver tourist coach lumbering up the rutted track toward the site. It had blank, wraparound windows of the kind you can only see through from the inside. It looked like a great armor-plated beetle, awkward and alien as it crept up the hillside.

"How the devil do you suppose he'll turn that thing?" asked Martin.

"With a great deal of difficulty, old lad," Jonathan predicted.

People around them stopped work to observe the coach's progress. They gathered in little knots.

"I thought this was supposed to be a closed site," said Martin. "General public not admitted while work in progress, et cetera, et cetera."

"In theory yes, but short of barricading the track off the main road, how would you keep them out?" replied Jonathan.

"What about a sign—'No Trespassing'—for instance? Anyone thought of that?"

"Several times so far this summer. They keep disappearing —the signs, not the people. And of course we get hikers off the Pennine Way all the time. Not much you can do about them."

"Do you mean that someone takes the signs down?" asked Penelope.

Jonathan nodded. "Hullo, somebody's roused Sir Kenneth."

A tall, thin figure in a khaki bush jacket had come out of the farmhouse. He paused and ran a hand through his great shock of grey hair. His head was thrust forward on his neck, his shoulders rounded as if from years of trying to disguise his extreme height. Penelope straightened her own instinctively at the sight of him; his posture was terrible.

The coach halted in the worn area that served as a parking lot; it dwarfed the other vehicles. It coughed and shuddered convulsively as if getting there had been an appalling experience, then the door hissed open. A compact woman with a furled umbrella disembarked immediately, followed by a rush of foreign-looking people. They were encumbered with tourist paraphernalia and small children, and as soon as they hit the ground they scattered across the field. Their leader stood immobile, like a rock in a flood, scanning the people on the site, obviously searching for the person in authority. While all this was going on, Sir Kenneth loitered by the farmhouse, and it was Valerie who came forward to declare herself. From all parts of Sulpitium the archaeology students shifted closer, anxious not to miss anything. Penelope, Martin, and Jonathan got up and shifted with the rest.

"Well," declared the woman from the bus on a note of triumph. "We have come. So. You tell us what are to see, please? We have little time here. Where are your ruins?"

"Underground, most of them," replied Valerie. "There's practically nothing to see yet, which is why Sulpitium isn't open to the public."

It was clear that the woman didn't understand English well, and Valerie's American accent puzzled her still further. She shook her head emphatically. "No, no, no. Says the guidebook Roman fort with impressive ruins, not to be missed, so we have come all this way to see. But"—she looked round the site—"I do *not* see."

"That's because we haven't dug them up yet." Valerie was making a great effort to be pleasant, but the color was rising in her face. "I think you must be looking for one of the other

Wall forts. I'm sorry, but we can't have your group climbing all over this site."

The umbrella woman was not making the same effort. Her face had settled into a stubborn, unfriendly expression. "We want," she said slowly and firmly, "postal cards, we want maps, we want washrooms and place to pick-nick. You sell Coke, yes?"

"No." Valerie was equally firm. In the voice she used with the twins when they were in iminent danger of going too far, she continued, "There's absolutely nothing here for you. I don't know how you found us, the only signs at the road say clearly 'No Trespassing'."

"Aha!" cried her opponent. "Yes, yes! You deliberately mistake the tourist, but I have experience in your country and I *ask*. Local boy say this is the place." She thumped her umbrella vigorously on the turf.

While this unsatisfactory but fascinating dialogue was taking place, Sir Kenneth had ambled leisurely down to the two women, his face carefully bland. "Problem?" he inquired. Valerie gave him a hard look, and the woman launched into a repetition of her demands.

"Mmmhmph," he interrupted her. "Sounds to me as if you've missed your turning, madam. You want to instruct your driver to take you back to the main road and turn left. You want Housesteads—it's clearly marked. You should have no trouble finding it."

She glared from Sir Kenneth to Valerie and back, as if she suspected them of conspiring between them to conceal the fort from her.

"Impass," murmured Jonathan. "She's a right battleax, that one."

At last, ungraciously accepting defeat, she said, "Ahhh, you Brrritish!" picked a black plastic whistle off the broad shelf of her bosom and blew three mighty blasts. Her group, now thoroughly spread across the site, searching in vain for an ice-cream or souvenir stall, a comfort station, a picnic area, or even something worth photographing, immediately stiffened to attention. Like well-trained dogs they turned and converged on their leader, who held her furled umbrella aloft like a weapon and motioned them back into the coach. The woman gave Valerie a last resentful glare, pronounced a short, emphatic, and unintelligible sentence, which caused the members of her tour still within earshot to snigger nervously, then climbed on board herself. With agonized whines of protest, the coach reversed back down the farm track.

Everyone stood spellbound, watching, until it was out of sight.

"Well," said Sir Kenneth. "Another international incident. Which country did we offend that time, anyone know?"

"Do you know what that woman said to me?" Valerie had gotten quite pink and her eyes glinted dangerously.

"No," admitted Sir Kenneth.

"Just as well," she replied tartly and took several deep breaths. "You could have been more help, and it was Turkey, for your information."

"It was good experience for you," he said. "That's been happening with startling frequency this summer and I thought you might as well have a turn."

"Thanks. I think it's time for lunch—I need some quick energy."

"Ah," said Jonathan gratefully. "I was hoping someone would think of that—I'm beginning to feel quite hollow." He laid a hand tenderly on his ample stomach.

Like a photograph suddenly come to life, people across the site began to move again. Penelope followed Martin and Jonathan in the direction of the farmhouse; others were heading for the parallelogram of shade it cast on the grass and flinging themselves down.

"—mean you've had other coaches arrive before this?" Edward was asking Sir Kenneth in the conversational tone that made Martin instantly suspicious. Penelope saw him glance sharply at his father, then away.

"God, yes," said Sir Kenneth wearily. "Four last week— that's our record. Two from London, one full of Swedes, and the fourth packed with retired Americans. People always take it so personally when we ask them to shove off." He sank onto the grass like a folding chair. "Of course everything comes to a stop while we sort it out—it's a frightful inconvenience. Jonathan, would you fetch my sandwich as well, there's a good chap."

55

"Seems like an unusual number of accidentals," Edward observed.

"Accidentals, my foot," snorted Valerie. "Excuse me, Kenneth!"

"Quite all right," said Sir Kenneth Foote with amusement.

"But didn't you hear that woman say they'd been directed here by a local boy? That sounds highly suspicious to me."

"Perhaps she misunderstood," suggested Martin. "She seemed capable of it."

"But why would anyone bother to send tour coaches up here?" asked Penelope. "What good does it do anyone?"

"Perhaps that's the point," said Edward. "It's a disruption. It hampers your work."

"But—" Martin protested.

"There are people who might want to do that," Valerie said thoughtfully. "Local people."

"There might be." Sir Kenneth was noncommittal.

Edward gave him a speculative look, but at that moment the twins arrived and pitched down to join them. "What have you done with my lunch, you wretched and untrustworthy boys?" he demanded, seeing Mark and Luke rucksack-less.

"You didn't think we were going to carry them everywhere, did you?" said Mark. "We stashed them. No sweat." He retrieved both packs from underneath a bramble bush that grew against the house.

"Who was in the bus?" asked Luke.

"Enemies," replied Lou with a certain amount of relish.

Valerie looked long-suffering. "Not enemies, they were ordinary Turkish tourists."

"A fine distinction in my experience," remarked Sir Kenneth. "There you are, Jonathan. Yes, that's right." Jonathan handed him a brown paper bag with a large foot drawn on it in red felt pen. "That way no one can possibly take it by mistake," he explained, catching Penelope's eye. She grinned at him. "Trouble with packing one's own lunch," he went on, beginning to rummage inside, "is that it's never a surprise."

"Perhaps you could do it blindfold," she suggested gravely.

"Hadn't occurred to me," he replied, equally grave, "Valerie, this must be your entire family."

Valerie nodded and introduced them all. The group in the

shade continued to grow until there was no one left on the site; everyone gathered to sprawl on the grass and share lunch. Valerie and Sir Kenneth, as codirectors of the dig, were the focus of a lopsided, informal circle. Conversation followed a variety of topics, though most concerned archaeology on the Wall and at Sulpitium in particular. Penelope sat in the midst of it and listened to fragments float past.

"How long d'you reckon it'll take us to dig out the bath-house?" one of the girls asked Valerie.

Valerie swallowed a mouthful of ham sandwich. "Can't say for sure. It depends on what kind of stuff we find as we go. No one's dug down to the Roman floor before so we'll have to sift every square foot—"

"It isn't as if I were going to *Africa*, I told him. It's only Northumberland, but the way he went on you'd have thought it was the dark side of the moon. I said if we were to have any kind of a relationship . . ." said another girl to her friend who nodded earnestly.

"—and he found a leather pouch with seven silver denarii and twenty-two sestertii in it just outside the temple. I keep wondering why shouldn't I find something like that?"

"But the wind was so strong on the top we couldn't stand upright. We had to take the photos lying flat on our stomachs which shot the perspective—"

"Just piles of rock and a few odd bones—"

Jonathan was deep in a technical discussion of carbon dating, to which Martin and Luke were listening with rapt attention. Penelope, who had no desire to try to follow its complexities, observed the two of them. Their faces were just similar enough so that a stranger might take them for natural brothers—until they opened their mouths, of course. She found it faintly disturbing and looked away.

Her father had zeroed in on Sir Kenneth, which didn't surprise her. He leaned back on his elbows, relaxed and casual, and asked question after question about Sulpitium and the excavation, and Sir Kenneth, equally relaxed and casual, answered them. He knew a tremendous amount, but if, as Valerie had told them, he was one of the foremost authorities on Roman Britain, he did not find it necessary to impress everyone with his importance, as so many people her father knew

57

seemed to. There was a well-used sense of humor just beneath his craggy surface, and shrewd kindness in his eyes. Penelope decided without reservation that she liked him.

"It was a marvelous stroke of luck for the University, being given an undeveloped Roman site by the Whitton family," he was saying. "It meant that we could use it as a kind of laboratory—give our students invaluable field experience in excavation from the ground down, so to speak. We have faculty to supervise and visiting experts we can call in to help."

"But I understand from Valerie that you've had some bad luck up here," said Edward. "How has it affected your operation?"

Sir Kenneth nodded soberly. "Excavation began in a burst of glory the first year and they had a terrible summer—poured with rain every day. All the trenches full of water, mud everywhere, and to finish it off, twenty-two of thirty-one students down with chicken pox."

"I had chicken pox when I was four," said Lou.

"We *all* had chicken pox when you were four, sweetie," Valerie said.

"That's what qualified you for this job, not your brilliant mind," Sir Kenneth told her. "Your immunity."

"To get back to Sulpitium," Edward prodded gently. "I'm really very interested."

Penelope hoped Martin wasn't listening; he still seemed to be involved in half-lifes and isotopes.

"Yes, well last year was another disaster. Peter Raymond had a serious heart attack in the third week and there was no one to take his place here, so that put paid to work almost before it began. In fact, it very nearly closed the site permanently."

"But they were all acts of God," said Valerie. "No one could be blamed for any of them."

"You'd be surprised how superstitious many educated people are," Sir Kenneth replied. "Sulpitium has a bad name in a lot of circles. It took a great deal of persuasion to convince the Board to give us even a small grant to operate with this summer. They've lost interest—nothing has come out of this site in two years. If *we* aren't a success I doubt very much that anyone will be back next year. And we're down to twenty-one students and two professionals. That's the main reason we've divided into two teams and Valerie's is working on the bath house. The west gate has to be excavated, but we stand more of a chance of finding something over there. We've *got* to have something to show for our efforts—it's vital."

There was a general silence when he finished; everyone looked serious. They had all been listening.

"Well," said Valerie, gathering up sandwich wrappers, "I'd say we ought to get back to work and discover something! Come on, you lazy slugs."

"Don't worry, Mom," said Mark confidently, "Luke and I'll find you something neat. Right, Luke?"

His twin nodded.

Sir Kenneth raised an eyebrow quizzically. "Really?"

"It's no idle boast," Valerie informed him. "Four years ago in Greece they were responsible for the prize find—a lovely silver mug. If their father hadn't been site director, I think we'd have been asked to leave. Professional archaeologists do not like being outdone by a pair of eight-year-olds."

"Brian didn't like it either," said Luke. "He was furious with us, wasn't he? You had a fight about it."

Valerie compressed her lips in a flat line.

"Frankly," Sir Kenneth said, "I will be the first to publicly congratulate anyone who finds anything good at Sulpitium. I don't care who it is."

"Let's get at it then," said Jonathan, heaving himself to his feet. People got up and stretched and began straggling back into the sunshine. Mark and Luke stowed the rucksacks again and loped away in the direction of the Wall.

"Would you mind," Edward asked, "if I stick around this afternoon? I promise not to get in the way."

"Not at all," replied Sir Kenneth affably. "I'll show you what we're doing with the gate and you can look at the plan we've drawn up if you like."

"Smashing," said Edward.

"Oh hell," Valerie said, shading her eyes with her hand. "Why aren't they waiting for me? They're putting those stakes in on the wrong side! Hang on!" She thrust a handful of trash at Penelope and raced off across the field toward her team of surveyors.

CHAPTER V

PENELOPE CRUSHED THE TRASH INTO A TIGHT BALL AND SAT staring at it.

"He was up to his usual tricks, wasn't he?"

She raised her head, startled, and found Martin frowning above her. "What tricks?" she asked cautiously.

"Oh, Pennie, don't be dense! You know perfectly well what I mean." Abruptly he sat down. "All during lunch he was going after Sir Kenneth—I could hear him, question after question. All sounding innocent and harmless, except he's packing the answers away in that mental filing cabinet of his. Everyone else thinks it's polite conversation, but we both know better than that. It's *material*, and he'll twist it into whatever shape suits him when he decides to use it. He's got absolutely no scruples!"

"I think," said Penelope, "that Sir Kenneth can look out for himself."

"How can he if he doesn't realize what Dad's doing?"

"What do you think he *is* doing?" she countered. "You know he expects the first proofs for his book from Uncle Richard any day now. He's got all his revising to do. And he hasn't said a word about beginning anything new while we're here."

"He never does say, does he? He just collects his information and goes ahead with it and by the time anyone finds out, it's to late. He *exploits* people, Pennie—and for what? His stuff isn't even great literature. He writes thrillers, the kind of thing you buy in a railway kiosk and then leave behind on the train." Martin drew up his knees and wrapped his arms glumly around them. "Remember what he did to that holiday camp in Devon? And what about Mrs. Holden?"

Penelope shuddered. "But that holiday camp really was a dreadful place," she said, remembering all too vividly the three weeks they had spent there: the used, musty smell; the seedy little caravans, and the desperate, garish gaiety. Her father had murdered several of his characters there, quite plausibly, and written a devastatingly accurate description of it. "And Mrs. Holden was thrilled when he put her in *Ashes, Ashes*, you know she was. She thought she was famous." Mrs. Holden was the Ibbetsons' last housekeeper but one; she had not stayed long with the family because her inseparable companion was a monstrous ginger tom cat, ironically called Fluffy. Edward was violently allergic to most dogs and all cats, he could not tolerate them in the same house. Both Mrs. Holden and Fluffy had, however, figured prominently in the book. "She gave all her relatives copies of it for Christmas. I think it's the only book she ever read."

"Oh, Pennie, you've missed the point!" Martin was disgusted with her. "He couldn't stand Mrs. Holden, and he *loathed* that cat—it gave him the worst attacks he ever had. He was making fun of them, using them without their knowing."

"But if they didn't know, where's the harm?"

"It's bloody well immoral!" her brother exploded. "And don't tell me you don't think so, too. But this time it's even worse. He agreed to take the summer off, remember—to keep house so Valerie could get on with her work. You know that was the arrangement. Not only is he going back on it, he's moving in on Valerie's territory as well. He's taking advantage of his own wife. Turning something serious and scholarly into cheap entertainment for the sake of a few quid."

Penelope sighed gustily. "I do hate it when you go all righteous, Martin. He's always managed to support us on those few quid, as you call it. He's successful at something he enjoys. And honestly, can you see Dad spending all summer being domestic? He'd go spare—and drive the rest of us mad as well. He can't stop being interested in things, that's the way he is. Besides, you're only doing the same thing yourself."

"And what does that mean?" demanded Martin, staring at her.

"Well, you're no archaeologist, but the first thing you did when you arrived was get involved with the excavation."

"That's quite different."

"How?"

"I volunteered to *work* for the dig, I'm not using it."

Instead of retreating in miserable silence to avoid further argument with her brother, Penelope found she was getting quite annoyed with him. He could be every bit as single-mindedly stubborn as their father when he chose, and equally unreasonable. "Of course you are," she retorted. "You're using it for something to do. You're using it to make friends. You care less about the excavation than Dad does! He's genuinely interested in it—you're only interested in the things *around* it."

For a moment Martin looked at her with astonishment, unused to hearing her answer him back. Then he shook his head disparagingly and said in an older-brother voice, "You're still too young to understand, I suppose." He picked himself up off the grass and walked away from her, back toward his trench and the new niche he was digging himself among the university students. If he'd glanced over his shoulder he would have seen her glaring furiously after him.

But he didn't afford her the satisfaction, and the glare dwindled to perplexed little lines between her eyebrows. She leaned back against the rough stones of the farmhouse and gazed down the long southward slope of the hill to where the countryside spread out in a rumpled green pattern of hills and valleys, splattered with the darker green of field rows and copses. The distance was vague with haze, the horizon white, wrung colorless as the sun remorselessly syphoned up every drop of moisture. Even the breeze was fretful with heat.

Gradually the angry and confused storm Martin's parting shot had triggered in her head calmed. There was a genuine and steadily growing muddle there, no question, but she was able to recognize his jibe for what it was: a thing to say because he couldn't think of a real answer for her. She wasn't too young to understand, not at all, and daily she was getting older. Old enough to see what he was trying to do and to resent it. He wanted her to come out and declare herself, to side with him against their father on this. Even if she agreed with some of the things Martin said—and she had to admit she did—she resented his pushing her to make a choice between them. She didn't want to side with Martin against her father any more than she wanted to side with her father against Martin. Why should she? They *both* did things that annoyed and upset her. She supposed, though she didn't want to dwell on it, they must feel the same about her. But they were all three of them members of the same family, and in spite of their individual faults, there was a bond of love holding them together as strong and abiding as the mortar in the Roman Wall. If Martin wanted to fight with their father she realized sadly she could not stop him, but she would not allow him to suck her into a fight that was not hers. She wondered suddenly how the twins and Lou must have felt, caught between Valerie and Brian.

A small noise pulled her out of the jungle of her thoughts; the sort of noise a person makes when he or she has been ignored long enough and wishes to let you know that you aren't alone. Penelope hit consciousness with a bump and blinked to find Lou sitting compactly not more than six feet from her. Penelope noticed that her fringe needed trimming; it fell straight and dark over her eyebrows, shadowing her narrow face, making her expression impenetrable.

"What are you going to do next?" asked Lou, now that she had Penelope's attention.

"I don't know." Penelope was deliberately noncommittal, but Lou waited. "I might go back to Wintergap," she amplified finally, expecting that Lou would want to stay with the rest of her family.

But Lou was not bound to the expected. "Can I come?"

"Why?" asked Penelope with a twinge of dismay. "There won't be anyone else there, and I have things of my own to do."

"What?"

"I have some letters to write and I might do some drawing." They were solitary activities, both of them.

Lou shook back her hair, exposing a triangle of forehead and changing the whole appearance of her face. It was open and hopeful. "I wouldn't bother you."

Penelope gave in. "If you're coming, you'd better tell your mother, then."

"Will you wait for me?"

She nodded, resigned, and watched Lou race off through the fierce white sunlight.

Wintergap stood waiting for them, lurking behind its trees, its expression blank. Penelope was struck by the uneasy feeling that by coming back early, she and Lou had interrupted something: almost as if they were "It" in a game of statues and had spun around quickly and only just missed catching the house move.

She had no idea what could have put that into her head and was ashamed of her childishness. A house was an inanimate object, and Wintergap was a house, therefore an inanimate object. Deliberately dismissing the whole thing, she went into the house and up to her bedroom where she collected her current sketchbook and pencils, some sheets of letter paper and envelopes. Then she took them outside and settled herself on the terrace. It was much too fine a day to stay indoors, even though it was cooler out of the sun.

Lou observed this silently, then mindful of her promise, wandered away by herself down into the steep little valley beside the house. Even though she couldn't see her, Penelope could still hear her rustling in the dry undergrowth, dislodging pebbles, and had to confess she was glad not to be completely alone.

She turned her attention firmly to her sketchbook. It was half-filled with the precise, painstaking drawings she had been working on last in London, drawings of the ornamental ironwork displayed along one corridor of the Victoria and Albert Museum: door hinges, keys and locks, balconies and fire irons. How wide the world had opened to her on the day two and a half years ago that she had first discovered the V and A! Within its dark Victorian walls were what seemed to her enchanted eyes a limitless number of objects to draw: costumes, porcelain, silver, pottery, jewelry. She had spent hours there since.

She didn't think of herself as an artist. She copied, she didn't create. But over a period of years she'd grown quite skilful and she had discovered a great satisfaction in the work. When she attempted to transfer something she was looking at to paper she saw and understood so much more about it. And the world was so full of objects she could draw, she felt secure in the knowledge that she never need run out of subjects. It was the perfect pastime; it required no awkward materials, no help, no company. Wherever she went she carried it unobtrusively with her.

Now she sat with her legs curled under her, the pad propped on a knee, and considered a blank sheet of paper. The range of subjects open to her at Wintergap was limited; she had an idea in the back of her mind, but she wasn't ready to commit herself to it just yet. In the meantime . . .

Without consciously deciding what to draw, she began to make lines with her pencil. Usually she sketched directly from her object, her eyes constantly shifting between it and the paper, gauging, probing for tiny details. But sometimes she drew from her memory of an object, then went back to it later to see how well she'd observed it and if she'd managed to find those features that made it unique.

She was doing that now—copying from memory. With a sense of detachment she watched the lines connect, saw a shape emerge among them. Later she supposed she must have known all along what she was drawing or she couldn't have done it. But as she worked her mind refused to give it an identity, leaving it to her hand to reveal the thing.

Two long parallel lines, joined top and bottom by short cross strokes: a tall, upright rectangle. A third of the way up it a panel with tiny hatches to indicate an inscription she could not recall. Then above the panel, a pattern of curving lines which gradually became a horse and rider; they were deliberately out of proportion: the horse small, less important than the man on its back.

By this time she had put a name to it: the Roman memorial stone at the foot of the nightstair in Hexham Abbey. Not surprising that she should have fished that out of her subconscious: it had impressed her and she remembered looking at it with considerable attention.

The horse's bridle wouldn't go right, and to her annoyance she couldn't picture the way the soldier held his standard. She fussed over these details until she'd done as well as she could with them, then went on to put in the third figure, the "naked Briton" crouched underneath. His body made a slightly dis-

65

torted S shape: legs, torso, and arms, then the upthrust knife, and the head with its wild halo of hair. He was crudely formed, but wound tight as a spring ready for release. She could feel the tension in him as she drew. Last, she filled in his features: almond-shaped eyes, slightly crooked nose, determined mouth. And it was done. She laid down her pencil and looked appraisingly at the sketch. As a piece of work it wasn't that bad. In spite of the mistakes, she knew that no one who had seen the original could fail to recognize her drawing; it communicated the same sensations, like a draft of clammy air down the back of the neck. She didn't like it now any more than she had on Tuesday, and the longer she looked, the less happy she felt about it.

There was a sudden explosion of sound just below the terrace. She jumped and dropped her pencil. There was a series of reports like muffled gunshots, and a frantic cry of alarm: "*Kok-kok-kok!*," then Lou's little gasping yelp. It had just occurred to Penelope that the best thing would be to destroy the sketch she'd done, when the commotion distracted her.

"Lou!" she called. "Louisa? What happened? Where are you?"

Crashing, scrambling noises, and a minute later Lou pushed her way out of the overgrown ravine, slightly breathless. "They were big and black, like chickens," she said. "I almost stepped on one."

"What were? One what?"

"Birds. There were four of them. Do you know what they were?"

Penelope shook her head.

"Luke probably will. I'd just got down to the brook. There's something that looks like a cave." She turned to go back down.

"Do you want some lemonade?" Now that the silence was broken, Penelope was reluctant to let it harden around her again.

"All right," said Lou. "Are you finished drawing?"

"Yes, for now."

"Can I see what you were doing?" The question was tentative, but Penelope was too preoccupied to pay attention. She

66

simply said "No," then pretended not to notice the way Lou's face closed at the rebuff. Well, why should she have to share her private things? Especially this sketch. But the moment for tearing it up was lost; she had closed it into the pad.

There really were letters she had intended to write: one to Alison in London, and another to Grannie Lawrence in the St. Albans' nursing home. But neither one was urgent. Instead, after lemonade and biscuits in the kitchen, Penelope went to scout the library shelves again and after a few minutes' search, found what she wanted: a small collection of garden and wild-flower books. She selected a couple and returned to the terrace.

During the years they had lived with Grannie Lawrence in St. Albans, Penelope had spent hours and hours helping in the garden behind the Georgian house. Sparrows chipped from the eaves and the sun lay like butterscotch over the long slow afternoons, and the little garden was full of bees and color and the warm smells of earth, grass clippings and herbs. That was before Grannie Lawrence had fallen and broken her hip, then begun to grow vague. Sometimes, in the hospital, she had not recognized her own family; at other times she was lost in the company of people who were invisible to everyone else.

Grannie Lawrence's practical-minded children had over-ridden Edward's gentle protests and installed their mother in a nursing home. That was when the Ibbetsons moved to London. The Georgian house and its garden belonged to someone else now, and Penelope found there wasn't any private space in London where she could plant flowers. The little square in front of the Ibbetsons' house belonged to everyone who lived around it, and there was a Pakistani gardener to look after the grass and rake leaves. It was a solemn square, dark with hollies and rhododendron, myrtle and ivy, here and there a small patch of autumn chrysanthemums, and tulips in the spring; nothing riotous or likely to get out of hand. So everything Penelope had learned about gardens from Grannie Lawrence she had stored in a back corner of her mind until she had the opportunity to use it again.

She didn't see why she couldn't bring out at least some of it now at Wintergap. She began by exploring the wildly over-grown garden around the terrace. Someone, presumably Charles or Anthony Whitton, had evidently spent consider-able effort to plan it. Among the tangle of weeds and rampant ivies, Penelope noticed a number of familiar plants. There were, she discovered, a great many herbs: wild garlic and chives, lemon balm, wild marjoram, and thyme in a matted carpet of lavender tumbling over the stone retaining walls into the valley. It hummed with bumblebees and gave off a warm, spicy aroma when bruised.

Underneath the seasons of neglect, it was possible to see the former order of things: the careful placing of flag step-ping-stones, a rockery, the once deliberate arrangement of shrubs, which had been left to spread unchecked. Systemat-ically Penelope began to examine the riches, feeling out the familiar names, and after a time, Lou came to join her. Before Penelope realized what she was doing, she had begun to name things aloud, and Lou moved nearer until they were crouched together, shoulder to shoulder, heads bent close over each new find.

Grannie Lawrence had taught Penelope country names, not Latin ones: clove pink, traveller's joy, columbine, wallflower, herb Robert. And when she didn't remember, or had never known, Penelope had the books to search through. Once, looking up from a little purple orchid, she found Lou watch-ing her expectantly and felt a tiny surge of pleasure. Lou was genuinely interested, she was absorbing the same things that Penelope herself had absorbed from her mother's mother.

Unnoticed, the sun slid down the sky spreading shadows across the afternoon. It was getting late when Lou sat back on her heels and gazed penetratingly over the little valley, into the dusk of the firs. "It feels," she stated, "as if we're being watched."

It took Penelope a minute or two to adjust her eyes from closeup to distance. She pushed the fair hair off her face. "You're imagining it," she said. "Who'd want to watch us grubbing about the garden all afternoon."

Lou hunched her thin shoulders. "Not all afternoon, not un-til a little while ago. What's that one?"

"Which? The yellow? I think that's woad. The ancient Britons used it as dye—it turns blue when it's boiled up, I think." But Penelope gave it only half her attention, because Lou's observation had suddenly brought into sharp focus a vague suspicion that had been lurking in the back of her own mind. She glanced around uneasily and found it difficult to concentrate again.

Hand in hand, Valerie and Edward walked slowly up the dusty track toward Wintergap. Valerie didn't bother to hide her delight at finding Lou and Penelope together, but to Penelope's relief she made no specific comment. She went in to wash up. "You can start thinking about supper, Ted. I'm not doing it all myself," she warned over her shoulder. "And you two can set the table, unless of course you've done it already to surprise me—"

"Dreamer," said Edward.

"No, I'm eternally optimistic." They heard her go upstairs whistling "Young At Heart" between her teeth.

Edward strolled over to see what Lou and Penelope were looking at and noticed the flower books lying on the terrace. "Those aren't yours, are they?"

Penelope shook her head. "I borrowed them from the library. I didn't think anyone would mind, and I'll be careful of them."

"Of course you will. You remind me of Grannie Lawrence—and your mother—sitting there," he said with a faint, remembering smile. Then, "I shall want a long, cool drink before I tackle the kitchen."

The twins had followed the footpath back. They came cantering around the house, empty rucksacks flapping on their backs.

"Whew, it's hot!" exclaimed Mark. "We've been exploring the Wall. Sir Kenneth says you can go from one side of England to the other following it."

"There's a map," said Luke. "I want to buy a copy of it the next time we go to Hexham—it shows all the Roman stuff, and where the roads were. There are temporary camps and signal towers all around Sulpitium, and hut circles north of the

Wall. There was even an aqueduct four miles long to carry water to the fort. We'll never have time to see it all! I copied a little piece of the map—where—" He rummaged through his pockets and came up with a handful of crumpled red paper, which he tossed on the ground in front of Lou. "Oh, yes—did you drop those? Mom would have an absolute fit if she'd found them instead of us—you know how she hates littering."

"The littering part isn't so bad," put in Mark, "but you might have shared."

"No," said Lou. "Those aren't ours." "Those" were two empty Toffee Crisp wrappers.

"It must have been a hiker," said Penelope.

But Luke shook his head. "We found them off the path—over there." He pointed to the far side of the valley, hidden by the fir trees. "There was a patch of grass all mashed down. I saw the red and went to see what it was."

A thought occurred to Penelope; she and Lou exchanged the briefest glance—it had occurred to them both. The paper was still shiny and bright, obviously fresh.

"I told you," said Lou.

"Where are the table-setters?" Valerie called from the house.

Martin did not come back for supper; Penelope could guess the reasons and she was just as glad. Unless his mood had changed radically since noon, he would only have spent the evening sparring with his father. He had gone instead, with a group of students, to investigate the nearest pub, an uninspired-looking place on the main road called The Centurion. Valerie had loaned him the Mini.

In the lingering summer twilight, Valerie, Edward, and Penelope relaxed together on the terrace. By unspoken but evidently mutual agreement, everyone seemed to find it the pleasantest part of Wintergap. It was certainly the least gloomy and overbearing. Lou and the twins had been prodded toward bed, Lou only willing if her brothers went too.

"I'd forgotten it stays light so long in the evenings this far north," said Valerie cradling a mug of coffee. "If it weren't for physical exhaustion we could work until nine or ten p.m."

70

"Dedication is so boring," said Edward with a grin. "Do you really think you're going to find a treasure?"

"Depends on your definition of 'treasure'," replied Valerie. "Based on *my* definition, I don't see why not. We have every reason to believe that Sulpitium's a good site. Parts of it have been excavated before, and the Whittons between them transported tons of the fort over here for their personal enjoyment. They've got rather a lot to answer for, those two antiquarians. But there's still plenty that hasn't been touched yet. Who knows what we'll find?"

"What happened here at the end?" asked Penelope. "When the Romans left, I mean. What happened to all the people who lived at Sulpitium; did they go, too?"

"No, probably not," said Valerie. "There's so much we still don't know. But remember that by the time Rome pulled out of Britain, the Romans had been here for about three hundred years. Most of the civilians would have been born here, had probably never seen Rome in their lives. A lot of them must have had British mothers—the soldiers married native women."

"So they stayed and became Britons."

Valerie nodded. "The ones who survived. We do know that the Wall was overrun at least three times by the British tribes. The last time was in 367, just before the Wall was abandoned, during the so-called Barbarian Conspiracy. This frontier must have been pretty thoroughly devastated and lots of people killed. Those who stayed alive would have had to join the natives for self-preservation. Kenneth believes that Sulpitium was very badly hit during that uprising."

"How can he tell that?" asked Edward.

"Very little has ever been found on the site that dates after 360–370 A.D. The implication is that Sulpitium was abandoned by everyone around that time."

"And what exactly are you hoping to find then?"

"Objects that were broken or lost before and during the Conspiracy. The fort's occupants couldn't pick up all their possessions and carry them away—many of the people must have been killed. The valuables would have been looted by the natives, of course, but we ought to turn up pottery, coins, small metal objects, broken tools, and weapons. Depending

71

on the soil conditions we may even be lucky enough to find preserved leather goods, wood, even cloth, like the archaeologists at Vindolanda."

"You people are nothing but educated scavengers," Edward observed amiably.

"So, in a manner of speaking, are you, my love," she returned. "We scavenge objects, you scavenge information and ideas."

Penelope started.

"Kenneth said you showed a flattering interest in the whole operation this afternoon."

"Only natural," said Edward. "Here I am camped right on the doorstep for the summer, seems daft not to find out a little about what goes on during an archaeological dig."

"Any special reason?"

"Not at the moment, no. Why? Has anyone any objections?" he asked, sounding faintly surprised.

"No, not as far as the excavation goes," replied Valerie. "But as to the rest—"

"Rest?" He raised his eyebrows questioningly.

"The local feud, the Whittons and the Robsons. *That* rest. You've obviously been looking into that as well, and I just want to say that what I told Mark the other night goes for everyone, Ted. We cannot afford any kind of trouble this summer."

"Very well, I shall certainly avoid physical combat with all local residents."

She gave him a considering look. "I'm quite serious, you know. I'm beginning to see the way your mind works, Ted."

"God forbid!" he exclaimed with horror. "I shall have nowhere safe to hide! What time d'you suppose that son of mine will get in?"

"Soon after the pub closes," said Penelope.

"I thought archaeologists kept early hours."

"Not students," said Valerie. "Never students. Only us grey-haired professionals." She yawned. "You've just reminded me of how tired I am. I think I'll go take a bath and turn in. Pennie, you'd better, too. Your eyes are closing."

CHAPTER VI

THE DAYS SLID EASILY INTO A SIMPLE PATTERN. AT WINTERGAP
there seemed very little to complicate it—at least to begin with.
Every morning the sun sprang, blazing, into the clear sky
and the Northumberland country parched and panted beneath it. After an early breakfast, Valerie and Martin would
set off together across the dry moorland to Sulpitium, where
they spent each day toiling with Sir Kenneth and the archaeology students. Weekends made no difference to the routine;
as Valerie explained, the summer season was short and they
had to make the best use of every day. The students got time
off, but there wasn't much for them to do with it: they could
hike or take a local bus into Hexham or expend considerably
more effort to get themselves to either Carlisle or Newcastle,
both larger, but farther away. Most chose to remain at the
site and keep on with the work.

Long hours of exposure turned Martin dark brown. His
body hardened, his hair grew shaggy and bleached to the
color of cream toffee, and his clothes acquired an authentic
seasoned look. When she visited Sulpitium, Penelope found
it impossible to distinguish him from the others without a
systematic scrutiny. At Wintergap, where he spent very little
of his time, he seemed like a familiar stranger. His conversation, if it could be called that, was almost entirely concerned
with his "mates" on the site: their lives at university, their
interests, their opinions, relationships, jokes. Personally, Penelope found his infatuation something of a bore, but it was
useful, too. It meant that he and Edward had minimal contact
with each other and spared everyone the friction that inevitably developed these days when they were together.

On Monday of the second week, Edward's proofs arrived,
and he plunged into the business of revising. He did most of
his rewriting on the first set of proofs; Uncle Richard, his
editor at Trowbridge Publishers and a family friend for
longer than Penelope could remember, had given up trying to
convince him that it would be far less expensive if he revised

before his manuscript was set in type, instead of afterwards. Edward always claimed he could tell better what he wanted to do with a novel once he'd seen it printed up on long galley pages.

He set himself up in Anthony Whitton's study and spent long hours behind the closed door, emerging for meals, occasional visits to Sulpitium to indulge his curiosity in the site, and undisclosed errands in the Volvo. He seemed in a very even temper.

It was anyone's guess what the twins did with themselves. Valerie allowed them to explore the countryside within a wide radius of Wintergap, and they turned up from time to time—and always at meals—at the house or Sulpitium. Luke could happily have spent most of his time hanging about the site, watching, helping when permitted, absorbing information. But Mark's attention span was nowhere near as long as his twin's. Impatiently he would drag Luke away from the excavation to involve him in some more vigorous, physical activity. Although reluctant, Luke always went.

That left Louisa and Penelope, odd ones out, to amuse themselves however they could. This was nothing new to either of them, but Lou suffered from a serious disadvantage; she was only eight and still too young, Valerie said firmly, to wander about entirely unsupervised. Therefore, if no one else planned to spend the day at Wintergap, Lou had no choice; she had to accompany her mother to Sulpitium whether she wanted to or not. Penelope worked hard, though not entirely successfully, not to feel sorry for her. She knew how unsatisfactory it was to have no control over one's life.

By the middle of the second week, Penelope was sure enough of her surroundings to take the bus to Hexham. She reveled in the almost-forgotten luxury of being alone, of doing exactly as she pleased without having to consider anyone else's wishes. She wandered the narrow, crooked streets and peered in shop windows, bought stamps and a couple of paperback novels and several packages of her favorite biscuits to stow in her suitcase, where she could count on finding them when she wanted one. Considering the twins' appetites and her experiences during the past eight weeks, it had occurred to her it mightn't be a bad idea to spend a little of her pocket money on emergency rations.

She left the shops well-pleased with her purchases and with her day. Before catching the return bus, however, she detoured down a side street and, without giving herself a chance for second thoughts, she walked toward the Abbey. She could see its towers above the other rooftops, and eventually she emerged in the marketplace, empty of stalls on a Wednesday afternoon. It seemed much smaller and was jammed with so much traffic it looked like a Dodgem at a fun fair.

Deliberately she wove her way across it and slipped in through the south door of the Abbey. When she set out from Wintergap that morning, she had taken her current sketchbook with her in case, she told herself, she found something she wanted to draw. There were a good many prospective subjects in the Abbey: carved stones, the figures on the rood screen, the misericords in the choir stalls. But it was none of these that had brought her here, and underneath the pretense she knew it.

She had come to look again at the Roman memorial, and she had brought her sketch pad so that she might compare her drawing with the real thing. It was almost as if she had no free choice in the matter; she was pulled to the stone, yet when she stood in front of it she didn't want to raise her eyes. As soon as she did she knew she had gotten something basic wrong when she'd put it on paper the week before. She couldn't think what until she opened her pad to the sketch, then it was obvious. She snapped the book shut as if it had bitten her and fled out of the Abbey, back to the welcome sunshine and bustle of the street. A bus was waiting when she reached the stop; she flung herself onto it and sank, out of breath, into an empty seat.

Her mistake had been in putting a face to the figure of the Briton. On the stone it had none. The features had been chipped away, leaving a blank except for one eye and a bit of nose. And yet Penelope had never hesitated when it came to drawing that face, had never questioned her memory of it. The face had come from somewhere; she had seen it and subconsciously fitted it where it didn't belong. Or did it? She was disproportionately upset by the whole incident. The obvious solution was to destroy the drawing and forget she'd ever done it; she recollected thinking that earlier. And now, as before, she couldn't bring herself to do it. So she left the sketch locked in the pad, and it hung like a clock weight in the back of her mind whether she allowed herself to think about it or not.

That night, Valerie returned from the excavation looking weary and discouraged with a thick bundle of papers under her arm. There had been two tourist coaches to deal with during the course of the day. The second was full of German archaeologists on a busman's holiday who had refused to leave quietly when requested. They spent more than an hour hopping in and out of the trenches and asking technical questions in impenetrable accents. Everyone's work had been thoroughly disrupted as a result, and even the usually calm Sir Kenneth had lost his temper. He all but tore his hair and gnashed his teeth, Valerie reported with a thin smile.

When Penelope wandered out to the kitchen for a glass of milk before bed, she found her stepmother sitting at the kitchen table surrounded by diagrams, ground plans, and work schedules. Valerie was wearing her glasses, a sure sign she was tired; normally she wore contact lenses. She seemed glad of her stepdaughter's interruption. She pushed the glasses up on her forehead, rubbed the back of her neck, and inquired about Penelope's day.

"Sorry I didn't ask earlier—I was too full of my own troubles," she apologized lightly. "Put the kettle on for me, would you, Pennie? I've got to make some sense of these before I go to bed."

So Penelope put the kettle on, sat down across from Valerie, and proceeded to tell her about Hexham. Not about her visit to the Abbey or the drawing, of course, but the farm women on the bus and the tea shop where she'd had lunch, and the newsagent's she'd discovered with a sign that said s. w. shaftoe and must belong to Jonathan's father. Valerie listened and the kettle boiled, so Penelope made coffee and a mug of cocoa for herself, and they talked some more. It was very peaceful in the kitchen.

She hadn't really meant to ask Valerie what Lou had spent the day doing, but somehow it slipped out and Valerie heaved a sigh.

"Being bored to tears mostly, I'm afraid. If only she were interested in the excavation like Luke, but she really isn't, God love her! She tried not to be a nuisance, but it's hard when there's no one at all to pay attention to her and nothing she can or wants to do. I just haven't time to spare for her right now, we're behind as it is."

If it was a trap, she had walked into it with her eyes open, Penelope realized glumly. She had no one to blame but herself, but she'd come this far, why not spring it? "She could stay with me," she offered reluctantly. "At least tomorrow anyway. I mean, I don't expect to be at Wintergap every day, but when I am . . ."

Valerie looked at her gratefully. "That would be a tremendous favor, Pennie. I just can't leave her here alone and the twins are no help. Luke's got a good sense of responsibility, but Mark's hopeless and he easily outweighs his brother." She got up and made herself another cup of coffee. "She's not a bad kid, Lou. She's independent and quite good at amusing herself most of the time."

"I will have other things to do," Penelope said quickly. "I'll want to go back to Hexham, and—"

"And you won't want an eight-year-old tagging after you all the time. Of course you won't, especially since you're not used to it. Don't worry, I understand and sympathize. But if she doesn't have to come with me every day she'll be much happier. She told me this morning you were teaching her the names of wildflowers. I didn't know you were interested in botany, Pennie."

"It's not really botany," said Penelope, embarrassed. "It's only a bit of gardening. My grandmother had a garden in St. Albans and I helped her with it when we lived there. I was just having a look round Wintergap. The garden is so overgrown—"

"Mmm," said Valerie thoughtfully. "How many of the flowers still growing here do you s'pose the Romans knew? They may even have brought plants with them from Italy— someone told me they grew herbs along the Wall, and that for years and years after they'd gone people would come specially to pick them for medicines. That would make a fascinating thesis—you could press specimens and mount them." She shook her head and grinned ruefully. "Listen to me! Once a teacher, always a teacher."

"I hadn't thought of that," said Penelope. "Actually, I'd thought more of drawing them." Then, quickly, to avoid any questions, "Who took care of Lou before, when you went on excavations and she was even younger?" It was surprising to realize how little she knew of the Prines' past life, but still more surprising to find she was genuinely curious. Such curiosity could be a dangerous thing; it threatened her detachment. The more she learned, the more involved she would become.

"I did. When I was really lucky I could con a student into baby-sitting at least part of the time, for the twins as well, but I couldn't count on it. And since Brian left, in order to get any work done at all I've had to hire someone. Don't misunderstand, Pennie, I love my children dearly, but I'm not a professional mother, I'm a professional archaeologist. God knows I need Mark, Luke, and Lou, but I need my job, too. I was rather hoping your father would—" She broke off with a little shrug. "But he has his own work, and I can't blame him. Lou isn't his responsibility."

"But she is now," said Penelope. "I mean, isn't she?"

Valerie regarded her quizzically. "And you and Martin are mine?"

"But we're older," she protested. She couldn't tell what Valerie was thinking and she felt awkward. Somehow she'd never bothered to consider any of this before, not in straightforward terms.

But Valerie didn't press her further. Instead she continued in another direction. "Responsibility for other people is a very tricky thing. Brian always maintained that once we had babies, looking after them was my responsibility. I had to give up everything else I was doing and devote all my time to it. It wasn't just Brian who felt that way, in fact. It was our parents and a lot of our friends, and I let them convince me they were right. It's taken me nine years to climb out from under that and I still feel guilty quite often."

"Guilty about what? What do you mean?"

"One of the main reasons Brian and I got divorced, Pennie, was that although Brian loved the idea of having a family, he refused to take any responsibility for the kids except financial. I did all the taking care, and he did all the earning money. I finally realized that there was nothing horribly wrong with me for wanting to continue my career even though I had three children—that, in fact, we'd all be better off if I did because I wouldn't be frustrated and miserable most of the time. I'd trained for my profession as hard as Brian had for his, damn it! If he'd been willing to *share* a little—" She lowered her glasses and peered at Penelope with an apologetic smile. "But you don't want to hear me rake through all that, I'm sure. If you really would be willing to keep an eye out for Lou, I'll have a talk with her in the morning. She won't be any trouble, I'm sure. She can amuse herself very well."

Friday morning, instead of taking the half-filled sketch pad downstairs with her, Penelope chose an empty one. That, she reasoned, was because she meant to begin a new project and it made sense to start with a new book. It was not because she had an illogical distaste for the old one.

One by one the family drifted away from Wintergap until Penelope and Lou were left alone there. Lou was greatly relieved not to have to spend another day at Sulpitium where there was even less for her to do than at Wintergap.

They explored the garden together until lunchtime, then ate their sandwiches in the relative cool of the dim, stone-floored kitchen. Lou was quiet and undemanding; Penelope wondered what Valerie had talked to her about before she left—Lou even helped clean up afterward, then got out a couple of Mark's *Tin Tin* books and stayed at the table to read them. Penelope left her at it and went back into the heat and dazzle of the afternoon. The sun blazed overhead at its fullest strength, and she soon found it difficult to keep her mind fixed on what she was doing. She looked the same flower up in Keble-Martin's *Concise British Flora* three times without being able to remember its name. Movement became more and more of an effort and she could feel the blood pulse inside her skull. She was just wondering what sunstroke felt

79

like and if perhaps she oughtn't to have a hat on, when she became aware once again of being watched. At first she thought it was Lou come silently to check on her, but when she looked up, the terrace was empty, the air undisturbed. The feeling swept her like a chill, causing her scalp to prickle. Lou's presence would not do that.

There was no sound except the hypnotic scouring of the breeze among the fir branches, no outward sign that anyone was spying on her, but she knew it for a certainty. Righteous indignation at such an intrusion revitalized her; her slack muscles tensed and she forgot her headache. Deliberately she collected her things: flower book, pad, pencils, art gum and piled them in a precise stack while she considered the situation. Whoever was watching had been there before and would doubtless come again unless stopped, and the only way Penelope could see of stopping the spy was by direct confrontation. She didn't much like the idea, but she liked even less having her privacy invaded. She wished she'd paid more attention to what the twins had said the other day about finding those candy wrappers; that was the spot, she was sure, on the opposite side of the valley, that she must aim for if she were going to track this spy down. Carefully casual, she picked up her pad and a pencil and began to walk slowly along the edge of the terrace, pausing now and then to examine something. There was a drop of about three feet from the terrace to the hillside below, where the ground fell away in a steep tangle of scrub down to the burn, which lay hidden at the bottom. Unlike the trees in a Forestry plantation, the firs that lined the valley were scattered and spaced far enough apart to let sunlight ooze between them. Though they were all the same size and had been planted deliberately, they were for appearance rather than timber. It was just possible to discern the vague suggestion of an old footpath winding among them toward the burn.

Penelope chose a clear spot, sat on the retaining wall, swung her legs over it, and jumped lightly down. Immediately she left the garden behind, and with it the blurred but unmistakable feeling of civilization. If there had been a sign nailed to one of the trees that said PASS AT YOUR OWN RISK, or even NO TRESPASSING, the message couldn't have been plainer.

80

She had not realized before what a tiny, precarious island the Whittons had built themselves in the midst of an alien country. On all sides the wilderness crowded Wintergap, sneaking up the valley, creeping closer and closer with each year of neglect. The garden, into which someone had obviously put much time and care, was a brave attempt to keep it at bay, but the battle had to be continually fought or all would be lost, the island inundated, reclaimed. It was a frightening thought.

By great effort of will, Penelope made herself dawdle until she reached the bottom of the valley. She reckoned that from there no one above could see her; the slope was too steep and the undergrowth too thick. She left her pad tucked into the roots of a large fir and hoped she would be able to find it again —it would be a pity to sacrifice a whole new one. The burn was dry; here and there among the boulders she found a patch of crusty mud, but there was no water. Penelope found it easiest to walk quietly in its sandy bed, where there were no dry twigs to snap underfoot. She followed it as it rose northward, until she judged she must have got past the house, then began to work her way cautiously up the far side of the valley. She kept low to the ground, eyes and ears alert for anything that would indicate her quarry, and shifted from one bit of cover to the next: a scrubby alder clump, a patch of withering bracken, a hummock of fescue, a boulder. The sun beat down upon her, dust tickled in her nose and the back of her throat, but she was resolute.

It was the drought that gave her away; everything was so brittle that when she leaned her weight accidentally on an old furze root it cracked like a pistol shot. Her heart gave a mighty jump. She hadn't time to recover, when quite close at hand she heard someone start up in the deep grass and leap away. There was no need for concealment now. She shot upright and fought a momentary giddiness; she must have been almost on top of the person. She could congratulate herself on that, but not now—there wasn't time. Ahead to her right, the spy was haring up the open fell. It was a boy, that much she could tell from his build, and he was familiar with the terrain. He had a good start and he was going fast, surefooted as a deer. Her breath caught as, out of the corner of her eye, she saw another movement. It hadn't occurred to her there might be more than *one* spy on the hillside. But no, the second figure wasn't human, it was a black and white dog bounding beside the boy. They reached and crossed the skyline, where Hadrian's Wall rode the crest of the fell, and Penelope set off after them, blundering over the uneven ground. Twice she caught her foot on one of the great knobs of grass and, unable to save herself, fell headlong, bruised, daunted, but refusing to give up.

Panting, she topped the ridge the boy had disappeared over and paused to scan the territory beyond. She felt an odd reluctance to cross the line of the Wall and realized that she had not done it before; she had stayed below, on the Roman side. But there he was, her spy, still in plain sight although there must have been dozens of places he could have found in which to hide. He was making for the great rounded bulk of Dodd Pike.

She took a last deep breath and plunged after him, determined not to let him get away. It was terribly hard work crossing that stretch of fell; she had to concentrate fiercely on her footing and even so missed it several times more. Feeling grim and streaming with sweat, bits of grass and twig tangled in her hair, Penelope pounded up the long low shoulder of the Pike, wondering if the boy would have vanished altogether by the time she reached the top. When at last she did, he had, but it was obvious where he'd gone. On the far side of the shoulder was a small plateau from which there was a great sweeping view northward. The plateau was protected on two sides naturally by the Pike, and on the other two by a thick loose wall of stones. In the center of the enclosed circle were more stones, seeming at first glance to be heaped at random into huge, haphazard cairns. Somewhere among the jumble the boy and dog had gone to earth—it was the only place they'd had time to reach.

But if Penelope had felt a reluctance to cross the Wall, she felt a positive aversion to entering that circle. As she stood above it looking down, the pattern began to emerge: the shadow-shapes of mounds and ditches lying beneath the bleached grass, the deliberate arrangement of the stones. It was the site of an ancient settlement, perhaps as old as the Wall, perhaps even older. She remembered Luke exclaiming over the number of remains that showed on the O.S. map of the area; this must be one. She would look when she got back to Wintergap. What, she wondered, had been the relationship between the people in the settlement and the Romans at Sulpitium? Openly hostile? Uneasy? Suspicious at best. That was how she felt, standing there now, in the safety of the twentieth century. How much had changed in eighteen hundred years? She twisted about. To her right loomed the mass of Dodd Pike; a sentinel posted on its summit would have an excellent view east and west along the Wall, would probably be able to watch all the business of Sulpitium. To the south, even from where she stood, the Wall was visible, and below it the smudge of trees that marked Wintergap and the long crooked seam showing the course of the burn. West and north spread acres and acres of wildness, with here and there a handful of specks: sheep or cattle; and one farm. It lay to the northwest; a little group of grey buildings clenched together like a fist in the midst of the green-brown fell.

A flicker of movement caught the corner of her eye. He *was* there. She could see no point in having got this far only to turn back at the last minute. Like it or not, she would make herself go and face the enemy. She started down the slope concentrating so hard on what she was daring to do she walked right into a cloud of midges without noticing them. The tiny insects whirled erratically round her head like flakes of soot, catching in her mouth and hair. She spat and tried to brush them away while continuing to move through them and felt one fly into her left eye. She rubbed and it stung. She tried pushing it toward the corner and for a moment thought it was gone, but she blinked and knew it wasn't. It lodged under her lower eyelid. Damnation! Well, it would just have to stay there then; she couldn't afford to let it stop her now. As much to hear her own voice as anything, she called, "I know someone's down there! You might as well come out."

Silence.

"I won't leave until you do." She stepped onto the plateau and it was as if the sun slid behind a bank of heavy cloud; the breeze was chilling. But on all sides the day was as hot and bright as ever. She tensed, felt an urgent need to keep the silence at bay. "If you're here," she said, "I'll find you. I will." The words sounded thin and small; they fell dead on the air without any kind of resonance and were instantly absorbed. Slowly, carefully, she moved forward into the alien settlement alert for the slightest sound. Now that she was among the heaps of stone she found they were quite large and some were still recognizable horseshoe-shaped shelters, roofless but remarkably complete—almost as if someone was keeping them in repair, perhaps still living here—rubbish! She felt her nerve failing and stopped, her feet planted slightly apart as if she were braced against something. There was a long moment of nothing; she thought it would suffocate her.

Then suddenly he broke cover and confronted her, coming out from behind one of the shelters on her right. And all she could do was stare at him, her mouth opened for an exclamation that wouldn't come. The blood drained from her cheeks and she was anchored to the spot. She knew him. She knew him as two separate individuals whom it had not before occurred to her to connect. He was the boy she had seen rolling about the dusty market place in Hexham locked in combat with Mark—now without the blood and dirt griming his face, but the telltale scab of a scratch along the left side of his chin. That boy was real enough, if alarming.

It was the other that paralyzed her: his was the face she had given the Briton in her drawing of the memorial stone. Simple as the features had been, they were unmistakable.

CHAPTER VII

"WHAT'RE YE GAWKIN' AT, WHEY?" RANDALL ROBSON DE-manded as Penelope continued to stare. His expression was hostile and challenging.

She couldn't answer. Her knees felt queer and she knew she had to sit down. She folded awkwardly onto a pile of stones and attempted to fight clear of the cold fog that enveloped her mind. If her legs had been working right, she would simply have cut and run, but she couldn't. The boy called Randall Robson was part of her world—he might be an enemy, but she was able to deal with him. The figure on the carved stone, however, was part of a world she had little or no understanding of; he filled her with an unreasoning panic.

There was a rattle of pebbles and she glanced quickly up. The dog had reappeared, its feathery tail waving, its ears cocked. It grinned at her in such an ordinary doglike way, pink tongue vibrating, that she took courage from it. "I know who you are," she stated defiantly, meeting the boy's eyes. "You're Randall Robson."

He was older than she'd thought when she'd only glimpsed him tangled with Mark. Then she'd assumed that since they were about the same size, they must be about the same age. Now she guessed him to be at least fifteen or sixteen—slight and tough, his dark face framed with wiry black hair.

"Ye divvent belong here. Ye shouldnae a come," he replied.

"You brought me yourself," retorted Penelope. "I wouldn't have come if it hadn't been for you. Why were you spying on me?"

His brows drew together threateningly. He took a step toward her. She was at a disadvantage, still sitting, and her eye had begun to bother her again. The dog's bright, interested gaze shifted from one to the other.

Sounding as belligerent as she could to hide her nervousness, Penelope went on quickly, "And why did you start that fight with Mark in Hexham? What have you got against us?"

"Aa just told ye, ye divvent belong, ony a ye. Ye shouldnae a come an ye shouldnae stay."

Her knees felt less treacherous, so she stood. He was only slightly taller. "But what difference can it make to you whether we're here or not? If you don't like us—and you don't even know us, so I don't see how you can have decided—you can just ignore us. It isn't as if we live right next door to each other. You make it sound as if we're trespassing on your property by being here."

"Aye."

"But we're not." She scrubbed unsuccessfully at the irritated eye. "*You* were trespassing down at Wintergap just now. The University owns that land and the fort. We've got at least as much right up here as you."

He shook his head impatiently. " 'Tis nowt to do wi' ownin'. There's land can be owned nice an' tame, an' there's land that aye belongs to none but those can live on it. Buyin' an' sellin' an' bits a paper make nae difference tae it."

"That's no kind of argument," objected Penelope. "What you're saying is that you belong here and we don't, but you can't prove that, can you?"

His eyes held hers for a minute, then she blinked, pretending it was only her eye again that made her. Randall's gaze was no longer hostile; it was uncomfortably penetrating, hard and sharp. "Aa neednae," he said simply. "Ye ken yersel 'tis true."

The worst of it was that she knew he was right. She had felt out of place ever since she crossed Hadrian's Wall. And she remembered all too vividly how reluctant she had been to enter the camp circle. To avoid confessing this, even to herself, she held her hand out to the dog. It stretched its muzzle forward and breathed on her fingers, its tail waved faster. Randall glowered but said nothing. "That doesn't explain why you were spying on me," said Penelope, now that she'd collected herself.

"Aa did nowt to harm ye."

"You invaded my privacy," she returned primly. "And it isn't the first time you've done it, either. I'd have thought you'd have better things to do with your time—or haven't you?"

His face grew stony; it was the image of the one she'd drawn and her stomach tensed. "Thon's nae affair a yers."

"It is if you bother me. Or any of the rest of my family." It was Mark she was thinking of, but he looked at her so sharply it caused her to wonder. The dog had inched close enough for Penelope to pat.

"Frit!" he snapped angrily, and the dog withdrew, ears flat. Without responding to Penelope, Randall turned and started to walk away. Before he'd gone half-a-dozen steps a thought struck her. "It's you, isn't it? You're the boy who's been sending tourist coaches to Sulpitium! That woman last week said they'd asked directions of a local boy."

It was a long shot, but she'd scored. He stopped, his back to her.

"But what's the point?" she asked baffled. "Why should you want to interrupt the excavation that way? Or fight with Mark and spy on me? If this is all your idea of a joke, I think it's stupid."

Randall Robson swung back and she saw at once from his face that whatever his reasons, none of it was a joke to him. "Ye ken nowt about it, ony a't—"

"You're right," she declared. "I don't understand, either."

"Ye're one a them, down thonder. 'Tis our land ye're on, *our* farm ye're howkin' up wi' yer bluddy great pits. Ye've nae thought for us—*ye divvent belong.*"

"*Your* farm—but that was years and years ago! You can't have been more than a baby when Anthony Whitton came up here to live. And he *owned* the land anyway. He only took what was his. Your family got another farm to live on."

"Ye make it sound se simple. Whey, it isn't." The blazing anger had gone out of him and for just an instant, before he hid it behind the stone mask, she glimpsed a bleak desolation. "Ma dad died account of it. Ma brother Archie cannae—*we* cannae forget thon."

"But what about us? We had nothing to do with any of it," she protested. "None of us even knew your father or the Whittons, so why should you blame us?"

"Because ye divvent belong."

"There you go again! You sound like a broken phonograph record!" she told him scornfully.

"Aa'll nae argue wi' ye! Ye cannae understand."

"But it's *over.*" Penelope dug the heel of her hand into her eye socket, attempting once more to rid herself of the bug. It was beginning to nag painfully; she couldn't let it alone and she couldn't dislodge it.

"It *is*nae over!" he almost shouted at her. " 'Twill never be over—nae se long as there are Robsons."

"That doesn't make any sense!" she shouted back. She was making the eye worse. It watered copiously.

87

"Aa told ye—Aa'll nae argue—what's wrong wi' ye, whey?" he demanded, coming a few steps closer and scowling fiercely at her.

"Nothing!" She turned her head away. "I've got something in my eye, that's all."

"Well, ye'll nae get it out doin' thon. Ye'll make it warse."

"Well, there isn't much else I can do, is there," she retorted, knowing he was right, but not about to admit it. He was, after all, the enemy.

They glared at each other in silence, Penelope doing her best one-eyed, but Randall won handily and she looked away again.

"Howway an' let me see." If it had been a request instead of a command she would have refused point-blank, but she was desperate enough to obey almost without thinking.

"It's very small," she said. "It was a midge, I think."

He moved close to her, his face suddenly only a few inches from her own. "Shift yer hand. Look up, whey. Divvent move, Aa'll nae harm ye," he told her impatiently as she flinched slightly when he pulled her lower eyelid down with a finger. "Aye, Aa see it," he said, after a minute.

"Can you get it out?"

"Whisht." He pulled something dark out of his pocket—she hoped it wasn't terribly dirty—uncrumpled it, and smoothed out one corner. She willed herself not to move. His hand was steady—a quick touch with the tip of the cloth, then he stepped back. She blinked. The eye felt sore and raspy, but the irritant was gone. The sensation of relief was so wonderful it was almost worth having gone through the agony for it.

He stuffed the handkerchief back into his trousers. She drew a deep breath. "Thank you." The two words sounded so small she thought he must not have heard, then he shrugged. She felt suddenly inadequate and cast about for something safe to say. "What's your dog's name?" It was the first thing that came into her head.

He glanced at her, startled and a little suspicious, hesitated, then grudgingly answered, "Frit. She's Frit." The dog wriggled happily at the sound of her name.

"Is she a sheepdog?" Penelope persisted gamely.

"Aye." Still the suspicion, wondering what she was leading up to. It was so plain on his face she almost challenged it, but instead she crouched and called softly, "Frit?"

The tail beat and the dog cocked her head at Randall as if begging permission. He said nothing but made the smallest gesture with his hand and she bounded forward. She was warm and silky, so full of life and joy she quivered under Penelope's fingers. Penelope liked dogs, but she had never had a chance to know any very well; her father's allergy made familiarity impossible. Alison's family owned a fat, middle-aged cocker spaniel called Honey, who slept a great deal and seemed to have very little brain. Penelope didn't really count Honey.

Frit rewarded Penelope's overture with a selection of wet kisses that surprised and pleased her.

"She's nowt but a puppy yet," said Randall. "But she's the sense for sheep an' her mam's a good bitch." There was a hint of pride in his voice.

"She's very friendly," said Penelope pointedly.

"Aye, she's a fond wee fool, Frit. She thinks the world's a friendly place still. She'll learn right enough, Aa warrand."

"Why should she?" asked Penelope. "A lot of the world *is* friendly."

Randall said nothing. Suddenly Frit went stiff under Penelope's hand, head up, ears alert. Penelope listened, but heard nothing remarkable. "What does she hear?" she asked Randall, then noticed that he had gone tense as well, like a wild creature testing the air. Across the hot afternoon came the faint bleating of sheep, the occasional fretful low of a cow. Rooks chacked somewhere out of sight, and the drone of a distant motor carried down the scorched breeze. She could hear nothing else.

"Howway home, Frit!" commanded Randall. Without hesitation the dog left Penelope and trotted toward the far edge of the camp, pausing there to wait for her master. He followed.

Penelope stood up. "Hang on! Wait—where are you going? You haven't told me what you were doing at Wintergap yet."

He looked back at her, eyes narowed. "Bide here till Aa've gone."

"Why should I? What is it?"

"Divvent ask—there's nae time. Just ye do it." His voice held a note of urgency. "Gi'us the chance to get off the Pike afore ye gan, d'ye ken? Then haddaway back as ye came. Aa mun gan." But still he hesitated. "Aa'll nae fash ye further," he said. "There's ma word—what's yer name, whey?"

She stared blankly at him. "Penelope, but I don't—"

"And mine's Ran, se ye ken."

"I told you, I already know who you are," she said, but he didn't hear. He'd gone before she'd spoken the words, and she was alone among the secretive piles of stone. Without Randall and Frit she felt exposed, vulnerable. She wondered what had caused his abrupt departure; surely more than just a desire to get away. And why did he want her to wait until he was gone before she herself left? More to the point, why on earth should she pay any attention to what Randall Robson told her to do?

But the urgency in his words was impossible to dismiss. And although she had to work to translate many of them, she realized that he had, in the end, promised to leave her alone. He'd given his name on it as though it were not something he did lightly. And she'd given hers—she felt vaguely disturbed by that, as if she'd done it without fully understanding its importance. But what possible harm could that do? It was just a name . . . The whole episode was fantastic.

Warily she picked her way between the hut circles in the direction Ran had gone. She hadn't the faintest idea what she was looking for: something that had made Ran bolt, something potentially threatening. But when she got to the rampart, all she could see was a long cloud of tawny dust moving across the fell: a car following a dirt track toward the huddled farm that she had noticed earlier. And there were Ran and Frit, already far away, two rapidly moving dots well quit of the Pike, also heading toward the farm. It was Dodd Moss, she knew it must be—Valerie had said you could almost see it from Sulpitium and there was none other in sight.

Then was it the sound of the car's engine that had sent him off so suddenly? And if so—she scoured her memory for information from that dinner table conversation—the driver was probably Ran's brother, Archie. She remembered him furiously shaking Mark—the angry face, the powerful thick hands, the thunder of his voice as he ordered Ran away. Her eyes went back to the yellow streak below.

When Penelope got back to Wintergap Louisa was waiting for her on the terrace, her face pinched with concern. Penelope, coming over the Wall and down the path behind the house, saw Lou first and felt a jab of guilt; she had forgotten the younger girl altogether. She had no idea how long she had been away.

"I didn't know where you were," Lou complained. "You didn't say you were going."

"I didn't know I was," Penelope countered brusquely. She told herself she had no need to make excuses to an eight-year-old for going off on her own in the middle of the afternoon.

"Where *did* you go?"

"Oh"—Penelope was vague—"up there." She discovered she wanted to think a good deal more about her encounter with Ran Robson before she might be willing to discuss it with anyone else.

"Have you been crying?" Lou frowned at her.

"Crying? No, why would—? I just had something in my eye."

"Well, you might have said. I didn't like being here alone."

"You could always have gone to Sulpitium," Penelope reminded her.

Lou subsided into a dissatisfied silence, which made Penelope feel even guiltier and therefore cross with her stepsister. She passed the remainder of the afternoon sitting in plain view on the terrace, reading *Puck of Pook's Hill*. She returned to the chapter called "On the Great Wall," where Dan and Una meet Parnesius, the Roman Centurion, and hear from him what it was like to be a soldier stationed on Hadrian's Wall; when a kind of informal truce existed between the Romans and the Picts, and they rode and hunted together in the wild country to the north.

Lou left her alone, but her mind kept straying from the words in the book to her own experiences north of the Wall that afternoon. When Edward drove in an hour or so later, she welcomed the distraction. He brought with him a large cold chicken and a paper sackful of fresh salad greens, and conscripted the two girls for kitchen duty.

The three of them set to work concocting supper. Edward was in good spirits and teased Lou out of her bad humor. The twins turned up magically almost as soon as the chicken was unwrapped and were sternly ordered to go and wash. "Thoroughly, and I mean *thoroughly!*" Edward chased them out of the kitchen waving a soup ladle while Lou applauded, and they thundered upstairs where it sounded as if they released a small typhoon in the bathroom.

"You must have had a good day," observed Penelope, deviling eggs.

"Oh, I did! Indeed. I solved a problem with the book that's been haunting me for months! So *simple*." He snapped his fingers.

Valerie and Martin were late, but when they arrived it was immediately obvious that they'd had a good day, too. Under her dust and blisters Valerie was positively radiant. It was impossible for the rest of her family to ignore the glow, but not until they were all seated at the table expressing impatience would she tell them the cause of her excitement.

"She's always like this when she's found something," Luke told Penelope and Edward. "It must be really good." There was undisguised envy in his voice.

"Well if you want to spend all your time hanging around watching other people dig holes," said Mark. "*I'd* rather be exploring. Who knows what we might find somewhere else?"

Luke nodded, not totally convinced.

"So?" prodded Edward, passing out plates. "Don't keep us in suspense."

"I'm not sure it's proper dinner table conversation," she said demurely, her eyes sparkling.

Martin snorted. "If you don't tell them, I will—and I wasn't even there when you made the discovery. I only saw afterward."

"Told you," said Luke.

"What was it?" Mark asked. "A broken pot or a handful of bent nails?"

"Oh ye of little faith," said his mother.

"I thought it was supposed to take months to find anything," said Edward, "and you've been at it less than a fortnight. It sounds like cheating to me."

"She can't tell us what it is if we don't let her," pointed out Penelope practically.

Valerie gave her a little nod, then looked round at her family, gathering everyone's attention. "We found a grave," she said and sat back.

"A grave?" Edward raised his eyebrows inquiringly. "Sounds promising."

"How could you if you were excavating the bathhouse?" demanded Luke. "They wouldn't have buried anyone in the bathhouse."

"Ah, but they did—or *some*one did," replied Valerie.

"You mean a grave with bones?" Mark was interested.

"Lots of bones," she confirmed happily. "Several peoples' worth."

Lou said, "I don't think I'd like finding them."

"What does it mean?" asked Edward. "Bones in the bathhouse—not a bad title."

Martin's brows drew together dangerously.

"We can't be entirely sure yet, but we think the bathhouse would most likely have been destroyed in 367, during the Barbarian Conspiracy."

"When the Wall was overrun?" Penelope said.

Valerie nodded. "It was outside the walls of the fort, and after 367 anyone living at Sulpitium would have been living inside in a sort of fortified village for protection against the northern tribes. We also know that both Charles and Anthony Whitton removed a great many stones from the bathhouse for the construction of Wintergap—it was one of their main sources of material."

"How do you know?" Edward asked.

"They left records. Charles's are the more detailed. Apparently, although he had no qualms about appropriating whole chunks of Sulpitium for his private use, he had enough sense of responsibility to keep account of where he put them. And when Wintergap came to the University a team of experts examined the house thoroughly and analyzed the stones in it. Satisfied?"

He nodded. "Continue."

"Thanks, I will. Last summer before the dig closed, they managed to do some preliminary surveying, so we were able to begin excavating relatively quickly. The first thing we came to, under a thick layer of turf and rubble, was a rough sort of platform constructed of large slabs of stone, rather like a floor. It had been deliberately laid, no question, which seemed odd. Today we began to lift the slabs and in a cavity underneath we found the bones. They were heaped together in the area of the bathhouse that would have been the caldarium, and it looked—"

"What?" asked Penelope. "What's a caldarium?"

"Steam room," said Luke with a glance at his mother for agreement.

"Right. The baths were rather like a sauna."

"Get back to the bones," said Mark.

"It looked to us as if we'd uncovered a mass grave of some kind—the victims of some calamity simply piled in and covered up. So far we haven't found any of the jewelry or coins usually associated with Roman burials, nor have we discovered any memorial stones. It's highly unlikely, anyway, that the Romans would have buried people in one of their own buildings—and it was illegal to dig graves within the boundaries of a town. Roman cemeteries are always outside civilian settlements."

"I still think it could have been a plague of some sort," said Martin. "Smallpox, typhoid—there must have been contagious diseases in the second century. And they would have had to bury the victims as fast as possible to keep it from spreading."

"Unclean, unclean," murmured Penelope.

"It's possible," said Valerie, "but I'm not convinced. In case of plague I think they would have burned the corpses. It is a thought, however."

"I suppose even Martin must have them sometimes," said Mark cheekily.

Martin attempted to kick him under the table, but missed and got Penelope, who scowled and kicked back.

"Enough!" declared Edward. "There are too many innocent ankles down here, including mine. Behave or I'll send you to bed without any lemon sponge."

94

"Try," challenged Martin.

"How could you tell the bones were human?" Luke asked his mother.

"Yes," said Mark, easily distracted. "Did you find a skull?"

"Several. Frances dug one up almost immediately and we knew we'd found a grave, not a midden."

"Hey, neat!" exclaimed Mark. "That's what we need to find, Luke. A skull of our own. Only if we find one, we're going to keep it."

Lou made a disgusted face at her brother. "Gross!"

"I've never seen one," said Luke, "only a plaster cast at school and that doesn't really count."

"Alas poor Yorick," remarked Edward. "What ghoulish children you've got, Val."

"It's only scientific curiosity," Luke said.

"How many skeletons are there?" asked Penelope, fascinated in a gruesome sort of way.

"We don't know yet. We won't until we've finished excavating this particular layer, and then we'll need a specialist to sort the bones out. I'd guess there are at least nine or ten, maybe more than a dozen. But with what we've got we've made two really important discoveries. The first is that at least two of the bodies were children, and the second—"

"You didn't tell me," said Martin accusingly. "Nothing specific."

"I was saving it. Rob and Frances found a skeleton almost intact, lying curled up. Kenneth thinks it's a man's. Anyway, lodged between the ribs about here"—she indicated on herself—"was the broken blade of a knife."

"Wow!" Mark was gratifyingly impressed. "A murder!"

Penelope's stomach gave a queer little lurch and she avoided looking at the half-eaten chicken salad still on her plate.

"You could have said that's why you thought I was wrong about an epidemic," Martin objected. "You withheld proof, which is jolly unfair!"

"Was it a massacre?" asked Luke.

"It's a good possibility," allowed Valerie. "We'll be extremely lucky if we can find anything to prove it, but you never know."

95

"A classical mystery," said Edward reflectively. "Intriguing. If I weren't so busy at the moment with *All Fall Down* . . ."

To head off Martin, who Penelope could feel was gathering himself for an attack, she said brightly, "Where did you go this afternoon, Dad?"

"Hmm? Oh, Hexham. Found rather a nice pub there—unpretentious, jolly sort of place. Called The Hand and Glove—did you know Hexham was a center for glovemaking in the nineteenth century? Hexham Tans, quite famous."

Valerie gave her husband a bemused smile, Martin subsided, and Penelope sighed, knowing the crisis had been averted. She was far too tired to be able to face being caught between her father and brother in an argument.

"—how desperately serious the drought is up here," Edward was going on. "That's almost all anyone talked about in the pub this afternoon. The farmers have begun moving their livestock in off the hills because there's no water in the burns. I had the devil's own time getting anything else out of them, I can tell you."

"It affects their livelihood, Ted," said Valerie. "We had a deputation at Sulpitium yesterday. The local farmers are terrified we'll set the countryside on fire. They didn't come right out and tell us to leave, but they certainly wanted to."

"Why?" asked Martin, shifting his aggression to the farmers. "They can't accuse you of being careless—there hasn't been so much as a campfire on the site since I've been working there, and no one even lights a cigarette except at the farmhouse. You've got signs up everywhere about the danger and stacks of fire brooms in plain sight."

"I know, I know," said Valerie soothingly. "We've taken every precaution we can think of. But remember, Martin, this is *their* country—we're intruders. They don't know us, they don't understand what we're doing. A fire up here would be devastating: the vegetation's like tinder and there's no water nearby. Here we are, playing our eccentric games at Sulpitium while they're trying to earn a living under very difficult circumstances. I wish they weren't so hostile, but I can't really blame them. They lead a pretty hand-to-mouth existence."

"What's 'hand-to-mouth'?" Lou wanted to know.

"It means you don't use silverware, dummy," said Mark.

"Does it really?" She appealed to her mother.

"No, sweetie, it means you work very hard for a living and you don't have any money to spare."

"Like us until last year," put in Luke helpfully.

"Not really," said Valerie. "Not at all."

"You had to work all the time," he reminded her.

"And you said we didn't have very much money," added Mark.

"We managed perfectly well—we never had to do without anything, did we?" she said firmly, fixing the twins with a steely look. "All right then."

Martin glanced at his watch. "Valerie, may I borrow your car? There's a group going down to the Centurion, and I said I might be able to drive—"

Glad to change the subject, she smiled at him and fished for the keys in the pocket of her jeans. "Just don't stay out late, we've got to have everybody at work early tomorrow morning."

"Promise!" With a wave of his hand, he was gone.

Edward looked after him thoughtfully, but by a miracle of restraint said nothing.

Before she went to bed, Penelope retrieved her sketch pad, the half-filled one, and sat with it on her knees in the silence of her room. She sat for a long time without opening it, her hand resting on the cover, then finally, with a sigh she gave in. She fumbled rather unnecessarily in finding the right page, but there it was: the drawing of the stone. And there he was, the Briton crouched beneath the Roman's horse, the Briton with Ran Robson's face. She made herself stare at him until she felt calm enough to think about it.

There was a perfectly logical explanation for the likeness; she reasoned it out carefully. It had been after she had seen the stone in the Abbey that she and Lou had found Mark and Ran fighting. Somehow the two things, both of which impressed her, had gotten twisted together. When the moment had come, in her drawing, for her to complete the figure of the Briton, instead of remembering the blank space, her mind had given her an image of Mark's opponent and her hand had drawn it.

The drawing swam out of focus as she sat, lost in her thoughts, and beyond her window the evening filled with darkness. Sulpitium sat at the middle of a spider's web; connected to everything around it by threads that looked deceptively fragile. Since its creation it had been a place of violence —Valerie's discovery was positive proof. In his hand, the Briton held a broad-bladed knife . . .

Wintergap itself was built of stones from the Roman bathhouse, which had last served not as a bathhouse at all, but as a burial cairn. That thought laid a chill on the back of her neck. Could anything that happened so long ago matter to a place now? Could it have any effect on Wintergap? Stones were inanimate, not dead—they had never been alive. How could they possibly carry any of their past with them?

And what had any of this to do with her and with Randall Robson? The answer to that, she told herself firmly, was nothing. At least not so far as she was concerned. Valerie wanted no trouble for the excavation, and the Robsons were trouble, so they should be avoided. Unless she wanted to confess that she had actually met and spoken to Randall, Penelope realized that meant she could not tell anyone that she suspected him of disrupting work on the site with coachloads of tourists. She was unexpectedly relieved to have that responsibility lifted from her.

The next morning she settled down to serious work, certain she would not be interrupted as she had been the day before. Ran would not come back to watch from the other side of the burn. It was hot and peaceful on the terrace. Bees bumbled among the thyme, stashing pollen in the swollen yellow sacs on their legs. Lost in the blazing sky overhead, larks spouted fountains of song, and insects chanted from the dry grass. Lou pottered among the trees below, making herself a private lair. She had found a place screened by scrub and curtains of ivy where the rock slabs supporting the terrace sloped inward, making a shallow cave. Penelope could hear her singing softly as she cleared it out.

To begin her sketchbook, Penelope chose a mountain pansy,

which she had found growing in a sunny square of garden near the front of the house. It had a small yellow face, rather like that of a violet. The next time she went into Hexham, she decided she would buy a set of colored pencils; she hadn't used color before in her sketches—it would be a challenge to try with the flowers. She worked with her usual painstaking care, thoroughly absorbed. There was no need to hurry, she had all the summer holiday ahead.

Gradually she realized that something was missing; there was a small hole in the fabric of the morning, a thread had broken. Puzzled, she raised her head and looked around. Nothing seemed out of place; the hillside beyond the trees was empty, she was sure. Then she knew it was Louisa. The song had stopped, there was no sound from below the terrace. She wondered a little that she should be that aware of Lou and was about to call to her, but Lou called first. "Pennie! I've found something! I really have. Come and see."

"What sort of thing?"

"You have to come and see it!" Lou's voice was pulled tight with excitement.

With a sigh, Penelope laid aside her pad and pencil, went down the front steps, and around the edge of the terrace. "Where are you?"

"Here!" Lou was sitting back on her heels behind a clump of hawthorn, her lower lip caught between her teeth, her eyes shining. "See what I found? What do you think it is?"

Penelope scrambled in beside her and saw that Lou had uncovered one of the flat stones that had been used to build the retaining wall. She had pulled ropes of ivy away from it, scraped off great scabs of silver-green lichen and dry clumps of moss, exposing a rectangle about three and a half feet tall and two feet wide. Its surface had been hollowed out to form a rough niche, in the center of which someone had carved a crude human figure: stick-legs supported a shapeless body that was clothed in a tuniclike garment; the arms and shoulders were cut in a simple horseshoe, and the head was a sphere with circles for eyes.

Penelope studied it in silence for several minutes. "It must have come from the fort," she said at last. "I don't know what it's meant to be."

99

"*I* found it," said Lou, her voice a mixture of wonder and jubilation. "It's important—don't you think it's important?"

Penelope looked from the stone to Lou's eager face and nodded.

"I'm going to tell Mom!" She sprang to her feet. "Will you come with me? She'll pay more attention if there are two of us."

Penelope contemplated the stone. "It would be even better if you could show her the stone instead of trying to describe it."

"But we can't move it."

"No, but I could make a sketch of it and you could take that to Valerie," Penelope offered, feeling virtuously generous.

For a moment Lou considered, then she flashed Penelope that rare wide smile of hers and nodded. "And will you come, too?"

Resigned, Penelope agreed. She went to fetch her pad and pencil, wriggled back in beside the stone and set to work. One of the Whittons had brought the stone here, of course. A personal Roman trophy, set in the Wintergap garden, to be admired and gloated over at leisure. There might well be others like it built into the walls, masked by years of neglected foliage. She almost said so to Lou, but Lou was too full of the thrill of discovery. It would be mean to point out that she was only the *re*-discoverer; she'd realize it soon enough herself. But Penelope found it impossible to concentrate while Lou crouched impatient at her elbow. She wasn't used to being watched intently as she drew. Finally she said, "Why don't you go and make us some sandwiches to take?"

Lou looked at her doubtfully. "Why can't I stay here?"

"Because I'll finish much faster by myself, and if you make lunch we can go as soon as I've done."

"But you don't have to get it exact," the younger girl objected.

"As exact as I can," said Penelope firmly. "I have to do it my own way or I shan't do it at all."

Lou made a face, but disappeared, climbing up the wall like a mountaineer. "What kind?" she called from the top.

"Hmmm?"

100

"Sandwiches."

"Don't care." Penelope was already deep in the task she'd set herself. With Lou gone, the drawing began to progress more satisfactorily. She reached out and picked a little hump of moss off the side of the figure, then traced it caressingly with her hand, relishing the feel of rough-shaped stone. She seldom got to touch what she drew—the objects were usually protected from handling by glass or museum guards who were particularly suspicious of unaccompanied children. And yet most of the objects were made by hands, for other hands: to touch, grasp, pick up and hold. She had learned through her drawing that she could feel them with her eyes, but it wasn't the same.

CHAPTER VIII

AS SOON AS THEY CAME WITHIN SIGHT OF SULPITIUM, PENELOPE could see that something was wrong. The cars and van were parked in their usual spot, the tents clumped on the brown grass like a colony of oddly shaped mushrooms; but the excavation was deserted. Valerie's bathhouse lay like a wound on the hillside, the turf stripped from it, but it too was abandoned.

Penelope slowed and stopped, and Lou who was ahead, carrying the precious sketch in one of Edward's used manilla envelopes, turned back to her questioningly.

"Where is everyone?" Penelope asked.

"Probably having lunch."

"It's too early. Perhaps they're having a meeting. It might not be a good time to talk to your mother, Lou. We could wait until she gets back to Wintergap."

"Not after you did the drawing. I'm going to show her *now*."

Penelope shrugged. "All right, but don't blame me if she's too busy to pay attention."

They found everyone clustered in and around the farmhouse, talking among themselves in little knots of concern. Penelope searched until she found Martin, Jonathan, and two other students huddled together looking serious. "Let's find out what's going on," she said to Lou.

"Well, it's not drinkable, I can vouch for that," one of the students said with a grimace as Lou and Penelope joined them.

"But, Dick, we can't manage up here without water," said the other. "Particularly not in weather like this. What'll we do?"

"Perhaps the Youth Hostel will let us use theirs," suggested Martin.

But Jonathan shook his head. "It's their busiest season, this, and with water as short as it is they won't have any to spare, I can promise you. No one round here will." His normally cheerful face was somber.

"What's the matter?" asked Penelope. "What's wrong with the water?"

The four exchanged glances and Martin said briefly, "The well's gone bad."

"What do you mean 'bad'? Valerie said just last night that the well here was such a deep one it wasn't likely to go dry."

"It's not dry, Pennie, it's *unusable*. It's been poisoned."

The student called Dick looked up sharply as he said that. "You make it sound as if someone's responsible for it. I thought it was an accident."

"No one knows," said Jonathan. "Perhaps it was, perhaps it wasn't."

"There have been a great many accidents up here, if you ask me," said Martin.

"Will you explain?" demanded Penelope. "What happened?"

"Where's my mother?" said Lou loudly, tired of being ignored.

"In the house," Martin told her. "But I wouldn't interrupt her just now—she and Sir Kenneth are having a council of war."

"There's a very dead sheep in our well," Jonathan said in answer to Penelope's question. "It's ruined the water, at least temporarily."

"I had no idea," said Dick, "how thoroughly a dead animal could contaminate a well." He rolled his eyes expressively.

"Oh, yes," said Jonathan.

"How did it get there?"

"Not by itself, I'll wager," said Martin. "What d'you think, Andrew?"

The other student said, "Fair means or foul, it really doesn't matter. What *does* matter is how it'll affect the excavation."

"I'm going to find Mom," announced Lou. "She'll be even gladder to see what we've brought, Pennie."

"Unless you've brought a solution to the present crisis, I wouldn't guarantee it," cautioned Jonathan.

"Why don't you just haul the sheep out?" asked Penelope. "Wouldn't that solve the problem?"

"Eventually," said Dick. "It was falling to bits—the water needs time to clear."

"Well, there's good water at Wintergap. It isn't terribly convenient, I suppose, but—"

"Champion!" exclaimed Jonathan, giving Penelope a friendly thump. "First constructive suggestion I've heard. Good for you, Pennie!"

She smiled at him and said modestly, "It seems rather obvious."

"I don't care, I'm going," Lou repeated. With a last look around, she darted off.

Dick and Andrew drifted away to see if they could learn anything more, and Penelope, Martin, and Jonathan were left together.

"Do you really think someone did it on purpose?" Penelope asked her brother. "Who would?"

"There are people up here who wouldn't mind seeing us leave."

"But there's no proof one way or the other," put in Jonathan. "The wretched beast could have fallen in by accident— the well cover was skewed to one side when we found it."

"And how did it get that way?" argued Martin. "It's heavy and it fits tight. In order to drown in that well a sheep would have to be bent on suicide, Jonathan."

"Even if they didn't want us, the people up here wouldn't deliberately spoil our water to be quit of us," said Jonathan, equally stubborn. "I've grown up with them, don't forget."

"What about the Robsons, then? You yourself said Archie Robson would stop at little to get this land back."

At the name Robson, Penelope froze momentarily. For an agonizing second everyone around her vanished.

"—the little girl—" Jonathan said from a very long distance.

"Lou," supplied Martin.

"What was Lou going to show Mrs. Ibbetson?" Jonathan asked, successfully changing the subject.

With a shuddering jolt Penelope was back in time and place. "Oh," she managed, catching her breath. "Oh, just a drawing of something she found at Wintergap." The stone had lost its importance, for the time being anyway.

There was a stir among the students and the tiny groups merged into one large one as Valerie and Sir Kenneth appeared in the doorway of the farmhouse. Their faces were grave. An expectant silence fell.

Sir Kenneth broke it. "I'm sure you must all know by now what's happened. It presents us with a serious problem, especially coming as it does in the middle of one of Northumberland's worst droughts. We've lost our source of fresh water for the time being, which means we've either got to find an alternative or we'll have to close down the site, at least until the well clears."

There were mutterings of dismay.

"Where would we go?" someone asked.

"That's another real problem," Valerie said. "At this time of year we can't think of any place locally that would have room to put you all up, even if we had money enough to pay. And if you scatter we'll never be able to collect you again."

"We don't want to close down," said Sir Kenneth firmly. "If we do, there's every chance that the excavation here will never be resumed. Too many things have gone wrong. I tell you this quite frankly so that we understand one another. If we stop work now, virtually everything we've done to this point will be wasted, and as you know we've just begun to make discoveries—important ones. This is a rich site, I'm convinced it is, and the bathhouse is only a start."

Penelope noticed Lou standing close to her mother, looking like a small thunderhead. She still clutched the envelope to her chest and Penelope guessed she'd been unsuccessful in her attempt to get Valerie's attention. If only she'd been able

104

to wait, to choose her moment for its maximum effect. Penelope knew only too well the disappointment that was bound to come from trying to attract the attention of a parent deeply involved in something else. She felt a tug of sympathy.

Valerie was saying, "—no matter what, it'll be a tremendous inconvenience for everybody."

"Bloody awful," said one of the students near Penelope.

"If anyone," she went on, looking round the semicircle, "if anyone thinks it's too much of an inconvenience for any reason at all, then he or she may certainly choose to leave without questions being asked. Otherwise we've decided to try to stick it out. Suggestions are welcome."

Nods and head shakes and rumbles of discussion on all sides.

"There's good water at Wintergap," Martin spoke up. "Why can't we use that?" Penelope gave him a sharp little nudge and he added with a grin, "That's Pennie's idea."

Sir Kenneth nodded, with the merest suggestion of a wink in Penelope's direction. "And an excellent one. But we'll have to be particularly careful about how much we draw. We can't afford to have that well go dry. In the meantime I shall scout up some barrels that we can use to transport water to the site for cooking and drinking. I know a councillor in Hexham who might be of use."

"What about the local farms?" asked the girl called Frances. "Wouldn't one of them give us water?"

Sir Kenneth hesitated visibly and Valerie replied, "We've telephoned the closest two—got no answer at one and were told by the other that there was neither equipment nor water to spare."

"Which one?" Martin asked, eyes narrowed as if he'd guessed.

"Doesn't matter," she answered with finality. "Now that the sheep's been hauled out, we need volunteers with strong stomachs to bury it and to clean out the well. Then we'll need people to haul water once the arrangements are made."

"What if the well goes dry while you're cleaning it out?" Dick wanted to know.

But Sir Kenneth shook his head. "No 'what ifs'—we've got too many 'in facts' that need to be dealt with to waste energy. Let's have lunch, then go to work."

Obediently the group began to disperse, buzzing softly like a hive of bees.

"What do you think?" Valerie asked Sir Kenneth. "Will they stay?"

"Oh, I think so. If it doesn't drag on too long. It's a good, enthusiastic group."

"We came mighty close to disaster, you know. If the well had gone dry instead of being contaminated we couldn't possibly have considered staying, not with the country as dry as it is. I expect the farmers would have driven us out in no time."

Sir Kenneth gave her an ironic grin. "Now *you*'re 'what-if-ing'."

"Sorry!" She caught sight of her stepdaughter. "Pennie, how lucky you're here. If you and Lou stay for lunch, I'll send some students back with you for enough water to last us the afternoon. I'm afraid it's going to make life a bit hectic, but that can't be helped."

"I don't want to stay," said Lou rebelliously. "I'm thirsty."

"Ah," said Sir Kenneth. "Everyone will be. Jonathan?"

"Yo?" At the sound of his name, Jonathan turned away from the girl to whom he'd been talking.

"How would you like to take the van and some money and go down to the pub for bottles of beer and shandy? Enough for two all round, I should think."

"There, sweetie," said Valerie to Lou. "Just tell him what you want."

"Or better still," suggested Jonathan, "come and help me pick it out. Ever ride in a van?"

"Lots of times," said Lou, only slightly mollified.

Not in the least daunted, he beamed at her. "Yes, I should have known you were a person of vast experience. Come on, mate!" He thrust a hand toward her, and caught by surprise, she took it, her small one vanishing among his enormous fingers. Valerie gave him a ten pound note and a grateful smile.

"She has something she wants to show you," said Penelope

rather sternly as they watched the two walk down to the Sulpitium van.

"Oh, help, Pennie, I know it! She came in while I was on the phone to Dodd Moss Farm and I'm afraid I hurt her feelings, but I just didn't have time for her at that moment. When they come back, I'll ask to see it, I promise." She sounded contrite and harried, so Penelope let the subject drop. She had, in fact, surprised herself by bringing it up in the first place.

Valerie kept her word, and when Lou and Jonathan returned laden with bottles and packets of crisps, she asked to see the sketch. Lou made rather a show of reluctance, but finally handed it over and waited with ill-concealed eagerness while her mother examined it. Valerie's reaction was entirely satisfactory; she at once wanted to know where and how Lou had found the stone, what its dimensions were, and if it had any discernible inscription.

Penelope, unenthusiastically nibbling a peanut butter and strawberry jam sandwich—her own fault for not being specific when Lou asked "what kind"—was slightly miffed. No one mentioned the drawing itself, which she considered a pretty decent effort. Valerie was only interested in the stone and said she'd speak to Sir Kenneth about it as soon as they had a chance to discuss anything but the immediate crisis.

By the time lunch was over, Lou had lost her desire to leave. She preferred to stay at Sulpitium to hear more about her discovery.

Feeling irritable, Penelope left her to it and walked back to Wintergap accompanied by four students and Martin. They carried thermoses and canteens. Now that the worst of the crisis was past and a course of action decided upon, the students were in good spirits again, able to joke about the situation. There was talk of "sheep-dip" and the advantages of switching permanently from water to beer for drinking purposes.

"It would put everyone to sleep in the afternoons," said Andrew. "Cut productivity in half."

"At least if *no* one can wash," observed a girl cheerfully, "we'll all smell the same."

107

"And that might keep the tourist coaches away," another said. "We could call it the Sulpitium Stench."

The mention of tourist coaches was like an elbow in Penelope's stomach. She glanced at her brother who was being unusually silent. "Martin," she began hesitantly.

"Hmmm?"

She could tell he wasn't really listening, he'd reacted to his name instinctively. She wasn't committed to going any further but she couldn't help herself. "Why do you think the sheep wasn't an accident?"

That registered. He turned his head to look at her. "There have been altogether too many accidents at Sulpitium: sheep loose on the site, another in the well, tourists disrupting work. Someone wants us out."

"But Jonathan said even if the farmers didn't want archaeologists here they wouldn't deliberately cause harm. Even the Robsons—"

His attention was totally engaged now. "What do you know about the Robsons?"

Too late she realized she'd put her foot in it. Best defense was an attack—Martin himself had taught her that. "What do you?"

His eyes narrowed and for a moment he didn't answer. She tried to look innocently curious. "I've seen Archie Robson in Hexham, and I've heard enough about him to know Valerie's right," he said then. "You don't want to get mixed up with that family."

"Why would I?"

He shrugged. "Damned if I know, Pennie! You brought them up, I didn't. Jonathan's from Hexham, you know, and in spite of what he says he's let enough information drop to make it clear that the Robsons are generally viewed with suspicion. Of course, you won't get anyone up here to say so outright to a stranger—they're a close lot. They'll gossip and criticize among themselves, but just let an outsider join in and they'll shut up and close ranks so fast you won't know what's hit."

"But," Penelope pointed out, "this is the third year there have been archaeologists here. Why should the accidents start now?"

"They haven't."

"But Valerie said—"

"Look, Pennie," he said sounding grown up and irritatingly patient, "there's been a history of difficulties at Sulpitium—not just the big ones that closed operations down. Tools missing, cars tampered with, windows broken, livestock trampling the site. Last year instead of sheep it was a dirty great bull rampaging through the camp. Scared four or five students witless. *Now* do you begin to understand?"

"But why does it have to be the Robsons?" she asked stubbornly.

"Use your head! They've never wanted anyone else on this land. I'd guess the son, Archie, is more than a little bonkers from what I've heard, and no one's seen Mrs. Robson for years. No one seems to have any idea what happened between her husband and Anthony Whitton at the end. One night Robson disappeared and a farmer found him a day or two later, lying face down at the bottom of an abandoned mine shaft. Anthony Whitton simply fell to pieces and no one could get any sense out of him, so his family scooped him up and took him—oh blast!"

"What?"

"Dad's in."

The Volvo was parked outside Wintergap, but Edward wasn't immediately in evidence. Penelope was too full of this new information to grasp the implications of his being there at all.

"Coo-er!" exclaimed Dick. "Posh digs you've got, Ibbetson!"

Making rude, friendly remarks, they all trooped up the broad steps. The front door stood half-open, admitting a wedge of dusty sunlight into the dark hall. "The kitchen's down at the end," directed Penelope. "And there are two bathrooms upstairs—one's on the left, and the other's straight back on the right."

"Righto!" they said cheerfully and clumped into the house. "Odd sort of place, isn't it?" observed a girl as she passed Penelope. "Don't think I'd like to stay here."

Martin led the way to the kitchen, but Penelope lingered on the doorstep, thinking about the things Martin had said.

The trouble was that if he were right and the poisoning of the well had been no accident, she knew even better than he who'd done it. And if the incident were only one in a series of similar carefully staged, premeditated incidents, what would the next be? Suppose it were bad enough to stop the excavation permanently? And suppose she herself was in a position to avert it but didn't because she didn't want to get involved? She knew it was Ran Robson who directed tourist coaches to Sulpitium, and he could well have let the flock of sheep loose on the site. If she told Valerie—

A sudden loud crack! made her jump. It was the sound of a door being flung open so hard it swung back against the wall. "What in hell is going on here?" her father roared. "And who in blazes are *you*?"

Oh, help! She should have warned everyone to be quiet. Penelope swallowed hard and slipped round the front door into the blinding darkness.

"Penelope, who are these people? Where did they come from? What do they mean bursting into my house this way, like a bloody football mob? What are they doing in *my* kitchen?"

She didn't have to see his expression to know that he had been interrupted at the worst possible time: in the middle of rewriting his proofs, when he was tailoring phrases and words to the exact requirements of his story, making the fit as precise as he was capable of. It was at this stage in the process that Martin and Penelope had learned to make themselves invisible and noiseless—Penelope out of respect, Martin out of grudging self-preservation. "It's our house, too, you know!" he'd grumble.

"They're students from Sulpitium, Dad," she said bravely. "Valerie sent them with us to get water." Now that her eyes were accustomed to the gloom she could see her father standing in the study doorway. There ought to have been lightning playing round his head. Dick was poised halfway up the stairs, an expression of alarm on his face; two of the others were squashed in the mouth of the kitchen. "I'm sorry we interrupted you."

"Water?" Edward looked from one to another, his face ominously rigid. Although he wasn't a tall man, he always seemed enormous to Penelope when he was in a temper. "*Water?*"

"Yes," said Martin, pushing through the kitchen door. "Water. The well at Sulpitium's gone bad, so we had to come here for enough water to get us through the afternoon."

"Bad? What d'you mean bad?" Edward asked crossly; at least he was no longer shouting.

"It's been poisoned," said Martin brusquely. "Now, if you don't mind, we'll finish filling our jugs so we can get back to work. They're waiting for us."

"And what about my work?" Edward inquired, his voice dangerously even.

"We'll leave you to get on with it," replied Martin coolly. Penelope tensed herself for the explosion.

"Oh you will, will you? Now that you've destroyed my concentration, totally disrupted coherent thought and made it impossible for me to recapture the mood of what I was doing. Thank you very much!"

"Dad," said Penelope, "it's an emergency. We're sorry if—"

"Don't apologize!" Martin cut in. "We have as much right here as he has. We had no way of knowing he'd be working."

Penelope glared at him down the length of the hall. "We didn't have to make so much noise."

"You're damn right you didn't!" exclaimed Edward. "Barging in here like that. What the hell are you standing about for? Get your bloody water and get out, why don't you!"

The students in the doorway uncorked themselves and disappeared. Dick went up the stairs, two at a time. There was no more joking, no more conversation, only the muffled sound of water running through pipes. Edward stood in the hall with his arms folded, looking for all the world like Louisa when Valerie ignored her.

"You could at least have given me some warning," he complained.

"How?" challenged Martin. "Wintergap isn't on the phone, and no one knew this was going to happen ahead of time."

"Bloody inconsiderate, I call it. Might know *you'd* be involved."

"It was Valerie who sent us," said Penelope. "And after

111

all, this house does belong to the University, so the students have a right here."

"What's got into you?" her father demanded irritably, glowering at her. "You sound like your brother!"

She faced him back, feeling miserable and helpless. She hated being caught between them, yet here she was, cross with them both: her father for being unreasonable, Martin for deliberately making no attempt to handle him with any tact. They were *both* at fault.

Martin took the subdued little party back to Sulpitium without further argument. Edward had withdrawn into the library again by that time, and the door was tight shut.

Penelope spent the remainder of the afternoon moving restlessly from place to place around the house, trying to shift away from her own thoughts and to convince herself that she hadn't any responsibility for any of this. She wished she'd never caught Ran spying on her, never met him face to face on Dodd Pike and talked to him, patted Frit. If only she hadn't guessed right about the coaches.

She thought of Ran's father lying dead at the bottom of an overgrown mine shaft and in spite of the heat felt clammy with cold. It wasn't enough to go to Valerie with a suspicion, that much she decided. Unless she knew for certain that Ran had put the sheep down the well, she could say nothing. But where did that leave her?

The crises of the day were not yet over. It was late again when Valerie returned to Wintergap, wound tight over the business of the well, her patience all but used up. She brought Lou and the twins with her, all three out of sorts because they'd been snapped at for one reason or another. Of Martin there was no sign. Penelope guessed he'd chosen to stay at Sulpitium rather than come back to face Edward. She found herself wishing *she* had somewhere else to take refuge and resenting her brother because he had.

Reluctantly she put aside the letter she'd been trying unsuccessfully to write to Grannie Lawrence and went into the house to give herself up to good works. She supposed she could set the table, even though it ought by right to be the twins' turn. The study door was still shut, and she could hear no sound from the other side as she passed it. Her father was evidently so deep in what he was doing he either hadn't heard, or chose to ignore, his wife's arrival.

Valerie was standing in the middle of the kitchen, tight-lipped and flint-eyed. The groceries Edward had bought that morning were heaped on the table, the iron skillet full of cold water and strings of breakfast egg was still in the sink, and the long counter under the windows was strewn with breadcrumbs, blobs of strawberry jam, and two knives smeared with peanut butter left over from Lou's lunch preparations, which Penelope had never thought to investigate. Of course not a thing had been done about supper, a menu hadn't even been contemplated. Valerie glanced at her as Penelope came in, and Penelope's heart sank.

Ominously silent, Valerie washed her hands and set to work, moving about the kitchen with a kind of violent efficiency that alarmed Penelope far more than ranting and raving would have. The twins and Lou had made themselves scarce. Penelope struggled to defend herself from the sharp insistent barbs of conscience that jabbed her. So what if she'd spent the past few hours sunk in fruitless meditation on the terrace while Valerie labored at the excavation. All these people weren't her responsibility—she was only a fourteen-year-old schoolgirl, for heaven's sake! Why should she feel guilty for not having made supper for six, especially when four of them weren't her blood family? But that argument made her feel worse than ever because she'd begun to see that distinction for what it really was: mean, small-minded, and unimportant. One meal did not commit her to an endless future of drudgery. While these thoughts warred in her head, Penelope stacked canned goods in the pantry, set the table, and side-stepped desperately to stay out of Valerie's way.

When Edward finally appeared, the look Valerie gave him was not one of affection. Edward didn't seem to notice; he kissed her lightly on the cheek. "Had a traumatic day I hear, love. Didn't you want a bath before supper?"

"As a matter of fact, I did," she replied with deadly calm. "But there didn't seem to be any supper to have one before, if you follow my drift."

Edward blinked and achieved an expression of innocent

113

question. Penelope wanted to kick him.

"Oh, don't play games, Ted! I've had a hell of a day, and I came back here—late—expecting to be able at last to relax, wash up, have a drink and some food, and what do I find? Nothing. *Worse* than nothing! You couldn't even put the groceries away. No supper started, no supper even *planned*—"

"Look, Val—"

"Ted, *you* look. We discussed this over and over last spring. Don't you remember? I told you I had accepted this job, I told you what that involved, I told you we could wait and get married afterwards if you'd rather. And you said— you *said*"—she levelled a kitchen fork at him—"no, that was fine. You'd be free to keep an eye on the kids and the house while I worked. You *offered*. You even bragged about your cooking, for God's sake!"

The twins braked to an abrupt halt in the kitchen doorway and exchanged uneasy glances. Lou's face was shut tight, lest any of her feelings escape and make her vulnerable.

Edward looked round the room, acknowledging the four children as if for the first time, then faced his wife. "All right," he said in a carefully controlled voice, "I apologize for allowing time to get away from me. I didn't realize it was so late. That often happens when I'm working." He bore down slightly on the word "working." "I had no idea, Valerie, when we made our arrangements, that they would necessarily exclude my being able to write at all. If *All Fall Down* is to be finished on time, I have got to do the revisions now." He paused and suddenly shifted ground; he went from defense to attack. "As a matter of fact, I lost track of the time because your students came blundering in here unannounced and completely disrupted my train of thought. It's taken me all afternoon to pick it up again."

"*My—?*"

"That's what they said. Mrs. Ibbetson sent them here for water. They burst in shouting and laughing—"

"They didn't know you were here," said Penelope.

He ignored her. "If Martin hadn't been with them I'd have had no idea at all who they were," continued Edward. "They could have been vandals, trespassers, hikers, *any*body!"

Valerie's cheeks were very pink. "Don't forget whose

114

house this is, Ted. Those students have every right to use it. And as for interrupting you—it could have been any of us who did that—the twins or me, for that matter. None of us knew you were planning to work here today."

"Mom?" said Luke tentatively. "Can we have supper?"

Valerie and Edward stared at each other in silence for a long moment, then Valerie said, "Such as it is, yes."

Whether by accident or design, the supper Valerie served consisted almost entirely of the kinds of food Penelope knew her father deplored: tinned spaghetti in vivid orange sauce, hard rolls and butter, and coleslaw made with cabbage, apple, and raisins. One glance at her stepmother's set face confirmed Penelope's worst suspicions. She felt completely out of her depth and rather frightened.

As she passed the plates around, Valerie kept her eyes on Edward, as if daring him to object and waiting to tell him that if he didn't like what she had fixed he knew what he could do about it.

But Edward said nothing. He tore his roll into small fragments and ate it slowly, ate several forkfuls of coleslaw, then picked the raisins out and passed them to Lou, who accepted them with a swift glance at her mother. He tested the spaghetti thoughtfully and asked, "What brand is this, Val? It isn't very nice—we ought to try something else next time."

There was an obstruction part way down Penelope's throat; she couldn't seem to swallow past it.

Valerie replied coolly, "It's what the twins like."

"Then I shall buy it only for the twins in future," replied Edward, equally cool.

"When I heat it, I shall only *give* it to the twins."

Penelope wanted to bang on the table and demand to know why they were arguing about tinned spaghetti when that wasn't the real issue. She was sure it wasn't. But she said nothing, she sat still and inconspicuous, and pushed the food around on her plate.

After dessert, which was instant caramel-flavored pudding— another of the twins' favorites judging by the way they fell on it—Penelope took a deep breath and said, "I'll do the washing up."

"Oh, no, Pennie," said Valerie, still watching Edward,

"I've fallen so completely into the routine this evening I might just as well finish."

Edward pushed back his untouched bowl of pudding and remarked, "I haven't had a meal like that one in ever so long."

Mark applied himself to scraping the last trace of pudding from his bowl. Luke tried to balance his spoon crossways on his water glass. Lou, her face inscrutable, made rings on the tabletop with her wet mug. Penelope ddn't know whether she ought to sit tight or get up and begin to take dishes to the sink. Valerie couldn't have meant what she'd said, but why had she said it? And why did her father keep needling Valerie? He and Martin were really very much alike in some ways, she had to agree with Grannie Lawrence, though Martin would hate her for saying so. What ought she to do? She was startled by a sudden gulping snort from her stepmother; Valerie's face was convulsed with violent emotion. Penelope's heart caught, then she realized that Valerie was choking on, of all things, *laughter*. Not fury, not tears, but laughter. She turned to her father and saw his mouth twitch, then loosen, and he too was laughing. They dissolved together over the remains of supper, while their children looked on with puzzled, uncertain faces.

"Pax!" declared Edward at last.

"Temporary truce," amended Valerie, wiping her eyes with a napkin. "Before we declare *peace* we've got some negotiating to do, Ted. I'm too old to face this kind of thing after a long day in a hot trench."

"Are you all right, Mom?" asked Lou with a suspicious glance at Edward.

"Yes, sweetie. Perfectly," her mother assured her. "Pennie, I will take you up on your offer, and you three"—she nodded at the twins and Lou—"can jolly well pitch in."

"But Luke and I've—" began Mark.

Luke made a face at him and he let the remainder of his objection hiss away between his teeth. "Oh, all *right*."

"And you," said Valerie to Edward, "can take me out and buy me a huge expensive gin and bitter lemon."

"Now there's the sensible woman I married," said Edward. "But what about all our little responsibilities, hmm?"

"Which?"

"I think he means us," said Penelope dryly.

"We can take care of ourselves," declared Mark. "We're not so little."

Edward said, "Beg pardon!"

"We won't be late," said Valerie, "and Martin should be in before very long."

"I wouldn't count on it," Edward said.

"Did you fight with him, too? No, don't answer that—I'd rather not know until I feel mellower. Honestly, Ted . . ." Valerie's words faded as the two adults left the kitchen. Curiously enough, Edward seemed in a much better humor than he had before the argument.

CHAPTER IX

BY THE TIME THE FOUR OF THEM HAD FINISHED CLEANING UP, Penelope was not at all convinced that Valerie had done her a favor by ordering the twins and Lou to help. The first thing Mark and Luke did was to divide Edward's uneaten pudding, then scrape the basin spotless.

Their dishwashing was extremely haphazard, and Penelope had to keep a sharp eye on what was being passed off as clean and dry, and where it was being put away. Luke added so much soap to the washing-up pan he was over his elbows in suds and kept blowing them at Mark, who retaliated by snapping him with a tea towel. They were in an abnormally silly mood and kept up a running patter of dreadful jokes—Luke as straight man for Mark, and both of them growing more and more hysterical.

"Ask me if my name's Sam," commanded Mark.

"Is your name Sam?" Luke obliged.

"No!" Mark yelped and collapsed over the drainboard. Luke howled.

"That," declared Penelope, regarding them with disbelief, "has got to be the dumbest joke I've ever heard!"

"Stick around," advised Lou, then added patronizingly, "They usually get like this when they're overtired. Brian taught them most of the jokes."

117

"Except," complained Mark, gasping, "Mom won't let us tell his best ones."

"What's the difference between a duck?" asked Luke.

"Easy!" crowed his twin. "It has one foot the same!" And they were off again.

As her contribution, Lou piled all the dirty dishes by the sink for Luke to wash—she only broke one glass—and sorted the clean cutlery once Mark had swiped at it with his towel. As she swept fragments of tumbler up from between the flagstones, Penelope asked herself whether compelling the three younger children to help was really worth the extra time and effort it cost to supervise them.

"Hey, Pennie," called Mark, and she glanced up. "Why did the owl fall out of the tree?" He was sitting on the edge of the counter, dangling his legs and grinning engagingly.

She hesitated a second or two while they all waited expectantly, then said obediently, "I don't know. Why?"

"Because it was dead."

It was terrible, not in the least funny, but her face relaxed uncontrollably into a smile; Mark slapped his knee in fiendish delight, Luke blew a handful of suds at him, and Lou giggled.

When at last the kitchen could pass as reasonably tidy, all four of them adjourned to the drawing room. In defiance of the darkness beyond the windows, Lou turned on all the lights. Luke produced two battered decks of cards, shuffled them with the skill of a cardsharp, and dealt out four hands. Without the awkwardness of having to ask or of being specifically invited, Penelope found herself included. She was immediately absorbed by the intricacies of a complicated game called Tournament Eights. For the first half hour or so it required all her concentration to master the rules.

Mark played cutthroat, fiercely, determined to win. Luke gave him no competition, which surprised Penelope until she caught on to the fact that he was playing a far more difficult game: he played to lose. Even Lou, her face keen with excitement, was beating Luke soundly. He gave Penelope a bland smile, when he caught her watching him, and deliberately played a two, causing his brother to pick up extra cards. "Fink!" said Mark, and Luke gave an apologetic shrug.

With the next hand, Penelope altered her own game. She

saw no reason why Luke should be allowed to lose unopposed; she'd give him a real run for last place. When the final scores were tallied, however, her lack of experience forced her to accept third.

"You'll do better next time," said Lou consolingly.

The evening slid by unobtrusively as they played; it was going on ten, and Lou was heavy-eyed with sleep. Even the twins had grown subdued, but no one made a move toward bed. At length Lou curled herself up on the horsehair sofa, like a small animal. The other three switched to Go Fish, a game that required minimal thought.

"Wonder how late they'll be," said Luke.

"Late," Mark said positively.

"Valerie said they wouldn't be."

Mark gave Penelope a pitying look. "What she said doesn't mean as much as how she said it."

Plucking up her courage, Penelope asked, "Did your parents used to fight a lot—I mean before—" She stopped, embarrassed.

"Not like that," replied Mark.

"Oh."

"It was much worse," Luke said. He glanced at his brother almost guiltily. Again Penelope sensed the wordless communication between them. And she knew that whatever had made that time much worse, they would neither one of them say more about it, and she would not ask.

"You aren't used to that kind of thing, are you?" said Mark like a kindly older brother.

She shook her head.

"Well, don't worry. Everyone fights sometimes—even Luke and I do."

"Thanks," she said wryly. "I'll remember that."

Martin came in shortly after eleven, unfocused and muzzy, and in no shape to take command of anything. It was obvious where and how he had spent the evening; even from a distance of several feet Penelope could smell the warm, thick aroma of beer on his breath.

"I hope you didn't drive back that way," she said disapprovingly.

119

"How else would I've get—'ve got here?"

"If you'd been stopped—"

"Wasn't." He grinned wickedly at her. " 'm going to bed."

"Jolly good idea!"

He must have fallen across his bed fully clothed and gone out like a light; she heard him stagger upstairs and along the hall to his room, then there was absolute silence. To the best of her knowledge, Martin had not come home before really tight. She thought it ought to shock her, but it didn't. It only made her sad; he was almost an adult, and she was growing up too and they were both leaving behind the world in which people were expected to take care of them. They had to learn to accept responsibility for themselves, but even more important, and perhaps first, to acknowledge responsibility for the people they loved. Mark and Luke were learning; they would not discuss their mother and father. She recognized and was grateful for their generosity in saying as much as they had.

And for that reason she pulled herself together, went into the drawing room, and said, "I think we'd better all go upstairs before our parents get back."

"Why?" challenged Mark as a matter of course.

"How're you going to get her upstairs?" Luke nodded at Lou who was sound asleep in a tight little ball.

"Wake her, I suppose," said Penelope doubtfully.

"It's your funeral," Mark said, "but *I* wouldn't. She hates being woken up."

At that point Valerie and Edward arrived, tired but happy, differences settled, at least for the time being. When she found her children not yet in bed, Valerie made a half-hearted attempt to be severe.

"What happened to Martin?" asked Edward as he picked Lou up off the sofa. "Why didn't he chase you out?"

"He was exhausted," said Penelope charitably. Luke gave her a disconcerting wink.

When she woke, the dilemma Penelope had postponed facing the day before was waiting for her. Her room was full of the brilliance of reflected sunlight and the premature heat of another blazing day. She guessed it was early; the house

120

was quiet, though it did not feel peaceful. Somehow she doubted that Wintergap had ever achieved the kind of equilibrium one associated with peace.

As soon as she opened her eyes, she was fully awake. There would be no drowsy period of grace between consciousness and subconsciousness this particular morning, so she got up and washed, dressed, then went out to the terrace with her sketch pad. The light lay thick as honey across the moors, the sun was well up the cloudless sky. From the valley below the house a wood pigeon cooed montonously; invisible insects twanged on all sides. She returned to her little yellow-faced pansy—the sketch Lou had interrupted the day before.

By the time she was finished and aware of being hungry, other people had begun to stir. Everyone except her father and Martin was milling around the kitchen.

"Hullo," said Valerie. "I thought you were still in bed." There were smudges under her eyes, but she was brisk and cheerful. "I had been thinking I might take the day off and loaf for a change."

"Well, why can't you?" said Lou. "You said we could have an expedition."

"That was before the crisis yesterday, sweetie. I've really got to spend the day at Sulpitium, I'm afraid. Here, Pennie."

Penelope accepted a mug of tea and sat down at the table, where Mark and Luke were deep in a private discussion with the O.S. map spread between them. From the fragments she overheard, Penelope concluded that they were planning an all-day hike along the Wall toward Housesteads. "We can at least get as far as the Cawfields milecastle," said Luke.

"Aw, that's *nothing*," exclaimed Mark with scorn. "We can do much better than that."

"I'm afraid there'll be students coming for water off and on all day," said Valerie.

"I hope they're quiet," Penelope said with feeling.

"I'll warn them," her stepmother promised. "At least Ted knows about them today. By the way, what happened to Martin last night? I looked in on him but he's totally unconscious this morning."

"Zonked," said Mark.

"I expect he's just very tired," replied Penelope evasively.

121

Valerie looked skeptical, but only said that she wouldn't wait for him; he could follow her to the site when he was ready. "And you," she said to the twins, "I don't know what you're planning for the day, and I think on the whole I'd rather not. But I want you back here no later than four o'clock. I'm not in the mood for argument, Mark. Four o'clock sharp, understand? Check the time when you leave and you'll know when to start back."

"I don't think that's long enough," said Luke when she'd gone.

"Course it is," declared his brother. "You can walk a mile in twenty minutes—that's three miles an hour—right? So it ought to take us three hours. It can't be more than nine miles from here."

"That's only if you walk at a constant speed and don't stop for anything," Luke pointed out. "I'm not sure we can do three miles an hour, Mark. It's up and down a lot."

"Well, as long as we sit here we're not going to get anywhere, that's for sure. Come on."

They packed their orange rucksacks full of food and set off, still arguing amiably about walking speed and distance.

Penelope bided her time, relieved that the twins would be out of the way. Lou went out to play by herself, and the morning dawdled by. Jonathan and two other students appeared with jugs and pails while Edward was having his breakfast in the kitchen, and he greeted them quite civilly. The fact that he'd been left in bed until half-past nine doubtless contibuted to his good temper.

Martin didn't emerge from his bedroom until after ten, and then seemed to spend an inordinate amount of time running water in the bathroom. When at last he came downstairs, he looked unusually solemn and a little pale around the edges. All he had for breakfast was toast and tea with nothing in it. On his way to Sulpitium, he paused to speak to Penelope in the front hall. "What about last night?" he asked in a low voice.

"What do you mean?" She was preoccupied, working out her own plans for the day.

"I mean what happened? What did they say?"

"It was a rather silly argument really—"

"I mean about *me*, you nit!" he whispered furiously.

"You?" She looked at him in astonishment. "They didn't say anything about you, except Valerie asked Dad if he'd had a fight with you." The light broke. "You mean *after*wards. Dad asked where you were when they got in."

"And what did you tell him?"

"I told him you'd gone to bed. You had."

"What did Valerie say this morning?"

She shook her head. "Nothing. I expect she thinks you were very tired last night."

He took a deep breath and straightened up. "And so," he said in a normal voice, "I was."

She watched him go off down the track with a mixture of irritation and affection. He couldn't really have believed she'd give him away, could he?

Edward closed himself into the library shortly after he finished his morning tea, which left Penelope only Lou to deal with. But that, she realized, was liable to be difficult. She couldn't simply disappear, as she had the other day. Then she had done it without thinking of Lou at all; she had forgotten everything in her pursuit of the spy. This time her conscience wouldn't let her.

Patience, she counseled herself, she must have patience, and she settled outside the back door of the house with her sketch pad to draw the white trumpet flower of the bindweed that crept over the low wall of a long-abandoned kitchen garden. Eventually Lou came and found her there, as she had hoped. The silence stretched tight while Lou watched Penelope work. It took considerable self-control on Penelope's part to keep sketching, and she was painfully aware of how badly she was doing—the lines were ugly and self-conscious, the effect all wrong. But she struggled on.

Finally Lou got tired of waiting to be noticed. "Are you going to do that all day?" she asked.

Penelope didn't answer immediately. She judged her moment, then looked up, deliberately vague. "Hmm? Oh, probably. Why?"

"I thought maybe we could do something else."

"But I want to draw."

123

"Oh." Lou was silent for a moment and Penelope bent again over her pad. "But what about when you're finished with that?"

"I thought I'd go looking for another flower up by the Wall." Penelope, trying to sound casual, kept her head down. "I saw some betony and I want to try that next."

"Everybody's busy except me," Lou complained, kicking at the wall with her sneaker. There was a hole coming in the toe.

"Can't you find something to be busy with, too?"

"By myself?"

"Why not? You found the stone yesterday by yourself. Maybe you could discover something else."

"I don't want to be left here alone."

"You won't be. Dad's in the house," Penelope pointed out, feeling traitorous. Strictly speaking, she knew that if her father was immersed in his writing, he might just as well not be there, and she wouldn't much like to be left at Wintergap on her own either.

Lou sighed gustily and Penelope went on drawing, putting extra leaves on the bindweed, adding nonexistent details to the blossom. Eventually Lou picked herself up off the warm flags and wandered discontentedly away. Penelope took some comfort from the fact that she'd disentangled herself from Lou openly, but not, she couldn't help feeling, with much honor.

Still, there was no way she could take Lou with her; she had no idea what she was getting herself into and didn't want witnesses. Just to be safe, she gave herself another half hour, but Lou didn't come back, so she put her pencils in her pocket, the pad under her arm, and climbed the path to the Wall.

But instead of stopping to look for betony, she stowed her pad in a convenient crack and continued across the Wall, feeling again as she did so that she was entering hostile territory. She paused and carefully surveyed the surrounding country; there was no sign of movement at Wintergap. Its slate roof shone among the trees. To the east she glimpsed a knot of people toiling along the Pennine Way, but they were far off and the twins were nowhere in sight. There was no one to observe her; she was on her own.

Once above the Wall she was committed, even though she realized mournfully that it was past midday and she'd come away without any lunch. At least this time there was no need to run, no one to keep in view, and she could watch her step. It seemed much further to Dodd Pike than she remembered.

Alone in the vast sweep of bracken and grass, she felt self-conscious, open to attack—but by whom she had no idea. She almost wished she had brought Lou along for company.

She had no intention of returning alone to the ancient settlement on the shoulder of the Pike. She couldn't rid herself of the notion, irrational as it might be, that she had been tolerated there before because she had been with Ran Robson and he belonged. Quite apart from that, she would gain nothing by going there now. She had something specific in mind.

So she walked instead around the Pike, holding her back very straight, trying to appear more confident than she felt. There was Dodd Moss Farm, stuck to the fell like a burr caught on a worn tweed coat. The sun poured down on it relentlessly, drowning it in heat and glare; the few trees only served to emphasize its nakedness and were too sparse to offer any real shelter. Even from a distance Penelope was disheartened by the farm's inhospitable appearance, and the closer she got, the less anxious she was to carry out her plan.

It had seemed sensible and honorable to her that morning: to go to Ran Robson and confront him directly with her suspicions and those she'd heard voiced at Sulpitium. To give him a chance to deny them before she said anything to Valerie. If he satisfied her that he and his family had had nothing to do with poisoning the Sulpitium well, she could forget the whole business with a clear conscience. If not—that was a problem she would meet when it faced her; she would not go rushing toward it.

She decided, under the circumstances, the best thing was to approach Dodd Moss straightforwardly, to walk right up to it boldly as if it had never occurred to her that its inhabitants might not welcome her. On the far side of the Pike she found the track that led to it. She plodded along in the

125

heat and the dust, considering what she would say when she arrived. And there was the question she tried to avoid of who would be at the farm? She was *not* anxious to confront Archie Robson, nor did she particularly want to meet his mother, a woman whom no one had seen for years. But suppose Ran himself wasn't there? She narrowed her eyes thoughtfully; in that case she would go away again without telling anyone what she'd come for. It was only Ran she'd talk to, that she decided. She would convince Archie or Mrs. Robson that she was a friend of his who happened to stop by. But even as she worked that out, she sensed the folly of it; it seemed unlikely that "friends" ever "stopped by" at Dodd Moss Farm. And there was the added hazard that Archie would remember her for her part in the fight between Mark and Ran in Hexham.

So absorbed was she in all this and in the effort it took to keep going that Penelope failed to notice the small figure following her until it sneezed. Then she spun round to find Lou some fifty feet behind her, frozen in her tracks and looking apprehensive.

"What are *you* doing here?" Penelope demanded.

The apprehension turned to obstinacy. "Exploring."

"You are not—you're following me."

"You happened to be going the way I wanted to explore."

"What a coincidence. Well, you can just find another direction—this one's taken."

"You said you were only going up to the Wall to draw flowers," Lou reminded her.

"I changed my mind, didn't I?"

"Who lives there?" Lou pointed ahead.

Penelope shrugged, watching Lou intently.

"You do too know, I bet you do. Anyhow, you can't stop me from walking along this road."

"If I'd wanted you to come, I would have asked you," said Penelope bluntly.

Lou looked stubbornly at the ground.

"You'd better go back to Wintergap."

"I don't want to."

Penelope sighed. What next? Underneath her righteous indignation at Lou's intrusion was a sneaky relief at not being

126

alone. It was easier to be brave when you were with someone who expected you to be. She turned away from Lou and started to walk again, waiting, listening for the slightest sound that would mean the younger girl was following. The track that had looked flat from Dodd Pike had a discouraging number of dips and rises in it, so that the farm appeared and disappeared as she walked toward it, but seemed to get no closer. Then she breasted a little hill and there it lay, just ahead: a clump of dour grey buildings penned behind a high stone wall. Across the track hung a crooked iron gate, its bars rusted. A sign—two boards nailed together and wired to it—proclaimed in faded letters: Dodd Moss Farm—PRIVATE—Close Gate.

Penelope stopped in front of the gate to muster her resolve, and Lou came up behind her. "Are you really going in there?" she asked in a voice scarcely above a whisper.

Penelope nodded. "That's why I came."

"But isn't it the farm Mom warned Mark and Luke to stay away from? Isn't that where the Robsons live?"

"Seeing as you've come this far you'd better stick with me," Penelope told her.

"But—"

"You oughtn't to have followed me." With that she unlatched the gate, fumbling a little with the bent wire hook that secured it. The hinges screeched, and she hastily caught at the bars before it swung wide. Lou hesitated, then slipped through after Penelope, who replaced the hook with particular care. From somewhere behind the house came a single short, sharp bark. Just one.

Penelope had the same sensation entering Dodd Moss Farm that she had experienced entering the camp circle on Dodd Pike; it prickled at the back of her neck and across her shoulders. The wall surrounding the farm was not there to imprison it, but to protect it, like the defensive rampart at the camp.

The only sign of life anywhere was a scraggle of hens lurching around the yard, looking heat dazed. Nowhere in the enclosure as far as Penelope could see were there any green growing things: no grass, no flowers to soften the hard angles or add a touch of color. The meager evergreens around

127

the house looked limp and discouraged, their roots like the veins in an old man's hands sticking up through the bare, hard-packed earth. Everything was shades of muddy grey and brown.

The farm was neat enough. There were no bits of rusting equipment lying about, no old tires or barrels and oil cans, no heaps of dirty straw and manure. The house and out-buildings were in good repair, wood trim and roofs sound. There was nothing obvious about the place to justify its over-whelming air of bleakness, its desolation. But the very thought of living here—of calling it home—filled Penelope with an un-focused despair. Lou must have felt it, too. She kept as close to Penelope as she could without actually touching her.

"I don't think anyone's here," she whispered hopefully.

"Well, we won't know till we've knocked," said Penelope and marched up to the front door of the house. There was a brass knocker on it that hadn't seen polish in a very long time. Penelope lifted it and rapped, then stepped back a pace and waited. Nothing happened.

"See?" Lou looked distinctly relieved.

Penelope banged the knocker again, harder. There were no sounds behind the door, but a thin voice somewhere inside suddenly called out. It seemed to come from a distance, per-haps upstairs—Penelope couldn't distinguish words, only a thread of sound. She glanced at Lou; Lou's eyes were round, her eyebrows had disappeared under her fringe.

But the door remained shut. Whoever was in the house evidently had no intention of answering the knock. Penelope wondered uneasily if they were being observed from one of the upstairs windows by someone who wanted them to go away. Then why the voice? Why not keep still and pretend there was no one home? Short of opening the door herself, Penelope could see nothing to do. At least she'd tried.

"All right," she said to Lou," "let's go."

"But who did you come to see?" asked the younger girl as they turned away from the house.

"It doesn't matter. I just—" She was interrupted by a loud erratic jangling—the sound of a handbell being rung.

The hens scattered awkwardly in front of Randall as he

strode around the house. He stopped short when he saw and recognized Penelope. The water in the bucket he carried slopped over the rim and made dark stains in the dust. Lou gave a little yelp of surprise and fright.

"What're ye doin' here?"

"I came to find you." The words sounded startlingly loud in Penelope's own ears.

"Why?"

"To ask you something."

He continued to stand, staring at her. If she had entertained even the slightest notion that he might be pleased to see her, that notion vanished. The bell jangled again, shattering the silence between them. Ran shook himself as a wet dog might. "Come here," he commanded, setting down his bucket. "Come on whey—Aa'll nae harm ye."

Warily Penelope did as he said, reaching to pull Lou along with her close to the house. "Why?"

"Se she'll nae see ye," he said tersely and went to the front door. He pulled it open and stepped inside. " 'Tis all right, Mam. Nowt but hikers off the Way."

Penelope heard the indistinct voice again, and Ran answered, "Aye, Mam. 'Tis all right, Aa'll do thon." He re-emerged and shut the door gently.

"Look here—" began Penelope, but he gave his head an emphatic shake. Motioning them to follow, he led the way back to the cobbled courtyard between the farmhouse and the barn, then turned to face Penelope. "Whisht—divvent talk se loud. She mun think ye've gone."

"But who—?" She knew, of course, before he answered, but she couldn't believe it.

"Ma mam. 'Tis her nap an' ye've woke her."

"I'm sorry, I didn't mean—" Why had he lied to his mother about them, she wondered.

He cut across her apology. "Why've ye come here?"

"Oh, look!" cried Lou. She had spotted the black-and-white dog, Frit, tied with a length of rope to an iron ring set into the barn wall. Frit was sitting high on her haunches at the very end of her tether, every muscle taut, ears stiff. The smallest thread of a whine escaped her, and she looked in-

129

stantly abashed as Ran's eyes flicked her direction. He chopped the air with his hand and she dropped to the ground as if she'd been clubbed.

"What made her do that?" demanded Lou who hadn't taken her eyes from the dog.

"Aa did."

Lou made a move toward the flattened animal and Frit's tail began to sweep the bare earth like a windshield wiper. Lou glanced at Ran doubtfully. "Can I pat him? He wants to make friends." For the moment at least the dog made everything else unimportant to her.

"Aye, ye can pat her. Thon's a bitch, nae a dog." Ran watched while Lou crouched down to Frit and began to fondle the black ears. With a small gesture of his hand he released the dog and she sprang to her feet, snuffling Lou's delighted face. Ran's eyes came back to Penelope. He waited for her to speak.

This was what she had come for, she reminded herself. To talk to him face to face, so that she could ask the question and judge his answer, then decide what she had to do. But accomplishing that in theory was a long way from accomplishing it in fact. Ran's physical presence made it much harder. It wasn't so much that she was afraid of him, she discovered, more that she was afraid of his answer. She felt awkward and she didn't like feeling awkward. Although she'd come to Dodd Moss openly, through the front gate, knocked on the front door, she was trespassing again—the message came through loud and clear. While this went around in her head, she groped for the right words and he continued to stare at her, his eyes unwavering.

"Whatever it is, it's nae good, is it," he said, not bothering with the question mark. "Ye'd best say an' be done."

"It's about Sulpitium."

"Wintergap. Aye?"

"Something's happened to disrupt the excavation. The well's been poisoned."

He didn't move but his eyelids flickered. "Poisoned how?"

"There was a dead sheep in it."

She had been sure that she would be able to tell from his expression whether or not he'd done it, but she found dis-

130

concertingly that she couldn't. "An' ye think it was me, whey." Flat statement.

"No," said Penelope firmly. "I don't know. That's why I came to ask you."

"Ye really thowt Aa'd be numb enough to tell ye gin Aa'd done it?"

It was her turn to be silent, to wait. He didn't seem surprised to hear about the well, but neither did he plunge into a suspiciously heated denial; he gave no clue. Instead he looked away from her, at Lou, completely involved with Frit. She had collapsed cross-legged on the ground and was scratching the dog's ribs while Frit grinned ecstatically.

"Would ye believe me gin Aa said Aa'd nowt to do wi' thon?" he asked finally.

"I wouldn't have come here otherwise," said Penelope. "There are people on the site who suspect it wasn't an accident, that someone—a Robson—put the sheep there."

He swung back to her, frowning. "Then why'd they send you, why not one a the gaffers?"

"Gaffers?"

"Aye, bosses," he said impatiently. "Them wha runs things."

"You mean my stepmother, or Sir Kenneth Foote? They didn't come because they haven't any proof. No one saw it happen. But no one sent me, either—I came on my own. I haven't said anything about you to anyone yet."

He shrugged. "Well?" The word was casual, his expression was not. "Aa warrand ye've nae proof yersel, have ye?"

"Not about the well, no," she replied sharply, "but I do know who's been sending the coaches, and who likely turned the sheep loose in the camp. If the well wasn't an accident . . ." She let the sentence fade.

"Aa had nowt to do wi' the bluddy well!" exclaimed Ran loudly enough to make Lou and Frit glance at him. "But ye believe what ye want."

"That's what I want to believe," said Penelope, realizing how true it was.

He gave her an odd look, almost a scowl, but she returned it with a sudden smile, and slowly, reluctantly, he smiled back. "Ye should never've come," he said, but without an-

131

tagonism. "Gin Archie'd been to home, or Mam's brother—"

"Don't you ever have visitors at all?" asked Lou curiously.

He shook his head. "Not now wi' Dad gone. 'Tisn't on the way anywhere, this. An' Mam divvent like strangers."

Instinctively Penelope looked at the house, trying to imagine the woman inside it. What kind of a mother must she be that Ran was afraid to introduce anyone to her? That she wouldn't see anyone who wasn't her family? She shivered.

"Why do you keep Frit tied up?" Lou had little time for anything but the dog.

"Aa divvent keep her tied," Ran answered. "Only when Archie's near, se she'll nae get in his road. He's nae patience wi' her."

"But she's so well trained," Lou protested.

"Aye, whey she's nae over fond a him either, are ye, Frit?" The tail thumped. "She's young yet, an' hasnae learned to gan canny round Archie."

"You mean he doesn't *like* her?" Lou was incredulous. "But she's beautiful!"

For the first time since they'd arrived, Penelope saw Ran relax. He became the person she'd caught a glimpse of up on Dodd Pike; someone it might be possible, even good, to be friends with. He lost his resemblance to the face in her sketch so completely she wondered if she'd imagined it. "Aye, she'll do," he said, then he really noticed Lou. "Aa divvent ken ye, do Aa? Aa've seen two lads—"

"I know *you*," she replied with some asperity. "You're the one who gave Mark a black eye in Hexham. Mom told us not to have anything more to do with you."

"Her name's Lou," said Penelope quickly, anticipating the slamming shut of the door he'd just opened and putting her foot in the crack. "She's my sister." The word came out more easily than she'd expected. Lou didn't seem to notice; Frit had her utterly infatuated.

"She divvent talk same as ye," Ran said.

"Stepsister," amended Penelope. "Her mother and my father got married two months ago. Lou's American."

Ran considered that in silence.

"Two months and six days," corrected Lou. She was right, Penelope discovered, counting back.

132

"Yer mam—" Ran began. Somewhere close at hand a cow suddenly lowed and he glanced guiltily over his shoulder. As clearly as if he had spoken it aloud Penelope sensed his anxiety: he was afraid to have them stay, but he didn't want to ask them to go. Yet the only thing they were doing that might be considered wrong was keeping Ran from his chores. It was obvious they'd interrupted him at work.

No matter. She had come to find something out, and she had accomplished that. She could keep silent at Wintergap with a clear conscience knowing that however the sheep had got into the Sulpitium well, Ran had not put it there. She refused to push her luck by inquiring about Archie; it was only Ran about whom she cared. "Lou," she said briskly, "we ought to start back. We didn't tell anyone where we were going, or even that we were going away at all."

Lou's face darkened with dismay at the prospect of leaving Frit. "Couldn't we stay just a little longer? Please?"

But Penelope shook her head, noticing the relief that eased Ran's mouth. Watching him, she said, "Maybe you can see Frit again."

Ran said nothing; it was impossible to tell what he was thinking, but at least he didn't deny the possibility.

"All right," said Lou, "but can I have a drink before we go? I'm so thirsty."

Ran hesitated, then said, "Aye, whey, ye'd best come in. Aa've nowt to give ye but water."

"That's all right," said Lou graciously. "Though I like lemonade better. Can Frit come?"

"She's nae allowed in the kitchen."

Lou frowned disapprovingly. It was plain she felt Frit was not properly appreciated. "If I ever have a dog she'll go with me *every*where."

Penelope was extremely curious about the inside of Ran's house, but she didn't want to risk confronting the forbidding Mrs. Robson. "Are you sure it's all right?'

"Aye," said Ran shortly. "She'll nae come down by hersel."

He led them in through the back door. The room was scrubbed spotless, every surface clean, not a speck of dust anywhere. But there was also nothing in the kitchen that was the least bit frivolous or colorful or comfortable. In the exact center stood a plain wood table, its top bare, set about with four straight plank-bottomed chairs. The sink was a huge soapstone affair with a pump in it. Instead of an electric cooker there was a black Rayburn stove with a woodbox beside it. There were no curtains at the windows, no pictures on the walls, no rug on the floor, no friendly clutter.

Ran filled a mug with water from the pump and handed it to Lou. It was a thick white crockery mug, the kind that could be dropped from a considerable height without damage. A whole world away from the Royal Worcester china with which Anthony Whitton had furnished Wintergap. Ran looked at Penelope questioningly.

"No thank you," she said—too politely, too fast, and blushed. The air in the house was static, heavy, as if it had been there unchanged for years. It oppressed and suffocated Penelope in much the same way as had the atmosphere in the Abbey crypt. She longed to give Lou, who was dawdling over her drink, a sharp nudge and tell her to hurry, but of course she couldn't do that. She and Ran stood and looked at one another and she wondered how badly her face betrayed what she was thinking, but his betrayed nothing. She supposed its very blankness was a clue to his feelings. Once her initial flood of self-consciousness began to recede, she found room for sympathy. She couldn't herself imagine *living* here, coming home to this.

"Can I go to the bathroom?" asked Lou over the rim of the mug.

All Penelope wanted to do was get out, away from Dodd Moss Farm, to relieve Ran of the awkwardness of their presence, but Lou seemed determined to delay them. Ran looked at her helplessly. "Aye," he said at last. " 'Tis out back."

"Out back?" she repeated.

"Aye, in the yard."

"You mean it's an *out*house," she said with disbelief. "Don't you have one inside? What do you do at night? Or if it rains?"

"Put on boots an' a mac," he told her flatly.

"Lots of people have outdoor loos," Penelope said. "Even in London—Dad has a friend in Neasden—" She didn't add that she herself had never known anyone with an outhouse.

134

"Really?" Lou was interested. "We used one when we were in Italy, but we all lived in tents. There weren't any houses."

"Come on," said Penelope. "If you have to go, hurry up!"

CHAPTER X

BUT IT WAS ALREADY TOO LATE. LOU HAD HER HAND ON THE doorknob when they heard the clash of studded boots on the stone doorstep outside, and the knob turned in her fingers. She leaped back as if she'd been burned, just in time to avoid being struck as the door was thrust inward. Without actually seeing him do it, Penelope found that Ran had edged in front of her, so that when Archie Robson entered the kitchen Ran himself was first to face him.

"Randall, divvent Aa tell ye to bring in the gimmers? What have ye been doin', lad?" he was asking before he was through the door. Then he caught sight of Penelope and Lou and stopped short. "Assa! An' wha be these two?" he demanded.

Ran answered him as he had his mother. "Hikers, Archie, Off the Way."

Archie peered at the two girls, his eyes adjusting from the glare of sun outside to the dimness of the kitchen. He took his time looking them up and down. Penelope thought she knew what a rabbit caught in a snare must feel like facing its captor. Her heart was thudding and her hands were damp. "An' how is it they're in our kitchen, whey?" he asked slowly. "Aa divvent see the bluddy Way leadin' through Dodd Moss farmyard."

As bravely as she could, Penelope said, "We lost the path and my sister wanted a drink of water. It's so hot." She willed Lou to keep her mouth shut, and Lou obliged, staring at Archie Robson with solemn eyes. He seemed to fill the kitchen, squeezing them back against the walls.

"Hikin' alone, bits a bairns like ye? Missed a path se clear ye could walk it blindfold an' nae put a foot wrong? Strayed frae it this far?" He clearly didn't believe any of it. He con-

135

tinued to stare fixedly at them, eyes narrowed under a suspicious frown.

Penelope's heart sank; she realized he knew he'd seen them before. It was just a matter of time until he placed them, and then—"The others went on ahead," she improvised desperately, trying to distract him. "We saw this house and came to ask the way. We're not familiar with the area, you see." It sounded terribly lame.

But even as she was trying to deflect Archie from their identity, hammering away in her head was something quite different. She dared a glance between the two brothers; the likeness was unmistakable: the shape of the face, the features. But while Ran's face had proven it still had the ability to change expression, Archie's was set hard as stone. It was *Archie* Robson's face she had drawn! The revelation flooded her with unexpected gladness in spite of their precarious position. It made her momentarily lightheaded.

"Aa saw them on the fell," Ran was saying. "Aa thowt Aa'd set them right—"

But Archie suddenly made the connection. "Aa've seen ye, Aa ken it!" he declared with triumph. "The both a ye! In Hexham, Aa saw ye, wi' the lad wha was fightin' wi'—" He broke off and turned on Ran. Penelope sensed violence in him, like a primed pistol, ready to explode at the merest touch. The frown thickened to a scowl. "What they doin' here, whey?"

"It wasn't Mark's fault—" began Lou in a small voice as she instinctively backed a step.

"We were just going," Penelope cut in hastily. "Come on." She held out her hand to the younger girl who took it gladly. Drawing a deep breath, Penelope walked quickly around Archie's bulky, threatening figure and out the door. "Thank you for the water," she called over her shoulder. "I'm sure we can find the way back." She was frantic to get away before Archie made any further connections. She had no idea whether he knew they were from Wintergap or not; or what Ran, the spy on the hillside, had told his brother before this about the people in that house, or about the boy he had had the fight with.

But Ran eeled out after them. "Aa promised, Archie. Aa'll be right back."

"Boogger that!" bellowed Archie from the kitchen. "Get back now or Aa'll skelp ye!"

"Ye'll wake Mam," Ran told him, and to the girls he said urgently, "Gan on wi' ye, hop it!" and gestured toward the front gate. "He's slow, but he'll get there, gin ye gi' him the time!" Penelope didn't need to be told twice. As they ran around the house, she heard the bell again and glanced at Ran. He had paused in the yard long enough to release the eager Frit from her tether. He cocked his head at the sound of the bell and gave a brief nod. " 'Twill keep Archie back—gi' him summick else to think on for a bit," he said and they made a dash for the gate.

"Over thonder," he commanded once they were on the other side. He pointed across the grey-green fell, toward Dodd Pike. "He'll nae follow. Aa cannae gan far wi' ye."

"But why?" asked Lou. "Why was he mad at us? Why wouldn't he let us stay?"

"It doesn't matter," said Penelope. "We were leaving."

"But that means he won't ever let us come back and I want to see Frit again."

They had slowed down so Penelope and Lou could navigate the rough ground without risking their necks, and Frit loped ahead to investigate a scent she'd picked up in a patch of bracken. Lou looked at her with undisguised longing.

" 'Tis just Archie. He divvent trust strangers," said Ran guardedly. "He's nae easy wi' folk. Perhaps"—he sounded carefully distant—"perhaps ye might see Frit somewheres else."

Lou seized the hope. "Oh, *yes!*"

"Do you really think we might?" asked Penelope in a voice she might use to ask about the weather.

Ran shrugged. "Ye never ken. We're round an' about, Frit an' me. Aa'm in Hexham wi' Archie most market days," he added, watching Penelope.

"Do you take Frit?" demanded Lou.

"Frit? Nae, not Frit. Archie'd nae have her."

"Then why'd you say?"

137

"Aa mun be gannin'," he said hastily. "Ye'll nae have trouble gin ye make for the circle up the Pike—ye ken it."

"Yes," said Penelope, "but we don't have to go there—we can go around Dodd Pike, can't we?"

Ran gave her a sideways look and said, "Aye, ye can. 'Tis longer to gan round."

"I know, but I don't like the circle," she admitted irritably.

He shrugged. "'Tis yer ain choice. Hi, Frit! Howway wi' ye!"

With an abrupt nod he left them and raced with Frit back toward the farm. The two girls set off in the opposite direction, to Wintergap.

"Pennie," said Lou after a while, "Pennie, do you think he really meant it about Frit? That we'll see her again?"

"Hmm? Yes, I think so."

"She's so beautiful." Lou sighed.

"If you like dogs so much why haven't you ever had one of your own?" asked Penelope curiously.

"Couldn't. Not in our apartment in Cambridge, not in London either. No pets allowed. We had a cat named Mimi once, but she wasn't a very good cat—she wasn't friendly. Mom didn't like her at all and Dad took her when he left. But oh, Pennie, I want a dog *so* much! And now we live in a real house instead of an apartment . . ." There was such a fierce yearning in her voice that Penelope hadn't the heart to tell Lou about her father's allergy. Let her find out later, from someone else.

Instead, she said, "Let's not tell anyone where we've been, or about Frit and Ran, Lou. Let's keep them a secret for now."

"Why?" Lou studied her narrowly. "Because of Mom?"

"Mmm." Penelope tried to sound noncommittal.

"I don't think I want to go back to that farm again—not even to see Frit. Did you know it was like that?"

"No."

"But he was nice once he got over being cross with us for coming, wasn't he? You like him, don't you, Pennie?"

The words were innocent enough—too innocent. Penelope suspected Lou of leading her into an ambush; she was scouting information for some purpose. "If you *do* want to see Frit

138

again, anywhere, you'd do well not to say anything," she told her sternly. "Not about Frit, not about Ran, not about the farm. Remember, I didn't invite you along today—I didn't expect you to follow me. The next time I'll manage to get away without you, see if I don't."

"I bet you can't."

"We'll see. I could always get your mother to take you to the fort with her."

"That's not fair!" declared Lou.

"Who said anything about fair?"

Lou struggled with this for a while in silence, then, as they reached the far side of the Pike she said, letting her guard down, "Please, Pennie, can I go with you again?"

"Even if I go to the farm?"

"No, but to play with Frit, if you see her again. Or maybe sometimes if you just go walking."

It was a direct appeal, and Penelope was disarmed. "All right," she agreed. "But not every time, Lou. Sometimes I like to be by myself."

"So do I," said Lou. "Only not always."

At Wintergap that evening Lou and Penelope had no difficulty keeping their secret. Everyone was tired and preoccupied and asked no questions about what they'd done or where they'd gone during the day. The twins were as close to worn out as Penelope had ever seen them. They hadn't got all the way to Housesteads, but they'd hiked a good ten miles, none of it easy going, and they were dragging. Luke could barely keep his eyes open, and Mark yawned all through supper. Valerie watched them with affectionate amusement and finally sent them off to bed before nine; Mark protested, but only for the sake of his reputation.

Martin still looked slightly ragged, but no longer actually ill. He and Valerie brought back reports of success. Sir Kenneth's Hexham connection had proved cooperative: they had been able to borrow half-a-dozen water-tight barrels from someone in the Works Department. Initially they had to be filled in town, but Sir Kenneth had hopes of being able to refill them, one or two at a time, somewhere closer: the Youth Hostel or the pub, perhaps.

In the meantime, excavation went forward, and small parties of students trekked across to Wintergap to do serious washing: selves, clothes, hair. Edward, although he did not complain, was clearly feeling the strain of interruption. He was out-of-sorts and uncharacteristically withdrawn, but at least there was no repetition of the previous night's scene.

Lou was still privately glowing over her encounter with Frit, and Penelope began to realize that she was also relishing the idea of having a real secret. It must usually be the twins who had the secrets, not Lou.

Coming back to the drawing room after putting her daughter to bed, Valerie remarked on Lou's good humor. "She obviously had a marvelous time with you today, Pennie. You've been very good with her and I do appreciate it—I know it can't be easy, adjusting to the pace of an eight-year-old."

Edward looked up from the day-old paper he was reading. "Nonsense," he said roundly. Martin caught Penelope's eye in a long-suffering way, inviting her to allow him to commiserate, but their father went on, "Pennie's flexible and sensitive." His voice softened. "Truth be known, Val, she's the nicest one of us."

Penelope blushed in spite of herself and said awkwardly, "I was glad to have Lou for company." It was perfectly true; once she'd gotten over her annoyance at being followed, she had been glad.

Valerie gave her a warm smile and came to sit beside her on the rustling horsehair sofa. Penelope noticed she had a manila envelope in her hand, but didn't recognize it until Valerie slid a sheet of white drawing paper out of it. Her sketch of the stone Lou had found; she had forgotten it. "I meant to say something to you about this last night, Pennie, but what with one thing and another I didn't get to. I didn't have much time to spare it yesterday, I'm afraid, but I showed it to Kenneth this morning and he was very interested."

"It was Lou who found it," said Penelope.

Valerie nodded. "But you did the drawing, didn't you?"

"Yes." Penelope was on her guard suddenly. She wondered what Valerie was leading to. "Is it a gravestone?" she asked, hoping to divert attention from her sketch. "I thought it might be."

"Mmmm. Gibson discovered it near Sulpitium in 1896 and made descriptive notes when he did his survey, but when people tried to find it again three years ago it had vanished. It's Kenneth's guess that Anthony Whitton carried it off as a personal trophy to ornament his garden."

"He has a lot to answer for, all in all, hasn't he?" remarked Edward.

"Indeed he has. I wonder how much else he relocated while he was here," Valerie said.

Martin asked, "Whose tombstone was it, do you know? I spent most of the day filling barrels in Hexham and missed all the interesting bits."

"According to Kenneth it commemorates a girl named Lucasta—it's a fascinating combination of Roman and native Briton. The figure's crude enough to suggest local work, but the inscription begins 'Dis Manibus' which is Roman. It was probably done at the end of the Roman occupation."

"How much longer do you expect the well to be undrinkable?" asked Edward who'd lost interest and progressed to the crossword.

Valerie sighed. "We'll give it another two days to be on the safe side. It should be all right by Wednesday. I did tell them specifically to be quiet today, Ted."

Martin gave his father a challenging look, but Edward merely nodded gravely and went on with his puzzle. "You might thank what's-his-name—Jonthan?—for troubling to bring me the Sunday paper. I do miss contact with the outside world."

It had been Martin's idea, actually. Penelope'd heard him talking to Valerie about it; they'd brought it back from Hexham with the barrels as kind of a sop against the invasion of the students.

"Pennie, have you been drawing long?" asked Valerie.

The question was unexpected; Penelope had thought she was safe, the conversation had moved well away from the sketch. "Quite a while," she answered cautiously.

"Years and years," put in Martin. "She's got cartons full of

141

sketchbooks on top of her wardrobe at Warburton Square."

"How do you know?" Penelope demanded.

"Well, I've seen the cartons and I've some idea how much you draw. Don't get shirty—I haven't been snooping!"

"Kenneth was very impressed with this," Valerie said. "I think he was more interested in your drawing, Pennie, than in the stone itself. Of course I didn't tell Lou that."

"But why?" Penelope felt a warm, treacherous trickle of pleasure; her work had been noticed after all. But her drawing was a very private thing—she did it for her own enjoyment, and she didn't want that enjoyment ruined by well-intentioned adults. "All I did was copy what I saw."

"Yes, but you copied it very precisely. Just by looking at this Kenneth was able to identify the stone positively. He knew it right away. He asked me if you did a lot of this kind of thing, and I had to confess I hadn't any idea. I've never seen your sketches before. You said something about drawing wildflowers the other day, didn't you? I'm afraid I didn't pay enough attention."

"I only do it for myself," hedged Penelope, "just for fun. There's always something I can find to draw when I want."

"Have you ever had lessons?"

"Lessons? In what?" Edward wrenched himself away from the newspaper, sensing the conversation had gone off gravestones. "Has Pennie had lessons in what?"

"Drawing, Dad," said Martin with exaggerated patience.

"No," said Penelope, feeling self-conscious.

"That art mistress of yours—what *was* her name—Dustbin? —wasn't she keen on it once?"

"Dustin," corrected Penelope.

"She wrote Dad a letter about it," said Martin. "I remember."

"Said you had 'potential,' whatever she meant by that. We discussed it, as I recall, and you said you didn't want extra lessons."

"I didn't."

Edward seemed relieved.

"Why not?" asked Valerie.

Penelope hesitated, on the brink of attempting to explain

something she hadn't talked over with anyone before. Her stepmother waited, not prompting, not prying, ready to listen if she wanted to try, and Penelope stepped over the edge. "Because I wouldn't have been any good at what Mrs. Dustin wanted me to do, and I wouldn't have enjoyed it, either. I like to copy things—objects—like the stone and the flowers in the garden here, but I don't care about *pictures*. She didn't think of my sketches as proper art, she thought they were sort of a first step, and I'd develop." She made a face. "But I didn't want to spoil the thing I enjoyed doing by trying to turn it into something else. I don't know if that makes sense," she finished lamely.

"It makes sense to me," Valerie assured her.

"And to me," agreed Edward. "Why the hell should you let someone interfere with what gives you satisfaction when it really doesn't concern anyone else?" He spoke with some heat.

Martin said nothing.

Penelope glanced from Valerie to her father gratefully and Edward slipped her a wink. So that, she thought, was that; she could maintain her privacy.

But it wasn't. After a couple of minutes, Valerie said conversationally, "Pennie, did you know that there are people who make a living professionally drawing objects like this?"

"There are?" She looked disbelievingly at the paper.

"How do you mean?" asked Martin with interest.

"Scientific illustration. It's one of those odd, specialized professions that no one thinks to mention when you're considering careers."

"Drawing objects?" He sounded skeptical. "For what?"

"Textbooks, catalogues, guidebooks, reports, exhibits. All those figures and diagrams have to be drawn by someone, Martin. Someone with an eye for detail and exact scale. What's needed for those isn't a pretty picture, but a precise representation of a specific object."

"Are you saying that Pennie should take this seriously?" asked Edward. "May I see that?"

Valerie handed him the sketch. "Yes, if she wants to. Kenneth suggested it first. Of course," she looked at Penelope, "you need training—any skilled job requires training, but there are places where you could get it without being forced into doing something you don't like. I'm sure there are people at the University of London who could help."

"I never thought," said Penelope slowly. "I mean—it never occurred to me."

Valerie gave a comfortable little laugh. "Why should it? The world is full of obvious things we never see. It never occurred to me that I could be an archaeologist, you know. I was all set to be a first grade teacher—I'd been accepted in a graduate training course. Then a friend of mine introduced me to Brian Prine and he introduced me to the joys of archaeology and I couldn't go back again. Wrecked all my plans— my mother wouldn't speak to me for months. *She'd* been a first grade teacher."

"I didn't know that," said Edward.

"There's a lot you don't know about me," she told him with a smile. "But you have plenty of time to find out, isn't that nice?"

"I thought Brian didn't want you to be a professional archaeologist," said Martin. "Why did he start you out?"

"It was all right as long as I was a wide-eyed beginner," said Valerie. "As long as he knew more than I did. But when I began catching up, he got less enthusiastic and started talking about having children. And when I got my Master's degree the problems began. Two professional archaeologists in the same family was one too many—it just didn't work. It was my fault, too—I *wanted* to compete with him. So here I am, and last I heard Brian was somewhere in Greece. But"— with a shake of the head she thrust the past away from her— "back to a more important matter. Pennie, if you'd be willing, Kenneth and I would very much like to have you make sketches for us of the most interesting objects we turn up at Sulpitium this summer. We want to use them in our report, to help convince the all-powerful Board of Governors that the excavation here really is important."

"Well," said Penelope, unaccountably shy of what she'd started, "I'm not sure."

"Think about it," urged Valerie. "The student who was supposed to do the sketches came down with hepatitis at the end of May, so we were resigned to doing without. We'll be disappointed if you say no, but I promise we won't hold it against you!"

"I think"—pause and deep breath—"I'd like to." Penelope gave her stepmother a tentative smile, then a thought occurred to her. "It wouldn't be bones, would it?"

Valerie laughed. "No, no bones, word of honor! Tell you what—why don't you come over to Sulpitium one day this week and have a look at what we've found so far. You'll get a better idea of what we want and whether you want to do it."

"Well, well, well," remarked Martin, as shortly afterward he followed Penelope up to bed. "Who'd have thought this would turn out to be such a family project!"

"I hope you aren't going to be beastly about me getting into the act," she said, remembering their conversation the first time she had visited Sulpitium.

"Beastly?" He sounded genuinely surprised. "No, why should I be? I think it's bloody marvelous that Valerie's enthusiastic about your drawing. It means that you can—well—" He broke off.

"I can do something," she finished for him.

"*I* didn't say that," he protested. "Don't alienate me, Pennie, I'm the only brother you've got."

She took her head. "Not anymore." On the top step she paused and turned to look down at him.

"Strewth, I suppose not! But do you really think of the twins as your brothers?"

"Not with*out* thinking, if you see what I mean. But it doesn't seem as impossible as it did once."

"Harder for me," said Martin. "This autumn when I start at university I won't see you very much—only at vac. I must say, I'm glad you've got Valerie, Pennie."

She gave a little nod. "But we would have managed perfectly well, you know, Dad and I."

"Without me stirring things up, you mean," he said dryly. "I can't help it, Pennie, Dad and I are so different—I can't see the world the way he does."

"He can't see it the way you do, either," she pointed out. "But isn't there room for both of you?"

"Maybe. But I say, I think it's worked better than we

imagined when we decided to back Valerie, don't you?"

"Yes." She was unable to keep just a hint of uncertainty out of her voice.

"But?"

"But life is a lot more complicated now than it was when there were only the three of us."

And Martin, who on occasion surprised everyone—even himself—with a flash of real perception, said, "The older you get, the more people you come to know, one way or another. And the more people you're involved with the more complicated life gets, Pennie. It's an accumulation—you started out uncluttered, but as time goes on you acquire more and more odds and sods. I'm beginning to see that's what life is. If it wasn't Valerie, Lou, and the twins, it'd be someone else—unless you ran away and lived like a hermit. Not for me, thanks all the same." He grinned and shrugged to cover the momentary embarrassment of being serious with his younger sister. "And having delivered myself of that profundity, I shall leave you reeling and fall into bed. That is, if you'll get out of my way."

"Last night it was you who were reeling," she observed and stepped nimbly out of reach. "Good night," she called after him.

She seemed to have been handed a great deal to think about all at once. Her perspective had shifted and she had to adjust to looking at life from a new angle. Ever since Grannie Lawrence had sold the cottage in St. Albans three years ago, Penelope had been traveling a long straight road, able to see ahead quite far into the distance and to recognize the landmarks as they approached. When her father married Valerie, Penelope reached a major intersection. She had seen it coming and been convinced that she could carry right through it—and perhaps she could have, but she hadn't. She had made a turn and left behind the straight and familiar to embark on a different road, narrower and meandering. A bit frightening, but exciting and full of surprises. The world was much wider than she had guessed.

CHAPTER XI

TUESDAY MORNING, BY HERSELF, PENELOPE WALKED THE dusty length of the Wintergap track, then followed the tarred road to the closest bus stop. There she joined two carefully dressed farm women with shopping bags, and three unfinished-looking boys with London accents and bulging rucksacks. She herself wore sandals and a respectable skirt for the journey to Hexham, out of deference to Grannie Lawrence who maintained that in public anyway "Girls should look like girls!" Lou hadn't been pleased at the prospect of spending the day at Sulpitium, but Edward had some mysterious errand about which he was irritatingly vague, and Penelope had reminded Lou of their bargain.

The bus service along the Roman Wall was a special summer one put on to accommodate the tourists. It ran between Haltwhistle and Hexham, calling at places like the Youth Hostel and Housesteads.

This particular morning it collected a large number of passengers at the Hostel and many local people at odd and frequent stops, so that by the time it arrived at the railway station in Hexham it was full. Penelope shared her seat with a hefty, red-faced young woman reading an article in a magazine titled *How to Win At the Marriage Game*. Not worth straining her eyes sideways to read, Penelope decided; it was full of advice on hair styles, matching accessories, makeup and provocative conversation. The young woman was utterly engrossed. Penelope preferred to look out the window and count sheep.

She had errands to do in Hexham, for herself and others: a new sketch pad that she could use at Sulpitium; shoelaces for Mark; Lou wanted crayons; a jar of instant coffee, a tube of toothpaste, drawing pins and four airmail stamps for Valerie; and a pair of socks for Martin. Very miscellaneous and none of it terribly exciting, but the list provided her with a good excuse to wander around the town while keeping her eyes open.

147

It was market day again, and Hexham was crammed with people, just as it had been the first day they'd come. And like that day, it was hot and sunny. Everywhere she went, threading her way through the crowds on the pavements and in the shops, Penelope heard people discussing the drought. It was good weather to be a tourist: floods of sunlight for photographs, dry feet, even the chance of a painful sunburn to prove a successful holiday. But the farmers had long faces and joyless eyes and spoke grimly of the danger of fire, the loss of livestock, and withering crops, wells running dry, and no relief in sight.

She took her time over the shopping, not wanting to finish too quickly. It gave her something safe and definite to accomplish; in case she didn't find Ran she wouldn't have wasted her time and needn't admit to anyone except herself that he was the reason she had chosen to come to Hexham on a market day.

For lunch she bought two huge apples and a wedge of cheese, and returned to the park where she could sit on the dry scratchy grass and watch people drift past. Each one of them had come from somewhere and had a destination; she tried to imagine what would happen if each person carried a ball of colored string, unrolling it behind through the day to mark his or her path. What a monumental tangle—what an incredible cat's cradle that would make . . .

"What ye smilin' at, whey?" asked Ran, crouching beside her. She wasn't surprised to see him although she hadn't heard him come. His expression was balanced on the thin edge between friendliness and withdrawal, poised for her reaction.

"People," she said. "You."

His face relaxed, but she noticed the violet and green of a bruise on his left cheek and her eyes widened.

"Aa wasnae sure ye'd come the day."

"I had errands to do." She held up her string bag of purchases. "Do you want an apple?"

He accepted and settled beside her. "The others?"

"I came by myself on the bus. They're all busy."

"Aa come wi' Archie, same as always," he said taking a

great chunk out of the apple. "Aa saw ye gannin' into the post office, but he was wi' me an' Aa lost ye."

"I didn't see you," she said and bit her lip. She'd just confessed she'd been looking for him and she saw from his expression he'd caught it. "Where's Archie now?"

"Over t' the White Hart, havin' a pint. Then he's got business wi' Jack Bell at the feed store. He told me to mind the pickup, but it can mind itsel, Aa warrand. Are ye busy, whey?" He didn't look at her.

"No, I've finished. I was going to have a last look around, then catch the bus back at half-past one."

"Aa could walk a bit wi' ye," he offered. "Gin ye want. Aa've just to pick up Mam's medicine over t' the surgery first."

"Medicine? Is she ill?"

"Aye, her tablets. 'Tis the heat frets her, she's wakin' most nights wi'out them an' she's nowt but two left." He finished the apple and stood up.

Penelope gathered her bundles and let Ran choose their direction, along the sun-stippled path through the park. He walked without speaking. He's probably wondering like me what we're doing together, thought Penelope wryly. It didn't make much sense for either of them, knowing as they did that neither family would approve. She swung her bag and tried to think of something inconsequential to talk about, but nothing would come. She had nowhere to start. She knew nothing about Ran except where he lived and that his family resented hers for being at Wintergap. That was not much to base a friendship—even an acquaintance—on, but that was what they had. It seemed silly to pretend otherwise.

"Your brother was angry about us being at your farm Sunday," she said at last, discarding any attempt at small talk.

"He's nae over fond a strangers, Aa told ye thon. We divvent get many." Ran thrust his hands into his pockets and hunched his shoulders. " 'Tis good ye left afore he kenned ye were frae Wintergap, or he'd nae have let ye gan se easy."

Penelope, who was walking on his left, glanced again at his cheek. She was unable to forget the bruise; like a sore tooth it nagged the edge of her consciousness. "He wouldn't have thought—I mean, he didn't—well, blame you because of us?" she asked awkwardly. "We were in the house, after all."

"Ay?" He was momentarily puzzled, then he understood and put a hand up to the tender spot. "Nae, it wasna to do wi' thon. 'Twas summick else altogether," he said off-handedly. "He was in a right takin' yesterday, Aa can tell ye!"

"But it was him?" she asked in a small, horrified voice. "He hit you?"

"Only on account Aa dinna shift smart enough. 'Twas ma own fault." He sounded rueful rather than bitter.

She didn't know what to say. Physical violence was totally outside her personal experience of the world. The worst that happened when people she knew got angry was that they shouted. She'd never been hit in her life, but Ran took it quite calmly.

At the edge of the park he led her across the street, dodging traffic, then around several corners into a pleasant, settled residential area. The building they entered had a row of discreet, neatly lettered nameplates beside the door. Penelope followed Ran into a waiting room papered with green and yellow flowers and lined with shabby, durable chairs. There were two middle-aged women sitting together, carefully disregarding the bald man across from them who was apparently sound asleep and snoring softly, and a girl who looked scarcely sixteen holding a chunky baby on her lap. The receptionist looked up as they came in and smiled at Ran.

"Hello, Randall. How's your mother, then?"

"She's nae over grand, Mrs. Noble. The weather has her fair beat an' she's nae sleepin' se well."

"Well, you can tell her I'm not either, if that's any comfort. This heat is dreadful. Dr. Samuel said he'd be out to the farm about eleven on Friday to see her, if that suits? He said he'd like to talk to your brother, and he's left the prescription for you. There you are."

"Thanks," said Ran and took the piece of paper. "Aa'll tell Archie. 'Twill cheer Mam, she likes to see the doctor."

Penelope, watching Mrs. Noble watch Ran, saw a look of real compassion in the woman's eyes. None of this fit with the mental picture Penelope had formed of Mrs. Robson. She imagined her as a grim, unsympathetic, rather fearsome old woman, an eccentric recluse who bullied her children relentlessly. But here were Ran and Mrs. Noble talking about her as if she were ill and helpless—and if the doctor was going to visit *her*, instead of the other way around, she must indeed be ill and helpless.

"Ran," she said, when they were outside again. "What's the matter with your mother?"

The question seemed to take him by surprise. "Ye divvent ken? Aa thowt everyone kenned about the accident." He was suspicious.

These were deep, murky waters; she had to feel her way with great care, she sensed, or she'd break the tenuous contact they'd established. But it was important to her that she understand, and she didn't yet know enough to understand. "I've heard a little," she said cautiously. "About your father and Anthony Whitton."

"Aye?" He waited for her to go on, and when she didn't, he said, "They've told ye she's a daft old woman, Aa warrand."

She didn't answer, she was afraid to. They walked back toward the center of Hexham and stopped in a chemist's so Ran could fill the prescription. While they waited the silence between them grew brittle. Penelope attempted to find distraction by reading the labels on bottles of shampoo, but the words were meaningless.

At last Ran said, " 'Twas the shock a findin' ma dad like thon. She had a stroke, Mam. She's been paralyzed down one side sin, thon's why she never leaves Dodd Moss. She cannae."

Penelope stood in the middle of her shattered image and stared at him. "Ran, I'm sorry. I didn't know."

"Did ye not?"

"But you—when we came—I thought—" She could not, of course, tell him what she'd thought. What other people had led her to believe about his mother.

"She divvent like folk to see her. It upsets her account a how she looks—crookit. Se no one but the doctor comes now."

As the numbness began to wear away questions crowded her head. "You take care of her?"

"Aye, me an' Archie. Tis nae se hard—she gets around wi'

help," he said matter-of-factly.

"And the house?"

"Aye. She divvent like it skew-wiff. It frets her gin we divvent keep it tidy."

The chemist reappeared, handed Ran a bulky white envelope, and they left.

"But there's the farm, too," said Penelope. "How can you do everything?"

Ran gave her a long, measuring look. He evidently found what he wanted in her face because the defensiveness left him. "Aye, 'tis enough to keep us busy, but we're three wi' Jonty to help as well, ye ken. An' the farm's only smaa, nae mair than enough for us to live on. Jonty's Mam's brother. He's been wi' us sin afore we lost Wintergap. He's gey good wi' the beasts, Jonty."

"What's 'gey'?" asked Penelope, feeling herself relax.

"Ay?"

"What does it mean—'gey'?"

"Ye divvent ken?"

"I wouldn't ask if I did."

"Well, it means—'gey' means"—he groped—"gin Aa tell ye he's gey good at summick, 'tis like—" and he broke off with a scowl. "Lukka, ye mun ken yersel!"

She thought for a moment. "It must mean 'very,'" she guessed.

"Aye, thon's it. What'd Aa tell ye?"

"Tell me about the farm," she said.

He was willing to talk about it, to answer her fascinated questions about the animals—beasts, he called them—and the kinds of chores he had: about lambing in the spring and weaning calves, digging sheep out of snow drifts, milking cows, hand-rearing orphan lambs, shearing, even mucking out the cow byre and pens and feeding the chickens. At first his answers were guarded, terse, as if he were afraid of saying too much—telling her more than she wanted to know. But as she persisted he grew confident and expansive.

His was a life in a world completely foreign to her, so totally unlike her own in London, she found it hard to believe they really coexisted. What she knew of farms and farming and living isolated in the country came from books. Now suddenly it took substance right before her eyes; it was close enough to touch.

From time to time she interrupted him to ask what he meant by "clarty" or "yett," "cuddy" and "lonnen"—words that were strange to her. He tried to explain, but lost patience quickly with himself and her when he couldn't find adequate words to substitute. He was no good at that, he got tangled and cross, and she gradually learned to stop pressing.

They neither one of them paid much attention to where they were going. They returned to the park and walked through it to the far side, then wound slowly through a maze of narrow back streets away from the market. These were working streets, where people lived and conducted ordinary, essential business. The houses were wedged in rows along the pavement, with here and there a newsagent's, a secondhand shop, a laundromat, a dingy garage scattered with spare parts.

Ran began to talk as if the words had been dammed inside and had finally found a crack to spill through. They came not in a great, overwhelming flood, but steadily, showing no sign of running dry, though every now and then he would give Penelope another of those long, gauging looks. He told her what it was like to see a calf actually born, in the middle of a hailstorm at three in the morning, and how Frit's mother had nearly died in a fight with a vixen that had been stealing hens.

They came to another park, Prior's Flat it was called, and beyond it lay the railway line and a golf course, and finally the River Tyne, shrunk small between its banks. Ran looked at it and gave a low whistle.

"Does it ever dry up completely?" asked Penelope, mistaking the reason for the whistle.

But he said instead, " 'Tis the time! Aa've been away too long—Archie'll be switherin' gin Aa divvent gan back right quick! How'd we get here, d'ye mind?" He looked round, searching for a landmark.

"I forgot about the time," said Penelope. "It was your stories."

Rather to her surprise, Ran left it to her to find the most direct way back to the marketplace. She accomplished it with only two wrong turns and a little hesitation. There was the

Abbey looming ahead, shouldering over the jumble of roofs, and she felt a glow of satisfaction as they came around its northeast corner into the busy square.

"I thought country people were supposed to have such a super sense of direction," she chided him.

"Aye, but nae in the city," he replied seriously and she laughed. " 'Tis true," he declared in an injured tone. "Aa can find ma way across the fell thonder an' nae bother, but city streets is summick else."

"I believe you," said Penelope, "but I'm from London, remember, and I'd hardly call Hexham a city."

His face clouded. "Aa'd nae ken about thon. Aa've nae seen London masel."

"It just depends on what you're used to," she said, not following his abrupt change of mood.

He was observing her closely. "Aye, well Aa'm nae used to much an' Hexham's all the city Aa'm likely ever to ken."

"What about Newcastle and Carlisle?" she encouraged. "You must have been there. They're cities."

Stubbornly he shook his head; his eyes had gone opaque, his face had the look on it she had first seen there: the look that reminded her of the drawing. He was not the Ran she wanted to be friends with, he was the image of his brother Archie. "No, Aa've nae been ayont Hexham. Ye've been havin' me on the day, askin' yer questions just se ye can gan home an' have a good laugh over the Robsons. Aa should've kenned ye were makin' game a me."

She was amazed, then outraged, "I—I have *not!*" she denied hotly. "I wouldn't do that—you've no right to say such a thing! Why would you even think so? That's a beastly thing to say!"

"Aa told ye the first day, ye divvent belong here. Ye should gan back to yer city an' leave us alone gin ye think we're sich fools," he continued doggedly. "Gin ye'd left when the well went off Archie'd nae be in sich a temper now. He'd nae be frettin' Mam wi' his carryin' on."

"Don't!" she said in dismay. "Don't say anything about it, Ran. I don't want to know who did it."

"Aye, 'twas Archie. Ye're se bonny an' clever ye must've

twigged it afore now. An' he's ma brother, se what'll ye do, whey?"

The anger left her and she discovered that underneath she was hurt; hurt that he could turn on her with no provocation and ruin what had been until then a good afternoon; hurt that he thought so little of her. She drew herself together. "You're right, I did guess that he'd done it," she answered defiantly. "But it doesn't matter—he didn't make us leave by poisoning the well. We aren't going."

"Why'd ye think Archie clipped me yesterday? He's thon het ye're still here."

"I can understand why Mark got into a fight with you," she replied with dignity. "I shall myself in another minute." Helpless with violent feelings of injustice and confusion, she pushed past him. She walked very fast through the rows of market stalls and traffic and snarls of people, paying no attention to anyone.

She spent most of the busride back to Wintergap seething. And he had accused *her* of leading him on—what had *he* been doing then? She was utterly unprepared for such contradictory behavior; either a person wanted to be friends, or he didn't. He should make it clear from the beginning, not hold out a hand to encourage you closer, then slap your face with it. Why had he done it?

She found it hard to believe that he could get so angry simply because she had laughed at him for calling Hexham a city. That was such a small thing! He might have been annoyed perhaps, or a little hurt, but not suddenly hostile.

All the way back from the river he had been silent. But then so had she—intent on finding their way and keeping her breath for hurrying so they'd get back before Archie was too angry with Ran. What had he been thinking all that time? What had she said that might have set him off? The harder she pushed to remember, the blanker she felt.

As a result of all this, she missed her stop and had to walk back from the next one. She'd trudged about a quarter of the way up the Wintergap track when a car horn blatted just behind her and she jumped like a rabbit. It was the Sulpitium van with Jonathan at the wheel and Martin in the seat beside him. They greeted her cheerfully and offered her a ride.

"You could have ridden all the way back with us," Martin told her as she climbed in. "I saw you in Hexham, but you were so absorbed in thought you cut me dead."

"I didn't know you were going to town."

"Had to collect supplies," said Jonathan. "Wire cutters, pick handles, whiskbrooms, toothbrushes, and torch batteries. And this is our last water run," he added with a note of triumph. "Positively."

"Super," Penelope dutifully responded, her mind still clogged with the problem of Ran.

"Polite but unenthusiastic," pronounced Jonathan.

"Did you get my socks?" asked Martin.

"What? Oh, yes. You could have gotten them yourself. Here." She fished in her bag and pulled out a brown parcel.

"Red?" he said in surprise, shaking them out.

"Bloody flaming scarlet, if you ask me!" commented Jonathan. "I never knew a chap with scarlet socks before."

"Why red?"

Penelope shrugged, unable to explain that when she had bought the socks she had been feeling gay and adventurous with all the posibility of the day ahead. "I liked the color," she said lamely.

Martin cocked an eyebrow at her. "Did I see you having an argument with someone in the marketplace, Pennie? I thought it was you, over by the Abbey."

She hadn't caught the full implication of what he'd said earlier, about seeing her in the town. Now she froze for a moment, then said carefully, "Oh, that was just someone I met today." In the strictly literal sense that was true, but it wasn't very honest. She didn't like not being honest with Martin. It wasn't that she felt she'd done wrong by seeing Ran—that was jolly well up to her if it didn't hurt anyone else—more that she didn't want to get into the muddle that was inevitable if she tried to explain. Anyway, there seemed very little point, as she doubted she'd see him again.

"—ran into someone we knew ourselves," Martin was saying, "and it wasn't very pleasant. Our friend Archie Robson was in the iron monger's. He didn't recognize us at first, and

I thought we might get away, then the clerk mentioned Sulpitium."

"He'd had a slowsh or two," said Jonathan.

"Or three or four," said Martin.

Jonathan sighed. "Beer makes some people mellower." He gave Martin a sidelong glance. "Makes *other* people foul-tempered."

"No marks for guessing which Robson is."

"He's not over friendly at the best of times," said Jonathan. "Don't know him except by sight and reputation myself. There are those say the old lady's done it to him, keeping that place shut up—it sounds a pretty grim life to me."

"But maybe—" began Penelope, then closed her mouth.

"My dad always said George Robson was a throwback, born out of his time. He'd have made a bloody marvelous Border raider, and his son takes after him. Obsolete and dangerous, the Robsons."

"Don't forget the young one," said Martin.

"Mmm, Randall." Jonathan nodded thoughtfully. "Wonder what chance he's got with only his mam and Archie for company? I suppose he'll turn out the same, won't be able to help it, poor sod."

Penelope was timid about her first official visit to the site. She wasn't sure what was expected of her; she knew only the barest minimum about Roman Britain from what she'd learned at school and was self-conscious about her ignorance. Once her delight at being asked to do the drawings had receded, doubts sneaked in: could she really do what Valerie and Sir Kenneth wanted? Did she want to make her drawings public in this manner? Would she even want to draw the objects when she saw them? Once she undertook this project there would be no going back; no matter what the result, she would never view her sketching in the same way again; it would never be purely personal and private.

But she had agreed to try, and try she would. Lou was even less pleased to discover this meant spending a second day at Sulpitium, for Penelope chose to start on Wednesday. The routine at the site was back to normal: the well was clean, and people were working with renewed energy to make up for time lost. Valerie's crew was opening the other rooms in the bathhouse; the skeletons found thus far had been packed off to Newcastle with extreme care to be examined by an expert. Excavation of the fort's west gate was virtually complete, and Sir Kenneth was beginning to dig in the northwest corner where the fort joined Hadrian's Wall, and the Romans had built an angle tower.

He took time to guide Penelope around as if she were a visiting dignitary instead of a schoolgirl. He was pleasant and easy, and answered her hesitant questions as if they were of the utmost importance.

"Of course the most discouraging fact is that we've done so little as yet that hasn't already been done by someone else. Valerie's had the real luck, finding her corpses."

"But if it's all been excavated before, I should think the digging would be easier," ventured Penelope.

"Oh, I suppose it is. We're progressing quite quickly, but all we're doing is uncovering masonry and carting away dirt. We're not finding any of the objects that make one feel one's really made a discovery—they've already been found. Your stepmother's unearthing objects in the bathhouse because no one's dug into it as far as she has. And once we get into the middle of the fort we'll do better. But for the time being, what my lot's doing simply requires saintly patience and strong backs!"

When she'd seen everything that was going on outside, Sir Kenneth took her into the farmhouse to show her the objects they'd found so far. As she crossed the threshold, Ran came uninvited to her mind; he had once lived in this house. She wondered if it had been any happier a place for him than Dodd Moss seemed.

Still, whatever it had been, now it was the working headquarters for the excavation: full of tools and general clutter, maps and charts, a bulletin board in the hall stuck with notices and lost and found items—Penelope recognized one of Martin's old blue socks with a hole in the heel. On a row of pegs was an assortment of rain gear, hanging in stiff, dusty folds. There were cartons of papers, empty milk bottles, bits of plastic sheeting, and empty grain sacks. The sitting room had been set up as an office with a battered metal desk, filing cabinets, and makeshift bookshelves spilling over with books and pamphlets. One of the students—Dick, Penelope thought his name was— was sitting on the floor surrounded by piles of papers.

"Filing," explained Sir Kenneth from the doorway.

Dick looked up and grinned ruefully. "Made the mistake of admitting I not only know the alphabet, but what order the letters come in," he said. "Still get me *l*'s and *k*'s mixed, though."

"Not to worry," Sir Kenneth assured him cheerfully. "No one'll notice."

"Even as I'd feared."

"Here we are, over here." Sir Kenneth ushered her into a room across the hall, where sheets of plywood had been set on sawhorses to make large worktables. "Frances, you know Penelope Ibbetson, don't you? Frances Allen. She's cataloging the finds for us, she can tell you better than I what there is, and you can work out between you which objects you think would be most effective to illustrate."

"Right," said Frances agreeably. She was a thin brown girl with short hair and a generous smile. "So you're to be our artist, are you? Super. I saw your drawing of the stone—it was jolly good."

"Thank you," said Penelope self-consciously, then turned back to Sir Kenneth. "What will happen about the stone? The one Lou found?"

"Happen? Nothing much I should think. Valerie says it would be very difficult to remove it—part of the retaining wall, isn't it? We'll send someone to finish cleaning it up, but I think we'll leave it where it is."

Penelope hesitated, then said a little diffidently, "You couldn't put Lou's name in your report, could you? I mean because she found it."

The craggy face broke into a smile. "Indeed, I don't see why not. Yes, splendid idea! I'll leave you two to get on with this, shall I? See you at lunch."

In the course of the day, Penelope's strangeness wore off. Frances was good company: knowledgeable and friendly, but perfectly willing to let Penelope work on her own, assuming Penelope knew best what she was doing. At first Penelope doubted that this was true, but she grew more confident as she lost herself in her drawing. The first object she chose was a small bronze boar, which Frances produced from a box with as much pride as if she were the craftsman. "He's lovely, he really is," she said. "*I* think he's the nicest thing we've found this summer. He'd look marvelous on the cover of the report." He was only about four inches long, smooth and simple rather than strictly realistic, but full of the essence of boar.

In addition, there were coins, pieces of pottery, fragments of clouded glass, two iron keys, a great many nails, a bridle bit and a handsomely patterned buckle, some pieces of tile, bone ornaments, a terra cotta figure with the head gone, and several spearheads. "Fancy people getting excited about stuff like this!" said Frances, making fun of herself. "We're daft, the lot of us."

Lou confronted Penelope at lunch. "Does this mean you're going to come here every day from now on?" she demanded.

"Not *every* day," Penelope hedged. "I doubt it."

"But most of the time." Lou sat with her arms clasped around her knees, looking glum. "I thought you liked Ran," she said after a while. "I thought you wanted to see him again, and I'd get to see Frit."

Penelope sighed and didn't answer. Lou had forcibly reminded her of the reason she'd come to Sulpitium today instead of tomorrow as she'd intended. She had wanted to get away from Wintergap and to think about something other than Ran and his queer family and Frit and Dodd Moss Farm.

"Well, you two seem sunk in gloom," said Valerie, folding up on the grass beside them. "How is it going, Pennie? Do you think you want to do the job for us, or is it too early to tell?"

"No, I do want to," she said, glad of the diversion. "Frances showed me the little boar you found by the bathhouse door. I think I'll start with him this afternoon, but I expect it'll take a while before I get it right. Perhaps, if I could show you what I've done in the evenings, you could tell me if it's what you want?"

"Terrific. But you don't have to spend all your time from

160

now on doing sketches for us. There are child labor laws to protect you, you know."

"I bet she will, though." Lou rolled over onto her stomach and began to pull discontentedly at the grass.

Valerie gave Penelope a helpless look over her daughter's head.

"Where are the twins?" asked Penelope to fill in the silence.

"Kenneth's got them off hunting for traces of the Roman aqueduct, God love him! He whipped them all up about it— told them it was at least three miles long, and somewhere near it there's supposed to be the ruins of a Mithraic temple. One of those things that's vanished, but mysteriously reappears every fifty or hundred years, if you believe local legends. Mark spent yesterday teasing me to let them go on an overnight hike. Even if it weren't so desperately dry, I couldn't seriously consider letting two twelve-year-olds loose on their own. Lord, he's a persistent kid!"

Once Penelope got over her self-consciousness, the drawing went quite well. She made a great many false starts that first day and was horrified at the number of sheets of paper she had to throw away and the amount of eraser she used rubbing out mistakes. Still, no one else remarked on the waste, or offered any criticism at all. And Valerie, when she saw the initial results, was warm in her praise. The suggestions she made were good ones and her encouragement very welcome. Penelope found it immensely gratifying to be told she did something well.

It wasn't that she was used to criticism from her brother or father; on the contrary. But the Ibbetsons in general seldom felt it necessary to hand out praise. You did your best because it was expected: you behaved well, you did a good job— and you got your satisfaction from knowing that, not from having other people tell you. Even Grannie Lawrence assumed it. Penelope was unable to remember her own mother well enough to know about her and wouldn't have been comfortable asking Martin. She was a little ashamed at how eagerly she accepted Valerie's praise, well-deserved or not, as if she were being vaguely disloyal to her own family by needing something they had not given her. But that dampened her pleasure only slightly.

She also enjoyed the sense of belonging that gradually crept up on her—of being a contributing part of the group at Sulpitium. She understood for the first time about her brother's craving for companionship; a little of what drove him to seek out people and make friends. It was his way of establishing himself, just as hers had always been to acquaint herself with her surroundings. She couldn't share his whole-hearted involvement, however, didn't envy him grubbing away in the trenches. She was more like her father, preferring independence, even at the risk of loneliness, to being constantly surrounded by people.

So Penelope worked conscientiously for the rest of the week at her new job, fixing her attention on it, viewing her work with a far more critical eye than anyone else. And she succeeded, partially, in blotting out other things. But several times she was reminded unavoidably of Ran, and no amount of concentration could prevent him from slipping into her consciousness.

The first reference to him was indirect—merely a casual remark made by Valerie one evening at supper, when Edward asked how things were progressing at Sulpitium. Very well, she told him. They were working undistracted now; the angle tower was beginning to emerge under Kenneth's super-vision, and her own group had been finding some very interesting odds and ends as they excavated that chamber in the bathhouse known as the apodyterium—the disrobing room. Among other items, they'd discovered several ladies' orna-ments and a number of hairpins. This in spite of the law pro-hibiting women from using the soldiers' bathhouse. "Either they were alloted a separate bathing time," Valerie speculated, "or the soldiers turned a blind eye to the law and enjoyed mixed bathing."

Martin gave a suggestive chuckle.

Edward said, "No more interruptions, then? No more dead sheep or tourists?"

"No, happily enough. I think our luck has changed. In fact, we haven't had a coach for almost two weeks, come to think of it."

"Over here," said Martin helpfully, "we call it a fortnight."

"Where would I be without you as an interpreter?"

"Lost," Martin assured her, and that was the end of the conversation concerning Sulpitium for the time being.

Penelope was sure that Ran Robson had been responsible for sending the coaches, which meant that he must also be responsible for *not* sending them. And he'd stopped, by her calculations, just about the time she'd confronted him on Dodd Pike.

Then on Friday, Mark reported having seen a black and white dog wandering loose north of Sulpitium. He and Luke were still searching for the aqueduct—Mark with a noticeable flagging of enthusiasm. They had called and whistled to the dog, which pricked its ears and studied them, but declined to come close enough for them to see if it wore a collar. There hadn't been anyone with it, as far as they could tell, but it didn't seem to be lost. Penelope willed Lou not to say anything about Ran, and she didn't, at least not to the twins. But later when she and Penelope were alone for a few minutes, she brought the subject up without hesitation.

"It was Frit," she said, "of course it was. See? If you hadn't spent the whole day at Sulpitium we could have gone up to play with her. She would have come to me, I bet she would have. Couldn't we stay here tomorrow, Pennie, in case she comes back? *Please?* I've had to go to the fort every day this week except Monday, and it's so boring."

Lou's expression was beseeching. She didn't bother to disguise her yearning, and Penelope's resolve crumbled in the face of it. It wasn't Lou she was avoiding, after all. Lou didn't know she'd met and quarreled with Ran in Hexham earlier that week. And just because the twins had spotted Frit near the Wall, it didn't necessarily mean Ran had been with her. She might have strayed off by herself chasing rabbits or grouse, any one of the enticing creatures that lived wild among the grasses and bracken. It was ridiculous for Penelope to allow the possibility of meeting Ran to dictate what she could and could not do with her own time, but that was just what she was doing. It took her all evening to work it out and to make up her mind, but by the time she finally fell asleep she had come to terms with the situation.

CHAPTER XII

"I THINK I'LL SPEND THE MORNING HERE, IF THAT'S ALL RIGHT," Penelope told her stepmother next day. They were alone in the kitchen enjoying one of those unexpected lulls that came, like the eye of a storm, in the midst of the most furious activity. Most of the family had had breakfast and scattered, Edward hadn't appeared yet.

Valerie, buttering a slice of toast with one hand and attempting without success to make sandwiches with the other, looked up and smiled briefly. "Of course it is, Pennie. I told you when you began that it was entirely up to you how often you came and how much time you spent. If you decided you never wanted to come back, you've already done some nice stuff for us."

"Oh, I won't," said Penelope hastily. "It's just that I've got some things I need to do." And, she added silently, I've decided not to let Randall Robson keep me from doing them.

Valerie, abandoning the toast, slapped the sandwiches together, piled them in a thick stack, and sawed through them with a dull-edged carving knife, muttering under her breath as the crusts on the bottom ripped. She wrapped them in wax paper, then gave Penelope her full attention, peering over the rims of her spectacles. "You sound weary this morning, love, or is it discouraged? You really are doing awfully well with the drawings. I wouldn't just say that."

Penelope gave her stepmother a tentative smile. It seemed easier to let Valerie think it was the drawings she was concerned about than to try to explain, even vaguely, about Ran, though for a moment or two she was really tempted. It would be such a relief to unbottle some of the tension inside by talking to another person, but it was so complicated and illogical and emotional she hadn't the energy to begin.

"What about Lou?" Valerie asked. "D'you want me to take her along just the same so you can have the time entirely to yourself, Pennie?"

"No, that's all right. She can stay with me. Really, I don't mind."

"Hmmm. She hasn't put you up to this, has she? Never mind. If you're sure, it would be a lovely break—for both of us. I'm awfully afraid the twins are beginning to get bored with their treasure hunt and I'll have to find something new to keep them occupied. But I don't want them wandering all over the landscape as long as the fire danger is so great."

"Luke still seems very enthusiastic about the aqueduct." This was a safe subject.

"Yes, *Luke* does. But Mark's getting restive, and when he's had enough he'll drag Luke off in some other direction willy-nilly. I wish Luke had inherited a little of his father's stubbornness, but Mark has it all." Valerie went on thoughtfully, "It's odd the way Brian got shared out between them when they were born: Mark has his stubbornness and energy, Luke has his curiosity and love of facts."

"Do they look like him?" It occurred to Penelope that she had never actually seen a photograph of Brian Prine.

"Mmm. Actually they do. Lou looks more like me, but her mouth and the set of her chin are Brian's. And you"—Valerie considered Penelope for a moment—"I think you must look like your mother. Martin looks like Ted."

"He does, doesn't he. But he wouldn't be pleased to hear you say it. He doesn't like to think of himself as being like Dad in any way."

"He'll get over that."

"I wish I thought so, but I'm not at all sure. It seems as if they've been getting further and further away from each other," said Penelope sadly. "They argue so much of the time."

"I didn't mean to sound flippant, Pennie. They're very different people, your father and brother, and I doubt that Martin will ever really understand what Ted does and why he does it. And Ted will always be scornful of the kinds of professions that Martin most respects. But that doesn't mean they will never be friends. It's just that right now Martin is starting to find out who he is, by himself, and he has begun by deciding he is *not* his father. So he has to cut himself loose, and that's painful for everyone. I don't know that I'm saying this very well—all I'm trying to tell you really is that I'm pretty sure if Ted lets him go now, Martin will come back again of his own accord before too long."

"You are?" Penelope looked doubtful.

"Yes, I am. In fact, I think your father is handling the whole business very well. If only I can do the right things when the twins get to be Martin's age!"

"Why do people have children if it's so hard?"

Valerie gave a snort of laughter. "Damn good question, Pennie. I could give you my answers, but there isn't much point because it's a question you'll have to find your own answers for when you're old enough."

"Suppose I decide not to?"

Valerie shrugged. "Then that'll be your answer, won't it?"

"What're you talking about?" demanded Mark, coming into the kitchen. "You look as if someone's dead."

"On the contrary," said Valerie. "We were discussing motherhood. What happened to the clean T-shirt I handed you last night? That one's dirty enough to stand up by itself."

"I don't know where it is."

"Go and have another look. I may be an unfit mother, but I'm not *that* unfit. Don't come down till you've found it— and *don't* stomp on the stairs, Ted is still asleep!"

"He wants us to try for Housesteads again," said Luke, who had slipped in behind his brother. His T-shirt was wrinkled but clean. "I wish we could find the temple at least. Then he'd want to keep on looking a bit longer."

"Don't be discouraged, pet, Kenneth says people have been trying to find it for years," Valerie said. "And Mark is going to have to stick around, for the weekend anyway. I don't want you going that far from Sulpitium."

Penelope spent the morning doing little personal chores at Wintergap: washing out blouses and underwear, sweeping the floor of her room, writing two very uninspired letters— one to Grannie Lawrence, the other to her friend Alison.

Lou mooched around the house discontentedly. After lunch she said, "But aren't we going to *do* anything?"

166

"I have been doing things, all morning," returned Penelope irritably. "You were the one who wanted to stay at Wintergap so badly—well, here we are."

"But this isn't what I meant. You know what I meant, Pennie. I thought we could go looking for Frit and Ran, in case they came back again. You heard what Mark said about seeing Frit yesterday. Couldn't we just—"

"No," said Penelope flatly: "I am not going to go looking for Randall Robson. And I'm quite sure he doesn't want us to find him, either."

"Why?" Lou's eyebrows shot up under her fringe. "He said —I thought you were friends?"

"Well, we aren't. He doesn't want anything more to do with us, Lou. He told me so. It would be a waste of time looking."

"But when, Pennie? When did he say that? I didn't hear him."

"You weren't there. It was in Hexham on Tuesday." Penelope was exaggeratedly brisk. "There's the end of it."

Lou was bitterly disappointed. "Then what's the point of staying at Wintergap today?"

"Once I've finished hanging out my laundry, there isn't any. I've decided to spend the afternoon at Sulpitium."

"But—"

"In a quarter of an hour," she went on relentlessly. She couldn't help it; she wasn't being fair to Lou, but Ran hadn't been fair to her, either. Lou didn't understand, of course, that what Penelope was passing on to her was some of the painful sense of rebuff Ran had given Penelope on Tuesday. And, as with Valerie, she simply couldn't find the energy to explain.

She pegged out the clothes, then collected her sketching things and her mutinous stepsister. When she started down the front steps toward the track that led to Sulpitium, Lou balked.

"Not that way. You could at least go by the path."

"Why?"

"Why not? It's shorter."

That argument was irrefutable, and Penelope knew it. "All right." She gave in with a bad grace. "But we're going *straight* to the fort, not taking any side trips."

They left Wintergap to close in on itself and brood and

167

took the path that led up to the Pennine Way. That afternoon there was not a hiker anywhere to be seen along it. It lay across the hazy fell, melting into the sunlight at either end. Lou sighed, but followed Penelope as she turned east without further argument.

Penelope wondered later how long he had been waiting. Frit met them first, loping joyfully down off the fell to greet an ecstatic Lou with a faceful of kisses. Penelope scarcely had time to hope the dog had come unaccompanied when Randall appeared, silent and unsmiling, rising from a patch of bracken above the Wall. Lou shot Penelope a triumphant look over Frit's head. Marshalling her wits, Penelope tried without much success to remember that the quarrel between them had been caused by Ran, and that she had no reason to feel defensive. She felt very defensive, and her heart was hammering unpleasantly. For what seemed like ages, neither of them spoke, then Penelope said in a voice slightly too loud, "I didn't expect to see you here. Or have you come to spy on us again?"

He shook his head. "No. Aa've come to see ye. Aa thowt to see ye afore this."

"I've been here," she said stiffly. "At the fort or at Wintergap, if you'd wanted to find me."

"Aa wouldnae gan either place. Aa'd a mind to catch ye alone."

"Why?" She challenged him directly. "I thought after Tuesday—"

"Aye, Aa've come to talk about Tuesday." He looked away from her.

"I don't see what there is to say. You don't want anything more to do with us, you said that quite plainly. I don't know why, or what I did to make you so furious—I'm sure I didn't mean to, but you wouldn't listen."

He glanced apprehensively toward Sulpitium, only just out of sight on the other side of a small rise. "Aa divvent ken how tae explain, but Aa'll have a try gin it wouldnae fash ye to walk wi' me a bit way—?" A nod of the head along the path back toward Wintergap.

"But we're going to the fort."

"We don't *have* to, Pennie, do we?" asked Lou. "We could walk a little way."

She made a show of reluctance, but yielded. She wanted, more than she cared admit, to learn from Ran why he'd come in search of her. She wanted to understand what had made him act with such anger toward her. As soon as Lou saw Penelope had agreed to Ran's invitation, she begged, "Can I go ahead with Frit? We're faster than you are. I won't go out of sight, I promise. Please?"

Penelope nodded; Lou and Frit were instantly away. As she and Ran followed, Penelope glanced at him and saw his face drawn inward in a scowl. He was chewing his lower lip. Well, the next move was his; she steeled herself to endure the silence until he made up his mind to break it.

Quite far in the distance now, Lou and Frit were playing a lopsided game of tag in which Frit was always it, and Lou always got caught. They both seemed to be suffering from an overabundance of energy and high spirits.

At last Ran said, for the second time, "Aa divvent ken how tae explain, but Aa've thowt about Tuesday an' what Aa said to ye, an' Aa see now Aa was wrong about ye. Aa've come to say Aa'm sorry."

"But I don't—"

"Hold yer whisht," he said with a kind of desperate rudeness. "Aa've worked it out—Aa cannae keep the words gin ye divvent give me the chance to say them."

She closed her lips and waited.

"Ye mun ken as well as Aa do there's a girt difference atween us. Ye were straight wi' me over Archie an' the well, se Aa owe it ye to be straight in return. 'Tisn't you, 'tis what ye are, an' where ye come frae. Ye should be able to see thon yersel."

As he struggled with the words, her indignation left her; it melted away like ice in summer and left her empty and hollow-feeling. "Are you saying you think we're too different to be friends? Is that it?"

"Aye. 'Twould nae be canny."

"But that's ridiculous! If we like each other, how can it matter? I *liked* hearing about your farm, Ran, really I did. I wasn't laughing at you. You didn't give me a chance to explain."

He looked at her helplessly. "Aa cannae help it, we're nae enough the same."

"But you can't—is it Archie? Are you afraid of Archie finding out?"

"Archie?" A flush of color darkened his face. "Ye think Aa'm fear'd a Archie, do ye? Aa am nae. Aa'm ma own man, divvent ye forget thon."

"Well he did—I mean, there was the bruise."

He stared blankly at her for a moment. Then he said, "Thon's nowt to do wi' any a this. Has nae one never laced ye for summick?"

Wordless, she shook her head.

That seemed to surprise him. "Gin ye do summick wrong, yer dad's nae laced ye for it? Or"—the merest suggestion of a smile touched his mouth—"divvent ye do nowt wrong, whey?"

On her dignity, she replied, "I've never seen my father hit anyone. If he's angry, he *says* so."

"Aye, words. Ye can run circles round about us wi' yer words! Wi' Archie now, gin he's het 'tis over quick an' forgot —he divvent hold a grudge. Thon's a good way. Ye ken where ye are wi' him."

It seemed to Penelope like an unnecessarily painful method of finding that out, but she didn't say so. It would only strengthen Ran's argument about their differences. Instead she asked, "Then is it because Archie—your family—wants the archaeologists out of Sulpitium? You think we oughtn't to be friends because we're on opposite sides?"

Ran sighed. "At the beginnin' Aa'd of said aye, but now Aa've given thon up, masel. Aa divvent believe Archie can win agyen't the pack a them thonder. He's nowt on his side. Gin he drives them out this year, they'll only be back next. Ma dad agyen't Anthony Whitton, now thon were different. Thon were one agyen't one. But 'twill never be like it again, Aa ken, though Archie willnae see it. He's lost an' cannae admit it—thon would mean everything afore was done for nowt: Dad, Mam, the farm. Aa cannae stop Archie masel,

170

but Aa neednae do what he says gin Aa divvent agree. Aa see thon now."

It was a long speech for Ran, and having delivered it, he lapsed into a brooding silence, as if he'd exhausted himself verbally.

Hesitant, Penelope said, "If you can decide that, I don't see why you can't decide about your own friends, Ran."

He favored her with a frown. "Aa do."

"Then you mustn't like me."

"Why d'ye say thon?"

"Otherwise why wouldn't you be friends?"

But he shook his head, frustrated and irritable, like a horse plagued by flies. "Aa've nae said thon! Ye're trappin' me wi' words. Aa like ye well enough or Aa'd nae of come here to find ye the day."

"Well then?"

"Have ye nae heard anything Aa been tellin' ye?" he demanded. "'Tis nae like or dislike! Thon's nowt to do wi' it!"

"But what else *is* there?" she burst out, exasperated.

"Why d'ye want to be friends wi' me, whey?" He stopped on the path and turned to look straight at her, his dark eyes probing.

She could think of a number of answers to that question: for something to do; because she was curious about him and his family; because she thought he might need friends; or just, why not? But instead she returned his look and answered, "Because I like you, too, though after Tuesday I didn't much at all."

"Aye, Aa've said—"

"I know, and it's all right." They began walking again. "But Ran, I can't understand why just our being different should get in the way of being friends. I've always been taught that it doesn't matter—or it shouldn't. I can make friends with anyone I please."

"An' ye believe thon?" he asked as if he couldn't.

"Yes," she said defiantly. "There's nothing to stop me."

"Aye, well, 'tis one mair difference atween us."

Arguments shoved each other rudely out of order in her head; there were so many she couldn't untangle them. What

171

Ran was saying to her went against everything she had grown up believing: that people could be anything they wanted if they tried hard enough; that you didn't hold a person's background against him—all that mattered was the kind of person he himself was; that class distinctions of any sort were archaic and artificial, shameful. But how could she begin to tell Randall any of this? She felt as if she had run into the hard stone wall of a house without seeing it first, and suddenly found herself lying winded on her back, dazed and shaken.

"There's nae future in it, ye ken," he said, watching her curiously. "Ye'll gan back to London an' Aa'll stay here." Something was going on behind his eyes, but she couldn't tell what. He gave a little shrug with one shoulder. "Aa hope nowt'll gan amiss."

"What do you mean?"

"Gin Aa gan on seein' ye."

"Why should it, if we're careful?" she said cautiously.

"An' what about the lassie?"

"Lou? As long as she can play with Frit, she'll not say anything to anyone."

With a nod he said, "Aa mun gan on home. Mam'll be frettin' gin Aa'm away much longer. An' Archie thinks Aa'm huntin' strays, se Frit an' me'd best find one or two." He called Frit back to him with a couple of short whistles, and Lou came puffing behind.

"What's the matter?"

"Nothing," said Penelope. "Ran has to go home, and we ought to start back ourselves, before anyone misses us."

"No one will," said Lou.

"Not yet perhaps, but we've walked a long way and it's beginning to get late." Penelope had only just realized herself that this was true. Her discussion with Ran had so occupied her attention that she hadn't noticed how far they'd walked —farther than she'd yet been along the Wall. The sun was visibly declining in the sky, though there were hours still of daylight. It wouldn't do to make anyone at Wintergap curious about where they'd been or with whom.

"When can I see Frit again?"

172

Ran hesitated, glancing from one to the other of them, then made up his mind. "The morn, gin ye want."

"Tomorrow? Do you mean it?" Lou couldn't believe her luck.

"Aye. Aa've an errand up to Greenrigg wi' Frit. Ye can come, gin ye've a mind."

"Neat!" Lou's eyes shone. "I can, can't I, Pennie?"

"Well—I ought to finish up the sketch I began yesterday—"

"You can do that later."

Penelope nodded. "All right." She suddenly felt unaccountably shy of Ran. He must have felt the same because he wouldn't look directly at her. Instead he called to Frit and with an abrupt "Aa'll see ye, whey," crossed the Wall and struck off north, toward Dodd Moss Farm. As she and Lou turned back toward Wintergap, Penelope wondered exactly what they'd agreed to do the next day. She had no idea where, or what, Greenrigg was, or what kind of errand Ran had there, or how long it would take, or when he meant to start out, or how he would arrange to meet them. With a sigh she resigned herself to leaving it entirely up to him; there was no choice. And she realized that she was happier than she'd been since Tuesday. Already she was looking forward to the next day.

All the way back to Wintergap Lou hummed happily to herself. When they reached the path that led down the slope to the house, Penelope paused. "Lou?"

"Mmm?"

She was uncertain how to proceed. "About this afternoon, I think—"

"You still want Frit and Ran to be a secret, don't you?" Lou said perceptively.

"Yes."

Lou grinned. "I don't mind having a secret with you, Pennie. Besides, Mom probably wouldn't let us see them again if she knew."

"Not saying isn't exactly being dishonest," said Penelope, as much to convince herself as the younger girl.

"Not the same as lying," agreed Lou. "Anyway, Mom just doesn't want any of us to cause trouble, and we're not going to. We aren't going to fight the way Mark did. Oh, Pennie, Frit is *so* beautiful! And smart, too. She listens to everything I tell her, you can see by the way she looks at me. If I ever have a dog I want it to be just like her. We'd do everything together and Mom wouldn't have to worry anymore about me being alone. It would be so neat."

"Yes," said Penelope absently, "wouldn't it."

When she came down to the kitchen the next morning, Penelope found Martin, the twins, and Lou already there. Valerie was on the terrace doing her exercises so as not to disturb Edward. Lou was composedly eating a banana, a small, private smile on her face, and Penelope could guess without effort what she was thinking about. The other three were listening intently to a static-y, anonymous voice coming out of Martin's transistor radio.

". . . all area footpaths, including major portions of the long-distance Pennine Way in Northumberland, Cumbria, and Borders have been closed to the public until further notice. All visitors to the region are urgently requested to keep to paved roads and be particularly careful when disposing of cigarettes, matches, and other flammable materials. Weather forecasters see no immediate relief in sight for the drought-stricken North of England, now entering its fifth rainless week. Rivers and reservoirs have fallen to their lowest levels in forty-three years, and farmers are reporting a widespread loss of livestock. A spokesman for the Forestry Commission said yesterday . . ."

"Aw, bloody hell," said Mark, then glanced furtively around to make sure his mother hadn't suddenly materialized.

"Sounds as if you won't be doing any more exploring, mate," said Martin, pouring himself a mug of instant coffee. "Must remember to buy new batteries for that thing." He reached over and switched off the radio.

"We can still look for the aqueduct, can't we?" asked Luke.

"You heard the man—all footpaths. Visitors stay on paved roads. That means they're closing off the countryside altogether to everyone but farmers. You could always take the *bus* to Housesteads, I suppose."

"Aw bloody—"

"What's up?" asked Valerie, giving Mark a narrow look as she came through the back door. She was pink in the face and a little out of breath.

"It's the drought," said Penelope. "They've just announced that they're closing off the footpaths until there's been some rain."

"A lot of rain, I should think. Jonathan was telling us yesterday about a fire on the moors south of Hexham," Valerie said. "They apparently had a terrible time getting it under control. We're just lucky no one's thought to ask us to close the site yet. If the well had dried up week before last, we would have had to. Kenneth and I keep expecting the roof to fall in, but so far we've been overlooked."

"But why should they make us leave?" asked Lou. "We don't set fires."

"*We* know that, sweetie, but they don't. They're terrified of anyone capable of striking a match up here. And we're expendable—we don't have to stay."

"Yeah, but what about us?" demanded Mark crossly. "What're Luke and I supposed to do? What's left if we can't *go* anywhere?"

At that, Lou glanced up in alarm.

"Come and give us a hand in the pits," suggested Martin. "We could do with a couple of stout backs."

"Who wants to dig holes all day?" said Mark, giving him a withering look. "That's *really* boring!"

"I can see this is going to be a problem," said Valerie, making a long face. "Well, my pets, I can give you two choices: you can come work on the bathhouse with me—and only if you promise to follow directions scrupulously—or you can stay here and amuse yourselves. There's nothing else for it."

Lou, Penelope noticed, seemed to be holding her breath, but was carefully not looking at anyone.

"Some choice," grumbled Mark. "Stay here and do nothing. Go there and work. Yeutch!"

"Well," said Luke, with an eye on his brother, "I'd kind of like to help at the bathhouse. I think it would be really inter—I mean it would be better than nothing." On an inspiration he added, "We might even find some more bones."

Mark was skeptical. "And we might not too." His tone of

voice indicated that he would give in to Luke on this, but he wanted to make his opinion abundantly clear.

Lou resumed breathing.

"What about you two?" Valerie asked Penelope.

"Oh, I think we'll stay here again, at least to start," she said carefully.

"What would we have done if they hadn't gone?" Lou said, when they were alone. "It would have been *awful!*"

"Well they have, so we don't have to worry about it."

They settled themselves on the terrace, in a meager patch of shade, where they could be seen by anyone across the valley who chose to look for them. Lou had cadged a piece of drawing paper from Penelope and was determinedly making pictures of dogs all over it: dogs lying down, standing up, begging, sitting, catching balls. Penelope knew what they were, and she tried hard not to look at them critically. She reminded herself that Lou was only eight, and that she was drawing a live animal, from memory; but still she itched to put some of the lines right, at least to make suggestions.

Presently Edward appeared, carrying a cup of tea. He was dressed, shaved, wide-awake and amiable, having been permitted to arise in his own time. Penelope had to give her stepmother full marks. Valerie was wise enough to know that there were concessions worth making in order to preserve peace within a family.

"What are you up to today, hmmm?" he inquired.

"Nothing much," said Penelope.

"Find it a bit dull around here, I shouldn't wonder," he remarked. "Not a lot you can do, is there?"

"It's okay," Lou assured him.

Penelope hoped he wasn't going to suddenly start making suggestions. Every now and then, she knew, he had an attack of conscience, usually when he'd just finished work on someing. It would occur to him as he resurfaced in the real world that perhaps he'd been neglecting his children.

When they were younger, there was very little either Penelope or Martin could do to prevent their father from suddenly bundling them off on a family outing—this no matter what they might have planned for themselves. Such outings were seldom very successful because Edward took them where he thought parents ought to take their young, rather than where any of them actually wanted to go. So they spent weary hours dutifully traipsing around museums, which Martin hated, or visiting zoos, which all of them hated. Once he'd even taken them to the pantomime, which proved an embarrassing disaster and never happened again. Penelope had been upset by the giant, and Martin had been sick to his stomach in the aisle.

Since Martin discovered, at age thirteen, that he was old enough, big enough, and stubborn enough to rebel successfully, Edward had done much less of this kind of thing. But with three new children, Penelope feared he might start up again.

"We thought we'd just take it easy today, Dad," she said. "It's so hot."

He gave her an appraising look in which there might have been just the hint of a smile. "Buzz off, Dad," he said.

"No, I didn't mean that," protested Penelope. "That's not what —"

"It's all right, quite all right. *I* don't mind in the least if my children tell me to get lost—either directly or by implication," he said, unruffled.

"You don't?" said Lou.

"Not really." He sat down on a folding chair to finish his tea. "I say the same to them often enough, God knows."

"That's true," agreed Penelope. "Only never by implication."

"Well, at least that way there's no doubt in your little minds, is there?"

"Absolutely none."

"Thought I might amble over to Sulpitium this morning and see what Val's turning up. It's been ages since I visited, but now that the proofs are finished I can relax for a bit. Then I'll give Richard a ring this afternoon to make sure the book reached him. I don't trust the post office. I'd much rather hand-carry the proofs. You'll be all right alone, I suppose?"

"We can cope," said Penelope with a touch of irony. "But you'd better hurry."

"Oh?" He raised his eyebrows.

"If you mean to get there this morning—it won't be much longer."

"Cheeky," he said with a smile. "You'll set Lou a bad example."

"Oh no," said Lou. "She's nothing like some of the babysitters I used to have."

"I think I'm glad to hear that. And I suppose you'll be glad to hear that I am leaving. I very much have the feeling that you can't wait to see the back of me for some reason. No, don't try to explain—I'm on my way!" He raised one hand in mock surrender, went in to deposit his cup and saucer and collect a few belongings. Then they heard him go out the front door, whistling "The Road to Mandalay."

Penelope and Lou looked at each other and broke into spontaneous giggles. "I was afraid he wouldn't go," said Penelope after a bit. "Or that he'd want us to go with him. He does that sometimes."

"I like it when he teases," said Lou, "because he really talks to you instead of only pretending to, like a lot of grown-ups. I don't always know when he means what he says, though. At first I was afraid of him," she admitted. "Just a little."

"You were?" That was something Penelope hadn't considered before. "He can be difficult, I suppose, but I never thought of Dad as frightening."

"Well, he's not at all like *my* dad," Lou said, giving it some thought. "You'd probably feel the same way about him, Pennie. It's just getting used to different people, and it takes time learning what to expect."

Penelope wasn't sure how she felt about words of wisdom from someone six years younger than she. "I suppose we could go up to the Wall and wait now that there's no one around to watch us."

"You do think he'll come?" Lou sounded anxious.

"He said so, didn't he?"

178

CHAPTER XIII

PENELOPE TOOK HER SKETCHBOOK AND AMUSED HERSELF BY drawing herb Robert, a little purple wildflower in the geranium family that she found growing near the Wall. It was a common plant, but one of Grannie Lawrence's favorites with its delicate blossom and lacy leaves. Lou scuffled about nearby, hunting for other specimens that might interest Penelope, while she kept her impatience in admirable check.

When at last Ran and Frit arrived, Penelope was too close to being finished to stop work. With any sketch it took time to warm to the subject, to begin to understand its shape and the way its petals fit together, to find the rhythm of it; and once she'd got that far, Penelope hated interruptions. She could never get the feeling back again without beginning from the beginning.

She ignored the joyous reunion between Lou and Frit, who greeted one another as if they'd been separated for months instead of merely overnight, and barely glanced up to acknowledge Ran, who stood about rather awkwardly, hands in pockets, watching Lou and Frit. Now and then his gaze slid curiously to Penelope, bent so intently over her work. To her relief, however, he kept a distance and did not come to peer over her shoulder and breathe beside her left ear as people sometimes did at the Victoria and Albert.

At last she had it to her satisfaction—she always knew her sketches could be better, but she was beginning to accept the mysterious and frustrating gulf between idea and reality. She was afraid she would never quite bridge it, no matter how much she improved. She straightened, put down her pencil, and looked critically at what she'd drawn.

"Can Aa see it?" asked Ran diffidently.

She nodded and he crouched to look. Usually people made polite noises or gave bright chirps of encouragement, but Ran studied in silence—which Penelope discovered was equally unsatisfactory. She couldn't tell what he was thinking. "Well?"

"Aye," said Ran. "Aye, well, Aa can see 'tis thon flower, but Aa divvent ken what the words mean."

"That's just the Latin name," she said with a touch of impatience. "*Geranium robertianum.* What do you think of the drawing?"

He seemed at a loss for words. " 'Tis bonny," he managed finally. "Aye, 'tis bonny right enough. What's it for, whey?"

"For?" she echoed. "What do you mean, what is it for? I just wanted to draw the flower—I've done quite a few different ones this summer. I like drawing." It was the first time anyone had asked to justify what she did, and she found it disconcerting. She had wanted Ran to be admiring.

"Ah," he said and lapsed back into silence.

End of critical conversation. Penelope shut the book decisively and gathered up her pencils. "All right," she said. "Where are we going?"

"Aa been thinkin'," said Ran, looking vaguely uncomfortable. "Aa doubt ye want to gan over the fell wi' me to Greenrigg—'tis a long way, an' hot in the sun. Aa brought Frit down as Aa told ye Aa would. Aa'll come for her on ma way back."

"Where *is* Greenrigg?" asked Penelope to cover a surprisingly acute disappointment. "What is it?"

" 'Tis Athertons' farm, up near the forest. Wark Forest."

"It's far?"

"Aye, a bit way."

She swallowed her pride .The prospect of spending another whole day at Wintergap alone—Lou would be totally involved with Frit, of course—had no appeal for Penelope at all suddenly. "Couldn't we go, too? It can't be that far—I could see the forest from Dodd Pike."

Ran looked at her doubtfully. "Aa divvent think—"

"What do you have to go for?" she asked quickly.

"Our gelding. Atherton borrowed him for some work."

"I could make a lunch for us to take," she offered. "We can have a picnic."

"Gin ye're sure," said Ran.

But Lou didn't want to go anywhere, even with a picnic. She wanted to stay at Wintergap with Frit. "Then she'll seem more like my own dog," she explained. "If we go with you and Ran, she'll still be his all the time."

"But you can't stay alone," objected Penelope. "Valerie doesn't want you here by yourself, you know that." The promise of the day was vanishing.

"I won't be alone," replied Lou promptly. "Frit will be with me. And your dad will be back this afternoon, so you needn't worry. I wish you would go, really I do."

Penelope was certain Valerie would not approve; she felt guilty just thinking about it, but there was Ran ready to be away, and Lou actually begging her to leave. Against her better judgment, she gave in. "Well, if you're sure—"

"Positive!"

"I'll make you some sandwiches, too, then," she said, to assuage her conscience, and started down toward the house. Lou and Frit bounced ahead, Ran followed slowly. Within sight of the kitchen door he stopped. "Ye'll nae be long, will ye?"

"Only a few minutes. Come on."

"Aa thowt Aa'd wait for ye here."

"You'd better come and tell me what you want," she called over her shoulder. When he didn't answer, she looked back. He stood still on the path, his expression wary, his eyes fixed on Wintergap. "There's no one here," she reassured him. "Really, there's not. They're all over at Sulpitium this morning." A thought struck her. "Have you ever been in this house?"

Reluctantly he shook his head.

"Come on then, I'll show you it."

All the time they were in Wintergap, Ran never relaxed. His tension was so palpable that Penelope herself felt nervous: her hands cold, her heart poised to leap at the slightest sound. There was an uneasiness in the very silence of Wintergap that she had not been fully aware of before. But that morning it was as noticeable as the stale smell of cigarette smoke many of her father's friends left behind them, and as oppressive to her. She wondered uncomfortably if Ran's presence in the house aggravated it in some way.

But that was a ridiculous notion, bordering on the superstitious. Defying it, she guided him through the rooms on the

181

ground floor, making good her promise but doing it as quickly as possible. They gave the dining room and sitting room each a brief look-in, Ran not saying much about either, and paused a little longer in the library.

"What'd anyone want wi' all them?" asked Ran, eyeing the shelves full of books. "Ye'd never read se many, nae in a hundred year, Aa warrand."

"Some people might."

"What, frae start to finish? Haddaway wi' ye!" he said in disbelief.

"We've got at least that many at home in London. Of course you wouldn't read them *all* straight through. Lots of them are for reference—to look things up in, encyclopedias and dictionaries, histories, anthologies."

"Aye." He made the word a full stop, and she sensed they were somehow precariously close to an argument again. She almost plunged in, then caught herself, realizing she had no way of winning.

Back in the kitchen, she raided the cupboards recklessly, heaping oranges, half a packet of shortcake biscuits, raisins, cream crackers, butter, and cheese on the table, while Ran stood impassive and watched her. Hastily she made two sandwiches for Lou, then cast about for something useful to stuff everything else in and hit on Martin's ancient school duffle, which he'd left hanging on the back of one of the chairs. She emptied out a limp football, two empty crisp packets, and a partially eaten petrified scone.

"They'll nae be in a swither gin ye take all thon?"

"They? You mean Valerie? Not likely. Food is fair game with the twins around. She probably won't even notice it's missing." If Valerie minded anything, Penelope reflected, it wouldn't be the loss of a few groceries, but she didn't want to dwell on that or she might have serious second thoughts about going along with Ran and leaving Lou. She packed the duffle and hefted it. "Ready."

It was indeed a long way to Greenrigg Farm, across the baking fell, and Ran led off at a pace Penelope had increasing difficulty matching. She felt the perspiration trickle down between her shoulder blades, and the duffle, which hadn't seemed so heavy to begin with, grew ever more cumbersome.

Once across the Wall, Ran headed northwest, around the far side of Dodd Pike. He followed no path as far as Penelope could see. The vast grassland spread away into distance on all sides, held down by the great weight of sky. Penelope felt very small and exposed in all that space. Here and there sheep with mottled faces paused in their nervous grass-snatching to watch the intruders pass, their eyes wide and unreliable. If Ran or Penelope got too close, they jumped and bolted, spreading the madness among their companions, and a ragged flock would thunder away.

"I thought you'd taken them all in because of the drought," said Penelope, using precious breath.

"D'ye see the daub a blue on them, whey?" Ran paused to point.

She nodded. Each sheep carried a round patch of blue dye on the left shoulder.

" 'Tis Atherton's. He's nae brought his gimmers in yet."

"Oh." She didn't ask what a gimmer was—some kind of sheep, that was obvious—and Ran was off again.

When first Penelope had viewed the country north of the Wall, she had assumed that because of its openness and great sweep it would be easy to find one's way around in without getting lost. One had merely to keep certain landmarks in sight, which ought to be simple where there was such visibility. She now realized that it wasn't simple at all; that its very openness was its greatest hazard. It was difficult—if not impossible—to keep specific features fixed. They shifted with perspective. What seemed unique and unmistakable from one angle became totally unrecognizable a hundred yards farther on. She had the vivid and unsettling impression that the country itself shifted and shape-changed, as though playing a subtle and frightening game with those people brave or foolish enough to intrude upon it. The unfamiliarity of the fells overwhelmed her; no matter how long she stayed here, or how diligently she set out to learn it, she knew she would always feel a stranger in this country. Ran was right when he said belonging had nothing to do with ownership. Belonging

183

couldn't be measured in money or square feet—it couldn't be measured at all. Nor was it something one could acquire; it was inborn.

Penelope struggled along in Ran's wake, keeping up as best she could for fear of being left behind, but finding it harder and harder, and the distance between them began to stretch noticeably until she could no longer ignore it. She had a sudden panicky vision of him vanishing, of being alone without the protection of his company, and called out, "Ran. Ran!" in a voice brittle with urgency.

He swung back instantly, responding to her tone, then stood waiting for her to catch up. "Aye?" he said when she did. "What is it, whey?"

"It's just I can't go that fast," she replied defensively. "I'm not used to rough walking. And," she added for good measure, "I'm carrying the lunch."

He opened his mouth to say something, thought better, and closed it again. "Well, ye gi' me thon an' Aa'll hump it," he said reaching for the bag. "There's a lonnen over thonder—a lane, ye'd call it. 'Tis long way round, but nae se hard gannin'."

They set off, Ran making an effort to walk slower, but Penelope could tell he didn't find it easy to shorten his normal stride to accommodate her. He changed direction, angling right, and after a quarter of an hour or so they struck a narrow, paved lane. Penelope's flagging spirits revived at the sight of it. "Ran," she said presently, "I don't really know what we're going to Greenrigg Farm for."

"Aa thought Aa told ye, to fetch our gelding."

"Yes, but what exactly is a gelding?"

"Ye divvent ken?" He looked at her in surprise.

"No," she said rather crossly. Why couldn't he just explain?

"'Tis a cuddy—a horse thon's been cut."

"Cut?"

"Aye. Castrated's yer fancy word. Se he'll work tawie."

"Oh." She left "tawie" alone. A little later, "Why do they have your horse?" From what she knew of him, it seemed unlikely that Archie Robson would voluntarily lend his property to anyone.

"Atherton needed a spare beast to hump stones to mend his sheepfold so he could bring in his yowes. An' Aa got Archie tae agree he could have the loan of ours for bit time. 'Tis nae a bad thing tae have a favor owin' ye." He gave his head a shake. "But Archie's in a hacky fettle the now an' Aa must gan canny wi' him. He wants the cuddy back at Dodd Moss, se Aa've to fetch it."

Penelope didn't follow everything Ran said, but she gathered that Archie was likely to give Ran trouble if he wasn't careful. She made herself walk faster so as to delay him as little as possible. She almost wished she hadn't come; her earlier visions of a pleasant day's outing disappeared: an easy, companionable walk across the fell, a picnic on the sunny grass, the chance to relax undisturbed. The errand was to have been no more than an excuse for all that, something conveniently dismissed for the best part of the day. But she now realized that the outing was incidental to the errand, not the other way around.

And there was the long, hot, dusty walk back to Wintergap to contemplate. Her heart sank, but her pride refused to let her admit to Ran that she might have made a mistake by coming, so there was nothing for it but to push ahead. She resolved not to mention the possibility of stopping for lunch and a rest; let Ran think of it. Then it occured to her that he had been quite prepared to come all this way without lunch, so there was a good chance he wouldn't think of it.

Once they passed close by a jumble of grey stone farm buildings, and several times they passed unpaved farm tracks leading away east or west off the lonnen. Then finally they topped a little rise and the edge of green forest lay before them in the distance, like the rind of a melon. Not much further on, Ran took a dirt track to the left. A sign on the stone gatepost said GREENRIGG. Penelope picked her way gingerly over the cattle grid—a piece of track that had been dug out and replaced with metal bars laid far enough apart to keep four-legged beasts from crossing; they would have caught their hooves between the pipes. A vehicle could drive over the grid, and with care a person could navigate it on foot, but animals had to be driven around it and through a gate on one side.

"But if you have to have a gate anyway, what's the point of having a cattle grid, too?" asked Penelope.

Ran gave her a perplexed look. "Wi' a grid ye can drive across wi'out havin' to get out an' open the gate," he said as if it were obvious. "An' ye divvent need to fash yersel about some numb hiker leavin' the gate unsnecked an' yer beasts strayin' all over the countryside. Aa wisht we had one at Dodd Moss. Aa'm workin' on Archie for it."

A high stone wall kept pace with the track on its south side; to the north lay open fields dotted with square hairy black cattle who viewed Penelope and Ran with interest but no particular alarm.

"Those're Galloways," volunteered Ran when he noticed Penelope looking at them. "Same as ours. Canny smaa' cows and tough wi'it. Ye can leave them out on the hills winter an' summer an' they'll do. Atherton's brought his in account a the drought."

"But it snows up here, doesn't it?" asked Penelope. "Do you mean you can leave them out in the snow?"

"Aye, they've the coat for it: long outside, thick in. There's some've never been in a byre in their lives."

Penelope was relieved to find the track to Greenrigg was considerably shorter than the one that led to Dodd Moss. They crossed another cattle grid and were in the farmyard. There could be no mistaking Greenrigg for anything but a working farm: its buildings and equipment had the same hard-used, practical appearance as those at Dodd Moss, but there were carefully fenced flower borders beside the Greenrigg house, and the wood trim was painted a bright green. Dogs barked and a rooster crowed somewhere.

A small child wearing only diapers and plastic pants gazed round-eyed at Penelope, three fingers jammed in its mouth, and a youngish woman was pegging more and more and more diapers to a clothesline strung back and forth between two posts. She stopped when she saw them and brushed the damp fluff of hair off her face.

"Now then!" she called with a smile. "How's yer mam, Ran? Not poorly, Aa hope?"

"No, she's nae se bad, thanks. Dr. Samuel was out to see her, an' he says she's comin' on amain."

"Aye, that's good. Ye mind me Aa've some green tomato chutney for her. Ye'll've come for the cuddy, will ye? Aye. Dad!" She turned her head and shouted. "Ran Robson's come. He'll be in the byre wi' Charlie an' Paul," she added to Ran.

"I'll wait for you here," said Penelope in a half-whisper. "Give me the duffle."

He handed it over and disappeared quickly around the house. Penelope stood self-consciously where he'd left her, trying to look at everything without seeming to stare. Although she felt a stranger here, she didn't feel unwelcome. There was none of the hostility that she had sensed at Dodd Moss.

The young woman continued to smile at her. "Gin ye'll watch the bairn, Aa'll fetch the chutney, se Aa'll nae forget it."

"All right," said Penelope, thinking that sounded simple enough. The child looked placid and biddable, its fingers still in its mouth. Its mother went into the farmhouse, leaving it with Penelope.

At that moment the baby caught sight of a small procession of cats: a marmalade mother, tail erect, followed by three fluffy wild-eyed little kittens, stalked out of the byre and across the front yard. With a gurgle of delight, the child staggered enthusiastically forward. The mother and two of the kittens escaped, the third did not. It yowled and wriggled as it felt the tiny, clumsy fingers clamp around its middle. Then, the next second it was free and streaking after its siblings, spiky with fright, and the baby had collapsed on the ground, howling in pain and fury. Its mouth opened in a great square, revealing a couple of tiny teeth; its eyes disappeared in folds of skin, and its face turned beet red.

Penelope dropped the duffle in dismay and hurried over to the child. She crouched beside it, wondering how best to comfort it, and put her arms around the little warm body. It continued to howl. Its mother came to the rescue, returning with a jar of chutney. She sat on the ground and gathered the baby to her. The kitten had left its mark on one chubby arm: four red threads strung with tiny beads. Useless and guilty, Penelope stepped back and watched. "I'm sorry."

187

The woman continued to rock the child who had begun to lose track of what it was yelling about. Looking over its head, she smiled at Penelope. "There's nae bairns in yer family, whey?"

"No, not that small. I'm the—I used to be the youngest."

"Aye, well. 'Tis a hard way to learn, Susie," she told the child, "but ye'll nae forget se smart this time, Aa warrand. Ye startled the wee beast, glaumin' ontae it like thon." She took a crumpled handkerchief out of her apron pocket, dampened it with spit, and wiped the beads of blood away. "All right now, off ye gan an' show yer dad what ye done." She gave the child a kiss and a gentle push, and it was up and staggering again. "What a pair a lungs she's got!" she said fondly. "Se ye come wi' young Ran, have ye?"

Penelope nodded.

"But ye're nae frae round here." It was a question disguised as a statement.

"No, from London. I'm with my family—we're spending the holidays at—up here." Instinctively she chose to remain anonymous.

"Oh aye, thon's a change for ye, Aa warrand! An' how are ye likin' it?"

Penelope groped frantically for some kind of simple, plausible answer that would be safe. She settled lamely for, "Quite well."

"Ran showin' ye round, is he? Thon's good," the woman continued, ignoring the inadequacy of Penelope's response. "He hasnae many friends, se far as Aa ken. Aye, but he's a grand help tae his mam. Ye've nae met Jean Robson? Na, ye wouldnae, poor soul! Aa've nae seen her masel' sin just after the accident. She dinna like folk to visit now, it frets her. Aa divvent ken what she'd do wi'out Ran—an' Archie in his own way, Aa warrand. Ran's a good lad. Have ye kenned him long, love?"

"No, not very," said Penelope. "We're staying near Dodd Moss."

"Oh?" Mrs. Atherton looked at her with interest. "Now where would thon be? Mrs. Ridley takes guests at Dykehead, an' there's Meggie Brown out-bye Haltwhistle—ye're never stayin' at the Centurion, are ye?"

188

Before she could pin Penelope down, however, Ran reappeared leading a shaggy brown horse by the halter. "We'd best be gannin'," he said.

"It's been nice talking to you," said Penelope, relieved.

"Gin ye can get a word in edgeways!" said Mrs. Atherton with a chuckle. "Aa've nae se much company up here masel an' Aa like to see folk. Dad and Charlie divvent talk much, an' the bairn hasnae started. Stop in for a bit crack gin ye're up this way again, love."

"Thank you."

"Aye," said Ran, "an' Mam'll be pleased wi' the chutney, Mrs. Atherton."

"Ye tell her Aa was askin' after her."

They trudged back along the lane; Penelope, with the duffle again, walked on one side of Ran, the horse plodded quietly on the other, its hoofs making plopping sounds in the dust. They reached the cattle grid at the lonnen and detoured through the gate beside it. Then Ran stopped to adjust the lead rope on the animal's halter.

"Ye'll want a leg up," he said.

"I beg your pardon?" She looked at him blankly.

"Ye'll've ridden wi'out a saddle afore?"

"You mean a horse?"

"Aye, an' what else would Aa be talkin' about, whey?"

She gazed at him helplessly. "Well, I have once," she admitted. That was at least six years ago near St. Albans, when one of the farmers, Jim Hadley, had let her sit astride his draft mare, Kitty. Her back was so broad Penelope's feet had stuck straight out on either side, and Jim had walked with her, his arm resting on Kitty's chestnut hide in case she needed steadying. She had not been so close to a horse since.

"How'd ye think we'd gan back? On foot?" asked Ran.

"I—yes, I suppose I did, if I thought about it at all. You didn't say anything about riding."

"T'would be numb to walk, an' us wi' a cuddy?" he declared. "Ye *can* ride, whey?"

"Not really."

Ran frowned in perplexity. After a long minute, he said with exaggerated patience, "Are ye feared of him, whey? Ye needna be, he's a tawie old beast—he'll nae harm ye."

Her chin went up. "No, I'm jolly well not afraid of him!" She caught a glint of something in those dark eyes: challenge? skepticism? amusement? Well, she had accepted his challenge now and she would make good on it or die in the attempt.

He nodded. "Aa'll get up first an' give ye a hand." Without waiting for her to reply, he set his hands on the horse's back and vaulted neatly up. He reached for the duffle and swung it over his shoulder. "Lukka. Climb onto thon stone thonder an' Aa'll come for ye."

Penelope did as he told her, and Ran maneuvered the horse alongside. He offered a hand, and the animal stood obligingly still, but she found it a very awkward business to clamber aboard. Once she was sitting astride there was nothing to hold onto but Ran himself, which was still more awkward. He gave her no time to think about it, however. As soon as he felt her in place behind him, he clapped his heels into the horse, and they were away. She had no choice but to grab him, at least until she'd gotten used to the motion and had her balance.

"Set, are ye?" he asked, half turning his head.

"Yes."

After a few minutes he prodded the horse into a trot and she really had to concentrate on staying up; there was no room to consider anything else for a while. But once she got used to the jolting and began to find a rhythm in it, she allowed herself to relax ever so slightly. Ran was solid and steady in front of her, the duffle swung and bumped against her thigh.

"Can we stop somewhere for lunch?" she ventured. "I mean, it seems a pity to have brought it all this way only to carry it back again. Besides, I'm hungry." She felt, rather than heard, him grunt. "I hope that means yes."

"Aye, we'll stop, when we get off the lonnen."

Now that she was more at ease, Penelope could appreciate the speed with which they were covering a distance that had seemed endless on foot. She hung onto Ran's belt and considered herself with detached amazement: how on earth had she gotten here? It seemed quite absurd actually, and she couldn't suppress a little gulp of delighted laughter.

Ran guided the horse out onto the fell, allowing it to drop

back to a walk. On and on they went, over the rough wild land. Penelope had given up trying to recognize anything as familiar. They crossed a dry burn, climbed a little hill, and Ran pulled the horse to a halt. Neither farm—Greenrigg or Dodd Moss—was visible, just acres and acres of uneven green-brown fell. The only immediate signs of life were a few sheep, the bubble of skylarks overhead, and somewhere—out of sight over the rim of the earth—the faint buzz of a tractor engine, thin and persistent, like a fly against a windowpane.

"This do, will it?"

"Yes."

The horse dropped its head and began to snuffle among the stiff, bleached grass for tender green blades.

"Do I get down first?"

"Aye."

Gingerly she shifted backward so she had room to lean forward as she swung her right leg behind. The horse's rump seemed higher than it had when she'd gotten on, but puffing a little, she managed to get over it, then slid not very grace-fully to the ground, only to discover when she got there that her knees had gone soft. She was too busy reminding herself how to stand to notice Ran dismount. Suddenly he was on the ground beside her. He let the horse's halter rope trail.

They picked a spot free of gorse and heather and settled on the warm sharp-smelling grass. Penelope emptied the duffle and began to spread cream crackers with very soft butter and slices of cheese. Food tasted very good, and once she pointed out that whatever they didn't eat they would only have to carry with them, Ran ate his share without further hesitation. Penelope lay on her back with her hands pillowing her head and gazed straight up into the shimmering blue sky, up and up, until she felt dizzy with its height. She could hear the horse's soft, hollow munchings; she was aware of Ran close by. She felt very peaceful, at ease with her surroundings for the first time that day. After a while she asked, "What d'you call him?"

"Ay?"

"The horse. He must have a name."

"Brown."

She raised her head and peered at him to see if he was

making fun of her. "Not really," she said. "You don't really call him that."

"An' what's wrong wi' it?" he asked in surprise. " 'Tis brown he is, se Brown we call him."

"Well, yes, but—there's nothing wrong with it," she conceded and wondered how Frit escaped being called "Spot." She was too conscious of the delicate balance between herself and Ran to pursue this, however. She shifted to something else. "Mrs. Atherton seems nice."

"Aye, over fond a talkin', but she's sonsie," he agreed. "Aa wish Mam'd let her come for a bit visit now an' then. 'Twould do her a world a good tae have company." He sighed.

"Is she—I mean, does she really look so bad?" asked Penelope hesitantly.

But Ran seemed not to take offense; he shook his head. "Nae se bad as she thinks, an' folk like Leezie Atherton wouldna mind. They ken what happened well enough. Aa keep workin' on it. Mebbe one day, gin Aa keep at her."

She rolled onto her stomach, the better to look at him. "Is that what you'll do, Ran? Stay here all your life?"

"Aye, an' why not? 'Tis ma hom. 'Tis what Aa ken." His eyes met hers levelly.

"But don't you want to see something you *don't* know ever? Don't you wonder what the rest of the world looks like? I do." She discovered as she said it that it was true. The world was too wide and fascinating to ignore.

But not to Ran. "Nay. This is where Aa belong, this is where Aa feel easy. 'Tis ma place—Aa'd be lost gin Aa left it. 'Tis what Aa am. Aa'm like Archie."

"Oh, but you aren't!" she denied. "You can't be!"

"An' why not? He's ma brother, should we nae be alike, whey?"

"But—"

"An' how would you ken anyway? Ye divvent ken either of us se well, do ye?"

"Well enough to know I wouldn't be here having lunch with your brother Archie," she replied with spirit.

The angles that had been sharpening in his face suddenly eased into a grin. "Aye, there's one to you." he conceded. "But he's still ma brother—Aa cannae change thon even gin

Aa wanted, an' "—he was serious again—"an' ye munna think Aa do. Ye'd be wrong."

"But, Ran, I'm frightened of him. Aren't you? He's so grim and angry."

"How can Aa—" He shook his head, searching for words, but all he could find to say was, "Ye divvent ken Archie, do ye? Not really."

"No, and I'm just as glad."

"Ye've a brother yersel, divvent ye?"

"Yes, but not like Archie."

She saw frustration in his eyes. "Ach! Aa cannae argue wi' ye—Aa've nae the words!" Abruptly he got to his feet.

She looked up at him with a sinking heart, afraid this afternoon was about to end as the one in Hexham had and furious with herself for having caused it. She was beginning to learn that there were subjects she could not argue with Ran about, but she'd be lucky if their relationship survived long enough for her to master her tongue.

With the ease of long practice, Ran recaptured Brown who had ambled away from them in the eternal quest for a mouthful of perfect grass. Preoccupied and silent, they remounted and Penelope hardly noticed the struggle this time. It took all her willpower not to carry on the debate with Ran—arguments kept bubbling up inside her and she kept forcing them back. But there was one thing she had to say, even if it did make him angry. "Ran?"

Pause. Then he said, "Aye?"

"You *are* different from Archie, even if he is your brother. Ran, stay different."

She felt him stiffen in front of her, then gradually relax again. "Aa divvent ken how things'll gan," he answered. "There are things we see different, Archie an' me, and there always will be, Aa warrand."

It was as close as he'd come to acknowledging he knew what she meant. She sensed with reluctant admiration that Ran's family loyalty was every bit as strong, if not stronger, than her own, and that he would not tolerate any further criticism, implied or obvious, of his brother.

"Hang onto me," he commanded, and obediently she tightened her hold. "Grip wi' yer knees." He shifted the empty duffle so it was pinned tight between them, then gave old Brown a mighty clap with his heels and Brown responded by stretching himself into a long, rocking canter. Penelope clenched every muscle in her body, clinging for life to the horse and to Ran. They seemed to be going at a furious pace over ground she knew from first-hand experience was a maze of pitfalls. If Brown stumbled and threw them, or worse, fell on top of them—visions of disaster flashed like forked lightning behind her eyes. But nothing happened. Minutes passed and still they were cantering across the fell, and she was suddenly aware that her arms and legs had begun to ache with the strain of staying rigid. Ran sat easy and secure in front of her and there seemed to be no panic in Brown's stride—at least none that she could feel. Muscle by muscle, she willed herself to unclamp—it was hard and she couldn't completely succeed, but like a snail she began to come out of herself and see the world again. She felt an odd vibration through Ran's belt and realized after a moment that he was laughing. At her, she supposed. He must have been aware of her panic. He ought to have told her what he was going to do—but if he had, wouldn't she have protested?

Little by little she began to enjoy herself. Brown, canny old horse that he was, never put a hoof wrong. And she noticed for the first time that instead of heading south toward the Wall, Ran had set Brown's nose toward the northwest. She guessed they were passing through the wide empty gap between Greenrigg and Dodd Moss, but why, or where they were going, she had no idea, nor had she any wish to ask even if conditions had permitted it.

After a while Ran slowed Brown to a trot, then a walk. " 'Tis too hot an' Aa divvent want him stammerin'," he told Penelope over his shoulder. "He's nae se young. Did ye like it?"

"Oh yes, once I got used to it," she replied honestly. "But I thought you were in a hurry to get back to the farm."

" 'Twill keep." He shrugged. "Aa thowt to show ye a wee bit a the country. Gin ye divvent mind."

"No, I don't mind." She settled herself more comfortably.

They ranged across the fells, leaving all traces of civilization behind. There were no roads, no farms, almost no animals. Usually, Ran told Penelope, they would have seen sheep and cattle, but because of the drought they had been rounded up and penned where there was water. Once Brown put up a frantic, whirring pair of birds—muirfowl, Ran called them. They looked like little dark chickens.

Here and there, hidden in the grass and bracken, were old abandoned mine scratchings: grownover spoil and chunks of rock, the shafts hidden and treacherous.

"Aren't you afraid of falling into one?" asked Penelope, when Ran pointed to an innocent-looking slope and told her it was riddled with pits. But he shook his head and said he knew how to look for them. It was hikers—strangers—who fell into them and broke their ankles or their necks and had to be fished out. "Ye neednae fash yersel up here wi' me," he told her with some pride, and she accepted that, knowing it was true. So long as she was up here with Ran she was under his protection and she was quite safe. She could not have explained it, but she didn't need to. They neither of them mentioned Ran's father.

At last Brown took them to the top of a hill, higher than Dodd Pike, and there they dismounted again. A hot wind blew around them and on all sides the Border country fell away, tumbled and green, spreading out forever to join the sky at the edge of vision. The dark mass of the forest lay like a huge cloud-shadow on the fells, and a river—the Irthing, Ran said —unwound across the dull green like a ribbon of light.

"Gin we'd the time Aa'd take ye thonder," he said. "When Aa was a lad"—he made it sound as if that were long ago—"Aa was all over these fells. Aa come up here wi' ma brother Dickie an' we'd stalk deer. There's lots a deer live in the forest, an' wildcats. Dickie was nae a hunter, mind, we come to look."

"There's so much," said Penelope, awed. "I never thought there'd be so much country, just wild, with no one in it."

"Aye, well, comin' frae London," he said, gently mocking.

"What about Dickie?" she asked. "Where is he?"

Ran chose a boulder and sat down on it. Penelope sat cross-legged in the grass. He took so long to answer she thought he wasn't going to, but finally he said, "When Dad went, Dickie left. He's nae been back sin. He wanted summick other'n Dodd Moss—'twasn't right for him. An' he'd nae use for what Archie's doin'."

"Neither have you—you said so yesterday."

"Aye, but Aa divvent want to gan, masel. An' there's Mam, as well. Archie couldna manage alone. 'Twas right for Dickie to leave, but 'tis wrong for me."

"Where did he go?"

"To Canada. He's a lumberman now, wi' a family of his own. Makes Mam that sad she's never seen the bairns. 'Twould break her heart to lose another of us. An' 'tis ma farm as well as Archie's."

Penelope rested her chin on her knees and reflected on how different this Ran was from the one she had first perceived. Underneath he wasn't at all as she had imagined him to be.

"What're ye thinkin'?"

She gave her head a shake. "Just that I'm glad I've got to know you a little."

"Ye mean it?"

"Of course I do. I like you, Ran."

"Aye, Aa dinnae think 'twould matter whether ye did or no, but it does," he said with a trace of surprise. "Aa'm glad ye came. But we mun start back. Aa've had time to fetch Brown three times over, an' me wi' chores to do."

Penelope discovered that straightening up wasn't quite as easy as Ran made it look—not for her at any rate. Her joints, unaccustomed to fitting around a horse, complained loudly. She guessed with resignation that the next day or two would be quite painful. On the summit of the hill some anonymous surveyor had kindly set a triangulation marker which she could use as a mounting block while she hoisted herself awkwardly over Brown's rump. Ran grasped her firmly by the shoulder and heaved, and finally she was in place.

The sun had begun to drop noticeably down the sky, and the afternoon light curdled as it lay across the fells, thick and rich. Ran let Brown choose the pace: a slow, steady jog that suited all three of them. Wrapped in silence, they moved through that vast, changeless, constantly shifting space. Penelope relaxed and let her mind float free; for the present, the present was enough. The past and wherever she and Ran had come from, the future and wherever they were going, were at that moment unimportant. Just then they were moving through time together, and nothing separated them.

CHAPTER XIV

"HEY! PENNIE!"

The unexpected shout startled Penelope out of her comfortable daze. Ran had left her at the Wall and kicked Brown into a reluctant canter toward Dodd Moss, and she was walking slowly down the path to Wintergap. She stopped short at the sound of her name and glanced apprehensively around to see who had hailed her. There was no one immediately visible.

"Hey!" It was Mark's voice, commanding and impatient, coming from the tumbledown garden hut he and Luke had appropriated. "Come here, will you? We want to talk to you."

The sign on the door said ENTER IF YOU DARE. She peered into the dusty gloom. The twins had liberated quite a few odd pieces of furniture: a garden chaise, a bookcase, a battered steamer trunk, even a square of carpet for the packed dirt floor. They were sitting together at a table on which lay the crumby remains of a Swiss Roll and three empty ginger beer bottles. Their expressions were not encouraging: Luke's worried, Mark's suspicious. She wondered for a moment if they'd seen her coming down off the fells with Ran, then decided it was unlikely. "I thought you were spending the day at Sulpitium," she said.

"Too hot. We came back early," said Mark. His eyes were narrowed against the light. "I want to know where *you've* been."

"Why?"

"Because. Where have you been, Pennie?"

"You sound like the Grand Inquisitor," she replied tartly. "I don't see that it's any of your business."

"It's because of Lou," put in Luke with a glance at his twin. "We want to know what happened."

197

"What do you mean?" She felt a chill of premonition. "Where is she? Is she all right?"

"No," said Mark.

"Gone to find Mom," said Luke.

"It's *your* father's fault," Mark said ominously. "He bawled her out for something—she wouldn't say what. She's really upset."

"We passed her on the road. All she told us was that he blew up about a dog, and she'd been crying. She hardly ever cries."

"A dog? Dad wouldn't shout at Lou about a—" She stopped, stricken. The premonition became a freezing certainty. Yes, he would shout about a dog, particularly if he'd found that dog in his house, and Penelope could all too easily imagine Lou inviting Frit in.

"What? What is it?" demanded Mark.

"It's my fault—I forgot to warn her," wailed Penelope. "I just forgot! He's allergic to animals. He can't breathe properly around them and he comes out in hives. It's something in their fur."

"But where'd she get a dog from?" Luke wanted to know.

Penelope bit her lip wondering how much she was going to have to explain, and to whom.

Mark said, "I bet it was that black and white one we saw hanging around here a couple of days ago. Maybe it's a stray —Lou was bound to make friends with it if she saw it. You know how she is about animals."

Luke nodded.

"But"—Mark swung accusingly back to Penelope—"how was *she* supposed to know he's allergic? He didn't have to yell at her, he could have just said."

She felt trapped. Mark was perfectly right—her father shouldn't have exploded at Lou, but she couldn't agree outright without being disloyal to her own family. "He really does get sick," she said finally.

"Lou's just a little kid!" Mark was indignant and unrelenting.

There was nothing she could say; she backed out of the hut and started toward the house.

"He's still down there," Luke called after her by way of

warning. "He nearly blew us out of the kitchen about half an hour ago."

"Hey! You never said where you'd been," said Mark. "You smell like a horse—where—"

Pretending she didn't hear him, Penelope beat a hasty retreat. All the warmth and brightness drained from her day. She hoped that Frit had had the good sense to clear off back to Dodd Moss Farm to wait for Ran when her father had started shouting.

Why did she have to pay so dearly for such a harmless bit of pleasure? It wasn't at all fair! She was filled with equal parts of guilt and resentment and wished she could slink off somewhere and hide until the storm had blown itself out. Wintergap was ominously silent. Penelope tiptoed along the hall and up the stairs, noticing the library door which was tight shut. If she were less cowardly, she reflected, she would march in and confront her father face to face. But she couldn't bring herself to. She washed her face and hands and brushed the snarls out of her hair, then crept back down to the kitchen. It occurred to her that the best thing she could do under the circumstances was begin to get supper. If it made no impression on her father, at least Valerie might take the gesture kindly.

She had just finished laboriously peeling eight large potatoes when she heard footsteps in the front hall. Steeling herself, she waited, while the boiling water writhed impatiently in its saucepan on the cooker. For what seemed like ages, nothing happened, then Martin appeared.

"Hullo, what's this then? The Galloping Gourmet?"

"Don't be funny," she snapped, nerves making her testy. "Did you—where's everyone else?"

He leaned nonchalantly against the doorjamb. "Valerie and Lou are upstairs washing."

For an instant she allowed herself the luxury of hope: Mark had been exaggerating—there was no crisis, just a disagreement. But the glint in Martin's eye banished that hope. She sighed.

"What the flipping hell happened here?" he asked conversationally. "What did Dad say to her anyway?"

"I don't know," Penelope confessed miserably.

199

"What do you mean, you don't know? You were here, weren't you?"

Helplessly she shook her head.

"But I thought—"

"I know, but I wasn't. I went up onto the fell," she said with a hint of challenge.

Her brother raised an eyebrow, but didn't ask. Instead he said, "Well, whatever it was, he must have laid it on with a trowel. Crippen! I've never seen a kid in such a rage. Not even you when you were little!"

"*You* were the one who had the rages, not me," Penelope returned. "What about Valerie? What d'you think's going to happen next?"

"Blessed if I know. If you were a few years older, Pennie, I'd suggest we do a bunk together—sneak off to the Centurion for pork pies and a pint and leave them to sort it out."

"I'm afraid a lot of it's my fault though," she said forlornly.

"Well, for cripes' sake don't ever admit it!" exclaimed Martin in horror. "Take my advice and lie doggo on this one —let Dad answer for it. It won't do him a bit of harm. He's bigger than you are, don't forget."

"Doggo's the right word," she said wryly and dropped the potatoes into the pot. "But, Martin—"

"Well?" Mark, with Luke close behind, came through the back door. "What's happened? We saw them come home."

"Nothing yet," said Penelope.

"You're in time for a front-row seat," remarked Martin and earned a frown from his sister.

"Look," said Mark. "I want to know what you were doing up by the Wall this afternoon, Pennie. If *we* couldn't go, I don't see why you could—especially since you were supposed to be taking care of Lou. This wouldn't have happened if you'd been here."

"But I—"

"Hang on a minute, mate," said Martin, suddenly gone serious. "You can't make Pennie take the blame for this one. It isn't any of your business what she was doing—she doesn't have to account for herself, certainly not to you."

Mark looked belligerent. "What about Lou? Pennie

shouldn't have left her alone like that. Mom doesn't want her left alone."

"I know, but I—"

"If you're so concerned about Lou, why haven't you been looking after her, come to that?" returned Martin, paying no attention to Penelope. "You're old enough to take a little responsibility for her, I should think. Whose sister is she, anyway?"

"Mom didn't ask us to," said Mark defensively.

"So far you've been able to do whatever you've jolly well wanted to without thinking about anyone else."

Luke looked chagrined.

"Well, so have you," Mark retorted.

"Ah, but *my* sister's old enough to take care of herself."

"I really don't mind having Lou around," began Penelope.

"But there's no reason why anyone should expect you to take *all* the responsibility for her while Mark and Luke go larking about enjoying themselves. Don't be a mug, Pennie."

"I don't know that Mom would let us take care of Lou," said Luke. "I guess I didn't think—"

"No, you didn't, did you," said Martin severely.

"Look," said Penelope with a trace of desperation. "None of this is getting us anywhere at all. Right now I think the best thing we can do is to keep anything else from going wrong. You could wash your hands and set the table," she suggested to the twins.

"Good idea," agreed Martin.

Mark opened his mouth to protest, but Luke jabbed him in the ribs. "She's right, it might help. Come on." Grumbling about the high-handedness of certain people, Mark gave in.

"Right," said Martin and made for the door.

"And *you* can chop onion."

He checked. "Me?"

"Yes." She was firm. "All I can think of is to make rissoles out of yesterday's lamb. And I'm doing mashed potato. Will it be all right, d'you think?"

With a sigh of resignation Martin nodded. "Show me your onions."

By the time Valerie came down, the table was almost fin-

201

ished, Martin—blinking hard—was mincing onion on a chopping board, and Penelope, red-faced, was pounding away at a potful of potatoes.

"Good Godfrey!" Valerie exclaimed, pausing to take it all in. "Such industry! I'm afraid to ask what all this is in aid of. It looks like four guilty consciences, but I *know* that couldn't be the case."

"Conscription, that's what it is," snorted Martin, wiping his eyes with his shirt collar.

"Don't expect us to do this all the time," warned Mark.

"No?" said his mother. "It looks good to me—all of you working together."

Penelope had to ask, "Where's Lou?"

Valerie met her worried gaze calmly. "Still upstairs. She'll be down for supper. All right, guys. I don't know exactly what happened this afternoon—no, Mark, just keep still and listen. I gather that none of you does either because you weren't here. Right? Then this is between Lou and Ted, and it's an argument—a fight, not to put too fine a point on it."

"I wouldn't give Lou much in the way of odds," said Martin darkly.

"You don't know her very well," replied his stepmother with a little smile. "She has all her father's temper and obstinacy, and that's an awesome combination. She's a pretty tough little girl. But what I don't want"—she glanced round at them all—"is to have the rest of us choose sides and square off against each other. It's all too easy to do that—to turn this from a misunderstanding between two members of a family into a pitched battle between the Ibbetsons and the Prines. Do you know what I'm saying?"

Penelope nodded, a little uncertainly.

"Yes," said Mark, "but what about—"

"*All* families have arguments," Valerie went on. "A family is made up of individuals and friction between them is inevitable. If you try to pretend it isn't you're headed for trouble. You can't heal a wound if you won't acknowledge it's there; it'll fester and fester until it's past healing." She paused, then said ruefully, "That's a lot of what went wrong between your father and me, Mark. I can finally admit it even if I don't like to. And I'm telling you because I don't intend to let it happen to me again—or to any of you, as long as I can prevent it."

"But he had no right to yell at Lou," Mark protested. "He's not even her father."

"That," said Valerie, "is precisely what I meant about squaring off. You're splitting us up instead of pulling us together."

"Do you mean you want us to pretend he's our father?" asked Luke with a worried frown. "I'm not sure I can. What about Brian?"

But Valerie shook her head. "I'm not asking any of you to pretend anything—you're all much too old and cynical. I don't know yet what we'll end up being to one another. It's going to take a long time to sort out. Friends at any rate, I hope. Ted and I discussed all of this before we got married, you know. We decided we could make it work with your cooperation—that it was very much worth trying. And you all had the chance to object before it was settled, you know you did."

Martin, who'd been standing back listening, nodded. "Fair enough. But what do we do right now? Act as if we don't know what's happened between Dad and Lou?"

"We don't," Luke pointed out. "Not really."

"Some of us can guess," replied Martin significantly.

"I'm sure you can, but I wish you wouldn't." Valerie gazed thoughtfully at the pot of half-mashed potatoes Penelope held. "Do me a favor, Martin, just hold off and let me handle this. Don't jump in with both feet this time, either you or Mark. All right?"

"What about them?" demanded Mark.

"Oh, I'm not worried about Pennie and Luke."

"You're implying that Mark and I are unreliable hotheads," said Martin, preparing to step up onto his dignity.

"You've got it," agreed Valerie cheerfully. "Now, what's for supper, Pennie, and what can I do to help?"

Penelope, who'd been prepared to defer to her stepmother, found Valerie ready and willing to follow her directions instead. Valerie assumed she knew what she was doing, and so indeed she did. It gave her a measure of confidence just when she needed it most.

"This ought to be quite a gathering," Martin observed as they put food on the table. Valerie took it upon herself to go announce supper to Lou and Edward.

"I still feel responsible," said Penelope.

"You're a minor, you can't be. Not legally."

She gave him a baleful look. "If that's meant as a joke, it's failed miserably."

"All right, wallow in self-pity then," he replied with a shrug.

"Thank you very much."

But he gave her a little thumbs-up sign for encouragement as they assembled around the table. Valerie reappeared with Lou whose face was closed tight as a clamshell. She sat on her chair without a word and looked at nobody. Penelope felt a knot tie itself in her stomach. Her lovely afternoon with Ran might as well never have happened.

The knot tightened when Edward joined them. He wore a bland, untouchable expression and acknowledged them all with a nod and an airy "Good evening." Martin's eyes narrowed, but he said nothing; Mark and Luke took one good look and withdrew into their exclusive fellowship. Valerie was composed and calm as she dealt out plates.

"What did you say these were, Pennie?"

"Rissoles," said Penelope, swallowed, then went on bravely, "Grannie Lawrence taught me how to make them. You can use any kind of leftover meat—you mince it with an egg and onion and bread crumbs. I couldn't find any tomatoes—I hope they're all right without."

"Excellent," pronounced Valerie after her first bite. "Like hash. You'll have to show me how to do it."

"They're very easy." Penelope felt like Sisyphus rolling his boulder uphill—the conversation weighed several tons. She and Valerie had their shoulders behind it, pushing for all they were worth, but they needed help. She glared at Martin and asked rather too brightly, "Have you found anything new at the bathhouse?"

Martin heaved a long-suffering sigh and joined them. "Strewth, Pennie—they aren't looking for anything *new!* Haven't you been paying attention? In order to be worthwhile the stuff has to be rusted and covered with dirt, bent, dented, broken into tiny fragments, full of holes, or otherwise smashed to bits."

"And at least fifteen hundred years old," added Valerie, grinning. "Don't forget that. As a matter of fact we did find a few old things today—buckles, hairpins, combs, and a nifty little enamel brooch that Frances thinks will clean up nicely. You might like to have a try at drawing it, Pennie."

"But it's all such *little* stuff," objected Mark. "You haven't dug up anything really valuable—like a gold plate, or even coins."

"Depends on how you define valuable, doesn't it?" said his mother. "The objects we've been finding may not be worth a lot in terms of money, but their value to me as an archaeologist is incalculable." She was warming to her subject. "The big stuff is exciting, but the little stuff is what tells me how people—ordinary people—lived at Sulpitium. What they ate, how they spent their spare time, what they wore, where they came from, how wealthy they were, what kinds of jobs they did. Those are the things I want to know. What was it like to be here in the year 300?"

"What difference can it make to us though?" pursued Mark.

Valerie, her mouth full of rissole, made a helpless, impatient gesture with her fork.

"Sounds to me as if you're fostering a heretic," remarked Edward.

"Well"—Luke looked doubtfully at his twin—"don't you think it's kind of interesting to know things like that?"

"No," said Mark bluntly. "Not specially. It hasn't got anything to do with *me, now.*"

"I must say," put in Martin with a sideways glance at Valerie, "it has occurred to me to wonder, as I clean my blisters and inspect my callouses every night, why exactly *are* we killing ourselves out there in that field?"

"But you keep doing it, don't you?" Penelope pointed out. "No one's making you."

Valerie swallowed too hastily and choked. Luke thumped her on the back and Penelope got her a fresh glass of water. She coughed until there were tears in her eyes.

"Hold your hands over your head," advised Mark.

"Or drink out of the wrong side of the glass upside down," said Martin helpfully.

"That's hiccups," Luke said.

Valerie waved her arms in the air and the coughing subsided.

"All right?" asked Edward and she nodded.

"Told you," said Mark.

"You don't think," Valerie began in a strangled sort of voice, "you don't think that history can make any real difference to us in the present?"

"How can it?" Martin was skeptical. "Oh, some of it's pretty interesting stuff—like those corpses—but I don't see that it's much different from a work of fiction, entertaining at best, diverting—" He gave a shrug.

Out of the corner of her eye, Penelope could see her father gearing himself for an attack. "History and fiction are two entirely different things, for your information," he began. "With fiction—"

"But don't you think that what people did in the past has some bearing on where we are now?" asked Valerie, interrupting him.

"Of course," replied Martin. "If the Romans hadn't built the Wall we'd never have come to Northumberland."

"That is not what I mean," Valerie made a face at him. "And you know it!"

"If you don't mind," broke in Edward, "I have a thing or two to say to my son."

Martin said dangerously, "I'll bet you have."

Edward fixed him with a flinty look.

Penelope stepped into the breach. In a loud voice she asked her stepmother, "Do you think things that happened here almost two thousand years ago can affect us now? Even if we don't know what they were?"

"What do you mean?" Mark wanted to know.

"Aha," said Edward, sitting back in his chair. "Let's hear you answer that one, Val."

"I'm not sure I understand what you're asking." Valerie frowned.

Penelope hesitated, uncertain about how to translate feelings, instincts, into adequately expressive words and felt a twinge of sympathy for Ran. She looked around the table; she had everyone's attention except Lou's. Lou was doing something private with her napkin under the table and didn't seem to be listening. "Do you like this place?" she asked finally.

"Like it?" Valerie looked surprised. "Sulpitium?"

"Mmhmm. Sulpitium, Wintergap, the Wall—all of it. Do you feel comfortable here?"

"Well, I haven't really given it much thought—"

"What's that got to do with the past?" asked Martin.

"Yes," said Mark.

Penelope wished she hadn't said anything, but it was too late now—they were interested, not about to let her drop it. "Suppose—suppose you live in a place where unpleasant things have happened in the past—not just once by accident, but over and over again throughout hundreds of years?"

"But—" said Martin.

"Shut up and let her go on," said Luke unexpectedly. He was leaning his elbows on the table, concentrating.

Penelope gave him an apologetic look. "I'm not really sure how to," she said. "I haven't tried to work it out before—it's more a feeling I've had since we arrived."

"Are you saying you *don't* like Wintergap, then?" asked Edward.

"There's nothing wrong with it," Penelope said hastily. "I mean nothing anyone can see. But I wouldn't want to live here. It's probably just my imagination . . ."

"You don't like the idea of it being built out of stones from the bathhouse," declared Mark. "Girls are always squeamish about things like that."

"Not at all," said his mother brusquely. "I don't believe Pennie's squeamish. But I'm still not sure I understand what you are driving at."

"I think," said Penelope carefully, "that it *does* have to do with the stones being taken from Sulpitium. But I think I felt this way about Wintergap before you discovered the grave. It has to do with the atmosphere here. Haven't you ever felt something about a house the first time you went into it? That it's a good place, or a happy one, or that it's sad?"

207

"That isn't the house, Pennie," said Martin. "That's the people living in it."

"Or the people who *have* lived in it," said Edward slowly. "Does a place accumulate feelings? That's a good question."

"It sounds highly unscientific," said Valerie the archaeologist.

"It sounds dumb," pronounced Mark. "I don't see anything wrong with Wintergap—I think it's neat."

"Has anything good ever happened here?" pursued Edward.

"What do you mean?" asked Martin.

"Well, the man who built it died of pneumonia before he could live here. His immediate family wouldn't stay in the house. His nephew came much later and spent his time warring with the local inhabitants. In five or six years he had a complete breakdown and his opponent was killed in an accident."

"But that could have been the family, not the house," Martin said stubbornly.

"But there's *still* trouble," said Luke. "Look at the fight Mark got into."

"And," Penelope added reluctantly, "the archaeologists haven't been very lucky here either. They have to keep canceling the excavations."

"But I don't see what any of that has to do with the fact that Wintergap is built from stones taken from Sulpitium," said Valerie. "Practically every house, barn, church and farmyard up here is built from Roman stone. According to your own line of reasoning the countryside along the entire Wall, from Wallsend to Bowness, ought to be declared a permanent disaster area. There wouldn't be a soul living here!"

Penelope was afraid to get herself in any deeper; she wasn't equipped with the right ammunition to refute her stepmother's blunt, practical arguments. But Luke wasn't so prepared to withdraw, now that he'd entered the discussion. "But everything isn't built of stones from Sulpitium," he said.

"I don't see that—"

"Maybe something awful happened here. You found all those bodies, and you said you thought the fort had been wiped out by the barbarians."

"That's not exactly what I said, and we can't be sure of anything, Luke."

"What about the knife in the skeleton?" asked Martin.

"That doesn't prove a mass tragedy. Unless we're extraordinarily lucky we'll probably never know precisely what happened. There just isn't enough hard evidence."

"Perhaps what Penelope's saying is that she thinks you'll never be lucky at Sulpitium," suggested Edward.

"That's a cheerful thought!" exclaimed Valerie.

Penelope felt her cheeks get hot. "Not really, I mean I couldn't—"

"It's odd in a way, when you think of it all," her father went on. "I mean the recorded history of this part of Britain. It's never been a peaceful place, has it? Always having to be defended, fought over, pillaged, captured and recaptured. And it hasn't really stopped. In a manner of speaking, Val, I suppose you're the new invaders."

"Thank you very much."

"People like the Robsons certainly regard you as such."

Penelope gave an involuntary start at the name and glanced at Lou. The little girl's head was down, her face hidden, but her hands had stopped moving in her lap and Penelope was sure she was paying attention.

"Well, among the lot of you, you could set archaeology back several centuries," declared Valerie. "Just don't go spreading your superstitions on the site, please. We have enough to contend with already."

"See?" Edward raised his eyebrows. "That's precisely what I mean."

"What?"

"Everything you've had to contend with."

"Oh, Ted, honestly! All our 'incidents' this summer are directly attributable to human interference."

"Archie Robson," said Martin.

"You said that, I didn't."

"And his brother," put in Mark belligerently. "Don't forget his brother."

Penelope bit her lip to keep silent.

"So there you are," said Valerie, looking at Edward with a gleam of triumph.

"Not really," he replied pleasantly. "That's only the top line, Val. Underneath it lies whatever compels him to go on fighting a battle even he must know he hasn't a prayer of winning. The natives hereabout may be a close-knit, loyal lot, but they're canny when it comes to self-preservation. If he goes too far, he'll run up against our civilized twentieth century law, Robson or not. And if he doesn't go too far, he'll never get the land back."

"Well personally, I don't know the man so I really can't say what his motives are, Ted. I can't even say for sure he's involved."

"But you know he is," said Martin, adding with relish, "and if he keeps on long enough we'll catch him at it dead to rights. *Then* there'll be hell to pay!"

"You'd like that, wouldn't you?" Penelope charged him.

Her fierceness caught him by surprise. "Certainly I'd like to see him stopped. The bloke's a menace."

She subsided like a snuffed candle, the flame gone instantly.

"I want to be excused," said Lou, speaking up for the first time.

Valerie glanced at Edward then at her daughter. "Lou—"

"Can I?" Lou glared challengingly back.

Valerie hesitated, then gave a little nod. "All right, sweetie. I think you ought to have an early night, though. Perhaps we all should. That is if none of us feels too peculiar about sleeping in a haunted house."

That remark Penelope considered unfair. She could feel herself close up even as Lou had. In future she would keep her thoughts private, not expose them to be made a joke of.

Luke, hesitating at the top of the stairs on the way to bed, tried to offer her a little awkward sympathy. "I don't think she was making fun of you, Pennie, not really. She was just trying to keep things light."

"I don't know what you're talking about," she replied stiffly.

He gave her an anxious look. "She was filling a gap—you know—between Lou and your—between Lou and Ted." He had obvious difficulty saying "Ted," she noticed.

"It's all right," she said with a sigh. There was no point in being irritable with Luke. But how curious, she thought, as she got undressed, that Luke should have trouble knowing what to call her father. She realized then that both the twins managed usually to avoid calling him anything and remembered what Valerie had said to them all in the kitchen before supper. They *didn't* yet know what they were going to end up being to one another. Everyone was struggling with it, not just Penelope herself, and that was comforting.

Before she slept, there was one thing she wanted to do. She sat on her bed, making a desk of her knees, and opened her sketch pad. Pausing to look at it for a moment, she flipped past the little drawing of herb Robert that she had done—it seemed much longer ago than that morning—and on a clean page she began to sketch from memory. She felt a sense of urgency; it was important she do this now, tonight, before the edges of it blurred. She wasn't much good at drawing people—she'd never cared to try, but she sat there, working, oblivious to the night and the settling noises in the house, and the face she wanted took shape under her pencil. And when it was done, she closed the pad carefully and lay back satisfied.

CHAPTER XV

THE FIERCE HEAT CONTINUED WITHOUT A LETUP. PENELOPE sat on the Wintergap terrace feeling oppressed and dull, her limbs almost too heavy to move, a vague, gritty aching behind her eyes. Beside her she had a stack of old *National Geographic* magazines, a complete run for the years 1948–1954, which the twins had discovered in a dusty corner of the attic.

The house was silent and deserted behind her; she was as aware of its presence as if it had been someone peering over her shoulder while she sketched. It made her uneasy, but she hadn't the energy to leave it this morning. She hadn't the energy to do anything much except sit and look in an unsystematic way at glossy photographs of exotic and unbelievable places.

Valerie, Martin, and the twins had gone straggling off to

Sulpitium, Mark predictably protesting. Edward for once had gotten up early and driven away without explanation. And Louisa, apparently still in a temper, had gone outside by herself before anyone else was properly awake.

"The only thing to do," Valerie said, "is to leave her alone until she mellows a little. She's absolutely intractable when she works herself up to it, but she'll get weary after a while. I keep thinking if I were a better, less distracted mother this wouldn't have happened."

"Rubbish," declared Martin. "It's Dad's fault."

"Or mine," said Penelope, feeling grim.

"And Mark's and Luke's then," Martin added. "That leaves only me, pure and blameless Martin Ibbetson, the best of a bad lot."

"Purely insufferable Martin Ibbetson," replied Valerie dryly. "Pennie, are you cross with me for some reason?"

"Why should I be?"

"I don't know, I just wondered."

Gingerly she shook her head. "I don't feel very well."

"Nothing serious, I hope?" Valerie sounded genuinely anxious. "Have you a temperature?"

"I don't think so."

"She's feeling antisocial," Martin decided with a sharp look at his sister. "She wishes the lot of us would clear out."

Valerie sighed. "All right, Pennie. You stay here and take it easy, why don't you? I'll find Lou on the way out and take her along with me so you won't have to worry about her. And don't brood about yesterday—everyone'll get over it."

A hot breeze worried the morning. In the valley the birds were silent, too hot and dispirited to sing; only the insects out in the burnt grass under the sun made noise: an endless, monotonous chain of sound.

Penelope found an article about New Zealand in one of the *Geographics* and sat staring at the pictures, trying to imagine the country her father had grown up in and to place him there. In the photographs it looked bright and mountainous and empty, with wide, sheep-spattered plains—different from Northumberland certainly, but not unrelated. For the first time she found herself wondering who she might have been if her father had not chosen to leave the Canterbury Plains for the twisted, civilized streets of Oxford and London. Would she then have been a person like Ran, used to wildness, isolation, and rough physical life? Familiar with sheep and dogs and weather and trackless fells, rather than with cities and people? Perhaps there wouldn't be such a gap between them.

Except an unbridgeable gap of continents and oceans—for if she had been born to that life in New Zealand she would not be here now, would never even have known of Ran's existence, much less talked to him, ridden bareback behind him. It was because of who she was that they had met one another, and it was because of who they both were that they would probably never see one another again once she left Wintergap. What had Ran said—there was no future in it? The thought made her feel sad and old, defeated somehow, without understanding by what. She wondered at herself a little for minding so much; she and Ran were inescapably different, he was right. He was probably the most different person she'd ever known, yet there was something instinctive between them that made them friends in spite of themselves, and in spite of their families. But what was it for? Why did she bother—why did either of them bother—if their friendship had no future beyond the end of summer?"

She closed the magazine and threw it down on the pile, filled with a resentful discontent. The morning passed slowly. At noon she ate a solitary and unexciting lunch: a boiled egg, some digestive biscuits, and an orange, then returned to the terrace taking with her one of Luke's crossword puzzle books. Had it been Mark's she would have left it in the drawing room rather than face his inevitable wrath at having his private property tampered with, but she knew Luke wouldn't grudge her a page or two of puzzles. They were very American and harder than she expected; they distracted her nicely. Odd to think that people who would claim to speak the same language might have such trouble understanding one another . . .

The sudden appearance of Frit jolted her out of the hazy trance she'd fallen into. Frit, the innocent catalyst for civil war. Penelope regarded the dog with blank dismay and Frit stood at the edge of the terrace looking back, her feathery tail swinging gently side to side as if she sensed her welcome was not a certain thing. Penelope shook herself, knowing that the dog had not come visiting alone. "Ran?"

Silence. She was getting tired of being stonewalled. He was there, she knew it, though keeping himself invisible. "Ran? Wherever you are, come out. I don't feel like playing games," she called crossly, getting to her feet. Frit's bright gaze was questioning. "Do you hear me?"

After a moment there was the merest scrape, leather on stone, and Ran materialized by the back corner of the house. She was about to demand what he meant by sneaking up on her again, opened her mouth, and caught the words just in time. It wasn't her he was sneaking up on, of course, it was the house and its other occupants. He wouldn't know she was alone. "It's all right," she said instead, a little stiffly. "No one else is here, not even Lou."

He looked distinctly relieved, but still not at ease. She sat down again. He stayed where he was. The silence was thick. "Well?" she said at last, unable to bear it any longer. "You didn't come just to stand and stare, did you?"

His face took on a hard, immobile expression that reminded her ominously of the face she'd given the figure on the memorial stone, and she was seized with something very like panic. "I'm sorry," she said, taking the edge from her voice. "It's been a beastly morning, and it was even more beastly last night when I got back and I'm not in a very good temper. There really isn't anyone else around, you needn't worry."

"Aye." He was unconvinced, but at least he'd spoken.

She waited, keeping her impatience in check, and finally he came across the terrace to sit beside her, cross-legged on the flagstones. Frit wriggled over to him and rolled onto her back, begging him to scratch her stomach. Automatically he obliged, his mind obviously elsewhere.

"Was he—Archie—cross with you for being late yesterday?"

He glanced up quickly and she saw the stony expression was gone, replaced by a glint of humor. "Ye might say a wee bit, aye. Nowt serious. Only called me names."

"Well, that's something," she said wryly. "My father was furious."

"Yer dad?" Ran was wary. "How'd he ken where ye'd gan? Ye never told him?"

"No, it wasn't me he was furious with. The row was about Frit and Lou. He doesn't know where I went."

Frit thumped her tail as she recognized her name. "What'd Frit do, whey?" Ran's fingers stopped moving, but he left his hand resting protectively on her ribs.

"Frit didn't do anything," said Penelope with a sigh. "It wasn't her fault, it was really mine. I forgot to tell Lou to keep her away from Dad. He's allergic to dogs and cats—they make him ill. I think Lou must have had Frit in the house when he came home yesterday and he shouted at her." Glumly she added, "It wouldn't have happened if I'd stayed here. I should have, I knew it."

"Then 'tis ma fault, too," said Ran unexpectedly.

"Yours? How could it possibly be yours?"

"For askin' ye to gan wi' me."

"But you didn't—I didn't think—I mean—"

He shrugged, looking faintly embarrassed. "Aa'm sorry it caused ye trouble, but Aa'm glad ye came."

She struggled valiantly to understand the movement of things dark and deep and unfamiliar. She was out of her depth, and so, she suddenly realized, was Ran. Nothing to do with two people was ever one-sided, that much she saw clearly. Was the whole of growing up going to be this difficult and bewildering? She sensed that Ran was struggling too. "Well," she said, catching hold of something solid in the middle of the morass, "what's happened, happened. There's no going back now, and it was lovely."

"Lovely?"

"Yesterday afternoon. Being up on the fell and the things you showed me."

"Nowt special," he said, frowning. "Nowt ye couldna've found for yersel gin ye'd a mind."

"But I wouldn't have," she persisted. "I wouldn't have done any of it without you taking me. And I'd never have ridden a horse."

215

At that the frown vanished. "Aa dinna believe ye when ye told me ye'd never ridden afore. Ye were feared at first, weren't ye?"

"Scared? No. Not really. It was just—well, a little," she admitted and was rewarded with a real grin.

"Aa'd nae of let ye fall, ye ken."

"I don't see how you could have stopped me!" she retorted. "But I didn't anyway."

"Nay, ye dinna," he agreed, then grew serious. "Aa divvent see how they'd still be angry today. Wi' Archie 'tis over an' forgot."

"Well, with my father it's not that simple. Nor with Lou."

"Aye," said Ran. " 'Tis bluddy words. Ye get all tangled in them—they divvent come right an' ye cannae get loose frae what ye've said."

"At least words don't hurt people," Penelope answered back.

"Mebbe not where ye can see."

She had no answer for that, so she countered with a question: "Why did you come here?"

He went still; his fingers which had gone back to teasing Frit's ears, ceased to move, and he sat looking hard at the ground. She sensed he had something important to say to her, but he was silent. She rolled Luke's book in her hands, then unrolled it and rolled it the other way. "Why?" she prodded gently.

"Divvent push me!" he exclaimed. The anger in his voice startled her.

"I didn't mean to. Ran—"

"Hold yer whisht."

She snapped her mouth shut. Whatever he had come to say she could feel him working it out, searching for words. It was terribly hard not to try to find them for him, but with an effort she throttled her impatience.

Suddenly he shook his head. "Aa cannae! 'Tis nae good. Aa cannae tell ye here."

"But why not? I told you there's no one here but us."

" 'Tis nae thon, 'tis the house. 'Twill nae let me think proper. Ye mun come away an' Aa'll tell ye."

"Away where?" she asked with a sinking heart.

"Up thonder." He nodded toward the fells beyond the Wall. "Aa cannae stay here. 'Tis unchancy." He sprang to his feet, Frit with him.

His words touched a spark of perversity in her. "It's too hot to go playing games out there in the sun," she said stubbornly. "I have a headache."

" 'Tis nae game," he assured her, his eyes somber.

"Then just tell me what it's about."

"Come wi' me."

"That's all superstitious rubbish!" she said crossly. "There's nothing wrong with Wintergap except that you're not used to it. That's what makes you afraid."

He looked at her long and hard, then turned away. Frit hesitated between them, then dashed after her owner.

Frit's decision broke the spell. Penelope jumped up. "Ran!"

He stopped but didn't look back. "All *right*," she said. "If it's so important, I'll come. But I don't see why you have to be so mysterious about it."

Once away from the shade, the sun caught them full in its searing light. Lost in the sky above the Wall a lark sang, a single brave, thin voice. Everything else was silent, defeated by the heat. Penelope's scalp prickled, and her legs encased in heavy denim felt damp and sticky. At least Ran didn't go racing ahead this time, he stayed with her. She felt the blood pound inside her skull. Ran was making for Dodd Pike; that came as no surprise, but it was such a long way. They walked and walked and seemed to get no closer.

Then at last the ground began to rise, and every step took even more effort. On and on he led her until they reached the shoulder of the Pike from which she had first looked down on the settlement. She paused there, breathing heavily, wishing the humming in her ears would stop. It lay shimmering in the heat of the afternoon, cupped between folds of scorched hillside: the same tumble of stone and mound. It had not lost its power to frighten her, to make her feel an alien. If it hadn't been for Ran she would have gone no farther, but she was safe in his company. They descended the slope and entered the circle.

He chose a pile of stone and sat. Gratefully, Penelope sank onto a sun-baked stone and closed her eyes. Time, like river water, flowed past and she let go and drifted with it until the thunder behind her eyes faded to a distant grumbling. The first thing she saw when she opened them again was Ran's face intent on her own. There was a concerned pucker between his dark brows. For a minute she couldn't find herself, couldn't quite remember what she was waiting for. Then she remembered he'd said he had something to tell her. "Well? Here I am," she said. "What is it?"

"All right, are ye?" he asked, still watching her. "Ye look gey pale. Aa thowt ye were gannin' off to sleep, sittin' there."

"Of course not. I was just resting."

"Aye." He sounded doubtful.

"Go on and tell me."

Unhappiness clouded his face. "Aa divvent ken—" he began and stopped. He took a long breath. " 'Tis Archie. He's got some idea in his mind—Aa divvent ken what, but Aa'm worried."

"Idea about what?"

Ran hesitated, giving her an uneasy glance. "About—'tis about Wintergap. He hadnae the time to lace me last night, he's too full a this. Wild he is that ye've nae left, d'ye ken? He's bound ye'll gan, one way or another."

"He's tried to drive us off before without succeeding," Penelope pointed out. "What is he going to do this time?"

"Aa told ye, Aa divvent ken. 'Twill be unchancy, ye can reckon. He's nae been thinkin' a owt else for days. Mam's dead fear'd he'll do summick real loopy. She wanted me to tell ye."

Penelope stared at him. "Your mother? She knows that— that we're friends?"

Ran flushed. "Aye, Aa told her. Aa divvent keep secrets frae her. She'd nae tell Archie gin Aa asked her not. 'Tis ma own life."

"But doesn't she mind about me? About my family?"

"Nay. Not Mam, not anymore. She kens ye've nowt to do wi' what happened—thon was atween ma dad an' the Whittons. 'Tis only Archie cannae see thon, an' we cannae stop him, Mam an' me."

Wearily, Penelope said, "You brought me all the way up

here to tell me that? That Archie's going to do something, but you don't know what?"

He turned abruptly from her. "All right, divvent listen. Gan back tae yer house an' see," he said in a tight voice.

"But Ran—"

"Divvent ye ken what Aa'm doin'? Divvent ye ken 'tis ma own brother Aa'm tellin' ye about? Aa've come tae ye agyen't Archie!" he burst out. "Aa divvent want to fight ye—Aa divvent want to fight anyone nae mair, Aa told ye thon. All Aa want is to stay here an' farm Dodd Moss, d'ye ken? But Archie's ma brother still." He hunched his shoulders miserably, drawing into himself.

"But if you can't tell me what he's going to do, what—" She caught herself. She'd been going to say, "What good does it do to tell me this?" Practically speaking, she could see that it did little. But to say so straight out would be to render Ran's gesture totally futile, and in spite of the fog in her brain she understood that the warning was the least important part of what he'd done. Ran's giving it to her was what mattered. But she had no chance to tell him she understood that, for just then Frit began to bark and Ran was instantly tense.

"There you are!" Mark cried.

Looking up, she saw him standing against the skyline, Luke beside him. For a handful of seconds everything froze, then the twins came pelting down the hill. "What're you doing here? What're you doing with him?" demanded Mark, pulling up some six feet from Ran and Penelope. "D'you know who he is?"

"Of course I—" She scrambled to her feet and her head began to thump again.

"Go on, tell me what you're doing here!" he challenged.

"What are you—"

"We were up by the Wall and we spotted him sneaking down toward the house, didn't we, Luke? We knew he was up to no good—spying and trespassing."

"He wasn't," Penelope denied, her temper rising at Mark's refusal to let her finish a sentence. "He was—"

"Get out of my way, Pennie," he commanded, paying no attention. "I'm going to finish what *he* started in Hexham!"

219

"Don't you dare!" she exclaimed furiously. "This has nothing to do with you, Mark Prine."

"Oh yeah?"

"Come wi' ye," Ran invited, his eyes narrowed. "Aa'm ready!"

"Ran—" said Penelope.

"Mark—" said Luke.

"Shut up, Luke," said Mark.

The two boys faced each other, radiating hostility, tight as stretched elastics ready to snap. Penelope looked from one to the other and saw a kind of murderous excitement in both pairs of eyes.

Frit, her feet braced, fired a volley of sharp, frantic little barks at Mark.

"Keep the dog out of it," said Mark.

"Frit, back!" ordered Ran, and her tail dropped and she crept out of the way, eyeing Mark suspiciously.

"Ran, remember what you just said about not fighting," said Penelope.

"And what Mom said to us," Luke added.

They were both ignored; they glanced at each other helplessly as Ran and Mark began to circle, knees bent, arms tensed. At the same moment they sprang, and it was Hexham market all over again, without the crowd of spectators: two grunting, growling figures locked together in a violent struggle. They swayed and staggered, each fighting furiously for the advantage. Mark kept trying to hook his right leg around Ran's and knock him off balance, while Ran fought to keep his arms free and push Mark over backwards.

"Can't we stop them?" Penelope demanded of Luke. She had the nightmarish feeling that they had all been in exactly the same place before, that it had all happened just this way.

"How?"

Ran stepped into one of the hut stones and lost his footing; the two boys crashed to the ground, rolling over and over—a tangle of flailing arms and kicking legs. With growing horror, Penelope saw them trying their best to hurt one another: ripping, punching, twisting like wild animals worked into a killing rage. They were too evenly matched for the fight to have a quick, decisive outcome. It would go on and on while

220

she and Luke stood by like dummies and watched Ran and Mark do serious damage to each other.

Then, beside her, she heard Luke: "Come on, Mark—come on! You've got him!" in a voice hoarse with excitement.

She opened her own mouth to encourage Ran and was struck with a sudden bolt of white-hot fury. How could they? How could *she* possibly encourage Ran to beat up Mark? Or Mark to beat up Ran? She couldn't take sides with either of them when she hated with every atom of her being what they were doing to each other. Without pausing to consider what she was doing, she grabbed Luke by the arm and yanked him out of her way. She saw him look at her with open-mouthed astonishment as she dove past, right into the middle of the writhing mass, not knowing which bits were Mark and which were Ran, and not caring. From outside herself she saw and heard the whole thing—heard Penelope shout, "Stop it! *Stop* it! *Listen* to me!"; saw Penelope caught in the thrashing heap—pulled in and snarled inextricably among the churning limbs. She heard Luke somewhere outside shouting, saw fragments of sky and turf and Ran and Mark. There was a sudden jarring thud that echoed through her skull and brought the two Penelopes together again with an anguished yell, and everything fell apart—became three separate bodies, panting and wild-eyed, torn, scratched, bleeding, and dirty.

Mark sprawled on the grass, his knuckles scraped raw and oozing, his hair on end, the neck of his T-shirt irreparably torn. Ran was several feet away, his chest heaving, two buttons off his shirt and a third hanging by a thread, a set of four wide crimson scratches plainly visible through the tatters of his shirt sleeve. And Penelope lay perfectly still on her back on the grass, her face wet with tears and blood.

"What'd you do *that* for?" Mark exclaimed furiously when he had enough breath.

"Mark, she's *hurt!*" cried Luke in horror. "Really hurt. She's *bleeding*."

Mark scrubbed the hair off his face and pulled himself up, scowling. The next moment he and Luke were on the ground beside Penelope, blotting out the light above her. She saw their faces hovering, frightened, angry, worried.

221

"You must have hit her," said Luke accusingly. "How could you?"

"Well, why didn't you stop her?" Mark shot back, genuinely alarmed. "Pennie? Pennie! I couldn't tell what was her and what wasn't. Besides, how do you know it was me? It was probably *him*."

They turned to look at Ran who had stayed where he was, kneeling on the grass.

"Oh, *stop* it, can't you?" snapped Penelope. She took a deep breath, blinked the tears out of her eyes, and sat up, almost knocking heads with Luke. Gingerly she put a hand to her nose. "Hasn't somebody got a handkerchief?" she asked thickly.

Luke, galvanized to action, felt frantically through his pockets and came up with a tattered lump of tissue, which he offered. She pushed it disgustedly away. "I meant *clean*." She tipped her head backward, breathing through her mouth. "It's only a nosebleed!"

"Serve you right," muttered Mark, limp with relief. "You shouldn't have gotten in the way like that."

"Here," said Ran, thrusting a worn cotton handkerchief into her free hand.

Mark glared at him. "Probably *crawling* with germs."

"Shut up," said Penelope and he lapsed into surprised silence. The blood stopped and she wiped most of it away, using her own spit to dampen the cloth. It was the same one Ran had used to take the midge out of her eye, it seemed like months ago.

"Who hit you?" asked Luke.

Penelope eyed all three of them balefully—Mark and Luke and Ran, who had withdrawn again. "I don't know and I don't want to know. It doesn't matter. It was stupid and you should both be ashamed."

"Now wait a minute—" began Mark.

" 'Twas nowt to do wi' ye," said Ran. " 'Twas atween him an' me."

"You make me so cross!" retorted Penelope. "Course it was to do with me! He's my brother and you're my friend—whether I like it or not—how could I just stand there and watch you rip each other to shreds? Tell me?"

Neither of them answered. Mark looked sulky, Ran stony. Luke said in a small voice, "It should have been me, Pennie."

"Personally, I don't think any of the three of you have much to be proud of," she said bluntly.

"Where do you get off giving us a lecture?" complained Mark. "If I'd known you were going to turn out like this, Pennie, I'd of never—"

But what he wouldn't have done remained a mystery because Frit interrupted him with a funny, muffled little bark, and Ran flung up his head and sniffed the air.

"What is it?" asked Luke.

"Whisht!" said Ran sharply. He jumped up and stood scanning the horizon, his face intent. Frit was quivering slightly. The other three looked at each other in puzzlement and Mark was in the act of tapping his head with his forefinger, when Penelope caught a whiff of something strange on the breeze—the merest trace. It was an odor she hadn't smelled up here before—it took her a second or two to place it, and when she did, it made the hair rise on her arms and prickle on the back of her neck.

By then Ran was away, racing full speed toward the summit of Dodd Pike with Frit beside him. Penelope jumped to her feet and went after them as fast as she dared, nosebleed forgotten.

"Pennie—!" yelled Mark, but she didn't stop.

She was out of breath and streaming with perspiration by the time she reached the top of the Pike. Her heart thundered so loud in her chest she could hear nothing else until it quieted. But it wasn't hearing that Ran had come up here for, it was seeing. They both could see all too well. Spread below them, across the fells to the east and south of the Pike was a vast billowing cloud of smoke.

CHAPTER XVI

THE BULK OF DODD PIKE HAD SHELTERED PENELOPE, THE TWINS, and Ran from the sight of the fells on fire, and they had been so absorbed in the fight that none of them had noticed the smell of smoke on the breeze, until Frit had barked.

Now, from the cairn at the top of the Pike, Penelope and Ran had a terrifying view: an immense grey blanket of smoke, fraying as it climbed into the pale sky, blotting out acres and acres of fell; and at its edges the red dance of flames racing out through the grass and bracken, flaring and falling, a long, uneven vanguard that met and overcame everything in its path. There was nothing as far as they could see to stop it—only an infinite supply of the best possible dry fuel.

Ran blew between his teeth and swore softly.

"But how," said Penelope in awe, "how could we not have known before this? It's a *huge* fire."

"It wouldnae take long for it to spread, not wi' the wind. Thon's nowt but tinder out thonder."

Even as they watched, the fire visibly spread farther: it lapped at the foot of Dodd Pike and raced through the grass below it to the south. It was cutting them off, Penelope realized with horror, stranding them on an island up which it would inevitably climb until it caught them. "We can't stay here!" she said, trying to swallow the panic that rose in her throat. "What can we do, Ran? How can we stop it?"

"Stop it? 'Twill take hundreds a men to do thon," he said grimly.

An impenetrable scrim of smoke hid Sulpitium and the country south of the Wall. Penelope, searching for the roofs of Wintergap, was distracted momentarily as she glimpsed a figure, distant and vague, running west along the course of the Wall, running out of the smoke and away from the fire. She clutched at Ran's arm.

"What? What is it, whey?"

She pointed and he looked. Neither of them spoke. The figure disappeared, hidden by trees and a dip in the fell. Penelope looked wide-eyed at Ran; his face was bleak.

"But not this," she said, her voice scarcely a whisper.

"Wow!" exclaimed Mark, as he and Luke joined them. "Oh, *wow!*"

"How did it start?" asked Luke, gazing about in wonder.

Penelope's hand was still on Ran's arm; she felt a tremor. "We don't know," she said as much to him as to Luke.

"Some bluddy fool wi' a match," said Ran expressionlessly.

"Hadn't we better try to get down?" asked Luke. "I mean, it's spreading awfully fast, isn't it, and the wind's carrying it right for Wintergap. We'll be trapped if we don't go pretty fast."

"What about Mom and everyone else at the site?" asked Mark.

"They must have smelled and seen it before we did," Penelope said practically. "Someone's probably called the fire brigade by this time—Jonathan said they were all ready, waiting in case there was a fire."

"But Mom won't know where *we* are," Luke pointed out.

"At least the sheep and cattle are off the fells," said Penelope, trying unsuccessfully to crack the misery on Ran's face.

"Aye," he said and shook himself. "Aa mun gan home." He turned to look straight at her, his eyes searching hers. "Howway, Aa'll set ye right for Wintergap, an' be off masel. There's nae time to stand about."

"Look," said Mark. Away to the northwest, coming down from the slate-colored forest were streaks of dust: vehicles being driven at speed over the dusty unpaved tracks that seamed the fells.

Ran nodded briefly. "Forestry. 'Twill need us all gin we're to stop it. Howway."

The fire had exploded across the fells; it was devouring acres of grass and bracken, heather, gorse, and scrub in a great confusion of smoke and flame. The wind drove it against the Wall and filled the air with grey flakes of ash like dirty snow. Smoke billowed dense into the sky, smudging the delicate blue, dimming the sun. It shone like a bloodshot eye through the shifting tatters. Penelope had a sharp, acid taste in her mouth, and her eyes were beginning to sting. She could hear the fire now: a muffled pulsing roar, punctuated with hissings and snappings.

"Ye mun gan back to the big house first," Ran was saying to her. "Ye cannae get to Wintergap Farm frae here now. Gan by the lonnen an' ye'll be all right, ye hear?"

"Yes," she gasped. They were stumbling and running down the Pike together, down past the camp without giving it a glance.

"Shouldn't we help fight the fire?" yelled Mark. "You said they'd need everyone."

"Have ye fought a fell fire afore?" asked Ran shortly.

"Well, no, but—"

"Aye, whey leave it to men wha have. Ye'll be mair help gin ye bide clear an' keep out the way."

There was no arguing with that tone of voice, even Mark realized it. He gave in with uncharacteristic meekness. "Well, at least no one can say we started it," he shouted back as they continued their erratic way down the Pike. "We were nowhere near the spot."

As they reached the level of the fire it was like running into a fog. All around the landscape was blurred, indistinct. The smoke collected in depressions, anywhere the wind couldn't worry it. But instead of being damp and clammy like fog, the air was blistering, dry, and full of the reek of burning. Penelope found herself wondering what would become of all the wild creatures: the grouse and mice, the owls, curlews and rabbits, even the crickets and cicadas. The plants had no chance, of course, they couldn't run. The distruction wrought by the fire was unimaginable; she couldn't get her mind around it, it was so vast.

It seemed to take forever to reach the Wall. The smoke blinded them and made their eyes water. There were no landmarks, nothing to catch hold of, to measure distances or reassure them that they were struggling in the right direction. They had to trust Ran who kept them moving as fast as possible and held them together, much as Frit would have done with a flock of sheep. Even he hesitated once or twice, but Penelope was certain that he could get them back to the house, and Mark finally gave up challenging him and accepted his lead.

Penelope knew instantly when they reached the Wall—it was there but not there. She would instinctively have known the feel of it blindfold in the dark. And Ran stopped. "Ye'll be all right—the house's down-bye, ye can see it there."

"But—" began Mark.

"Aa've to gan home. There's the farm an' all the beasts, an' Mam'll be in a swither."

226

"What'll you do?" asked Penelope fearfully. "There's nothing to stop Dodd Moss from burning, is there?"

Ran glanced around. "Gin the wind keeps steady the fire could miss us. Gin it shifts, we mun save what we can. Mam'll fret an' Aa'm nae back sharp." He spoke to her as if they were alone. "Ye'll be safe gin ye gan canny."

She nodded. "Don't worry about us, Ran. You be careful."

"Aye." He gave a grim little smile and was gone, disappearing into the smoke.

She, Mark, and Luke hurried down from the Wall. Trees loomed ahead of them wreathed in smoke; smoke lay like a skein of wool along the course of the small burn. Mark resumed his place as leader now that Ran had left them, and in ten minutes they reached the house. It was silent. As soon as she crossed the threshold, Penelope knew Wintergap was deserted.

"Hello?" called Mark and got no response. "Hey, where is everybody?"

The front door was standing open. Penelope was sure she hadn't left it that way. Mark called again, but they all realized by then that no one would answer.

"Well, I like that!" Mark was indignant. "They aren't even worried enough about us to come looking. We might be burned to a crisp while they're busy saving their broken pots and skeletons!"

"We've got to go to Sulpitium," said Penelope urgently. "Don't you see? Someone *has* been here, looking for us. They'll be worried sick."

"She's right," said Luke. "They'll send out search parties."

"We've got to let them know we're all right." Penelope was decisive; this time she took the lead, down the front steps and along the track toward the site.

"What about the shortcut?" Mark hesitated on the bottom step.

"I think we should do what Ran told us and take the lonnen—the track," she called back. "We don't know where the fire has spread to—it might have come across the Wall up there."

"You go that way and Luke and I'll take the shortcut. That way we won't miss anyone looking for us."

227

"No, we've got to stay together."

"I think so, too," Luke agreed.

Mark made a disgusted face at them but yielded, and the three set off at a quick jog. The smoke was thinner down this far; if it weren't for the smell it might almost have been heat haze.

"Pennie," said Mark after a few minutes, "what about that guy, Randall Robson. You don't mean he's really a friend of yours?"

"Yes, I do," she said curtly.

"Then you've been seeing him all this time?"

"Now and then."

"Well, I like that! Mom forbids us to have anything to do with him and his family, and you—"

Martin suddenly appeared, coming full tilt along the track toward them. The relief that flooded his face at the sight of them metamorphosed instantly to irritation. "Where in hell have *you* been?" he demanded. "I thought I was going to have to tell Valerie you were lost somewhere in *that!*" He waved a hand at the mounding smoke to the north.

"We were never lost," said Mark. "We came as soon as we noticed the fire."

"Noticed—! When I found the house empty—hang on, one of you's missing."

Luke looked from Mark to Penelope to Martin. "We're all here."

"Where's Lou?"

"She hasn't been with us all morning."

"Pennie?"

Penelope shook her head. "I haven't seen her. Valerie said she was going to take Lou to the site this morning."

"She couldn't find her—we decided she was just being bloody-minded, so we went without her," said Martin with a groan. "Where the flippin' h could she be?"

Ice formed in the pit of Penelope's stomach. "Are you sure she isn't at the fort?"

"Of course I'm sure!" snapped her brother. "Valerie sent me back to collect all *four* of you."

"What'll we do?" asked Luke looking stricken.

228

"Go back and have another look," said Martin grimly. "Come on, we'll all hunt, top to bottom."

They searched Wintergap from the attic to Edward's library, the back pantry, and the dank unused cellar, to Lou's cubbyhole bedroom. She wasn't there. Martin dispatched the twins to check the outbuildings while he and Penelope combed the garden and valley. After twenty minutes of fruitless hunting and calling, they met again on the terrace. Even Mark looked worried. Penelope felt as if she had a great solid block of ice lodged in her chest.

"Ideas?" Martin looked from one to another.

Mark shook his head, silent for once.

"Suppose," said Penelope miserably, "suppose she followed us? Either you and Luke or me?"

"Followed you where?" said Martin.

"She wouldn't have done that," Mark said, but he sounded uncertain.

"She might have. I never thought to look back, did you? She followed me once before when I went to—when I went up on the fells."

"What are you talking about? *Where* did you go?" demanded Martin impatiently.

"Up to Dodd Pike," said Luke.

They stood staring at each other. Martin rubbed his face with fingers that left streaks of grey down his cheek. "Oh, cor!"

"We'll have to go back up and look," said Penelope.

But Martin made up his mind. "No. Valerie told me to bring you back—and I shall at least take the three of you. Then we'll organize a proper searching party to go after Lou. I shan't take responsibility for losing any more of you."

"Won't that take too long?"

"Smoke's getting thicker all the time," put in Mark.

"Every minute you argue is wasted," Martin said, adult and obstinate.

"Come on then!" said Penelope.

Sulpitium was chaos. There were great heaps of equipment scattered about. The tents were being taken down and rolled in hasty, bulky bundles, leaving bleached white patches on the turf. Several students were lugging cartons of papers and small objects out of the farmhouse, down to the car park which was full of strange Landrovers and vans and pickups. The wigwam of fire brooms had vanished; three or four lay about on the ground where not long before there had been at least two dozen.

"Where is everyone?" asked Penelope, gazing around.

"Gone above the Wall to help fight the fire," said Martin. "That's where I'd be if it weren't for you lot."

"And those?" Mark pointed at the unfamiliar vehicles.

"There're men from all over the district—they're still coming in. There'll be masses more at Cawfields and the Forestry teams down from Wark. What they want to do is burn a wide strip ahead of the fire, so when it gets there it'll burn out for lack of fuel. Or they'll dig a ditch, except the ground's so hard they'd have to use dynamite to make it effective soon enough. Don't stop here. The sooner we find Valerie, the sooner I can get back to doing something useful."

"The sooner we can find Lou," Penelope said.

As they approached the farmhouse, Valerie appeared in the doorway as if she'd been waiting for them. Her eyes ran over them, counting—Penelope could see her coming up one short. She counted again, then looked beyond, down the sloping field toward the farm track. She came back to Martin then, her expression one of question, potential alarm. "Where's Lou?"

"We don't know," blurted Mark. "We haven't seen her."

"What do you mean? Pennie—?"

Martin glared at Mark. "She's probably all right, we just couldn't find her at the house, that's all."

"*All?*" repeated Valerie. "She was there this morning when we left. I should have told you she wouldn't come with me, Pennie, but I thought—"

"I didn't see her," Penelope said, the ice expanding, threatening to choke her. "She didn't come in for lunch. I thought she was with *you.*"

"No." The word was short and sharp and definite. "Anyone have any ideas?"

"Yes," said Martin. "These three twits went north of the

230

Wall this afternoon, in spite of being warned not to. They think she might have followed them."

"North of the—" Valerie turned her head and glanced up into the great rolling swell of smoke moving inexorably down from the fells.

"We didn't see her, Mom, any of us," said Luke miserably. "We ought to have seen her from the top of Dodd Pike if she was following us."

"Except that we were looking at the fire," Mark reminded him.

And Penelope thought, I *did* see someone but it wasn't Lou. And it wouldn't help the present situation to mention it. With a feeling of relief she pushed the memory of the figure into a far-back corner of her mind.

"None of this matters," broke in Martin. "The main thing now is to find her."

"Right." Valerie was suddenly brisk and decisive. "We'll have to send people up there to look. Martin, see who you can round up here on the site. If you can find Jonathan—"

He nodded and sped off.

"We'll go," vounteered Mark.

"You will not. You're staying put so I know where you are."

"But, Mom, we know where we went," he pointed out. "We know where to look."

There was a flicker of uncertainty in Valerie's expression. "Well—"

"I'll go," said Luke. "I can find the way better than you, Mark, I'm better at remembering." He looked as if he'd rather do anything than plunge back into the heat and smoke above the Wall.

"It's my idea," said Mark aggressively.

"I oughtn't to let either of you go, but it would make sense to send one of you along—" Valerie glanced doubtfully at the twins, then made up her mind. "All right, Luke."

"Hey!" protested Mark. "He doesn't even want to, look at him!"

"But he offered," said Penelope.

"Who asked you?"

"The thing is to find Lou, not fight over who goes with

231

the search party," Valerie said sternly. "There'll be plenty for you to do here, Mark, never fear. Luke, if you really *can* help—I only wish—well, you must stay close to Martin and do exactly what you're told. Understand?"

"Yes, Mom."

Penelope, looking at Valerie's hard-set, anxious face, caught an unwelcome glimpse of the problems of being a parent. She was totally involved in the struggle of growing up—learning to take responsibility for herself. But Valerie had taken on responsibility for three other people as well—her children—who as they got older were frequently beyond her immediate control. And the responsibility was hopelessly tangled in worry and love, sympathy and pain—the untidiest of emotions. And Penelope saw it now because her resolve to remain uninvolved had fallen apart: she was worried sick about Lou herself.

Sir Kenneth joined them at that moment, his arms full of flies and notebooks. When he learned what was wrong he immediately volunteered his services for the search. "A matter of priorities. You can oversee the evacuation, Val. It doesn't need both of us. I'll go and you stay in case she turns up on her own—she's quite likely to, you know. Here." He distributed his load between Mark and Penelope, and ducked back into the house, to reemerge in a minute wearing his felt hat and carrying a thick, knobbled walking stick.

Martin, Jonathan, Luke, Sir Kenneth, and two other students hastily assembled, then divided into two groups and set out for Wintergap—three on the track, three following the shortcut, so they wouldn't miss Lou if she were somewhere between the house and Sulpitium.

"No time to stand around gaping," said Valerie once they'd gone. "Much better to keep busy, and there's more than enough to go around." She was lecturing herself as well as Penelope and Mark. "Take those papers down and pile them beside the other files. As soon as Frances gets back with the Mini we'll load it again."

"Where is she? Where are you taking everything?" asked Penelope.

"The Youth Hostel. They've offered us a field for the tents and a lean-to for the papers and equipment."

"Maybe," said Mark to Penelope as they hurried down the slope, "maybe you were right—this *is* an unlucky place."

They worked steadily through the afternoon. Penelope carried load after load out of the farmhouse as Valerie piled things into cartons and bags, and Mark commandeered a wheelbarrow in which to cart it all to the parking area. He flung himself into the job with violent energy, to work off, Penelope suspected, his disappointment at not being allowed to take part in the search. It was astonishing how much stuff had accumulated in the six weeks or so the archaeologists had been at Sulpitium. The Mini came panting up the track, followed shortly by the blue University van, and then it was all hands to pack both vehicles for another run to the Youth Hostel. Frances assured Penelope that the artifacts had been among the first things removed to safety.

Penelope lost track of time, and it wasn't until Mark tipped his barrow on end and declared loudly, "I'm *starving!* Isn't anyone else hungry?" that she realized the hollow chill in her stomach might at least partly be the result of lack of food. It was almost five—lunch was ancient history, part of another life: before Ran, before the fight, before the fire. Valerie gave up her packing with reluctance, admitting that perhaps a break and some sustenance would do them all good. She and Frances and Penelope scrabbled through mounds of gear to find food enough for a makeshift meal: the inevitable oranges, a four-fingered hand of splotchy bananas, some cream crackers and a lump of solid, partially dry cheese, some chocolate, and a large bottle of cider.

"We've almost finished," Valerie told them as they sprawled on the grass, faces shiny and streaked with soot, hair in stribbles, clothes damp and dirty. Ash drifted down to settle on them, the hillside was tarnished grey with smoke. Everything tasted of it, smelled of it. There were seven of them—a subdued, weary little cluster. When they sat still there was time to think, to begin to grapple with what was happening around them: the inevitable disruption of everything they had worked on so long and hard, the hideous devastation that had swept down on them, that lay just the other side of the Wall.

"Now I know what the Romans must have felt like, facing attack from the Britons," said Frances, blowing ash off a biscuit. She spoke aloud what Penelope had been thinking and Penelope glanced at her startled. "Only they had to stay and fight."

"That's what I want to do," exclaimed Mark. "I don't want to go on lugging this garbage around—I want to *do* something. I want to fight!"

"Absolutely not," said Valerie. "You don't know anything about fire fighting, Mark. The last thing they need up there right now is to have you—any of us—getting underfoot."

"What about everyone else—Dick and Charles and Colin and all the rest of the students?" he countered. "They don't know either, but you let them go."

"I couldn't stop them," replied his mother. "But I can stop you—you're my kid. I have more than enough to worry about already."

"I wonder where they are—the searching parties," said Penelope, then wished she hadn't as anxiety flooded her stepmother's face. It was gone in an instant as Valerie slid a protective mask over it, but Penelope realized it lay just below the surface, ready to reappear as soon as Valerie let her guard down.

"This is like the last day of Pompeii," said a girl called Ann.

Frances shook her head. "That happened much faster. No one had any idea what was coming until it was too late. They all got buried in volcanic ash and lava while they were doing perfectly ordinary things."

Mark shot his mother a calculating look. "I'm going up to the Wall to see what's happening," he announced, scrambling to his feet.

"Mark—"

"Just to the Wall, I promise!"

Valerie could not bear to sit idle any longer. Even before they had all finished eating, she'd begun packing things up again. Penelope followed her into the nearly empty farmhouse. "They've got to be all right," she said. "They're probably just having to come back a longer way around the fire."

"Mmm," said Valerie. "I wish your father would come back."

234

"What could he do?"

"Be here," Valerie answered simply. "Come on, Pennie, two more loads should do it, then we'll have to decide what next." She glanced up at Penelope's solemn face and smiled. "I'm sure you're right and everyone'll turn up before long." It was after six when the van bounced off down the track with the last of the equipment stowed inside. The site looked derelict and desolate. Mark had come down from his lookout on the Wall to report that the fire line was dangerously close and the men were going to burn the scrub in the Romans' fighting ditch in a desperate effort to contain the flames above the Wall.

"They want everybody out of here," he told them.

"Did you see any of our chaps?" asked Ann, who was particularly concerned about Dick.

"Couldn't tell. Everybody up there looks the same—covered with charcoal. You can't recognize anyone."

"Look!" cried Penelope. "Isn't that Dad's car?"

"Where?"

"Coming along the track, down farther, see?"

CHAPTER XVII

IT WAS INDEED EDWARD'S YELLOW VOLVO, BEING DRIVEN WITH unusual recklessness up the rough track toward Sulpitium. The cloud of dust it raised was almost indistinguishable from the smoke that came rolling down the hillside to meet it. Mark waved both arms in the air, and Valerie and Penelope joined him as the car bucketed past the turnoff, heading for Wintergap. It jerked to a sudden halt and began to reverse.

"He's seen us!" cried Penelope with relief. "Hullo, there's someone with him. But who—?"

The same thought struck all three of them simultaneously.

"Oh, no!" Valerie exclaimed.

"He can't have!" said Penelope.

"At least she's not lost," Mark said.

"But what about the searchers? What about Martin and Luke and Jonathan and the others?" Penelope demanded.

Valerie had gone very still; she stood with her hands dropped at her sides, waiting for the car to reach them. As soon as it stopped, Edward's door burst open and he sprang out and ran toward them. The other door opened a minute later and out climbed Lou.

"Thank God you're all right!" exclaimed Edward. "We started back as soon as we heard about the fire, but we had a hell of a time getting through and no one could tell us exactly where it had spread to or if Sulpitium had gone up. How did it start, do you know?" He stopped short as he registered Valerie's peculiar expression. "What is it, love? What's wrong? Where're the others? Is someone hurt?"

"Why on earth did you do it?" she demanded, furious and unbelieving. "Why, for the love of God, Ted?"

"What? What have I done?" he asked in surprise.

"Louisa," she said in a choked voice.

Lou looked frightened. "Mommy?"

"This is going to be bad," Mark predicted in an undertone to Penelope. She heard him but was too intent on the others to reply. A liberating tidal wave of relief had swept through her at the sight of Lou, whole and safe, getting out of the Volvo. It was receding now, and in its place there came a sickening fear for the members of the searching party, out somewhere on the charred and blinding fells, hunting desperately for an eight-year-old girl who wasn't there at all and never had been.

"Now, Valerie, calm down and explain what's wrong," said Edward.

"The two of you, that's what's wrong!" Valerie had regained control of her voice. "You went off with Louisa this morning and didn't *tell* anyone. You just took her! We didn't know where she was, Ted. *We had no idea!*"

"But you do now," he replied reasonably. "She's quite safe, as you can see for yourself. We've had an expedition to Newcastle, just the two of us. I thought you'd be pleased," he continued, sounding faintly aggrieved. "We've managed to patch up our differences quite amicably, haven't we, Louisa?"

Lou nodded silently, her eyes not leaving her mother's

face. Valerie's expression did not soften as she looked at the two of them. "It was a thoughtless, stupid thing to do, Ted. I wouldn't have believed it of you."

"Now hold on a minute—" Edward was regrouping to defend himself, but she gave him no chance.

"We didn't discover she was missing until after the fire broke out, and I sent Martin back to Wintergap for Pennie, Lou, and the twins. Pennie and the twins thought she was here at the site. Do you know where Martin and Luke and four other people are right now? Do you?"

"How should I?" asked Edward impatiently. "Look here, Val—"

"I'll tell you then, Edward Ibbetson! They're out on the fells searching for Lou!"

"Why did you think she'd gone up there, for pity's sake! Has she ever before?"

"Because Pennie and the twins were up there this afternoon and all we could think of when we couldn't find her was that she'd followed them, then gotten lost in the smoke."

"When did they go? Oh hell, Valerie, that's not fair! I can't defend myself against that, and you know it," said Edward.

Penelope was shattered to discover that Valerie was actually crying. Tears spilled out of her left eye making a long shining track down her cheek. She had her lower lip caught hard between her teeth. Lou ran to her and flung her arms around her mother with a gulping sob of sympathy. Mark looked horror-struck at them, then turned to glare furiously at the monster who had caused this whole crisis.

Edward looked helplessly at his daughter for support. "Pennie, when did they go?"

"Hours ago," she said, struggling to keep her voice neutral. She felt wrenched and bleeding, torn in two; but the inescapable fact was that her father had been terribly wrong—he *had* been stupid and thoughtless, just as Valerie said.

He sighed. "Well, I shall just have to go find them, I suppose."

"But you haven't any idea where they are—none of us has! You'll only go missing yourself," she protested.

Valerie looked up from comforting Lou, her face quite wet, but determined. "Pennie's right. It won't do anyone any good if you get lost as well."

"You both have flattering faith in my sense of direction and ability to take care of myself, I must say," Edward replied acidly.

"I could take him," Mark suggested, ever hopeful. "Then again maybe I couldn't," he added after a glance at his mother.

"We could at least all go back to Wintergap," said Penelope. "We're almost finished here and the searchers are bound to stop at the house on their way back, to check a last time."

"True," said Edward brusquely. "You can all pile into the Volvo and I'll drive you."

"Thank you," returned Valerie, "I'd rather walk."

"Val, for God's sake—"

But she had already started, holding Lou tightly by the hand, neither of them looking back. Mark shrugged at Penelope and went after them.

"Damnation!" exclaimed Edward. "I suppose you're going to desert me as well?"

"No." Penelope got into the car. Her father slid in behind the steering wheel, started the motor, and they drove to Wintergap in silence, passing the three Prines on the way.

There was a welcome sight to greet them on the terrace when they arrived: half the searching party, exhausted, streaked with soot, and red-eyed. Martin, Luke, and Roddy Stewart. Penelope was so glad to see Martin and Luke that she felt like crying.

Before anyone else had a chance to speak, Luke burst out miserably. "We didn't find her!"

"The others are having one last look along the burn north of the Wall," said Martin, sounding bleak. "It's pretty awful up there. They reckon there isn't much time left before we've all got to get out."

"It's all right!" cried Penelope. "She's safe, Martin. She's coming with Valerie and Mark."

"You mean she found her way back alone?" demanded Martin.

"Not exactly." She hesitated, hunting frantically for a way to explain without igniting Martin's dangerously short fuse. Words failed her.

"Louisa was with me, actually," Edward cut in coolly. "We spent the day in Newcastle."

"With *you?*" Martin's voice rose incredulously. "She was with *you?* Why didn't anyone know that? You didn't, did you, Pennie? Valerie didn't or she wouldn't have let us go—" He stared at his father in disbelief. "You mean we've been tramping around the flaming fells all this time, shouting ourselves hoarse, blinded and blistered, and damn near suffocated, for *nothing?*"

"There was a regrettable lapse of communication this morning," returned Edward, still cool and very formal. "I'm sorry, but I had no way of knowing that some careless joker would set the countryside on fire today. In any event, Louisa is quite unharmed and will be here in a few minutes. So, I take it, will the rest of your party."

"As if that makes everything all right!" retorted Martin. "You breeze in here and say the alarm's over, and that's it."

"You've caught the gist quite well, I'd say," observed his father dryly.

"Oh, *stop* it!" cried Penelope, furious with them both. She was being pulled too many directions at once and it hurt—in spite of all this, her father's comment about "some careless joker" setting the countryside on fire had struck home, adding to the intolerable confusion she felt. "Here they come. At least everyone's all right."

"No thanks to *him*," said Martin between his teeth. "And the others haven't come down yet."

Valerie, Lou, and Mark came up the front steps just as the remaining three searchers came around the house: Jonathan, Sir Kenneth, and Jeannie Parsons, as grimy and weary as their counterparts. Sir Kenneth's left forearm was wrapped in Jonathan's bandana, but his sooty face split in a wide white grin as he caught sight of Lou, who was still holding Valerie's hand. "All's well that ends well, to borrow a phrase! I had the feeling she'd be here to meet us. Everyone and everything safely off the site, Val?"

Valerie had obviously made good use of the walk. She was

composed and dry-eyed now, though her mouth was tight at the corners. "Yes, just barely. Ann and Paul took the last load down half an hour ago, and Frances just drove off with the odds and ends in my car. I don't think we missed anything. What have you done to your arm?"

"Just a trifle singed, nothing serious." Sir Kenneth dismissed her concern. "Not to worry! Well, troops, I suppose we ought to push on. Those chaps we met by the Wall told us in no uncertain terms we had no business still here. What about all your gear in the house, Val?"

Valerie looked around at the group. "You've done more than enough already, Kenneth. Thank you all so much for going to hunt for Lou. I can't tell you how grateful I am."

Jonathan beamed at her through his damp beard. "Glad we could help," he said, and the others nodded.

"What's going on up there?" asked Edward. "Do they really think it'll come over the Wall?"

Jonathan's smile vanished. "More than likely, sir. Everything's so dry and the wind's driving it southwest faster than they can contain it. They're evacuating all the farms along the Wall in this direction."

"Even the Robsons'?" asked Mark. Penelope swung on him, hardly daring to breathe.

Jonathan gave his head a shake and said wryly, "Not they. No one'll shift Archie Robson unless he makes up his mind to leave. Tom Powers said they've tried."

"But surely if the fire—" began Edward, frowning.

"If it's meant to burn them out it will. If not, they'll be safe," said Jonathan simply.

Roddy said, "There are hundreds of people up there, literally hundreds—leaping and swotting away like lunatics with fire brooms. It's an incredible sight!"

"Aye, and there'll be more coming all the time," Jonathan added. "I don't mean to rush you, Mrs. Ibbetson, but I think you ought to collect what you need here and go. The fire's moving very fast."

"But where'll we go?" Lou wanted to know, her eyes round and fearful.

"To the Hostel along with everyone else, sweetie," said Valerie. "Bedding and food first, and whatever clothing you can lay your hands on. Paul promised to bring the van back as soon as they'd unloaded, Kenneth, so if you go back to Sulpitium you can get a ride with him. We'll cram ourselves into Ted's car."

"Well, I'm away to help fight the fire," Jonathan said. "I'll find you later."

"I'll go, too," said Martin.

Penelope, Edward, and Valerie began to object, but it was Sir Kenneth who settled the matter. "I'm afraid I can't have that, Ibbetson," he said. "I can't prevent Shaftoe from going if he chooses—this is his territory and he knows enough about it to be useful, but the rest of us are too exhausted and ignorant to be any help."

"What about the other students who are up there?" asked Jeannie.

"They haven't spent the afternoon trudging about, hunting for people. Besides, we'll need all available hands down at the Hostel to set up camp."

"Oh, lord!" said Valerie. "That's quite right. I'd forgotten we'll have to sort everything out immediately. Let's step on it!"

They looted Wintergap, using pillow slips, rucksacks, carrier bags, and cartons to collect things in. If Paul hadn't arrived with the van while they were working, the Volvo would have had to make at least two trips. But by stuffing people and equipment into both vehicles, they managed to find room for everything. They drove in procession down the dusty track for the last time that day, leaving Wintergap to its fate.

Wedged in the back seat of the Volvo, between Luke and Lou, with a box full of Edward's papers on her lap, Penelope craned backward for a last look at the house. It stood four-square on its hillside, closed and secretive. She spared a thought for all the things in it: the Roman stones, the Royal Worcester dinner service, all the Whittons' books, their own least important odds and ends. Somehow the certainty filled her that Wintergap would outlast the fire; nothing of this world would destroy it. The Hexham verger's words rang clear in her head: "These stones'll bide." In one form or another they would, carrying like radioactivity through the years all they had absorbed in their centuries of existence. In spite of the pounding heat, her arms came up in gooseflesh, and Lou, noticing, sat closer.

The new campsite was a walled field behind the Youth Hostel. Although four miles east and well below Sulpitium, the searing smell of smoke lay like a smothering shroud over it. The picture it presented to the refugees was unutterably disheartening. The field itself was small and scattered with rusting skeletons of abandoned farm equipment and little heaps of petrified sheep pellets. Along one stone wall ran an open-sided lean-to with a corrugated tin roof. In it were stacked all those objects, either wornout or superceded, that had been retired from active service in the Hostel but never thrown away: cracked plastic buckets, old mops, moldy sacking, odd bits of rotting lumber and cinder block.

All the gear from Sulpitium lay strewn about in jumbled heaps, just as it had been unloaded from the van and the Mini after each trip. Ann and Frances were doggedly stifting through the chaotic mounds, ferreting out tents and sleeping bags. They greeted the reinforcements warmly, but the reinforcements just stood and looked bleakly at the mess, feeling totally unequal to the task that faced them: to make some kind of habitable order out of it all by nightfall.

"I'm sorry," apologized Frances, two deep creases between her eyebrows. "I thought we'd have more done, but there's so *much*."

"I don't know how we'll ever sort it out," added Ann.

"Fire fighting's got to be easier!" said Martin.

Edward viewed the field with undisguised horror. "We can't possibly spend the night here. It's out of the question!"

Although it was obvious that other people shared his opinion, as soon as he voiced it, everyone immediately took sides against him. It was all that was needed to push the group into action.

"It's not as bad as it looks," said Sir Kenneth encouragingly. "Once we've got the tents up, you'll see."

"Nothing'll get done if we stand here." Roddy began to pick through the closest heap. "I say, does anyone know how many tents there are supposed to be?"

242

Valerie said shortly, "This is what there is, and we're lucky to have it."

Martin watched Edward with grim satisfaction, and Penelope could see her father throw up an invisible defensive wall between himself and everyone else. To her dismay, she found she had very little sympathy for him herself. The truth, as she saw it in uncompromising light, was that he had a horror of being caught in the wrong about anything. He was deft at turning situations around so that he wouldn't be—time and again he'd done it. But this time things had gotten out of hand, and there was no escape for him. If she hadn't been so worried about Lou and Luke and Martin, Penelope might have allowed her loyalty to overwhelm her sense of right. But she couldn't and it upset her more than she cared to admit.

When Valerie discovered that beneath the bandana Sir Kenneth's arm was scarlet and blistered, it only made things worse; that was Edward's fault, too, though Sir Kenneth didn't blame him. Valerie and Martin did. She instructed Frances to drop what she was doing and take Sir Kenneth up to the Hostel to have the director's wife attend to it. The Sulpitium first-aid kit was hopelessly buried, and there was no way of guessing when or where it might surface.

In the meantime, everyone but Edward turned to, and by working like donkeys, they managed to disentangle and pitch nine of the tents. Mr. Farer, the director of the Hostel, came out ostensibly to lend a hand and to offer the use of the kitchen once the paying guests were fed. But the penetrating way he looked over the camp and sized up its occupants made it obvious that his primary concern was how his field was to be used. "Shouldn't think you'd want to set up more than you need for the night," he said, adding hopefully, "If they contain the fire you may be able to go back tomorrow."

He was a lean, wiry man with clever hands and a watchful expression. He put up a tent by himself in less than half the time it took any two of the others.

When Valerie thanked him for allowing them to camp on the property and use the Hostel's facilities, he replied bluntly that it was less inconvenient to him than running the risk of another fire if they used camp stoves in the field. Martin glowered a little at this implication of carelessness, but Valerie stared him into silence.

"Thinks we're a bunch of irresponsible morons," he growled as Mr. Farer, after a final inspection, departed. "Probably thinks we started the bloody fire!"

"But we know we didn't," said Valerie, "so it doesn't matter."

"I can guess who might have."

Penelope's stomach gave a sudden twisting lurch.

"Unless you have proof, you're better off saying nothing," Valerie warned him. "This is much too serious to play with."

"Sooner or later someone's going to catch that bloke dead to rights," said Martin.

"You don't know it was him, do you?" asked Penelope, holding her breath.

"Who?" Martin challenged her.

"I thought—from the way you were talking—" Her voice trailed off lamely.

"No, he doesn't," Valerie answered briskly. "And I really think, Martin, that it's highly unlikely that Archie Robson or anyone else who earns a living from the country around here would have deliberately started a fire on the fells, no matter *how* much he might want to get rid of us. So follow my advice and drop it."

"Where do you want these files to go?" asked Ann.

"Under the lean-to. Here, Martin, give her a hand, will you?"

Penelope glanced carefully around to see who else, if anyone, had overheard the exchange between her brother and stepmother. No one had, it seemed. Edward was brooding over his papers beside the Volvo. The twins were squabbling amiably over which of the guy ropes on the tent they had appropriated ought to be pegged out first, and Lou was sitting on the ground beside Paul, helping to sort out food. The thing she knew burned like a live coal inside Penelope's chest.

"Do you really think we'll get back to Sulpitium tomorrow?" Roddy asked Valerie.

She shrugged as if her shoulders ached. "I have no idea, Roddy. But to be honest, I don't see how."

Involuntarily, everyone looked up to the northwest where the sun was sinking into an angry smudge. It looked, if anything, larger than before. Penelope thought of all the people up on the blazing fells, desperately fighting the fire: Jonathan Shaftoe, other students she knew, the Athertons from Greenrigg Farm, men from the Forestry Commission, and Ran. Yes, wouldn't he and his uncle Jonty, and even Archie himself, be there battling with the rest? Her mind was unable to picture what it must be like up there in the thick of it. Bitterness rose in her throat and her skin prickled as if she were ill. She felt a despair quite beyond fear. What had Jonathan said? *If it's meant to burn them out, it will. If not, they'll be safe.* Cold, hard fatalism. Then she shook herself angrily; she was exhausted, worn raw and vulnerable by everything that had happened. Supper and a night's sleep were what she needed.

But she wasn't going to get either very soon, that was evident. The handful of tents huddled forlornly together against one of the field walls, as if for protection. Under Valerie's supervision, people had begun to spread groundsheets over the lumpy piles of gear. Martin's face was distant and somber as he and Paul heaved and stacked and rummaged, trying to get the most valuable and fragile things organized in the lean-to. People's expressions were set and weary. Edward kept himself aloof and uninvolved. Only the twins, still struggling with their tent and refusing all offers of assistance, seemed able to view the present situation as an adventure. Penelope envied them their unconsciousness.

Sir Kenneth, his arm now coated with antibiotic and swathed loosely in gauze, joined them in the Hostel kitchen for a slapdash supper of corned beef, cabbage, and fried eggs. No one commented on the menu, they simply consumed every scrap; their hunger was so basic they couldn't bother about the taste. Sir Kenneth was as drawn-looking as the rest of them, but he managed to sound cheerful. They had, he pointed out, come away from the fire remarkably unscathed and with all their equipment. When Frances inquired about the future of the dig, he replied that it was too early to make any decisions. But they all knew that the likelihood of being able to continue it was growing slimmer by the hour.

They took turns washing up in the kitchen sink and the Hostel lavatory. Valerie and Penelope discovered that the family had only two bath towels and no soap to its name, so they had to make do sharing. Nothing was easy to find in the general muddle—many small items like toothpaste had either disappeared or been left behind.

Penelope thought she knew what a refugee must feel like, displaced from everything familiar, with only the barest handful of personal belongings, dependent on charity and the roughest of shelter. It was disorienting, bewildering, frightening. She found herself sharing a tent with Lou and Valerie. Everyone went to bed at the same time; there was little point in sitting up. They made unsatisfactory mattresses out of blankets and used spare clothing as pillows, rolled themselves up in sheets and tried to sleep.

But even enveloped in the darkness of the tent, Penelope was conscious of the fire; the air was thick with its reek, and every time she closed her eyes she saw again the fells spread below Dodd Pike, crawling with flame, heard the snapping and explosive flare of the dry scrub igniting, felt the scorching wind like the breath of an enormous dragon. And worse than any of it, she saw the figure, bent and furtive, emerging from the smoke and running away. It crossed and recrossed her memory, writing itself indelibly there.

Through the thin layer of blankets under her, she felt every root and rock, each unfriendly clump of grass. The ground refused to compromise with her in any way. Beneath her head the sweater she had folded was hot and prickly and one of its buttons bit into her left cheek. The tent was intended to accommodate two full-sized bodies, and Penelope was very aware in the close darkness of Lou lying on her back, and Valerie just beyond. She could hear them breathing and knew they could feel and hear her, so she endured as long as she could in one position. When it became absolutely unbearable, she struggled to shift as unnoticeably as possible, but the sheet had gotten tangled around her legs and the new position was even worse than the one before. She was suffocating; she was so tired she couldn't sleep, afraid to close her eyes for fear of what that would shut her in with. She tried desperately to think of something else: London, school, Alison, the Victoria & Albert. But then she thought of drawing and remembered the sketch pad she had deliberately left behind in her room at Wintergap—the one in which she had drawn the memorial stone from Hexham Abbey. If Wintergap was destroyed, then so would that sketch be. And there she was, back with Archie Robson and his brother Ran.

The wind plucked spitefully at the canvas walls of the tent, as if to prove how insubstantial its protection was—only an illusion of security. Penelope's head throbbed. If she slept at all, and it hardly seemed she could have, she was plagued with hot, restless dreams that slid unpleasantly out of her grasp the moment she became conscious of them.

Lou offered no comfort at all. When Penelope eased onto her other side, she discovered Lou sleeping soundly, her dark hair shadowing her face, one pale hand cradled under her cheek.

Then, the final straw: she realized she had to go to the bathroom. Among the things that had been misplaced was her electric torch. She shuddered at the idea of crawling blindly out of her stuffy canvas cocoon into the gaping pit of darkness, of stumbling across the unfamiliar ground, exposed to whatever lurked out there. Rubbish, she told herself crossly. It was Lou who didn't like the dark, not her. The worst that could happen would be to trip over a guy rope or put her foot on a pile of sheep droppings. Rubbish, rubbish, rubbish!

She sat up and felt her hair brush the roof of the tent. Anything was better than lying there and imagining herself into terrified immobility! She felt for and found the wad of tissues she'd somehow remembered to snatch from the box in the car. Jealous of Lou's and Valerie's sound sleep, Penelope unwound her sheet and eeled between the canvas flaps, which Valerie had tied back to give them a little air. Drawing a deep breath, she stood up. It was much lighter outside the tent; to the north the sky glowed a deep infernal red where the fire illuminated its own billowing cloud. She was so transfixed by it that she noticed nothing else for a moment. Then Valerie slid an arm around her shoulders. "It's like the beginning of the end of the world, Pennie," she said softly.

CHAPTER XVIII

THEY STOOD TOGETHER IN SILENCE WATCHING THE FIRE, A FALSE dawn, light the sky above the fells. Then Penelope said, "I thought you were asleep."

Valerie shook her touseled head and looked at Penelope with a smile. "I thought *you* were. I was feeling very envious. At least Lou's unconscious, poor baby. She had such a good time with Ted today—she couldn't understand what went wrong."

Penelope felt herself shy away from the subject; she was ill-prepared and tired out. She didn't even want to think about it. Valerie must have sensed as much; she gave Penelope a little squeeze and let go. "Did you know," she said conversationally, "that there's an outhouse on the other side of the wall behind the lean-to?"

"A what?"

"A latrine—a loo. Mr. Farer kindly pointed it out to me earlier, but I forgot to mention it. Much easier than going up to the Hostel. Just around there, see?"

Gratefully, Penelope nodded. When she came back, she found her stepmother sitting on the ground with Sir Kenneth. They were leaning against the field wall, talking together softly, companionably. She hesitated at the sight of them. She had no desire to crawl back into the stuffy tent and lie for hours, sleepless, beside Lou. But she also didn't want to intrude on Valerie and Sir Kenneth, who were, after all, adults.

"If you can't sleep, Pennie, come and keep us company," suggested Valerie, reading her mind. "It's no good being alone tonight, is it?"

"No," she agreed, relieved.

They made space for her in the middle, between them. She sank down and felt the stones, rough and still warm from the day, at her back. Roman stones probably, but not from Sulpitium she was sure.

"Quite a day we've had," said Sir Kenneth quietly. "I was just saying to your stepmother that I'd give my right arm for a

248

pipesmoke just now, but I can't bring myself to strike a match to light it." He sighed regretfully. "I don't want to be known as the 'Bloody Fool Who Started the Second Fire.' "

"What about the man who started the first?" said Valerie, and Penelope tensed. "Any idea who it was?"

"Do they know it was a man?" Penelope asked in a thin voice.

"Had to have been a person, at any rate," Sir Kenneth replied. "No other way for it to have happened. A cigarette, a match, even a hot car exhaust, I suppose—the country's dry enough. That's why the ban on hikers."

Penelope's heart resumed a more or less normal pulse. For just a second she thought of telling them what she'd seen from Dodd Pike, but the words scattered around her head like ash and were lost.

"Such a tiny thing to set off such enormous destruction," murmured Valerie. "Will it burn people out, Kenneth?"

He gave his untidy head a shake. "If it does they'll be back. They're a stubborn lot—survivors—used to fighting for everything they have. This is cruel country, but their roots are locked in it. They don't expect life to be easy—it never has been up here, has it?" He was silent a minute, then continued musingly, "I've done a lot of thinking about the Wall and what it means—what it meant to the Romans and to every group of people that's lived along it since. It's wedded to the land in more ways than we can ever hope to understand scientifically. It *had* to be built here, and even though it's in ruins, most of it quite vanished—it's still here. If there weren't a stone left in place, it would *still* be here."

"Yes," said Penelope. "I know."

"Do you, indeed?" He gave her a kind, shrewd look.

She pulled herself together. "How's your arm?"

"Very much better, thank you," he replied gravely. "I threw it up to protect my face when I slipped and fell. I was reminded of a chap I knew at school who had his eyebrows singed off by a Roman candle on Guy Fawkes' Day. They never grew in again—it gave him the oddest expression. I couldn't bear to think of losing mine. Ah, vanity!" He chuckled—a comfortable, solid sound.

"He's lucky he wasn't blinded," declared Valerie.

"Spoken like a mother," Sir Kenneth observed.

"Occupational hazard. Once you start, you can never stop," said Valerie a little wistfully. "What about Sulpitium? What do you think will happen?"

"I think that, if the fire has swept across the site, we shall find we have no choice but to fold our tents and steal softly away."

"Mmm. I was afraid of that."

He hunched his shoulders tiredly. "Like the Romans, we must withdraw. That'll be cause for rejoicing in some quarters, I shouldn't wonder. And I promise you, I shan't stop trying to get back again, but the University won't fund it, at least not until all this is forgotten. If I were a superstitious man I would say Sulpitium is jinxed."

Valerie gave a little snort. "But you are, aren't you?"

"What? Superstitious? Oh indeed yes."

Penelope frowned, trying to absorb all this into a head that felt stuffed with wet flannel. "You mean you believe—"

"I don't think we're welcome here," he said gently. "I don't know why we aren't and I doubt I ever shall. It's not a question with a tidy, quantitative answer. Ah, well."

"I hope all the kids are safe," said Valerie. "The ones up fighting the fire. I must say, I hate the idea of being beaten, Kenneth."

Slowly and stiffly he stood up. "Can't be helped, my dear. We have been. Think I'll just have a look round, then try to get some sleep."

"Good luck to you," Valerie called after him softly. "What about you?" She turned to Penelope. "Feel like trying it again?"

But Penelope shook her head. "Can you be too tired to sleep?"

"Or too wound up."

They sat on together. Penelope said, "I like him very much."

"Sir Kenneth? He's a duck," said Valerie warmly. "He's a human scientist—my favorite kind."

"Then why didn't you—I mean, he's so much more like you than . . ." Embarrassed, she let the sentence trail away.

"Than Ted?" Valerie let the words stand alone for a

minute or two. "Not really," she said then. "We have the same profession, that's all. And remember I married an archaeologist the first time and it did not work. To be honest, a lot of the reasons it didn't work were impermanent ones: my age and insecurities, two small children and a baby, Brian's early ambitions and his fear of competition. I'm sure we're both different people now. Who knows what it would be like if we met at this point?" She was half talking to herself. "But we didn't. The person I am at present met the person your father is at present."

"Do you wish you hadn't?"

"Why would I—because of today, you mean?"

"Yes," said Penelope unhappily.

Instead of giving her a glib and reassuring answer, Valerie said, "For a while, I suppose I might have said yes if you'd asked me that. But emotions are very tricky things to deal with—powerful and intoxicating. When you're under the influence of one like rage or terror—or love, come to that—you don't behave rationally. You do and say things you may well regret later."

"You're not sorry you got angry with him?"

Valerie scrabbled vigorously through her short hair. "No, I'm not. What your father did was very stupid, Pennie, there's no point in glossing over it. And he *knows* it was stupid, but he won't let himself admit it was more than a slight miscalculation. I don't think Ted's very good at accepting blame for things, is he? No, that's not a fair question to ask you. We got married on the condition that none of you children would be called on to make choices between us—I told you that the other day."

"I was really afraid for Lou," said Penelope. "And for Luke and Martin when they went after her. It didn't seem to make much difference which was which, if you see what I mean."

"Yes, I know. But they're all safe. It was too bad that it happened—Ted didn't use his head—but it's over now, and he did it with good intentions, bless him! So we go on from here instead of rerunning it over and over. That's something I had to learn the hard way. But now we need to give your father a little space to recover himself in, do you see that? Jumping on him anymore won't help."

"Does that mean you've forgiven him?"

Valerie nodded. "Yes. But I think I'll just let him find that out for himself instead of telling him outright."

Penelope leaned forward, drawing up her knees and resting her chin on them so her face was hidden. "Valerie, I've been thinking about you—and my father—and wondering . . ." She groped for words that wouldn't offend and was reminded of Ran's frustration over trying to say what he meant. She might as well ask what she wanted to ask and be done. "Why did you marry him?" she blurted.

"Your father?" Valerie gave her an amused, considering look. "You mean you don't believe we simply fell in love?"

"It's none of my business," said Penelope hastily, "it's just that I'm trying to understand—so many things, all at once, and I thought—"

"Listen, love. If I can help you understand anything, I'll do it. It's no fun stumbling around in the dark, especially when you don't have to. If only life were like school where you're told what to study and everything has a right answer. I keep wanting to shout, 'That's not fair—we haven't had that yet! I didn't know I was going to be tested on it!' "

"Do you really? I used to think being an adult must be like passing A-level exams—suddenly you'd know everything."

"But it isn't. So I'll admit something to you, Pennie. Something I haven't admitted to another soul, except finally myself. I do love your father, very much, and I wouldn't have married him if I didn't. That's the truth. But I also married him be- cause—" She paused, watching her fingers dig little holes in the grass. Penelope waited. "I married him because I was scared," Valerie said finally.

Penelope regarded her with disbelief. "You? Scared of what?"

"My God," said Valerie wryly, "where do I begin! If I look brave to you, love, it's because I've been working thirty- nine years on the disguise. Oh Pennie, I'm scared of getting old and being alone, of making mistakes with the twins and Lou, of not having enough money, of having the muffler fall off my car, of getting fat and being bitchy, of never accom- plishing anything worthwhile—there! I could go on and on, but I don't need to, do I? The worst is being alone and not

252

having someone with whom I can share life, someone who sees the world from the same narrow ledge I'm standing on and who understands without always having to be explained to. That's why I married your father, and I think—I think he married me for the same reason."

Penelope and Valerie looked at each other in the murky half-light. Penelope saw a long and difficult road ahead of her; she would have to walk every step of it by herself because that was the only way she'd find out what was at the end. But all along the way there would be people like Valerie, sometimes the most unexpected people—like Ran—who would help and offer comfort if she was willing to ask. And equally important, no matter who they were they would need help and comfort from her, too.

They put their arms around each other as they sat.

"I'm glad," whispered Penelope.

"So am I," said Valerie. "So am I."

Penelope was stiff when she woke. She and Valerie were still sitting against the wall, leaning together like bookends with nothing between them, Valerie's arm around her shoulders. Someone had draped a blanket over each of them. It was early morning; the sun was lifting over the low rim of hills to the east and the sky was a translucent blue, caught between darkness and light. There were no clouds; it would be hot again.

She had no idea how long she had been asleep, but now that she was awake, she realized how uncomfortable she was. She didn't want to disturb Valerie, but she had to move.

Valerie gave a little groan of protest, then caught her balance and straightened up. There were circles under her eyes, and her face was creased and puffy with sleep, her hair fearfully tangled. She gave Penelope a vague, half-conscious look, then smiled and tilted her head back against the wall. With her left hand she began to massage her right shoulder, the one Penelope had been propped against. She looked rumpled and grubby, just the way Penelope felt, and Penelope was flooded with a rush of affection for her, quite unlike anything she'd experienced since they'd left Grannie Lawrence and moved to London. Before she gave herself time to consider, she gave

Valerie a quick, awkward hug. Valerie's eyes opened wide, and they looked at each other in silence for a moment, remembering what they had talked about the night before. Then Penelope struggled to her feet and stretched to cover an attack of shyness.

All Valerie said was, "At least there's no wind this morning."

Jonathan Shaftoe found them while they were still at breakfast, which consisted mainly of oranges and cold cereal, milk bought from the Farers, and a huge pot of super-strength coffee brewed up at the Hostel. No one was quick off the mark that morning; they all looked heavy-eyed and bleary, except Mark, Luke, and Lou. Edward had spent the night in the Volvo, not sleeping, Penelope guessed by the look of him. He joined them for breakfast, but sat wrapped in silence, brooding.

Jonathan himself looked like the survivor of a particularly nasty train wreck: hair wild about his head, clothes filthy and torn, eyes bloodshot, and hands black. But he brought the first hopeful news. When the wind began to die, just before dawn, the fire fighters had finally been able to create an effective firebreak ahead of the flames. The fell was still smouldering and burning in isolated pockets, but the worst was over, and it would not spread any farther.

"What's a firebreak?" Luke asked immediately.

"Let the poor man have some breakfast," chided Valerie.

Between mouthfuls, Jonathan explained that a firebreak was a barrier of some kind designed to stop a wildfire. What the men had done was to burn off a wide strip of land in the path of the flames. When the fire reached that strip it died because there was no fuel to feed it.

"So you set a fire to stop a fire," Mark said. "Wouldn't you be afraid the fire you started would get out of control, and then you'd be worse off?"

"You have to know exactly what you're about, mate, and no mistake," Jonathan agreed.

"What news of the rest of our crew?" asked Sir Kenneth. "Have you seen them?"

254

"A few. They'll find their way down here during the morning, I shouldn't wonder. Everyone's all right, sir. No injuries that I've heard of—a couple of cases of smoke inhalation, nothing worse."

"Nothing short of a miracle," said Valerie. "Any farms damaged?"

"Todd Nichols out by Greenlee lost his hay barn and there's stock gone, but the fire seems to have started between the farms and the Wall and been driven south by the wind. Trapped a caravan full in the Cawfields picnic area, but they got out safe."

Penelope sat listening, her mouth firmly shut, telegraphing a mental question, over and over.

Martin seemed to pick it out of the air and asked it for her. "What about the Robsons? Anything happen to Dodd Moss?"

"Never touched it," replied Jonathan, an odd quirk to his mouth.

"Did you see any of them fighting the fire?" he pressed.

"No, but there's lots I didn't see, and lots I saw I didn't know." He shrugged. "It was a big fire."

"What about Sulpitium?" asked Valerie with a glance at Sir Kenneth.

"And Wintergap," added Edward, proving he had been paying careful attention to the conversation.

"Wintergap's all right, sir. The fire never crossed the burn below the Wall. But Sulpitium's in pretty rough shape, I'm afraid. The farmhouse looks like a dead loss, and the area all round the fort's been burned off."

A bleak silence greeted this news as the members of the dig stared glumly at one another. Sir Kenneth finally broke it. "Well, we must wait until it's safe and we shan't interfere, then we'll go have a look round. In the meantime we'll have to break the news to Mr. Farer that we shall need his field at least one more night."

"Right." Valerie took a deep breath. "There's lots to do. We might as well get to work—finish making camp, sort out the supplies, do some shopping, and get the equipment organized. It's in an awful mess."

"Look here," said Edward unexpectedly, "I realize I'm intruding, but if Wintergap's intact, why not shift everything up there? It's not as convenient as being on the site, but it's better than *this*." He gestured around at the camp.

"You just don't want to spend another night in this field," said Martin accusingly.

Edward returned his son's glare calmly. "You're damn well told," he said. "And I *shan't* spend another night in this field, even if the rest of you choose to. I have no intention of it. But I'm willing to, as it were, share the wealth. If Sulpitium is uninhabitable and our house is undamaged, I'm perfectly willing to open it up."

"It might be an alternative." Sir Kenneth didn't sound overly optimistic. "In any event, it's certainly worth considering."

The morning passed in strenuous activity. Mr. Farer walked down to see how they were managing and surveyed the confusion they were creating in the process of getting organized. "Fair amount of gear," he commented. He did not seem overjoyed at the prospect of having them on his doorstep another night, but he did not seem surprised either. He nodded somberly and stumped away again.

"I wish he was a little friendlier." Valerie sighed. "Still, we takes what we can get. Pennie, how are you coming with the shopping list?"

"Almost finished, that is if no one uncovers another carton of food." Penelope and Frances were collecting and inventorying the salvaged supplies. "I don't think we've left anything essential out—"

"Chocolate," said Mark. "Has anyone seen my jackknife?"

"Already thought of," Frances said. "Teach your grandmother."

"Where's Jonathan got to?" asked Martin, leaning on a shovel.

"He's out cold in Roddy's tent, snoring like a seal."

"Do seals really snore?" asked Lou.

"Good for him," said Valerie. "He needs it. What are you up to, Ted?"

Edward joined them, his expression determined. Penelope noticed with a sharp little jab of concern that he really looked terrible, the lines around his mouth had deepened, there was a haze of greyish stubble on his cheeks and chin, and his eyes were shadowed with weariness. This was not the appearance he normally presented to the world. He caught her looking at him and raised an eyebrow in her direction. "I wanted to tell you, that unless I'm needed for anything, Valerie, I shall drive myself back to Wintergap."

"But you can't do that," protested Martin.

"I'd like to know why not? The house is still standing and the danger over. I intend to have a hot bath, a shave, and a decent cup of tea."

Martin looked ready to argue, but Valerie intervened. "That's a good idea, Ted. At least some of us will be up later this afternoon to see what's left of the site."

"Look, Valerie," said Martin as they watched the Volvo disappear through the gate, "maybe it's none of my business—"

"You're right," she answered briskly. "It won't do him or us any good if he stays, Martin. He had a miserable night last night."

"He wasn't the only one."

"No, but what does it matter? Let's just leave him alone for a little while, Martin. Keeping him here doesn't serve any purpose, does it?"

Martin hesitated, then shook his head. The antagonism left his face and he actually grinned. "All right. I give up."

By noon the rest of the students had begun to trickle into camp. They were dazed and too tired to eat, but full of a peculiar comradely euphoria. They had helped to fight a raging fell fire, and working at the top of their endurance—together —they had won. Right now nothing was as important as winning. The grim devastation left behind would be reckoned later. They were intoxicated with smoke and a jubilation that was contagious. It spread throughout the camp, infecting even those who had not been on the fire line.

Mrs. Farer generously acknowledged the students' contribution to the victory by sending down from the Hostel four huge fruit tarts and a basket full of fresh scones, butter, and strawberry jam. Mr. Farer almost smiled as he brought them.

257

If Valerie hadn't laid down the law in ringing declaratives, Mark and Luke would have eaten far more than their share of scones.

It was midafternoon before anyone was in shape to leave the camp. Then Frances and Martin volunteered to take the van to Hexham to buy enough staples to feed everyone for at least twenty-four hours. Mark, Luke, and Lou begged to go along, and Valerie granted them permission, under pain of corporal punishment if they did not follow orders.

Once they'd gone, Valerie turned to Sir Kenneth. "I suppose we can't put it off any longer, can we?"

He gave his head an unenthusiastic shake.

"Can I go, too?" Penelope crawled out of the tent where she'd been unsuccessfully trying to take a nap. "If you're going to Sulpitium?"

"All right," said Valerie.

In the end Jonathan came as well, stuffing himself into the back seat of the Mini next to Penelope and rubbing the sleep out of his eyes. "I don't know why waking up in the middle of the day always seems so awful," he muttered into his beard. "I feel slow and bloated."

Everyone else in camp was unconscious, stretched out in tents or lying in the scanty shade of the lean-to. It looked like a scene out of *Sleeping Beauty*.

CHAPTER XIX

PENELOPE THOUGHT SHE WAS PREPARED FOR THE SIGHT THAT awaited them at Sulpitium—she knew the fire had swept over it, she knew the farmhouse had burned. But as they drove up the hill, it hit her like a short, vicious blow to the stomach. Instead of the broad, dusty green expanse of grass shouldering up to the Wall, there was a vast blackened wasteland. Even where the turf was still green there were charred patches where escaping sparks had taken hold, like a virulent kind of mange scarring the hillside. No one spoke as Valerie guided the little car into the desert. She pulled up where the parking area had been, and there was still a rough square of bare earth vaguely distinguishable, and in silence they climbed out and stood looking.

Some half-dozen men spread raggedly over the area were still combing it for any last trace of fire among the tussocks and whin roots. Methodically they stamped, crushed, and beat as they went. The acrid smell of smoke was strong everywhere. Never in her life had Penelope seen a place so desolate and dead.

"I suppose we'd better go see what's left, though there can't be much," said Sir Kenneth at last. "Thank God we all got away."

Valerie only nodded.

Close together, they picked their way slowly across the scorched ground toward the fort and the farmhouse. The grass had burned to black tufts. Little ghosts of ash eddied around their feet and they could still feel heat rising from the earth.

The shrubs around the house were ebony skeletons. The house itself was little more than a shell. The fire had raced through it devouring everything but stone and metal.

But at Sulpitium the stones remained; the stones of the house, the fort, the Wall. They were black with soot, some of them heat-cracked, but virtually unchanged in spite of the destruction on all sides.

While the others went to examine the house, Penelope stood in the excavated West Gate and gazed about. Fire and ruin. The enemy from the North, watching and waiting, then sweeping down on the fort . . . again and again it happened: the Romans, the Vikings, the Border raiders, the Whittons, the Robsons . . .

"Looks awful, doesn't it?" said Valerie, joining her.

"I very much fear that we must accept defeat," Sir Kenneth said quietly.

"But sir," said Jonathan, "it's only the top layer that's been destroyed—the stuff we're after is still safe underground."

Sir Kenneth shook his head. "Can you imagine what everyone would look and feel like after a day working here? Excavation's a dirty job, I'll grant you, but this—" He stooped and put his hands flat on the ground. When he raised them they were covered with soot. "People might be willing to stay at first, but I shouldn't like to bet how quickly disenchantment would set in. No, I've been considering it. Far better to close down now—take what we've got, which is jolly good for six weeks' work—and try to make a case for coming back in a year or so, than continue in the face of these odds and give poor old Sulpitium a permanently black name—literally and figuratively—among students and archaeologists. What do you say, Val?"

Grimly, she answered, "I'd like to lay my hands on whoever started the fire!"

Penelope surprised a worried frown on Jonathan's normally unworried face and looked away quickly in case he should see anything he oughtn't to on hers.

"That wouldn't do the present situation any good," Sir Kenneth pointed out. "It wouldn't alter any of this."

"No, but it would have a therapeutic effect on me." She sighed. "You're right, of course—we haven't much choice. How long will it take us to pack up and disperse, d'you think?"

"If we announce it tonight we ought to be away by tomorrow afternoon. No point in hanging about, and the faster we can finish up the better for all of us, including the long-suffering Mr. Farer." Sir Kenneth was decisive.

"Well, I'm going to have a look at my bathhouse."

"If you don't mind, I'll walk over to Wintergap and see what Dad's doing," said Penelope, suddenly desperate to get away from Sulpitium.

"Good idea." Valerie gave her a brief, preoccupied smile. "We'll pick you up when we're through here."

Penelope watched the three of them trudge dispiritedly across the blackened fort, then she turned and took the track to Wintergap. Now that Lou was safe, and Martin and the others, now that Valerie had forgiven Edward and relations within the family were settling back to normal, now there was nothing to distract her from Ran and Archie Robson. It wasn't right that whoever started the fire, particularly if it had been set on purpose, should go unaccused, unpunished. The fire was wrong, and there was nothing that could excuse it.

She had only to look around at the hideous devastation it had caused to feel angry. She didn't understand how anyone could have done it, could have deliberately struck the spark that ignited acres and acres of heather and gorse, grass and bracken and all the tiny plants that grew on the fells. And yet she knew someone had.

Well, no, that wasn't really true. She hastily backed away from that bald statement. She hadn't seen him do it. What she had done was put together two things she knew for certain: one, that Ran had come to warn her that his brother meant to have another, serious attempt at getting rid of the archaeologists; two, that from the top of Dodd Pike she had seen Archie Robson running from the fire. If she told Valerie and Sir Kenneth those two facts, she knew they would immediately connect them as she had, and they were in a position to take action. They could confront Archie Robson; they could probably get the truth from him—she didn't doubt that he, even more than Ran, was uncomfortable with words. They would see him punished, under the law, for the destruction he had caused.

Civilized people were brought up to believe that if you did wrong you were punished for it. It was such a simple, straightforward statement. Unarguable—or so she had always thought.

But like everything else she had believed she had a grasp on, she discovered when she opened her hands she hadn't got hold of it at all, not properly. It *wasn't* simple. For if Archie was accused and punished, what would become of Ran and Mrs. Robson? What would happen to the farm? What *good* would it do? The damage had been done—nothing, as Sir Kenneth said, would alter any of what had already happened. The dig would still be disbanded, all the students sent home. They would still have to leave. It couldn't give anyone back anything that had been lost—the fells, Todd Nichols's haybarn, the Sulpitium farmhouse, the sheep and wild beasts.

It was Ran she kept coming back to, of course. Ran with whom she was friends, although they neither of them seemed to understand quite why. Would it be worse to keep what she knew a guilty secret, or to hurt Ran, a person she would probably never see again? That was the question all this came down to.

261

The house, the garden, the firs, and the little valley with the burn at the bottom, all looked just as they had the morning before: dusty, dry, but miraculously unscathed. In fact, if Wintergap was all you saw, you would not know there had been a fire. It was as if the house and its immediate surrounding had been enclosed in a gigantic glass bell jar.

The Volvo was parked in its accustomed place, her father was there. She climbed the front steps and went into the dim hall. Memories crowded out of the shadows: Valerie on the stairs in her old bathrobe, Luke playing cards to lose, Lou's face lit with the excitement of discovery, Martin stumbling over the doorsill blurry with beer, Mark telling awful jokes in the kitchen, her father and stepmother glaring at each other over plates of tinned spaghetti, the hours she'd spent drawing on the terrace. Those things happened in a family; they belonged to her not to the house, and she would take them with her when she left.

"Dad? Dad!" she called, then stopped and made a face at herself in the hall mirror. Suppose he was upstairs asleep and she woke him?

But he wasn't. He was in the kitchen; he came to the doorway and smiled at her. She saw he'd washed and shaved and changed his clothes; he looked in control again. "Hullo, Pennie. Where are the others?"

"Valerie, Sir Kenneth, and Jonathan came up to look at Sulpitium, they'll be along later."

He nodded. "What's the verdict?"

"They've decided to close the excavation."

"Valerie disappointed?"

"Mmm, terribly. It's all so horrid-looking." She followed him back to the kitchen and sat at the table. "I didn't realize that I liked it so much."

"Well, I can't honestly say I'll be sorry to leave, myself. This place is interesting, but distinctly uncomfortable!" He gave her a considering look. "I think you were righter than perhaps you knew the other night."

Slowly she shook her head. "No, I knew I was right, Dad. This isn't a *good* place."

"Perhaps what we need is an exorcism," he replied humor-ously. His smile faded when he saw she wouldn't share it. "Are you still cross with me?"

"Me?" she said, startled.

"Yes, Penelope my love, you. Don't tell me you weren't cross yesterday along with everyone else. It was written all over your face. None of you liked me the least little bit."

"But I didn't—"

"No, you didn't have to. I had the devil's own time convincing Louisa to come away with me, you know. She caught me at a very bad moment the day before, with that bloody dog of hers. I had just learned from Richard that he hadn't received the proofs I sent—the ones I labored so long over. They appear to have been swallowed by Her Majesty's P.O. somewhere between this godforsaken spot and London."

"Why didn't you say?"

"Why should I have? You were all so busy painting Louisa as the innocent victim of Edward Ibbetson's unreasonable brutality, I thought I wouldn't spoil your fun. Besides, why should I have to make excuses for myself? You know perfectly well about my wretched allergy."

"Yes, but *Lou* didn't. She—"

He held up his hands. "Stop! Don't let's get into that again. It's past and done."

"That's what Valerie said."

"Oh, she did? Did she mean the whole business?"

Penelope felt her cheeks grow warm under his scrutiny. He gave a short little laugh. "It's all right, I'll ask her. Furthermore I shall put the kettle on and make some tea against their arrival. A peace offering. By the way—" He finished filling the kettle and lit the burner under it, then turned back to her. "A friend of yours came calling while I was shaving."

"A friend?" she said rather too quickly.

"Mmm." Her father's expression was bland, but his eyes were alert. "I told him you were down at the Hostel if he wanted to see you, but I don't expect he ever got there, did he? He left you a note. I put it up here for safekeeping." It was a folded sheet of paper torn from a school exercise book. Edward took it from the window ledge and handed it to her. "Odd I haven't seen him around before, Pennie. I didn't know you knew anyone up here."

263

"Why should you? You've been working or away a great deal of the time," she said evasively. She didn't know whether to read the note at once, or to put it in her pocket for later when she was alone. She hesitated.

Edward watched her for a moment, then began to get cups and saucers out of the cupboard and to arrange biscuits on a Spode plate. He made a great show of being busy, although she knew he was curious, and she acknowledged the gesture by unfolding the paper.

On it Ran had written in a black, deliberate script: "Dear Penelopy, I hoped you would be here, so I could talk with you. But I don't know what good talking would do. Never mind. I am sorry. Randall Robson." She thought of everything the note didn't say: what they had to talk about, how difficult it must have been for him to come to Wintergap, to approach her father, to try to find the right words among all those treacherous, deceptive ones, to risk getting himself tied up in them, to write his whole name there, as if she wouldn't have known "Ran." With a sigh she refolded it and put it away.

"The dog was with him," said Edward conversationally. "They were both pretty grubby—covered with soot and ash."

"She belongs to him."

The others appeared then as if they'd heard a tea bell rung. There was a moment or two of awkwardness, but it disappeared with the steam from the kettle as they all sat down around the table. Valerie, Sir Kenneth, and Jonathan were too full of the tragedy that had befallen Sulpitium and planning the logistics of evacuation to spend energy on anything that had already happened.

"There're buses to both Carlisle and Newcastle, where most of the students can get trains," said Sir Kenneth. "The worst will be packing all the objects and University equipment."

"—may have to make two trips."

"—don't see why *we* couldn't—"

"—nothing pressing in London."

Penelope watched the leaves float on the top of her tea and let the conversation wash gently around her. She was beginning to realize something far more important about Ran's note. It was goodbye. The end. He did not expect to see her again. He didn't know what she would do about Archie, nor had he asked. It wasn't fair.

"Pennie, you're far away," said Valerie. "I was just saying that we ought to get back to camp."

Obediently, her mind only half-listening, Penelope stood up. Edward stayed where he was. She looked from him to Valerie.

"Ted is going to stay here," Valerie answered, guessing the question. "He's offered to pack the stuff we left in the house yesterday."

"I could help," Penelope heard herself say and despised the telltale eagerness in her voice. "I mean, we ought to put the dustsheets back and clean things a little before we go, don't you think?" She was grabbing at memories of vacating other summer cottages.

"That would be a tremendous help," Valerie said. "If you don't mind? And I'm sure Ted would welcome the company."

Penelope glanced at her father doubtfully. "Would you?"

He nodded and put a hand on her shoulder. "Yes, as a matter of fact, love."

There was indeed a tremendous amount to do, and Penelope had to give her father full marks: he pitched in with a will. They first went through Wintergap and collected all the Prine–Ibbetson belongings, and Penelope recovered her sketchbook. She considered it carefully while she packed other things, then made up her mind. With resolution she tore from it the first drawing she had done at Wintergap, the drawing she had made from memory of the Roman memorial stone in Hexham Abbey, the drawing that had disturbed her so much. It wasn't bad work, in spite of its inaccuracies, but as she looked at it she knew she couldn't possibly keep it. She didn't want that face; she had another, which she would take home with her, the one of Ran she had drawn after their day on the fells. As a piece of work it wasn't as good, but that had nothing to do with why she'd drawn it or why she would keep it. The picture was Ran as she had come to know him: vital and human, doubtful, confident, loyal. Her friend.

Once the packing was done, Edward and Penelope began

to clean the house. It was less a matter of being meticulous, as Edward pointed out, more a matter of just straightening things up, making sure things were back in their proper places, or almost. Penelope even remembered the bits of furniture the twins had pirated for their club house.

While Edward was busy upstairs, Penelope found an opportunity to slip into the library. She knelt on the hearth in front of the very clean fireplace, and with fingers that shook just a little, she crumpled the sketch into a loose ball and put a match to it. The paper burned quickly, dissolving into a fragile black husk, and the little figure of the Briton was gone. She considered it an appropriate end; with it she was burning all thought of telling anyone what she knew.

She was still kneeling there, gazing at the ash, when Edward came looking for her to help start supper. "Classified information?" he asked, glancing from her to the fireplace. "Burning secret documents?"

"Sort of." His levity broke the spell she was under, and she looked up and smiled. He didn't push her to tell him what it was that she had destroyed. He had always allowed his children the same privacy he demanded for himself.

They had a sketchy supper in the kitchen. Edward said, "Once we're away from here, the first thing I shall do is take us all out to a proper, bang-up meal. Even the twins—how will they ever know what good food is if they don't experience it?" He scowled at his plate of sausage and egg. "These are bad enough for dinner! I can't imagine anyone voluntarily eating them for breakfast!"

"Usually it's children who're the fussy eaters."

"I'm not fussy, I am discriminating, Penelope. There is a world of difference."

That evening she worked so hard she gave her mind no more room to think of anything. And when she went to bed she was too tired to lie awake, worrying. Lack of sleep and physical exhaustion knocked her out as soon as she was horizontal, and when she woke it was broad daylight, her head was clear and her mind settled. She had finished sweeping out the drawing room and reshrouding the furniture when

Edward came down, yawning and stretching and looking completely his old self.

"I was thinking," she began as he poured himself a cup of tea. "Do you suppose anyone will notice if we don't sweep the attic?"

"Good God, no!" He looked genuinely horrified, as if the idea had never crossed his mind. "I don't suppose anyone will notice much about anything, so long as we don't leave dirty crockery in the sink. Who knows when there'll be anyone in this house again? Remember what it was like when we came?"

"I'm sorry about your proofs," she said.

"So'm I after all the work I put into them. And I was fool enough not to keep copies of the major revisions. Well, can't be helped. At least I'll be able to sit down with Richard in London and bash out another set."

There was no way around it, hard as she looked. Too much of the trouble that summer had been caused by people going off without telling other people where they were going. She braced herself and said, "Dad, if everything's been done here, would you mind—do you think I could—"

"Mind what?" He looked up from the book he'd opened to go with his tea and gave her his attention. His eyes were the same hazel green as Martin's.

"I want to visit someone before we leave. I thought it would be easier if I went before Valerie and the others come back."

Gently he rocked his cup round and round, making a little whirlpool. "How would you get there?" he said at last.

Not, "Where are you going?" or "Whom are you visiting?," the questions she had expected. "I'll walk."

"Across the fells, isn't it?"

"Yes." He knew.

"But it's all been burnt over up there, don't forget. It'll be nasty going."

Incredible as it seemed, she had forgotten that. It was Wintergap playing tricks—because everything was as usual here. She'd forgotten it had changed above the Wall.

"I think," said Edward, "perhaps I should drive you."

Penelope stared at him. "But—" she said. "But—"

A flicker of irritation crossed his face. "I haven't meddled so far, have I? I said *drive* you—I needn't go in with you, Penelope. I don't have to go within sight of D—wherever you're going. I'll park and stay in the car like a good chauffeur. I can read my book."

That was something she hadn't even considered. But the more she thought about it, the clearer she saw the merits of his proposal. It would certainly be faster, and he was right, it would be far pleasanter than to struggle across that expanse of burned fell, getting herself covered in soot. If she saw the destruction close up again, actually walked through the middle of it, she might change her mind about what she had decided to do.

So she agreed. And just after lunch they set out in the Volvo for Dodd Moss Farm. They left Valerie a note in case she arrived at Wintergap before they got back; it said simply that they had gone on an errand.

"It's not a lie," said Penelope. "It is an errand."

It was easier to pretend that her father didn't know where he was taking her. She directed him along the farm lane off which she knew the Dodd Moss track turned, without mentioning the name of the farm. She had brought with her two things: Ran's note and a manilla envelope, and she tried not to think what would happen if Archie were at Dodd Moss when she got there. It was possible that she was making a terrible mistake and that both she and Ran would regret it.

Neither she nor Edward spoke much during the trip. The sight of the ravaged fells, stretching away on either side of the car was unutterably depressing. Penelope kept thinking, but we are going away from this—we are leaving it. The people who live here can't. And it wasn't just the hideous fire scar.

At the gate to Dodd Moss Farm she asked her father to wait. He obligingly pulled the Volvo off the track and cut the engine. "Are you sure?" he asked. "Are you sure you want to go in there by yourself?"

"It wouldn't help if you came," she answered.

He wanted to protest, she saw it in his eyes, but he didn't. He gave a little shrug and settled himself comfortably in the seat.

Jonathan had reported accurately. Dodd Moss, like Wintergap, had escaped the fire. It was as bleak and inhospitable as ever, but not a stone in it had been scorched.

Her heart pounding, Penelope walked boldly across the front yard, scattering the straggle of hens. The pickup was nowhere to be seen; that gave her courage. But perhaps it meant that Ran was away as well? She went slowly around the house toward the kitchen—no knocking at the front door to disturb Mrs. Robson this time—and Frit came bounding at her, barking and wagging her tail.

"Frit! Whisht, ye daft beast!" came Ran's impatient voice from one of the sheds. "What ye yammerin' about, whey? Ye'll wake Mam."

He was cleaning out Brown's stall. The horse stood patiently whisking at flies with his stringy tail and every now and then gave his head a shake. Penelope bent to pat Frit, and when she looked up Ran was standing watching her.

She didn't know how to start, so she blurted, "We're going this afternoon."

"Aye."

"I got your note yesterday. That was my father."

This time only a nod.

"I'm glad Dodd Moss wasn't damaged." She was running out of things to say, and he was giving her no help at all. "Well, you might talk to me, after I've come up here just to see you," she exclaimed crossly. "Frit's friendlier than you are."

"Aa dinna ask ye to come."

She glared at him, swamped by a mixture of anger and frustration. "I came to say goodbye," she said finally in a tight voice.

"Aa divvent want to say goodbye," he answered in the same flat tone.

"Then don't!" she flung at him and turned away.

"Aa mun say it now, mun't Aa, as ye've come?"

She looked suspiciously at him over her shoulder. He had moved and was standing with a hand on Brown's rump. Brown gave his tail a sudden twitch and it caught Ran across the face. The nervousness bubbled up in her throat and she

269

gave a hiccuppy giggle. Ran brushed the hair away and the stone was gone from his expression; in its place she saw the boy who was her friend.

"Ye shouldnae a come across the fells."

"I didn't. My father brought me—he's waiting at the gate. I don't want to say goodbye, either, Ran, but I didn't want to leave without."

"Aye. Ye took a girt chance comin'. Suppose Archie'd been here?"

"I know, I thought of that. But he's not. I brought you something."

"Ye what?"

"Here." She handed him the envelope. He reached for it, then pulled his hand back and wiped it on the seat of his trousers first. "It isn't much—it's just—what I could find," she finished lamely, suddenly embarrassed. She had never given one of her sketches to anyone as a present before.

Slowly and carefully he opened the flap and drew out the sheet of paper. It was the sketch she had been finishing of the herb Robert that grew along the Wall that day so long ago now that they had spent together. He looked at it in silence and it was impossible to tell from his face what he was thinking. He hadn't understood then, she remembered, why she was drawing it. He probably didn't know what it was or why she'd bothered to come all the way up here to bring it to him. It was a stupid gesture.

Then he raised his eyes to her. "Ye did thon yersel."

She nodded.

"Aa mind. 'Twas the day we fetched Brown."

Well, that was something. "I thought you might like to have it."

"Aye." He put it back in the envelope. "But why?"

She blushed, she couldn't help it. "So you'll remember me."

He gave her an odd look. "Aa'll nae forget ye. But Aa've nowt to give ye back, ye ken."

"Doesn't matter." She hesitated, then said, "You could give me a promise. You never did that day."

"What?" He was wary, still open but wary. She'd seen that look before.

Go carefully, she warned herself. But how could she?

There was no time left; she must just say it and go. "That you won't let yourself be like Archie."

"Now how can Aa promise thon?" he asked reasonably. "Aa divvent ken what Aa'll be—anyway, he's ma brother."

There was the sound of a bell from the house. Penelope jumped.

" 'Tis only Mam. Aa mun gan see what she wants. The fire upset her bad. We couldnae all gan out to fight at once, one of us had to bide wi' her, se we took it in turns. Archie's gan to see the doctor."

But she refused to be distracted. "Ran, you know what I mean. You could promise."

"Ye dinnae tell them what we saw, did ye?"

Penelope shook her head.

A frown deepened between his brows. "An' ye willnae?"

"No. I've thought about it, but I can't."

"Aye. You said yersel we was different, Archie an' me, d'ye mind? Aa promise ye Aa'd never've done it."

She knew he meant the fire; it was on the tip of her tongue to ask, "Did Archie?" Then she knew Ran would tell her and she couldn't risk that. She didn't want to know for a fact.

He gave her a nod, stepped into the brilliant yard, and walked to the house without looking back.

"Ran," she called after him. "Goodbye."

271